SHIELD OF SECUNDA

ADRIAN COLLINS

DEDICATION

For my mother and father.

For her beautiful creative flair and his brilliant linguistic skills that gifted me whatever talent I may possess. For a life of love and support and for the future, wherever it takes us.

ACKNOWLEDGEMENTS

To Eliot, Simon, and Bob; thank you so much lads, your feedback throughout this experience was invaluable. To Fiona for putting up with my obsessive writing habits. To dad for your help editing and mum for turning my effort at a cover into something to be proud of.

PROLOGUE

What must the gods think of us? Why did they abandon us?

Armenius Faramon closed his eyes and sought inner calm as a light wind whispered across the shin-high luscious green grass covering the broad plain. The gust created gentle waves of motion and colour before him until it eventually brushed the heavy stubble on his gaunt cheek. The sun, a glorious illuminator and giver of life, coated the picture before him in a warm and loving embrace. *Let me die well today.*

Despite the welcome golden warmth, tempered by the cool breeze, the captain shifted uncomfortably in his heavy armour. Sweat trickled down the back of his neck and his skin prickled with no small amount of fear. Slowly, Armenius looked skywards, above the ranks of steel. Word had it that those who still clung to the old deities were saying the endless blue ocean above would provide a clear window for the gods to view the coming sacrifice. Armenius snorted in derision, sucking his teeth before fighting off the urge to spit. *If you are even still up there, mocking our predicament. Useless bastards. Not worth spit.*

The murmuring of vanquished men in their thousands drifted across the plain to him like lost souls looking for a home. Finding one, they mixed in with the soft clinking of metal on metal, horses whinnying, and canvas fluttering in the breeze. *A different melody to the one we all dreamed of. The roars of victory are not for us. All that remains is a symphony of defeat with the final crescendo not far from where we stand.*

Atop a long, crescent shaped hill, a little over three and a half thousand men stood in ordered ranks looking down upon him. They would be heroes, to those who would live to remember these days. Heroes not for their glorious deeds, but because they stood beside him, awaiting the great evil and the momentous sacrifice to come. A mere three and a half thousand battered, defeated, heartbroken men. His men. *Men? If half of them are more than boys or less than greybeards I'll take my pauldron from my shoulder and eat it.*

He admired them; the remaining glory of the Secundan Empire, in the tattered ruins of their finery. All that remained of an army hundreds of thousands strong. The only martial prowess left to defend their people. *A ruined dam in the way of a rushing flood.*

He watched as soldiers clapped each other on the shoulder and took forearms in warrior's handshakes, steeling their hearts. Grim faced to the last, the sons of Secunda were solemn in anticipation of the legacy forged in their own blood they would leave on this plain.

Armenius' gaze shifted once more, his chin squashing against the steel gorget that protected his throat. He drank in the figures that stood apart from the host, knelt before him. They were men who had remained regal and heroic through the war, figures of legend from stories as old as the mountains.

They were the last knights of Secunda, ever at the fiercest point of battle, ever the stalwart centre. The ninety-three lords and men of the elite knightly Orders were at ease in their glorious suits of plate and mail armour. Each man's helm rested on the ground in front of Armenius. Large pauldrons with ear-high inner collars partially hid their open faces as they looked to him. Eyes, the same Secundan blues as his own, betrayed each man's fear and hopelessness. The knights' thin, ice cold, veneers were unable to truly hide each man's dread. *They want hope. There is none I can give them.*

A tall oblong banner fluttered in the air above the small steel circle they created around Armenius. The gold-woven figure of their dead King was emblazoned upon ruined white canvas. *Rest well, my liege. Rest, in whatever plain of existence the gods vacated when they abandoned us to our fate. Perhaps we shall meet you there today.*

As he began to speak, three and a half thousand sets of ears desperately strained to hear.

"Secunda is gone."

He could almost hear the soldiers' hearts break.

"There is no victory for us. No glorious charge to take back our homes. We no longer have homes."

Somewhere, he heard the quivering mewl of a stifled sob.

"A million and more of our countrymen and women put to the sword. Our sons. Our daughters. Brothers and sisters. Mothers and fathers.

"All of them gone."

He turned and pointed into the west, away from where they had abandoned their lands.

"Secunda is that way now. Secunda is sixty thousand people. Perhaps some day it will be dirt and walls once more. Perhaps some day.

"But not this day. The Black Lands have taken our homes. They have taken our loved ones. They have taken our king. The gods themselves have abandoned us for fear of the dark horde that approaches!"

He could see men begin to rebuild themselves with his growing anger. His fists clenched and unclenched as the mood of the host set his blood afire.

"I say those gods are cowards! I say I would have the sons of Secunda stand by my side sooner than they! I say Secunda shall live on, not because some invisible being allowed it, but because we choose to die to make it so!"

A roar of approval spread from the ranks surrounding him. Fists pounded the air, swords and pike hafts crashed against shields. *I wonder how many truly realise they shall not draw breath beyond this day? How many truly understand that there is no retreat, no surrender; that we are here to delay and die?*

3

Few have seen battle. Few will survive their first. No matter. We must all meet our end sooner or later.

Armenius drank in the explosion of noise. He drew his gleaming sword and pointed towards the heavens, daring gods or man to try to strike him down.

His eyes glinted fiercely and reflected the gold trimming of the pauldrons upon his shoulders and cuirass upon his chest. A soft smile spread across his hard yet handsome features as he ran a leather-gloved hand through his jet black hair and then absent mindedly toyed with a small wolf head symbol hanging around his neck.

One long single trumpet note blew discordantly off in the distance and as one, three and a half thousand soldiers of Secunda looked across the plain. Not three miles away, thousands of dark shapes began to spill onto the plain, heading straight for the Secundan lines. Great hordes massed on the move in their eagerness to find battle.

Armenius turned to his soldiers. *It's time.*

He was solemn as he addressed him men. "My brothers, you are all that remains of the best men Secunda has to offer. It has been my honour to fight with and lead you these past eight years. We have all lost, but I ask of you this one last battle."

Slowly the hardened warriors began to stand, muttering their approval of the captain's words.

"One last battle to show that our brotherhood holds strong to protect our people."

"They need all of you!" he cried, pushing his voice to be heard all over the hill. "All of you to stand tall and stain the grass bloody this one last. We die so that Secunda may live!"

Shouts of defiance of the enemy erupted in a chorus sung only by those knowing that they had seen their last sunrise. Armenius spied tears rolling down more than a few mens' faces. It was all he could do to hold back his own. *Perhaps they do understand.*

Composing himself as the din died down, he began walking through the circle of knights towards the ranks of mail armoured men on the hill. He stopped not twenty feet from their front rank and spoke once more. "My brothers, Secunda's sons and daughters thank you for the blood you are about to spill. If I am lucky enough to fall with you by my side, I shall see you wherever the sons and daughters of Secunda now reside in the sky!"

With humility, he donned his helmet. The darkness of his full-faced helmet blinded him momentarily until the two eye slits aligned with his sight. As he and his remaining knight elite strode to the centre of the line, a chant began.

"Faramon. Faramon. *Faramon!*"

Signalling to his trumpeter, he ordered the call for the archers. A few hundred men in stiff leather tunics made their orderly way through the lines of men to take their place twenty feet out in front of the army. As one, each struck a quiver of arrows into the soft dirt in front of them and began attaching their bowstrings.

Armenius Faramon waited, and as the enemy drew within a mile, he ordered a second trumpet blast from his man. Those remaining war mounts were ridden by more knights and soldiers away from the formation and dropped behind the hill, out of the line of sight of the enemy. He listened to the thunder of their hooves as they made their way around to the right flank.

The enemy held up well out of bow shot, allowing their numbers to mass before the inevitable charge. Within the hour, Armenius stopped bothering to estimate their numbers. There was no point as hundreds more joined the horde each moment. A gurgling horn blast, followed by a cacophony of similar blasts, signalled the charge. *Let me die well.*

The Secundan line glittered in the afternoon sun as shields were hefted and swords drawn. The sound of wood poles cracking against each other as pikes were levelled down the gradient of the hill filled Armenius Faramon's ears. He could pick out individual men now across the field. Bloodshed would be soon.

At two hundred yards, the long bows unleashed their first volley. A dense cloud of steel tipped widow makers cut through the air as they rose to the pinnacle of their arc. A war cry louder than the breaking of a mountain erupted from the masses of barbarians flowing towards the Secundan lines as the arc of the arrows started downwards. Screams began to mix in with the war cries as hundreds of fur and dirty leather clad men were ended or wounded by a hail of Armenian fury. *Music to my ears.*

As the fourth volley was released, Armenius waved the men back. The archers streamed back through the Secundan lines. With the hammering of boots upon the earth, the Secundans closed ranks to present a wall of metal and raw, brazen courage to the enemy.

A ragged volley from the enemy's short bows flew into the Secundan lines. A few men fell, their screams pulling at Armenius. *Men die in battle. Their screams are terrible wind. There is naught to be done.* Rusted and blood stained axes and mauls pointed at the Secundans, held by gauntly muscled savages thirsting for battle as the wave of the enemy bore down on the beach head of Secunda.

Armenius's heart thumped in his ears. His nostrils flared as ragged breaths of excitement tore into his lungs. His mouth snarled as he raised his sword, leading his men in their war cry.

"For Mother Secunda!"

Armenius lay on his back, helmetless. His eyes focussed on the stars in the night sky and then closed in agony as his head and every limb exploded in white pain. The barrage to his dimmed senses continued as the eerie silence of a post battlefield of combat heavily lay itself upon him. Tattered banners flapped in the light wind and carrion birds tore cold wet chunks of flesh. Soft moans of men too stubborn to know they were already dead peeled out and the even softer sighs of those finally coming to their morbid realisation whispered in his ears.

He coughed and gasped, running his tongue over his dry, cracked lips and tasted the coppery wetness of his own blood. Looking around as the pain flare began to dampen he saw the heaped death and destruction surrounding him.

Faces frozen in soundless death-cries called to him. Fresh dirt had been turned to blood soaked mud and limbs hacked and hewn from bodies lay everywhere like mortar between bricks. The dull glint of moon and firelight on battered armour created horrors before his very eyes and broken weapons stabbed upwards like a forest of steel and wood. A soldier's worst nightmare and the reality of his existence.

Flashes of memory assaulted his consciousness. The first wave of the enemy horde crashing into the pikes on his right. The screams. Raising his sword in the air and bracing his shield with his metal clad shoulder. The push of the men beside and behind him, readying the line to take the force of the impact. The screams. Stabbing out at the first filthy, fur covered, blood spattered, salivating, axe wielding monstrosity. Being gloriously doused in its hot, steaming blood. And then the impact. The crush. The animal rage and finally blackness filled with screams. Always the screams.

Armenius slowly rolled on to his side. His anxious and pained eyes searched desperately for the form of a friend. Picking himself up into a crouch, he forced his wobbling legs to stand and then attempted to walk. Not two paces later, his ankle rolled as he misstepped on the face of a fallen friend. Armenius Faramon, first captain of the king's royal guard, found himself face first in the dark red sodden earth among the press of bodies.

In the bulk of his armour, it took all that was left of his strength to lift himself and crawl away from the main line of death and destruction. Mucus bubbled from his nose and tears welled in his eyes as he crawled over piles of his comrades, five bodies deep. Bursts of anguish whimpered from his lips as he recognised a friend here or a brother there. Fits of hateful anger pathetically ruptured out as he pitifully struck at the bodies of fallen foes.

From the dark, low, guttural voices cut through the post-battle sounds. They swirled and eddied through the piles of bodies like the sickly bitter voice of Death herself. Armenius peered over a tall pile of corpses and saw the silhouettes of distended jaws and whipping elongated limbs snapping through the dank torchlight in a sickeningly heathen ritual movement. His head pounded all the harder as the chanting voices rose and then sank, attacking and then retreating to strengthen and once more assault all that were alive to listen. Another sound drew his fragmented and frayed attention away from the grotesque figures before him.

Wet footsteps. Coming closer.

Eyes wide with fear, he quickly sought out a pile of bodies and burrowed in head first, crying and gagging quietly at the stink of death while the final vestiges of his courage failed in the face of such horror. Hands grappled at his legs and he cried out woefully as he curled into the foetal position.

"Brother-captain..." came a dry whisper. "My captain..."

Armenius looked up through red eyes to see a shape, one he knew very well. Clenching his jaw and desperately trying to rebuild his bastions of valour before speaking, he allowed himself to be hauled up to his knees.

"My captain, we must leave," the voice whispered again. "Quietly now, sir, there are still some of those barbarians wandering around looting our dead."

With pleading eyes Armenius looked up to the knight. "Are we victorious this day?"

The man ignored him, getting more urgent. "We must away, my captain."

Armenius grabbed the knight by the neck of his cuirass, recognising the stern features of one of the men who had stood gallantly with him in the centre of the line. "Did our people make Gall, Archenon? Answer me, damn it!"

Archenon pushed a gloved hand over Armenius's mouth, urgently looking around.

"My captain, be silent!" he hissed. "What little survivors we have are hidden nearby. We've linked up with the remnants of the mounted knights and archers a few miles to the west."

"How long..." started Armenius.

"Two hours have passed since we were defeated and routed. Now come." Archenon helped Armenius to his feet.

Armenius stood to a low crouch and together they began to trudge through the valleys of bodies, catching glimpses of the enemy over the ridges and hills of the slain. As his legs moved and his chest began to burn once more with life and anger, Armenius' jaw set.

"Brother Archenon, find me a horse," he whispered fiercely. "These cow-shit covered sons of whores will not reach our people unharried."

CHAPTER ONE

Trethore loved this moment. His mind tingled with anticipation, as he envisioned the immense battle of legend and prepared to launch himself in to the crescendo of his delivery. He'd delivered this sermon a hundred times, perhaps a thousand, and each time brought him a step closer to his god.

"For three days the Eternal Lord of the Secundan people led the tattered remnants of his warriors, constantly harrying the barbarian demons from the Black Lands, slaying hundreds with his own blade. Eventually our young and yet almighty god Armenius Faramon, now over four hundred years ascended to lead our mighty people in the shield wall in the sky, faced off against the evil warlord, Xantis. Their duel lasted almost a half day. Twelve gruelling hours of hacking, slashing, parrying and bloodletting. The combat came to a head with Armenius standing tall, his steady blade held between the collarbones of the bloody, bearded beast.

"An almighty cry of fear erupted from Xantis' foul horde as the imminent death of their leader dawned on them. With one fell stroke, Armenius broke the backbone of what remained of the enemy. One gleaming, glorious arc of sun reflecting steel as he carved his way into the annals of history as the saviour of Secunda."

Trethore paused a moment to give well practiced weight to the moment.

"He is our father, our protector, and our shining guidance against the dark night that lingers menacingly beyond the White Frontier. The dark night that strives ever towards the destruction of all we value and deem holy. It is the dark night that will stop at nothing to murder everything that you hold dear in this world – everything that your soon-to-be brothers spill their blood every day to protect and everything that you will soon spill your blood to protect.

"I want you to close your eyes," finished the Trethore, his breath misting before him in the cold air. "Close your eyes and pray to Armenius Faramon, our Eternal Lord, to guide your sword and strengthen your armour. But most importantly of all, pray to him to steel your courage and allow you to protect those who cannot protect themselves from the Dark beyond the Light that is our Eternal Lord and his chosen representative here; the King."

As the soft murmuring of the one-hundred youthful voices droned throughout the cathedral, Father Trethore allowed himself an inward sigh. His weathered and scarred features pushed the assumption of his age well past his forty-three summers. His black hair greying severely at the temples added to this supposition. *Forty-three hard years, training Secunda's best.*

He smiled to himself as he looked down the chest plate of the cuirass he wore, allowing his stubbled chin to press onto the painstakingly inscribed gorget. His fingers traced over the twenty-seven names engraved in the polished plate down the left side: the names of his ancestors who had worn the armour over the last four centuries. Finally his callused hand rested on the original owner of the holy metal. *Brother Standard Bearer Archenon Sokar.* The family line beginning with the name of the man who stood, and drew heathen blood, with the Eternal Lord finished with Trethore's own.

Trethore loved his armour. He could polish and marvel, one after the other and over again, for hours on end. *Imagine, just try to imagine, the things this ancient steel has seen,* he would tell his students. *Imagine what it was like to be my ancestor, standing next to Armenius. Just try to picture it!*

The ancient gousset and vambrance covering his well-muscled arms clinked quietly as he folded them across his broad chest. His blue gaze focussed upon the hundred young men he was about to induct into the elite knightly orders of Secunda. These youths were one-hundred of the most resilient and martially talented sons of Secunda, each with their own dreams of glory on the battlefield. They dreamed as he'd dreamed as a youth: of defeating great foes, shoulder to shoulder with the brothers they had been training with since early youth. He could almost feel their eagerness and anticipation, each youth keener than a honed blade's edge to be chosen by a knightly order and leave for the White Frontier. *Just like I was, once.*

In the front two rows of twenty youths, Trethore picked out a small group of his personal charges. All looked fit and strong, no less than was expected after four years of punishing training and tests to weed out the weak of limb and mind. Each young man was deep in communion with the Eternal Lord, their lips murmuring almost beyond Trethore's hearing. He need not hear them, he knew the prayer like he knew his own hand. *Eternal Lord. Saviour of our nation. Purify our souls so that we may become a clean slate to be moulded into a defender of Secunda and a purger of evil.*

There was the stout Branor, a cheeky grin never far below his deep Secundan blues and his short-cropped pitch-black hair. Sour faced Amorn, his massive frame already the match of most full grown knights. Sandy haired and almost translucently blue-eyed, Uthiel stuck out from amongst the other initiates, if only by looks alone. Sharp eyed Keldon, his prowess with a crossbow matched only by his big mouth. Quiet voiced Linton, ever the butt of jokes for his rather large ears. His eyes finally rested on Nikhael; disconcertingly, his face and eyes always devoid of expression.

Like mine own sons. Most dark haired, deep blue-eyed, and ready for what is to come. Well, as close can be with a vow of chastity, anyhow. Trethore suppressed a chuckle and a pang of regret.

As the last vestiges of the sun's rays disappeared outside, the cathedral was blanketed in darkness. Young thralls of the Armenius priesthood quietly moved about the outskirts of the massive building, lighting small torches spaced along the limestone walls. A dim glow slowly filled the room, but added no heat to the rapidly dropping temperature. Mist from the noses of the one hundred initiates slowly emanated towards the ceiling as if their very essence reached up to commune with Armenius.

Trethore broke his stance and, with an almost imperceptible nod to his one hundred charges, departed. The initiates noticed him no more than they noticed any of the young men next to themselves.

Three hours after the torches had burned themselves to nothing, a murky darkness entombed the cathedral. The darkness was broken only by three fresh torches placed in a fifteen foot tall enclave at the head of the room. The enclave held a six foot stone image of Armenius Faramon. He stood upon a dais half his own height and made of solid black granite expertly engraved with the holy words of his worship. Upon each shoulder an unfurled eagle's wing reached up towards the ceiling.

In his left arm he held a stricken young woman to his wide chest, the word "Secunda" carved into a small pendant around her neck. In his right arm a plain solid metal shield was held as if protecting the young woman. His face was flawless despite having watched over countless congregations of his followers.

Despite the exquisite rendition of their Eternal Lord watching over them, this was not the most impressive part of the vision before the still praying initiates. Four century old armour adorned the statue, its surface still gleaming immaculately with polish. Glorious chainmail filled the gaps between the flawless vambrances and goussets, and then flowed down to the knees in serpent skin like waves of reflection. Large pauldrons with tall inner collars, stereotypical of the Secundan knights, rested upon the gleaming cuirass. One single name was engraved into the left pectoral.

Armenius Faramon.

The soft Secundan sunlight crept over the smooth stones on the floor of the cathedral. Throughout the first three hours of the morning, it eventually caressed the black marble of the dais. As one, the hundred youthful faces opened their eyes and, with clarity borne of purity, looked upon the visage of their Eternal Lord. Eyes squinted as the light reflected off the polished metal.

"Initiates." A deep voice boomed throughout the cathedral, echoing off the stone walls.

"Initiates, rise, the cleansing of your souls is done," said Trethore, having quietly re-entered the cathedral. "Today is your last day as an initiate. You may spend it as you will. See your families and your sweethearts, for this may very well be the last time you see them. Tomorrow, we go to see the lords of the knight Orders."

Uthiel Caellar rose from the stone floor, his stiff joints protesting but his mouth smiling in eagerness of the adventures to come. He ran a hand through his short-cut sandy hair and locked eyes on the armour of his Eternal Lord. Swallowing nervously, he stepped forward and slowly walked to the dais, reaching out a shaking hand as he bent at the knee. The steel was so well polished he could see the reflection of his almost translucent blue eyes in it. His warm palm met the cold of the marble and he reverently bowed his head. *Let me win glory.*

"My soul, my blood, my life for you, my Eternal Lord. Praise be to you Armenius, for my life and my family's I thank you," intoned the youth.

With a final look at the statue he turned and walked past his fellow novices, through the rows of long wooden pews, back towards the entrance. As he passed, another novice stood and walked towards the dais to perform the same prayer.

Uthiel eventually reached the solid oak doors and, with great effort, pushed them open to allow the sunlight to fully flood the room behind him. He squinted once more as his eyes adjusted to the bright midmorning light and absorbed the beauty laid out before him. His shoulders straightened and his chest swelled with pride as he looked at the city and the land beyond that his forefathers had helped create. *Home.*

Reaching to the sky above him, the cathedral was the second highest point in the city, sitting before the mighty castle keep. Uthiel gazed over the vast network of streets and buildings that led down to the city's fortress walls. The rich and the noble had their large, multi-storeyed homes in a thick ring of well-kept grey stone walls and black slate roofs. Many flew their family standard above their homes, showing the world their holy link to the original fallen empire of Secunda through a plethora of colours and sewn images. House servants had begun the move around the streets, often dressed in garments far better than Uthiel had ever seen where he grew up in the poorer quarters.

From the mighty house of Lord Mirator, six household guard exited a side barracks on the estate and took up an honour guard stance. One of the house's sons emerged on a horse with four more armed and armoured household guard in tow and headed down the main thoroughfare. One of the guards looked up and saw Uthiel, and with a curt nod of approval turned on his heel and returned from whence he came. The rhythm of the five horses' hooves beating down the road was a pleasant break to the morning quiet.

While one major thoroughfare joined the castle and cathedral to the main city gate, many other clean cobblestone streets spider-webbed their way through the homesteads of the well off to the rest of the city. Eventually they reached the more crowded sections of the commoners. Older or cheaper stone, often mixed with worn wood, walled the thickly clustered abodes and thatch frequently replaced the roofing. The smoke and steam of morning cook fires lazily rolled and dissipated into the clear blue of the morning sky in a thousand different places while the streets were quietly filling with market stalls and people. *Home. The smells and the dark alleys and the colourful people of the life I have but one day left to live in. Glory beckons.*

Uthiel's stare met the immense stone walls that surrounded and protected the city of Secunda. Over a century of design and construction, Father Trethore had said during one of their lessons. Seventy foot tall and forty foot thick, the walls of Secunda were like mountains to the young initiate. *Surely no other walls in the Lands of the Light compare to such majesty?*

The main gate, the better part of three miles distant and a colossus of ancient Secundan engineering, had been opened for the day's business. A steady stream of trade wagons flowed to and from the city. Tall flags with the Secundan colours flapped beautifully in the morning wind from atop the battlements. The white background of the banners with the golden King's coat of arms stitched into the material shone beautifully as they flowed above the barely visible guards.

Beyond those walls stretched vast plains covered in farms. Crops sat in neat rows tended, by sturdy men, women and their beasts of burden. Herds of animals were being rounded up and moved to feed, breed, or be butchered by their shepherds. From this far away the wagon trains of the traders, groups of travellers or pilgrims, and the Secundan guard patrols looked like tiny ant columns to Uthiel as they made their way across his vast homeland.

To the left, the Faramon mountain range stretched off into the distance. Uthiel had heard their dull grey oft described as like the wall of steel a Secundan battle line presents to the enemies of the Light. *A comparison I shall soon be able to make!*

He shaded his eyes with his hand and stared off into the distance. Beyond the capability of Uthiel's sight, somewhere out on the borderlands of his nation, sat the fortresses of the seven knightly Orders. Uthiel dreamed almost nightly about those tall and noble bastions of honour and glory, when he wasn't dreaming about young women, that was. Tomorrow, one of those glorious knight Orders would become his home.

Standing on the steps of the Cathedral Armenius, lost in the wonder of his home, Uthiel didn't see or hear it coming until the impact. Something slammed into his back and he tripped down two or three stairs before regaining his balance and turning, crouched low with fists balled. His eyes narrowed with undisguised hatred as he saw his assailant. *Amorn.*

"You need to clear the way for your betters, gutter scum," came Amorn's deep voice, his eyes blaring with a desperate need to fight Uthiel.

Uthiel bared his teeth. *Come on, you bastard.*

A bare moment before Uthiel's rage ignited into violence, Branor intervened from behind Amorn as he pushed past the large cathedral doors. "Well, obviously your sister found him good enough to lie with last summer, arse-face."

Amorn turned on Branor as Keldon walked out and stood by his shoulder. A moment of tension followed before Amorn's huge clenched fists finally relaxed. His face did not follow suit. His massive frame turned back to Uthiel.

"One day, filth," he growled, his malevolent stare focussed on Uthiel. "One day your friends will not be around to help you. And on that day I'll have the pleasure of watching the life drain from your eyes, as I watched the joy drain from my sister's."

Not something I take pride in.

More initiates had come out of the citadel and stood watching the spectacle of impending violence. Uthiel still stood ready to fight. *Come on you bastard.* His eyes focussed on his enemy's and his peripheral vision was ever watchful for movement through Amorn's torso or limbs. Branor strode down and stood next to him. *Come on. Fight me.*

"Time to go kiss your life of wealth away Amorn," sneered Branor. "No servants to wipe your arse for you where we're going. Leave."

Behind Amorn, Linton and Nikhael had joined Keldon. Nikhael stepped down and gave Amorn a light shove down the stairs. Amorn allowed himself to be led down a few steps before snapping and turning to shove at Nikhael. The dark-eyed youth's hand twisted and grabbed Amorn by the wrist and with a vicious bend brought the bigger man into submission. As usual, Nikhael's face remained passive, his almost black eyes unwavering in their nonchalance as he leant in and whispered into Amorn's ear before allowing the bigger man free.

Amorn stormed off, his massive shoulders shaking in anger and his face the red of skin burned by flame. The other initiates not involved began to stream past them once more on their way into the city. Uthiel closed his eyes and took in a deep, calming breath as Branor put an arm around his friend. With an ear to ear cheeky smile Branor looked to his four companions.

"My friends, we have fasted twelve hours and at this point I'm so hungry I'm keeping an eye out for low flying birds. Will you join me for an ale or three and some food?"

All five young men headed down the stairs and in unison cried out, "To the Blue Goose!"

It wasn't long before Uthiel and his friends were in high spirits and laughing as they walked through the cobblestone streets away from the outer fences of the Cathedral Armenius. As they walked they joked, mock wrestled and yelled out the great deeds they were going to accomplish as knights. They would lead crusades and stand high on the walls of the White Frontier battle fortresses. The banners of Secunda and their knightly orders would stand atop piles of the enemy they had slain upon blood soaked battlefields. Of course, they would also court the finest maidens from across the land. They joked and laughed loudly, but even the sound of Keldon's bawdy banter was quickly lost in the sounds of a city brought to life by the morning.

An hour later they were amongst the older and more rundown buildings where they had been born and grown up. Friendly faces waved and offered wishes of luck. The baker they had grown up constantly trying, and rarely succeeding, to steal tasty pastries from even came out and gave them a small basket of freshly baked muffins. The passed Uthiel and Branor's houses. Their fathers were both on top of Uthiel's family house, mending a hole in the thatching. A quick wave, some playful banter about slacking off on their chores from Branor's father, and a promise of seeing them at dinner was all there was time for as the initiates swept on to finally arrive at the Blue Goose.

Uthiel loved the Blue Goose. He'd grown up eating with his father there, listening to tales of soldiering glory. His father's friends, soldiers from old days, had helped bring him of age there. Some of his favourite memories were of the loud and raucous common room with both ale and stories of battle flowing with equal reckless abandon. Provided you could withstand the stench of sweat, woodsmoke and ale, many a fine, drastically embellished, story of heroism could be found in the telling.

This time of the morning, the five young men were amongst the first to walk through its open doors. Inside, some small fires burned in the four hearths that surrounded the common area, the smoke tickling Uthiel's throat. A massive wooden table ringed by stubby stools ruled the centre of the room with smaller tables and stalls lining the walls.

Sawdust crunched underfoot and the strong smells of stale ale, sweat and woodsmoke greeted them. The walls were festooned with items brought home and donated by the soldiers from battlefields afar. Old suits of battle mail from Secundan foot soldiers, a dented helm from one of the soldiers of neighbouring Gall, two gladiator short swords from the distant desert land of Imonetia sat among paintings and scripted battle poems and songs for the benefit of those that could read, constantly drawing the eye from one wonder to another with promises of glory and lands far away.

At the far end of the room was the bar and entry to the kitchen. A tall, well built man in an old Secundan foot soldier's tabard stood with his meaty arms folded across his chest.

"And what trouble do I see here?" his deep voice boomed. "Five sons of Armenius in the livery of initiates come to grace us with their presence? Antony! Antony, roll yourself out here and help me remove these upstarts from our hall!"

From the kitchen boomed another strong voice. "Initiates!? Is any of them Tanin Caellar's boy?"

Uthiel stepped forward, his chest puffed out and his back straight in the presence of true war veterans. "You know me. May we..."

The man behind the bar interrupted him. "That's Tanin's boy alright!"

A short fat man, also wearing foot soldiers tabard, stormed from the kitchen, his scarred face red and his hands covered in flour. His beady eyes narrowed on Uthiel and his hands reached down to unbuckle his well worn narrow leather belt.

"Armenius damn it," he snarled as he folded the belt and snapped it onto his meaty hand. "Tanin told me about this one, Argo, told me this one thinks he can skip out on his chores because he and his skinny little friends are off to join the Orders tomorrow! Thinks he's too good to help his father, who served Armenius and Secunda for twenty years in the army leading the mighty and invincible Fifth, fix the very roof they sleep under!"

Argo's face hardened and the thick, corded muscles in his arms visibly flexed as they tensed.

Uthiel stepped forward, his face stormy but uncertain. "Now just you wait..."

"And this piece of rotten fruit?" roared Antony, pointing at Branor with his belt. "What I heard, he's fallen pretty far from the family tree. How a good and honest mining family managed to birth this one I'll never know!"

With surprising speed for such a big man Argo vaulted over the bar and landed within arm's distance of Antony. Together they advanced on the five initiates menacingly. The five held their ground in the face of the bigger, more experienced men. Each adopted an identical fighting stance with their left shoulder forward. A cheeky smile slowly spread across Uthiel's face.

Without warning there was a clamour behind Antony.

"Antony Hulfar!" yelled a husky female voice. "You will stop harassing those fine young boys immediately!"

Uthiel looked from the kitchen back to Antony and Argo and then back to the kitchen, his face betraying the seriousness he was trying to portray. Only a moment passed before Argo and Antony erupted into laughter. Argo doubled over, gripping his stomach. Their stony features softened to warm and welcoming in the briefest of moments by the laughter that echoed off the walls.

Lonetta Hulfar bounded her large girth through the kitchen door and out into the common room. She looked sweaty and flustered, her cheeks blowing out with exasperated breaths. She was laughing as she bustled past the two ex-foot soldiers and handed them both meaty slaps to the back of the head. She came to a gradual halt before the five initiates, puffing her big rosy cheeks out with a huge smile. Grabbing both Uthiel and Branor by their hands she pulled them into a sweaty hug.

"Lonetta!" yelled out Uthiel, a large smile spreading across his and Branor's faces.

"My boys! Oh my boys! Don't listen to these two oafs," she cried, her words piling out at an almost unbelievable rate. "I can't believe it! All grown up and about to head out into the world."

She pulled back for a moment, long enough for them to see the tears falling down her full rosy cheeks, before grabbing them in a hug even more rib crushing that the last.

"Your fathers and mothers will be here once the hole in the Caellars' roof is fixed. They've organised some drinks and food. On the house of course! Please, sit down."

She turned and glared at Antony who was rubbing at the red hand mark on the back of his head. "Antony! Argo! Ale and bread for these fine young boys. Tanin will have both of your hides for this stunt!"

Antony grumbled something about Tanin having set up the jest before flashing a grin at Uthiel and heading back into the kitchen. Argo, still laughing, clapped Uthiel and Branor on the shoulders and then moved past them and offered his hand to Keldon.

"My friends," he began. "My apologies, my name is Argo, I served under Uthiel's father in the Fifth."

Motioning towards the kitchen he continued. "That fat oaf is Antony, also a veteran of the Fifth. And finally his lovely wife Lonetta, finest cook in all of Secunda I'll wager! Along with a few other veterans we own the Blue Goose, the finest establishment ever to be graced by his Majesty's foot soldiers. I have known Uthiel and Bran since birth but I have not met you three before. And you are?"

Keldon stepped forward first. "Keldon Tremorne, soon to be the finest crossbowman the Lands of the Light have ever seen."

Argo nodded his head. "We need every one of you fine shots on the White Frontier, young lad. Well met."

Nikhael offered his hand next, grabbing Argo's forearm in a firm warrior's hand shake. "Nikhael Rokarn, it is my honour to meet you sir."

Argo nodded once more. "Well met, young man. I look forward to regaling you tonight with stories of battles long past."

Finally Linton offered his hand and spoke in his quiet voice. "Linton Lonnell sir."

"Speak up boy!" laughed Argo.

Branor snorted. "Speak up Linton, just because you can hear yourself with those massive ears doesn't mean anyone else can!"

Linton's face, and most predominantly his ears, reddened as everyone laughed. Argo wrapped one of his massive arms around Linton's shoulders and the other over Keldon's and led them to the bar stools around the table in the centre of the room.

"Come, my friends, take a seat!" he called, also motioning towards the three other young men.

Laughing and joking, mostly about Linton's ears, Uthiel and his brothers took their seats. Antony burst out of the kitchen with a platter of breads surrounding a wheel of cheese in one hand and a smaller barrel of ale under his other arm. Argo jogged over to the bar and grabbed an armful of wooden mugs and dumped them into the middle of the table, quickly throwing them to each initiate before setting out a few more mugs for people yet to arrive, and himself.

Antony uncorked the ale and started pouring the frothing dark brown liquid into the mugs as discussion began to fly back and forth across the table. Uthiel laughed and joined in, trying to keep track of every line of conversation as he dipped his top lip into the frothy head.

"You'll be asleep on your back before I feel a thing!" boasted Keldon to Uthiel before they both drew deeply from their flagons, challenges in their eyes.

"I was about to hand you the beating of a lifetime!" joked Branor to a mockingly fearful Argo.

"That smells amazing! Did you bake it this morning?"

"You think the Knights Aggressor will want a scrawny whelp like you!?" bellowed one of the veterans.

"In the lands of Imonetia, word has it a man's not restricted to one wife. Is that true?" Uthiel hadn't seen who'd spoken, but Branor owned that voice. He'd stake his right arm on it.

"I've not been there, lad. But I'd say to you, young man, that here in Secunda you may not call her a wife but most men don't feel restricted to one woman!"

Uthiel laughed with the rest of them, his sides beginning to ache.

"Did my little sister teach you how to drink!?"

"Did your little sister tell you about her and I last summer?"

"To little sisters!"

"To Amorn's sister! May those long legs remind Amorn of your bare arse between them forevermore!" Uthiel raised his mug with the rest of them, a flash of embarrassment spreading across his cheeks. *And perhaps a little shame. Yes, most definitely a little shame.*

Their non-stop banter had continued through the first three mugs of ale and well into their second platter of cheese and bread before Tanin Caellar and Branor's father entered. Uthiel and Branor both stood and moved to stand before their fathers, heads bowed.

"Father," said Uthiel.

"Father," said Branor.

In unison, the two fathers stepped forward and hugged their boys as their mothers entered the Blue Goose behind them. Quiet words were spoken. Private words of pride, honour, and fear of loss passed from father to son. Eventually the two fathers released their sons to the embrace of their

23

mothers. Tears were shed and words of pride, love and hopeful safety passed from mother to son. Eventually the boys were released to a few playful jeers from their friends and all were seated.

With his mug full and held high, Tanin Caellar stood and looked down on his boy. His chin quivered ever so slightly and his jaw muscles clenched as his eyes became tinged with red.

"My son and soon to be little brothers in arms," he said, his translucent blue eyes locked on Uthiel. "For the glory of Secunda. May Armenius watch over you."

Uthiel and his friends stood. "And you," they intoned.

Captain Phyrus stood tall and proud, resplendent in his immaculately polished battle armour as he entered the war room. Large metal reinforced doors, with two of the lord general's personal guard standing either side, swung open to reveal a fire lit room with a solid oak table in the centre. Detailed maps of the Secundan realm and surrounding kingdoms adorned the walls. Four men stood around the massive table in the centre. Each was an ageing yet stereotypical Secundan; tall, broad, jet black hair, pale skin and dark blue eyes. Upon first glance it could be said they looked as four brothers would, separated only by the different scars on their faces.

Captain Phyrus knelt before the masters of his Order.

"Lord general," he said, addressing the foremost man, with his head bowed in respect.

He then turned to the other three in similar fashion. "My lords."

Lord General Thomak's cold hard gaze fell upon the young captain. He waved Phyrus to stand and join them. As Phyrus approached the circle, he took stock of what lay on the table: an immense and intricately detailed map of the Secundan lands all the way east past stout and proud Gall. To the south the map traversed through the smaller kingdoms of Lemug and Pandur until it finally met with the mountains many hundreds of miles distant, at an acute angle. To the north, the desert realm of Imonetia sat proud and immense on the far end of the Lands of the Light.

Phyrus could only stand and admire the five kingdoms, all but Gall with their backs to the mountains. He marvelled at the sheer scale of the realm. *Truly, I never envisaged it to be so large.*

The Lands of the Light took up only half the map. The other half remained blank und undetailed. The Lands of Light were separated from the dark mystery beyond their realms only by the thin ink line running down the centre of the map. Beyond the line, to the east, were the lands lost during the last Great Incursion over four centuries ago. Small points dotted the line of the White Frontier, signifying the fortresses and towns where the five kingdoms held those that would destroy them back with the blood of their sons.

"Brother Captain Phyrus," said Thomak. "You are late. Not the best beginning to your captaincy."

Phyrus' head dipped lower. "Lord general, please accept my apologies. I've no excuse for my delay."

"I expected better of you, Captain Phyrus. Turn your attention to the table, most specifically the frontier fortress at Archenon Creek. At your leisure of course."

The young captain's face reddened as the lord general began to detail the enemy troop movements around the frontier. Captain Phyrus looked up under his eyebrows at the other three men surrounding the table. Lords Pomen and Ryun stood beside Thomak. *Mighty heroes. Old. Past wielding swords as weapons and on to using regiments and armies to shield our nation from the darkness.*

The third was a legend among knights. A hero to lead heroes. First Captain Solanthur Verutus. *The Light Bringer.*

Phyrus felt like a child looking up to a great hero towering over him. *Captain of captains. I stand before the Light Bringer!* The first captain was everything Phyrus wished he could be. Tall, immensely broad of shoulder, barrel chested, he seemed the epitome of knightly strength. The Light Bringer's handsome and noble features were marred only by a thin scar running from his right eyebrow and over the bridge of his nose to finally come to an end on his left cheek. His reputation as a warrior of duty, honour, a leader of men, was only surpassed by his ferocious prowess in combat. Solanthur's head turned suddenly and his eyes rested on Phyrus.

"Something the matter, brother captain?" asked Solanthur. All of a sudden all eyes were on Phyrus. Once again his face reddened as he quickly looked down at the table.

Phyrus could feel the lord general's stare upon him.

"Captain Phyrus," growled Thomak. "I warn you, my patience is short. You will pay attention to the details you see in front of you, or I will have your commission."

Phyrus stood dead straight. *Stupid! Stupid! Stupid boy! All your hard work for naught!*

"My lord general, I... I apologise. Won't happen again," said Phyrus, his face having quickly turned from the red of embarrassment to the ashen colour of fear.

"Apologies, Light Bringer," continued Phyrus, nodding to the first captain.

Solanthur winced at the name in annoyance but paid Phyrus no further attention.

"Don't force me to question further my decision to elevate you above your other brothers, Captain Phyrus," growled Thomak.

Tossing a sheet of paper in front of Phyrus, Thomak continued.

"On that sheet are the details of the company to be assigned to you. I have given you a small command as your first. You'll have twenty of your brother knights, including fourteen young initiates fresh from Secunda herself. Six more experienced brothers including your lieutenant, brother Ghurkar Storm, who will take control of the training of your young initiates. You have one year to sculpt these young men into brother knights. Once - "

"One year, my lord general?" asked Phyrus. "One year until what?"

"By Armenius boy! Will you let me finish?" roared Thomak, finally losing his patience. Phyrus let the silence grow.

Thomak huffed in annoyance once more, then leaned forwards. "Until you march to the Archenon Creek fortress on the White Frontier. You will be charged with our people's defence and there you will be tested by the wilderness of the Black Lands. That is, if you haven't disappointed me further."

Thomak turned his back on Phyrus. "Your young charges arrive in just under a week. I suggest you go make ready for their arrival. Lieutenant Storm and your five other brothers will await your orders tomorrow. You are dismissed from my presence."

Phyrus immediately placed his closed fist over his chest. Inside either his heart quailed or his soul raged at the embarrassment, as yet he could not discern which.

"For Armenius," said Phyrus and then, without further ceremony, left.

Nothing was said as the great oak doors closed behind the young captain. An uncomfortable silence grew and Thomak did his best to burn a hole through the door with his eyes. Finally he could no longer stand the accusing silence.

"Well, our forces won't deploy themselves to the White Frontier," he said gruffly. "Best we get on with it."

The Lord Pomen looked to him. "You were hard on the boy. He made a mistake, but he will learn."

"He's not a boy any longer, brother. Upon the frontier one hundred of our men will place their lives in his hands," said Thomak. "Him not waking up early enough to reach a strategic council may mean his company is misplaced or ill prepared and he will cost lives. I'll not stand for it."

"If you did not think him fit for command you would not have promoted him. Just remember who he stood amongst. We may be old and past the years of thrashing countless foes in a day with our blades, but we are still heroes in the eyes of the young. He is young. Tested in battle but not yet tried in leadership," said Pomen.

"Speak for yourself old man!" said Solanthur, only half joking as he cocked an arm out to the side. "I sport the strength of an ox and can easily outwit a few old men."

Pomen smiled. "Were it that I was thirty years younger, I would hand you a thrashing for that remark."

Solanthur straightened, his face hard and his stare challenging.

Thomak held up a hand. "My friends, let us not squabble. First captain, you forget yourself. Lord Pomen, you are right and I get your meaning but I will not go easy on any of our brothers, be they a lowly initiate or one of you. I am not here to be liked, nor to hold the hands of those freshly given the responsibility of leading men into combat. I am here to direct this order of brother knights through the days of bloody glory that rest on the horizon. I need men whose spirits are as steel as the armour we wear.

"These captains are to our men and initiates as the blacksmith is to the sword. If we have strong, hard, and intelligent blacksmiths, unafraid to put their flesh close to the fire and unrelenting in their hammering of the hot metal in order to temper the blade, then we shall have strong and sharp brothers to lead into battle. Else the weapons we take to war will be brittle, easily bent or dimmed.

"In the months to come we must be as hard as we can be on our brothers for when the time comes to sally forth into the Black Lands, the great enemy will show no mercy. They will cut the chaff from the ranks of the Lands of the Light brutally and without mercy. To succeed, there must be no chaff among our brothers. Each of our men must be worth ten of theirs for Secunda looks to us to deliver victory."

"My friends," he said, his tone and face enlivening with the fires of ambition. "In twelve months we shall be at the forefront of the greatest holy crusade our age has seen."

The four men of the council leaned over the table, attention solely fixed on the broken shield marked on the map where four centuries ago mother Secunda had been raped by the great enemy.

"In twelve months, the Order of the Grey Wolf will be a part of the spearhead of ten thousand knights of the seven orders and forty thousand soldiers of Secunda carving forwards from the White Frontier. Four months of fighting and marching later, and we will have reclaimed the lands of our forefathers. From Archenon Creek, all the way to our holy soil.

"History, my lords, will favour us with fame that will echo in the halls of our sons for a millennia."

CHAPTER TWO

Uthiel awoke to Branor's smiling face. Drawing his cracked lips back he tried to work some spit into his mouth, grimacing at the taste.

"Tastes like a cow shit in your mouth, doesn't it?" laughed Branor.

Uthiel groaned and pushed himself up from his small hay-filled mattress. As he sat up, his face dropped immediately into his hands as his mind threatened to explode out of his ears. Branor handed him a mug of water. Uthiel filled his mouth and then tipped the remainder over the back and top of his head. His red-rimmed eyes focussed slowly on his friend.

"Time?"

"You've one hour to prepare, my ale-addled friend!" chirped Branor cheerily, enjoying every moment of Uthiel's pain. "The lords of the knightly Orders wait for no man!"

Uthiel weakly threw his cup at his friend and rose to his feet. Branor tossed him a threadbare towel and they both trudged from Uthiel's family home and made short work of the walk to the community well. Branor attempted light conversation more than once and each time he was repaid with either a swipe of the folded towel or a glare that rivalled that usually reserved for a murderer from the victim's father.

30

With the sun still only just peeking its dazzling face above the horizon, there were few people in the streets. Uthiel's mood was as foul as his own stink of stale alcohol and sweat. The young man pulled a bucket of water up from the well and dunked his entire head into it. Ice cold did its best to tear through his fog. When he tried to pull out, Branor pushed his head under again with a laugh. Uthiel came up sputtering, spitting water to the ground in a gush filled with small pieces of ice.

"Brother," said Branor, "if we could unleash your breath on the great enemy, we'd win the fastest and most cruel victory in Secundan history. Another quick splash down the throat would help me bear your presence this morning."

Uthiel's mouth quivered and held hard for a moment before breaking into a broad smile. Red spider-webbed eyes closed as he ruffled the excess water from his hair with his hands. Looking at his fingers he could see some of the short blonde strands from his head stuck there with some mystery residue of the night's excesses. Reaching out, he clapped Branor on the shoulder, and wiped his hand dry on his friend.

"Come, Bran, you chubby bastard," he laughed. "Let us see if mother has baked something for breakfast."

"Ah, but Uthiel, lord of morning grumpiness, I'll not rob your father of his last chance to see you for what may be some years," replied Branor. "Last time he gave my arse a strapping for disobedience it was so severe I spent a week lying on my stomach."

"You did try to look up mother's dress," retorted Uthiel. "For a twelve year old you received a just sentence."

"Pah, a fair sentence would have been for him to look up my skirt."

Uthiel's eyebrows rose in feigned shock. He laughed and clapped his friend on his shoulder again as they parted ways, each to his family. Still chuckling to himself, he was quite happily surprised to see both his parents waiting outside their home for him.

His mother made it to him first. Once again more tears of pride and fear rolled down her cheeks as she tried her best to crush his much larger form. After a moment Tanin put his arm on his wife's shoulder and gently prompted her away.

"Come, my lady," he soothed. "Give me a moment with the boy before he leaves."

Uthiel's mother departed, her eyes never breaking from her son as she walked back inside the Caellar home. Her sobs were still just barely audible through the front window. Tanin put a hand on each of Uthiel's shoulders, stooping slightly to his son's eye level. Uthiel looked at his father, noticing the bags under the old man's sleepless eyes.

"My son. My last remaining son," he said, his eyes closing for longer than a blink. "I prayed to Armenius from the moment I put you to bed last night, to the moment Branor walked in and woke you up this morning."

"Father - " Uthiel started.

"Firstly, Uthiel," continued Tanin, tightening his grip slightly on his sons shoulders, "I prayed to our Eternal lord that I would see the sun rise on a world where my last remaining son was a blacksmith, or a teacher, or some such honourable commodity of Secunda that did not force him to draw blood unless in defence of his home or family.

"I prayed for this for hours, but the memory of my time on the Frontier reminded me of the horrors that lay beyond our lands. It reminded me that the White Frontier is the best tool for defending our lands from the immense threat without. The fortresses and towns of the Frontier are the extended walls of Secunda. The Land of the Light *is* our home. When I saw this, I came to the realisation that I already had what I had been praying for all night, in part at least."

Tanin smiled a weak smile. "My boy, do you know what I prayed for after that?" he asked.

Uthiel shook his head. Seeing his father this way unnerved him.

"I prayed that he would allow just one of my four sons to be with me when Armenius calls me to his side. Just one of my sons."

A lone tear rolled down the scarred veterans face.

"Father - " started Uthiel once more.

32

"No. No, my son. Do not listen to me, I am growing soft in my old age." As more tears rolled down his cheek he dropped his head. "I am being selfish, we are a soldiering family and I expect no less from you. My heart beams with pride so bright it rivals the sun. Your brothers are looking down at you from the Shield Wall in the Sky, their hearts also bursting with pride."

With a short movement Uthiel pressed his father's forehead to his own.

"Father, do not fear. I will come back. I'll bring glory to our family name, this I swear to Armenius."

Tanin jerked back, his face set hard as his hands gripped his son's shoulders even harder.

"Glory? Do not wish for glory, my son. Glory brings pain, Glory brings death," said Tanin, his eyes fixed on Uthiel's. "Most of the glorious heroes I knew died bloody deaths, screaming in agony, leaving their family to mourn at home."

Uthiel said nothing and silence remained for some time.

"They saved ten brothers, they slew the enemies' heroes. Pah... Always they ended up lifeless on the dirt."

Finally, Tanin regained his full composure.

"My son, remember that the strength in arms we Secundans have comes from three things..."

Uthiel cut his father off. "Your lord, your armour, and the man locking shields with yours beside you. I know, father."

Tanin grinned. "That's my boy. Now give your grey-haired old fool of a father a hug before you go. I imagine you've not got long to gather your clothes and leave."

Uthiel put his arms around his father just as Branor bounded around the corner calling for Uthiel.

"By Armenius' finely chiselled arse, have you not even got dressed yet!?" shouted Branor.

Tanin reached out and lightly cuffed Branor behind the ear. "Remember your manners, Bran, I'll not stand for blasphemy."

Branor rubbed the back of his head, looking sorry for himself. Tanin smiled and put a hand on his shoulder. "Now, you look after yourself and my boy. Apart from Mrs Caellar, he's all I've got."

Branor nodded, his eyes taking on a rare set of seriousness. "He is my brother."

Nothing further needed to be said.

Father embraced son once more. With no further word, Uthiel sprinted inside and was very quickly back out on the cobblestone street in his initiate's tabard, saying goodbye to his parents. As he moved to leave, Tanin grabbed his arm in a warrior's handshake and as their hands separated, passed something cold and metallic to Uthiel. Uthiel looked down to see a small silver chain with a small wolf's head on it which he pushed into his pocket.

As he ran to join Branor, who had already started up the street complaining about how Uthiel took longer than his sister to get ready for anything, he turned to hear his father call.

"Your lord. Your armour. The man beside you." The old soldier gave him a final wave. "Proud of you my boy."

Uthiel and Branor were in awe as they approached the Bastion of the Chosen. It was immense, almost twice as tall as the section of city wall that it immersed. Crenellated battlements sat high above them and arrow slits remained dormant. Like an immense castle in its own right, Uthiel imagined that it could resist all but the most determined or canny foe.

Heavy timber double gates stood open, beckoning them in with flickering torchlight. The two initiates walked through the immense gates and into the Bastion of the Chosen. *This is it. All my work. All my sacrifice. Time for the Knights Aggressor to welcome Brother Uthiel Caellar to their glorious ranks. Time to be chosen.*

As the two brothers passed through a long corridor, their other friends found them. Keldon, Linton and Nikhael were all in some state of dishevelled morning grogginess mixed with youthful excitement and exuberance. Branor instantly pounced on any opportunity to cause annoyance to them. Very quickly their demeanours turned from sour to awe as they began passing trophies, display weapons, and shields engraved with the names of the fallen at historic battles where more than one of the knight Orders had partaken.

Uthiel reached out and traced his fingers across a name, trying to wipe away the dust and grime. Too many had done as he had in the centuries the bastion had stood, and the letters were unreadable. *Will that be me one day? Will all my glory come down to a single, unreadable name, and perhaps a legend or two? Will I be remembered?*

The morbid thought struck him hard. He looked at his friends. Each youth had a look of unrestrained excitement and wonder as they read and touched and imagined. *No. No! I shall be the most glorious of knights. Glory awaits me!*

Uthiel's self-assurance quickly returned. *I am to be a knight. None shall stand in my way.*

As the corridor came to its end, they found the other initiates waiting in front of a cast iron door easily three times Uthiel's width. In front of the door stood two tall knights in full battle armour, their closed-face helms hiding their identity while their plain black shields and tabards sank them into shadow.

"Bastion Guard," whispered Branor.

"But from which Order do they hail?" wondered Uthiel under his breath.

Branor shrugged with an excited smile.

As the remainder of the initiates came up behind them, the group instinctively formed into equal columns and stood at the ready. They stood for what seemed like an hour, waiting for their destiny to beckon them through the iron door. Just when Uthiel thought he would explode with anticipation, the sound of metal scraping against metal broke the silence. The two Bastion Guards, immobile to this point, turned away. They swung their shields over their shoulders and leant their full weight into the door. After a brief moment of resistance born of sheer weight, the door opened inwards into pitch black.

The two knights strode through and in their black livery seemed to melt and disappear into the darkness within. No instructions were passed on to the initiates through the gaping doorway. Some initiates licked their lips and looked at each other unsure of which action, if any, to take. Up front the massively tall and broad form of Amorn turned to sneer at the other ninety-nine initiates before he strode purposefully forward, muttering a curse for the cowards he left behind.

Swearing, Uthiel made to follow. Before either could reach the door a voice boomed.

"Initiates. Enter."

The boys tried to keep a semblance of order as they entered the room, squinting and willing their eyes to adjust to the dark. Slowly, shapes and the faintest of reflections of polished armour began to reveal themselves.

"Stop. Kneel."

As one the initiates dropped to their right knees.

"Darkness, brother initiates," once again boomed the strong and authoritative voice. "It is what drove our forefathers from their homes and to the mountains."

Uthiel started as yellow flames erupted from a dais in front of the boys, illuminating a knight standing some ten feet above them. His white, full-length tabard flowed over his dark, polished armour.

"The Light of our Eternal Lord is what binds us against the darkness as brothers," continued the helmed knight.

The flames spread across in both directions from the knight to reveal three more figures on either side, each with different armour and tabards covering them from neck to just above the knee, leaving their metal-shod arms and greaves to gleam in the light.

Removing his helm, the white-clad knight revealed a face in its forties that looked chiselled from stone in both its hard lines and its coldness of gaze. Black shoulder length hair flowed around his brown, scarred skin. Ice blue eyes regarded them each in turn.

"I am the Lord General Loghan Faramon of the Order of the Knights Aggressor, field marshal of the mighty Secundan army, and leader of the council of the seven knightly Orders of our mighty mother land."

Uthiel swooned collectively with the other initiates in absolute awe of the individual they knelt before. The young initiate spared a quick glance at Branor and the others around him. *The White General. The king's younger brother! Here!*

Away from the White Frontier? There was not one young face that did not appreciate the significance of the moment.

"Before you stand six representatives of the Orders of Secunda," continued Field Marshal Faramon. "These are the men who have deliberated long and hard over the types of knights you may become. And I do say 'may become,' young initiates. For being chosen at this point is not a guarantee that you house within yourselves the fortitude of will and strength to fight by our sides against the darkness that would consume our proud nation."

"As the Order of the Knights Aggressor is the foremost in both size and glory of the seven Orders," continued Faramon, "we shall choose those initiates deemed to have the qualities we desire first."

Uthiel's licked his lips in anticipation. The Knights Aggressor were the most famous knights in the land. They were the men that not only held the walls of the White Frontier but also delved into the black lands. Their glorious deeds and honour rolls went back for centuries. That was where Uthiel belonged. The anticipation of receiving a white tabard to slip over his armour was almost too much to bear. Pictures of him standing next to the king's brother in defence of the Lands of the Light flashed through his mind's eye. He could already feel it in his hands, coarse white cloth against his callused palms. He could taste the glory he would achieve.

"The following initiates will follow me at the end of the ceremony. Arkhenon Faramar. Dugan Faramar. Amorn Loren."

Uthiel clenched his jaw, growing more anxious at every word. Twenty more names came forth.

"Nikhael Rokarn. That is all."

Uthiel's heart sank. Four years of blood and sweat, bruises and exhaustion, endless sacrifices. All for nothing. He pictured the look on his father's face, dark with disappointment with his second rate initiate looked over by the glorious Knights Aggressor. *A second rate son not worthy of his dead brothers.*

His lips shook and a tear rolled down his cheek as he struggled to control his disappointment. His mind raced through troughs and mountain peaks of anger, misery, hatred and distress. It was only the pain of his fingertips being mercilessly driven into the palms of his hands that finally allowed him to regain his self control.

He looked up as his hearing returned, his fists uncurling. A second knight lord had stepped forward in a red tabard with a white rose emblazoned on his chest. A few initiates down to his right he could see Nikhael looking over to him. For the first time that he could remember Uthiel saw genuine sorrow streak briefly across his face as Nikhael grimaced his pity to him. The expression passed quickly as Nikhael once again looked at the dais as the second knight lord stepped backwards.

To Lord Faramon's right a wiry, white haired knight now advanced. His steps were slow and purposeful, his back still straight despite his apparent age. His skin bore not only the lines of age but the scars of battle and the weariness of command. A mail-gloved right hand gave his chin a quick rub before he spoke.

"I am Lord Pomen of the Order of the Grey Wolf," his voice grated. "The following initiates will come with me at the end of the ceremony. Tobias Sential. Branor Styren..."

Uthiel glanced at Branor beside him. Branor ever so slightly mouthed a curse under his breath.

"Keldon Tremorne. Lokhi Dorn. Uthiel Caellar..."

Uthiel's world stopped. He didn't even hear his other friends get selected for the same Order. *No! The Wolves are weak! All but destroyed a decade ago upon the Frontier. No! I am meant for greater things, not a bunch of old men content to sit behind their walls!*

Uthiel looked at Branor again. Resignation sat heavily on the youth's face. They both knew the stories of the Grey Wolves. Great mystery surrounded the battle where they'd been decimated. There were no heroes of battle named nor villains cursed in the stories, no hills or cities or plains or landmarks named. Campfire and tavern stories always seemed to come from someone else who knew someone else who was a relative or friend of someone who had been there.

Uthiel sighed. Years ago the Grey Wolves had been a power amongst the Secundan Orders, brave and stout and easily the equal of any other force in the Lands of the Light. Now, their glory was a spent resource.

Before long a small group of Armenius priests entered to stand below the representatives of the seven Orders. One of those was Father Trethore. As always, Uthiel's eyes involuntarily followed each of the five suits of ancient armour linking the priests' family name to the brave knights who stood beside Armenius over four centuries ago. Trethore produced an antique leather book and placed it on a wooden podium and then began to read in a smooth, well-spoken voice.

"In the last year of our Eternal Lord's life in his mortal body, before his ascendancy above to lead his people in the Shield Wall in the Sky, he lay upon his death bed wracked by holy visions as his soul transformed from a mortal god, to that of an immortal being.

"All but one of his friends of youth already waiting for him in the shield wall above, his seven sons sat by his side having dutifully taken down his every word and teaching through the two years our Eternal Lord was bedridden before his ascendancy.

"Two of these writings I will read to you today. The first is what is considered by many a prophecy yet to be fulfilled. The second is his recount of his words to the first ever group of initiates after the rear-guard action that revealed Him in our people's time of most need.

"The book of Armenius, Chapter seventeen."

> *One hundred souls,*
> *Outside the circle,*
> *The beasts within awoken.*

> *One hundred souls,*
> *Infused with one hundred spirits,*
> *The instincts of a thousand years,*
> *Coursing through their veins.*

> *One hundred souls,*
> *Led by one,*

The strongest and bravest of them all.

One Hundred souls,
Doomed to stand,
When all around them fall.

The priests allowed the initiates to think on what had been said before turning a few pages and starting again.

"The Book of Armenius, chapter twenty seven, verses eleven through twelve, recorded by his brother knights;"

"And as I look each of you in the eye, my little brothers in arms, I see such pride in what it is to be a Secundan in these times. Most of our families and friends are dead and all of our homes are destroyed so I say to you all, while these walls of Gall may be our temporary home, the man beside you is now ever your brother.

"My little brothers, you are young of body and soul, and the burden I place upon you is huge. I do not ask you to live for your people, I ask you to die for them. I ask you to take this shield, and this sword, and this crossbow, and this suit of armour, and to smite the enemies of our people wherever they may be found. I ask you to fight for Secunda, a new Secunda, from whence, one day, we shall begin a great crusade to reclaim that which once belonged to us.

"As a symbol of our pact of brotherhood, I pass on to you these tokens, the very image of mine and me, may they bind you together behind my flag like wolves behind the pack leader. Remember always, what will matter most to us is your lord, your armour, and the man beside you.

"My little brothers," continued the priest. "Armenius spoke to us of many things. It's not until we join him that we are able to fully understand what he was trying to say to us. Each of us will find our own meaning in His words and ask our own questions. What was the token he gave his first group of initiates? Could one of you be among the hundred knights He referred to in His prophecy? In His transcendence, could His prophecy have referred to the near one hundred knights who stood with him at the very end and therefore been speaking of a past battle instead of voicing a prophecy?

"Initiates, the life you are embarking on is hard and fraught with danger. It is a rare knight who survives long enough to allow old age to take him. You will have many questions about His writings, and we will be happy to help you as best we can. But the best person you can ask is Armenius himself. Live your life as a knight with honour. Seek glory for Secunda and your king before yourself. Protect the defenceless with your blood. Smite the great enemy wherever you find him and one day you will meet Armenius. And on that day you will draw swords with him on the battlefield in the sky and on that day, little brothers, if you can call to him over the din of battle, you'll get an answer."

When the priest finished speaking, the knight lords above them stepped back from their dais and turned to disappear from sight. Not too long after, Lord Faramon appeared at a small side entrance.

"The initiates chosen for the Order of the Knights Aggressor will follow me, now," he said, and then turned and walked into the dull light beyond.

With the sound of shuffling robes and feet of the initiates that had been chosen followed their new lord to their new lives. Uthiel could not help but notice the smirk of self-satisfaction on Amorn's face, directed at him, as the big lad left the room. Next, the lord sent from the Order of the White Rose came forth and a smaller group of initiates followed him out. Finally, Lord Pomen appeared at the door.

"Initiates of the order of the Grey Wolf," he said. "You will follow me now."

Uthiel pushed himself up from the stone floor and fell into line with his other brother initiates. Despite his sadness at being looked over by the Knights Aggressor, it did his spirit some good to see Branor, Keldon and Linton stand to take their places with the new Grey Wolf initiates. With a small sigh of resignation Uthiel let go of his disappointment. *I am still going to become a knight. I am still going to be the best.*

CHAPTER THREE

Captain Lucien Phyrus stood shoulder to shoulder with Father Trethore as he looked over his small group of charges. *Twenty knights as my first command: fourteen raw initiates and six hardened veterans. And eighty men on the frontier.* To the far right stood his lieutenant, Ghurkar Storm, in full battle armour with a sword strapped to both his left hip and over his right shoulder. The grey tabard of the Order clung snugly to him and rustled lightly in the wind.

Phyrus glanced over his other veterans with a small smile that quickly disappeared when his grey eyes settled on the initiates. They stood dead straight, awaiting his word with the eager anticipation of youth, their travel-stained grey initiate tabards now lying over their baked leather and chain armour. The early afternoon sun shone over his shoulder and not only onto the fronts of his charges, but also onto the immense fortress behind them.

It would have taken the initiates and Father Trethore three days to ride from the city to the fortress of the Order of the Grey Wolf. Father Trethore had come with them with a group of ponies destined to be battle mounts for the knight lords. Phyrus called out to Storm to join he and the father. As the lieutenant made his way over, Phyrus turned to Trethore.

"I remember when I was an initiate, we had to walk here from Secunda," Phyrus grumbled, half jokingly.

Father Trethore smiled, but seemed otherwise to ignore the comment. "Just remember, captain, that your men are a direct reflection of yourself and your methods. Use Storm to train them hard. Lead by your own example, and you will be a successful captain. You're not here to be their friend; you're here to train them until you can confidently lead them into battle."

Phyrus nodded. *Leading men into battle.* He took a calming breath as Storm arrived.

Uthiel watched his captain as Phyrus explained, for the hundredth time, the premise of a shield wall. A month in to his training, he had become well-used to the sight of the young knight captain who had pushed him and his brothers cruelly, and brutally, every day for the last thirty. Phyrus was a hard young warrior. Handsome, but chastened by battle, Uthiel knew from experience that he was not a captain who allowed himself to be crossed.

It had begun with one dread sentence, roared in Storm's harsh voice. One dread sentence.

"Now my little brothers," his voice had boomed, *"let us see how far I can push your scrawny bodies today."*

That horrible statement had started the hardest month of Uthiel's young life. He and his brothers ran up and down hills until his chest burned and his stomach rebelled and his legs gave way. *I can still taste the vomit.* They lifted logs until his back ached and his shoulders turned to jelly. *But I am stronger for it.* They learned to swim in the local lake, oft coming near to drowning in their efforts as they were pushed harder and harder and further into the icy deep. *I shall never forget the biting cold, long or short as I live I shall thank Armenius for warmth.* They ate simple, tasteless, food and each bitterly cold night slept in a run-down barracks outside of the fortress. *My next mutton or steak or pork shall be divine.*

Uthiel reflected on his last month in comparison to his years of training under Trethore. The old priest had been hard, but the lessons in swordplay and tactics had become fun. His body hadn't ached every morning and pounded with pain every night, neither had his training compatriots been so strong and brutal and fast. The veterans they'd trained beside had been unwelcoming and brutal.

It had taken only three weeks for the first initiate to fail, his arm and leg broken after a vicious fall during a training run. The memory of the horrible injury was burned into Uthiel's memory like none before it. *A ruined forearm hanging grotesquely limp from halfway up the limb. White bone jutting from pink and red torn jelly flesh. Screams of agony. Blue eyes open in horrified awe and shock as Aran stared at his mangled body.*

Uthiel shuddered at the memory. It had been a stark lesson on youthful invulnerability. A second memory followed the first. One of things to come and a glimpse of brotherhood to be earned.

"Goodbye Aran," Uthiel had whispered under his breath.

"He'll lose the arm, and perhaps the leg," had come a voice beside him. *"Sad way for one so promising to spend the rest of his life."*

Uthiel had looked up to see Captain Phyrus there. The captain's gaze was sorrowful for a heartbeat before hardening under Uthiel's quickly withdrawn stare. Without further word Phyrus had turned, muttering loudly about which lord he had insulted to be given such soft-bellied initiates. *A show of harshness. No true malice towards those he wants as brothers.*

Uthiel turned away from his captain and stole a glance at the young men around him. After the first month of punishing training, Uthiel had begun to notice a difference in the surviving young men around him. Gone were the days of moaning and groaning about not learning to fight, the pains of their exercises, and how unpleasant the food or uncomfortable their dwellings were. Gone was the puppy fat of youth, a lust for personal glory, and a lot of the stupid youthful pranks. Instead this was replaced by a bond of hardship and effort based on the solid constitution of a team. *They are becoming my brothers.*

"Uthiel!"

"Uthiel you little bastard! Pay attention!"

Something struck him half-heartedly up the side of the head. Uthiel winced at the sharp strike, yelping in surprise more than pain as he winced at his aggressor. Storm stood there, his face cold with disappointment.

"Apologies, captain!" shouted Uthiel.

Phyrus glared at him a while before continuing. Storm continued to glare at him. Uthiel knew exactly what that glare meant.

I'll pay for that later.

Uthiel's legs ached, each descending step jarring his knees, hips and back. Gooseflesh covered him, the cold making him paler than usual. His breath was ragged, but strong and deep, within his chest. *Three months of running this damned hill -*

To his right there was a sudden cry which jerked to a painful explosion of breath with a loud thump as Lokhi's ankle twisted and he slammed into the hard ground. Lokhi rolled thirty or so strides downhill as Uthiel tried to chase him, Branor's pounding footsteps directly behind him. Finally, the youth slid to a stop with a muffled cry of pain.

Uthiel and Branor were there to help him struggle to his feet. Lokhi stood, but on but within a few steps crumpled to the ground.

"Come on, brother, stand tall," hissed Uthiel, his glance racing to find Storm before he saw Lokhi's falter.

It was too late. Storm spotted the fall immediately and was trudging over, jets of mist rhythmically bursting from his flared nostrils.

"Boy!" he yelled. "You'll stand and run with the rest of the initiates or I'll..."

Before he could stop himself, Uthiel interposed himself between the Wolf and his prey. He felt his friends form up beside him.

"We've got him," said Branor as he and Keldon each took one of Lokhi's arms over their own shoulders and hefted him from the ground.

45

Uthiel looked back to Storm. The big lieutenant was right in front of him. Uthiel prepared himself to take a beating, his shoulders squaring while he quailed inside. He forced his lip to draw back into a silent snarl. *Come on, get it over with.* A wry smile spread across Storm's lips.

"Took you long enough."

Uthiel stood, disbelieving as Storm turned and trudged back away down the hill. His guts were in a knot of turmoil and wind rushed in his ears as he tried to calm himself. Captain Phyrus met Storm at the bottom of the hill. They spoke for a time as the initiates helped Lokhi down the hill.

"Thanks, my brothers. Storm would have handed me a beating to remember for that. I owe you," hissed Lokhi through pain-pursed lips.

"And then some," said Branor. "I imagine you could have used your head as a shield to take some of the brunt though."

Lokhi huffed a painful laugh.

"Think nothing of it. Here, we are brothers, in spirit if not yet in title," said Uthiel.

Keldon reached over with his free hand and patted Lokhi on the chest, his own red face cooling as he got his breath back. "As Uthiel says, think nothing of it. We *are* brothers. And there is the foe."

Uthiel looked up and saw his two commanders watching him.

"Best we get down there quickly."

They trudged down the rest of the hill, their booted feet slipping and sliding in the mud, tripping when they found buried stone. Lokhi cried out in pain more than once as he did his best to walk unaided. By the time they reached the base of the hill, Uthiel was breathless once more.

"Captain, I believe the first lesson has been learned," said Storm. "Perhaps it is time for the next lesson to begin?"

Captain Phyrus was quiet for a moment as he watched initiates gather at the bottom of the hill. With a quick motion to a servant a cart was unveiled revealing a small pile of training weapons. Uthiel felt his anticipation rise, a smile tugging at his raw lips.

Storm walked over and picked up two wooden swords and two wooden bucklers. Walking back towards the young initiates he dropped a sword and a buckler on the ground and then started swishing his weapon through the air in a host of fast warm up exercises. To finish, he rolled his shoulders cockily and then called out for a challenger.

"Who amongst you would like to try your lot against me?" he called, laughing as if in the midst of a joke.

The initiates stood still, unsure of what to do. Uthiel felt his face flush. *I'll take you.*

"What!? Not one of you brave or foolish enough to try to strike me a single blow?"

Keldon flashed a smile at Uthiel before striding forward. *Damn.* Within three heartbeats of picking up the sword and buckler and taking his first swing at Storm, he lay as a groaning heap on the ground. *Damn.* Storm stood over him, calling out the next challenger.

Before Uthiel could react, his mind still trying to recount just how Storm had felled Keldon, Branor strode forward. He lasted two heartbeats longer, actually managing to parry a single one of Storm's strikes. But soon he was face down in the soft earth with Storm's boot on the back of his shoulders. Uthiel's eyes narrowed, *Damn, he's strong. Fast too. Arrogant bastard though.*

This gamecock show of martial prowess got Uthiel's ire up and he strode forward. The wooden sword was deceptively heavy and had been well weighted. Looking at the handle he saw that a rod of steel had been inserted to give the practice weapon a weight more like the real thing. Taking a quick couple of practice swings Uthiel got the blade's measure quickly and strode towards Storm.

Uthiel recounted, once more, Storm's movements. He knew that his opponent had allowed each initiate to strike first and then used the weight of their stroke to cleverly parry and with a swift movement put them off balance. A cracking strike to the head had followed both times.

I can beat him. Uthiel chanced his arm and swung. This time Storm stepped into the strike and swatted the blade away with his buckler, stabbing the point of the practice sword at Uthiel's torso. Only quick reflexes saved him as Uthiel twisted out of the way and stung Storm a light, off balance blow on the cheek with his own buckler.

Smiling cruelly as Uthiel re-took his stance, Storm attacked with lightning speed. Uthiel dodged the first blow, stopped the second but lost his sword as his wrist jarred, and then finally saw stars as he was swatted in the face by Storm's buckler. The blunt sword slammed in to his stomach and doubled him over, his breath gone and stars flashing before his eyes. As he stumbled forwards, Storm brought his knee up and Uthiel was out cold in a moment of blinding pain. The last thing he heard was his nose crunching.

He came around a moment later, the mud soaking through the back of his pants, clothes and hair. "Did I win?"

The youths around him chuckled. Branor offered him a hand up.

"Give them the rest of the day off," said Phyrus. "Armenius knows they're going to need all the strength they can muster tomorrow."

"As you command, my captain," nodded Storm in agreement, turning away from the fallen three and dumping his weapons back into the cart.

Uthiel jumped away from a wild swing that caught the end of his initiate's tabard. Quickly crouching in a fighting stance, he blocked two more swings with his metal weighted wooden sword, the impact sending hard vibrations through his hand and arms. He lunged forward inside of his opponent's reach and delivered a swift shoulder barge, which dropped the other initiate to the ground. A vicious downward swing was blocked before Uthiel kicked the sword from Branor's hand and placed the tip of his own at his friend's neck.

"Do you yield?" asked Uthiel.

Branor nodded, his open mouth sucking in huge lungfuls of air after their bout. Uthiel stepped back and offered his friend a hand.

"Bran, you need to stop leaving yourself open to that lunge," said Uthiel. "I get you the same way almost every time when we spar."

"Indeed he does, young Branor," said Captain Phyrus, having warmed to them somewhat during the youths' gruelling combat training.

Taking Branor aside, Phyrus quickly tutored Uthiel's friend in a few different techniques to avoid and counter Uthiel's lunge. Quickly, Uthiel found himself standing across the mud practice circle from Branor once more. Three victorious bouts later Uthiel eventually found himself on the wrong end of Branor's practice sword, stars exploding into view as his lunge was deftly avoided and a curt crack to his temple was delivered.

"Break!" called out Phyrus and the practice yard went from being filled with grunts and the crack of wood on wood, to the exhausted panting of the thirteen initiates and five veterans as they tried to regain their breath after their training. Branor sat next to Uthiel.

"How's the head, brother?" asked Branor.

Uthiel smiled dumbly as he used both his arms to prop himself up. "Lucky strike Bran, lucky strike."

A young boy came by with a small bucket of water that both Uthiel and Branor drank from. Thanking the lad, they sent him on to the next small group of initiates. Eight months into their training and the boys had begun to look like young men. Uthiel's shoulders were squarer and wider. His body was filling out with muscle and when he looked at Branor, he could see his friend's face had begun to take on the harder edge of a fit fighting man. Uthiel imagined his face had begun to look the same. He ran his hand over his jaw where a sparse and fluffy stubble had taken root on the angular bone.

Uthiel ran over what he had learned this day. He had drawn blades with Storm, the Lieutenant wielding his sword left handed. Awkward and difficult, he winced at the myriad of bruises he'd received in the morning. His hands were muddied from where their small company had formed a mock shield wall and he'd dragged back an injured man from the front line. His back was caked in filth from where he himself had been dragged back as the injured man. He smiled to himself. *This is where I am meant to be.*

It wasn't until a pleasant November morning that they were finally pulled out from under the blacksmith's hammer, having been beaten into useful soldiers as far as training could take them. That snowy, gloomy day Uthiel woke to the doors of the barracks being slammed open and captain Phyrus marching in with his six veterans in tow.

"Little brothers!" he yelled at the top of his voice. "Get up. Get dressed. Get outside in formation."

Lieutenant Storm was beside the captain. "Time to wake from your wet dreams and pull your sticky hands from your breeches young ones! Up! Up! Get up!"

The initiates were well used to Lieutenant Ghurkar Storm's methods and were quickly up and awake, moving about in organised chaos. Uthiel moved about quickly, getting dressed and wrapping on a leather belt. In short order the thirteen initiates fell into line on the dirt road outside the barracks with their brothers. Last out was Linton, who fell into line under the hard stare of Captain Phyrus.

"Initiates!" yelled Phyrus. "You will fall into line behind me on the march!"

Uthiel and his brothers followed him the short distance to the fortress gates at a brisk pace. There they stopped and once more stood to attention. The gates opened enough for two men to exit with Father Trethore following behind them. Uthiel craned his neck to see past and in to through the gate, but there was nothing to see.

Father Trethore bade the two men stop and place down their load. The sweating thralls carefully put down an iron brazier with bright orange coals glowing with heat. A long, thin metal prod had its head resting within the brazier, glowing a dull red almost a quarter of the way up its length.

Phyrus stood dead straight before them, as if on parade. His voice coated generously in the tone of ceremony, he addressed them. "Initiates, you have passed all of the tests our order can throw at you. There is but one final test. As a knight we are the property of Secunda, to do with as our king wills. There is one sacrifice of submission we ask before you don our colours and our armour and call us your brothers. A sign of Secundan purity to be seared onto the flesh. You will not balk. You will not shy away. You will not cry out. Purity by fire, little brothers. Purity by fire."

Phyrus pointed at Uthiel, and then waved him forward. Uthiel's heart quickened its pace and sweat began to trickle down from his brow. *What now?* His legs pulled him forwards before his mind could even register what he was walking towards. One of the men next to the brazier motioned for him to remove his tabard and shirt. He did so without hesitation, baring the naked flesh of his torso and arms to the elements. The same man motioned for him to raise his right arm and place his hand behind his head. Once again, almost mechanically, Uthiel complied. *What is he going to -*

As the white-hot wolf head symbol came from the brazier Uthiel fully comprehended just what was about to happen. Gripping a fist full of hair and clenching his teeth, he tried to mentally prepare himself as the skin of his side was lit up by the poke and started to sweat vigorously. Then it pressed against him.

White pain exploded from his side and his vision went black as he clenched his eyes. The smell of his own burning flesh filled his nostrils. His mind screamed wordlessly but no sound passed. The taste of blood whet his tongue as his teeth ripped through a small part of his lip. The moment of pain that seemed to last forever was over in a few short heart beats. It left only the searing of still burning skin and the muscle ache of having clenched every sinew within his body to its limit to obey his captain's words.

You will not balk. You will not shy away. You will not cry out. Purity by fire, little brothers. Purity by fire.

Uthiel struggled to get his shaking legs to obey him and keep him upright. Never in his young life had he ever experienced such pain. Looking down his side with eyes wet with unspent tears, he saw there was a massive red welt on his pale skin. The raw burnt flesh at its centre in the made the hard-edged shape of a simple wolf's head. The man holding the poker waved him past and into the door. Captain Phyrus placed a hand on his shoulder.

"Welcome, brother."

Uthiel did his best not to show the pain of his branding as he allowed himself to be led into the gates. *Wait. Brother?*

Inside he walked in to a hall full of knights, hundreds of them. As he entered they looked up from their conversation, plates of food, or mugs of ale. Those that were sitting stood, eyes locked on him. Broad smiled split grim face and a roar of welcome buffeted Uthiel.

Somewhat dumbfounded the young knight stood with his mouth agape as Branor walked into him from behind and a mug brimming with ale was pressed into his hand. Men in the livery of the Grey Wolves shook his hand in welcome. Some he'd trained with but never spoken to. Others he'd trained under or seen entering or exiting the Grey Wolves' fortress. All had been seemingly indifferent to his existence.

The straight backed form of Lord Pomen walked in flanked by the first captain and another one of the high ranking Grey Wolves he'd not seen before and shook his and then Branor's hands, a broad grin spread across his usually stern features.

"Welcome, my brothers."

"Aye!" cheered the knights surrounding them, "Welcome to our newest brothers!"

Nikhael Rokarn stood tall against the walls of the fortress. His gaze steadily and nonchalantly swinging from left to right across the plains and the horizon before him. His fresh white tabard flowed lazily over his polished plate armour. With the first slow waves of boredom creeping over his mind he shrugged his shoulders and pauldrons up to his ears and arched his back to stretch out the tiring muscles.

He thought of the past year of training as an initiate of the Knights Aggressor, and how its hardships had stripped away what little fat he'd had from his earlier teens. His body had grown with long and lean muscle along a frame that had his as tall as most of his brothers. His pitch-black shoulder length hair hung lank past his well stubbled square jaw. Something minute grabbed his attention on the horizon, a tiny dark smudge in the waning light.

Swinging his head right and left, he looked at the hunched forms of the other brother knights standing vigilant along the stone wall. He spotted the captain of the watch some hundred feet away, and then the bulky form of Amorn half way in between. He called out to the burly knight. Amorn's sour expression rested on him for a moment as he listened and then he turned to show his immensely broad back, its size exacerbated by the stereotypically large pauldrons of his armour, and called to the captain of the watch.

Within moments Captain Tybar was by his side.

"How goes it, brother?" he asked amiably. "Enjoying your time on the White Frontier defending our nation?"

I'm about to be. Nikhael motioned with his head, and then followed with his arm, to point to the spot on the horizon he had spotted earlier. "Brother captain, I think it's about to get a bit more enjoyable."

Tybar's eyes narrowed as he squinted to see. After a moment he spotted the smudge, then a few miles to either side he spotted some more small smudges, a few bunched here, a few bunched there. His jaw clenched as he placed his hand on Nikhael's pauldron.

"Brother, fetch the lord field marshal."

Nikhael jogged down from the battlement, a thin smile crossing his face. *Finally.* He straightened his face out with a quick moment of self-discipline as he approached the lord field marshal's war room. Two of his brothers opened the door for him and he walked straight in.

Inside, the lord field marshal, brother of the king, stood next to a great oak table pushing small wood figurines around a large parchment map. Nikhael waited for him to finish his discussion with his lords before moving forward, clearing his throat loudly to announce his presence as he lowered himself to one knee.

"My lord field marshal," started Nikhael, his voice firm and unwavering despite the legend he was addressing. "The captain of the watch humbly requests your presence atop the west facing battlement. Urgently my lord."

Lord Field Marshal Loghan Faramon turned to face him. Nikhael lowered his gaze as was expected.

"Rise, my brother knight," said the Lord Faramon quietly. "Lead the way."

As the sun dipped below the mountains, the Lord Faramon, with his entourage of captains, generals and advisors, set foot once again on the battlements. The captain of the watch met them and their eyes turned to the faint orange glow that lined easily ten miles worth of the horizon. Close by, the young knight Nikhael stood, levelly staring out to the plain.

The Lord Field Marshall turned to the captain of the watch. "Captain Tybar. Take your men. Five mounted scouting groups of twenty. Do not enter into any engagements; I want to know exactly how far away their main forces are. Go, now. I'll expect you back by midday tomorrow."

Captain Tybar called his men from their section of the battlement and to arms.

Turning to one of his advisors, Lord Faramon continued. "Seven riders. One to each of the fortresses either side of us, they can warn the frontier towns on their way. Three to each of the army camps to mobilise. The Third army to strengthen the lines to our south, the Fifth to the north, and the Fourth in reserve here."

"And the last two riders, my lord?" asked the advisor.

With a deep breath he dragged his eyes from the horizon. "Unless I'm mistaken, within two days we will be facing the greatest incursion of our age. Gall will want her sons here to share in the glory. Request King Grenhel to move his reserve armies into the frontier to the far left and far right of our forces and try to link up with the forces of our brother orders in the north and south. Send two hundred and fifty of our brothers with each of the four armies. "

"Our line will be thin, my lord."

I don't need you to tell me that. "I concur, but it is necessary. Their raiding groups will cause havoc otherwise and we need our supply and reinforcement lines clear."

"And the king?"

"Yes, my friend, best let my brother know what's happening."

The lord field marshal's eyes moved back to the horizon. The orange glow had spread a further four miles wide across the darkening horizon. *My time for glory approaches. Time to show my worth. Time to be truly worthy of my bloodline.*

CHAPTER FOUR

Before the light of the sun had completely disappeared below the mountains, Nikhael sat on a war mount in his group of twenty knights. He felt naked without his plate, stripped off and left at Archenon Creek for speed, and looked with questioning disdain at the dark hard leather armour with dark green cloak that sat light upon his shoulders. The silver of his buckles was blackened with dampened charcoal.

His brothers sat saddled around him, similarly clad. Even the light spots on their horses had been darkened to help them blend into the night.

At the head of Nikhael's scouting column, Captain Tybar watched as the other four parties of twenty knights disappeared into the darkness led by his lieutenants. The soft pounding of their horses' hooves was the only evidence of their existence as the darkness of distance enveloped them on the plain. With an exaggerated wave of his gloved hand Tybar spurred his horse away. Nikhael and his brothers followed into the night.

Almost twelve hours of hard riding later, Nikhael and his brothers came to a halt as Captain Tybar tried to confirm their position in the waning darkness of the morning. The light of the early sun creeping over the plain had long hidden the fires of the enemy and had made seeing their camps extremely difficult. Looking back to the mountains and the distant fortress back across the plain, Tybar nodded to Nikhael and waved his men into the forest but remained stationary himself. As each knight passed, he spoke in a low voice.

"Silence herein, brother," he whispered to Nikhael as the young knight passed. "The enemy will be close and they must not see nor hear us."

In front of them, a small forest sat thick with foliage. With the sun rising on the other side dark shadows lay heavy throughout and were very rarely pierced by a spear of sunshine. Motioning to Nikhael and brother Karkas to scout on ahead on foot, Tybar trotted his horse back to the head of his column as the thick canopy of the forest cut off almost all light once more from above.

Behind Nikhael and Karkas, their eighteen brothers disappeared from view quickly as they surged ahead into the undergrowth. Nikhael could hear Karkas' breathing and footsteps as they cut through the forest at a steady but quiet jog. Suddenly, another sound caught Nikhael's attention. There was something out of place in this quiet forest, something unnatural and not of this leafy land. Nikhael's fist rose to shoulder height as he quietly slowed himself and hid behind a fallen tree. Karkas joined him immediately and just as stealthily.

Nikhael glanced over the moss-covered trunk. He moved cautiously, allowing his eyes to gradually adjust to the different light levels. Long, slow breaths soon slowed his heart from the exertion of their jog. Ahead, atop a light rise in the middle of a clearing not a stone throw wide, three silhouetted figures stood in quiet discussion punctuated with animated hand gestures. As Nikhael's eyes adjusted, details began to pull themselves from the shadowy figures.

Two were dressed in light armour and patchy furs. Leather straps over bare, tattooed muscles held their garments together. A brutal short handled axe hung in a loop from each hip and a long bladed hunting knife was scabbarded across their chest. Each man's head was shaved with a single tail of plaited hair hanging from the base of their bald skull.

The third was a taller and far more imposing man, the strong lines of plate metal armour barely visible in the shadow he stood in. There was no movement but Nikhael felt an unnatural shiver travel up his spine when looking at the figure, as if he could feel the man's anger or hatred emanating from his shadowed face. Nikhael could almost sense those invisible, baleful eyes on him. For the first time in his young life, Nikhael thought he might just understand fear.

He placed a firm hand on Karkas' shoulder to ensure his brother did not get curious. A single movement or sound and they would be undone. The quiet of the forest almost startled him. No bird calls. No sounds of creatures or wind whistling through the foliage above. Nothing. He looked back. The man in armour was gone. The two men in lighter armour still stood atop the rise but eventually separated and moved in opposite directions about forty feet to either side of Nikhael and Karkas' position.

Nikhael ducked down and faced his brother. Placing his forefinger and middle finger under each of his eyes he motioned Karkas to watch one of the enemy while he watched the other. Nikhael's mark walked in a hunched fashion, his eyes always on the area around him. He moved with confidence and almost perfect balance. The movement of his shoulders suggested a cocky swagger and his right hand quickly, but smoothly, dropped to his hip axe whenever he became suspicious or startled.

Placing a hand on his brother behind him once more, Nikhael rose into a crouch smoothly, quickly exchanging a glance with Karkas as he drew a finger across his throat. Karkas nodded and also rose into a crouch. Nikhael turned away from Karkas and refocussed on his enemy. His eyes flicked at a furious rate between where he was walking and where his mark was. Slowly but surely he gained on the man, his movements silent and his dark clothes blending him into the shadows he moved through. *You are mine.*

Thirty feet from his mark, he slipstreamed into the man's footsteps and slowly drew a foot long blade from his hip. The whisper of metal sliding through leather roared in Nikhael's ears, but the man before him paid it no heed. *My first.*

Twenty feet. Nikhael's heart remained calm, his eyes still flickering from the man to the ground. His footsteps were sure and stealthy, still moving quicker than his prey. Fifteen feet. *A quick stab through the throat.*

At ten feet away, he smoothly reversed the grip on his blade, facing the point to the ground. The man stopped all of a sudden, his hand dropping to his axe. *Shit.* In an instant Nikhael considered charging the man and quashed the thought, allowing his final step to deftly land him partially hidden by a tree. The man scanned the bushes in front of him for a moment before moving on. *Patience.*

Nikhael started moving again. Seven feet. The man started to turn. Nikhael burst into a sprint, his feet landing on some pre-sighted thick roots, and then leapt. The sound of his swifter movements startled the man, who turned more swiftly, hand flicking down and catching his axe from its loop in a surprisingly quick movement. The barbarian scout's eyes widened and his mouth opened to sound an alarm.

The warning never came as Nikhael rammed the full foot of his blade through the man's throat from right to left. With a quick wrench of his wrist Nikhael tore the blade through and out of the left side of the scout's neck, neatly semi-decapitating the man. The young knight closed his eyes as a thick, hot spray of blood splashed across his front and face. His quick and strong hands caught the falling foe and lowered him to the ground soundlessly. The man's eyes flickered for only a moment longer before he died with Nikhael crouched over him. *All that I had hoped for.*

Nikhael smiled as he felt the back end of the momentary surge of excitement and danger flow through him, like a spark of life burning within. Licking his lips he savoured the feeling of his first kill. The power of having bested an enemy one on one; the supremacy of his bloodletting. A cry in the direction of his brother followed by three furiously fast clashes of steel broke him from his moment.

In one instant of rash carelessness he stood without looking at his surroundings and was instantly spotted by the two scouts behind him. Two men from further down the picket line come to check on their comrades. Nikhael muttered a curse as he broke into a hard run towards where he had heard the sounds. Behind him a cry erupted and he heard an arrow fly by his head and saw it embed itself into a tree in front of him.

Swerving as a second arrow flew past him, he spotted the scuffle ahead. Karkas had his adversary in a headlock and was slowly suffocating his sluggishly thrashing foe. Still twenty feet away on the run, Karkas' bloodied face looked up just in time to see Nikhael draw his short blade once more and hurl it towards him. Instinctively he released his foe's neck and fell back to the ground, using the man's body as a cover. Nikhael's knife thudded into the scout's chest, burying half its length into his tattooed right pectoral.

"Up brother!" shouted Nikhael. "We must get to the captain!"

Karkas shook off his initial shock and stood to run with Nikhael. His arm up to steady his balance, Karkas never saw the three foot arrow that sliced through the unprotected skin of his underarm, through his lung, and burst into his heart. Nikhael turned away and ran harder. Karkas was dead before his body collapsed to the ground.

Mind cool, but his body pounding with hot blood, Nikhael ran as fast as he could. His feet slipped and slithered on leaves and mud, but he kept upright. He needed to find his captain and get his brothers out of the forest. They needed to get back to the plain. They needed to notify the lord field marshal. They'd found the forward markers of the enemy. A few days march and they would be at the walls of the White Frontier. *Two days till killing on an almost unprecedented level. Two days till I sate my thirst for battle, my hunger that has starved me since birth. I need only get back to the Frontier alive. Just need to make it alive. Just -*

At full sprint, Nikhael didn't even see the body he tripped over. There was no doubt, however, that he saw the opened stomach that he face planted into. Choking and coughing up blood and intestinal fluid, he looked up and cleared his eyes to find his eighteen brothers and most of their horses slaughtered upon blood-soaked ground. The bodies of three or four of the enemy lay amongst them, but the black-feathered arrows of the barbarians jutted from many of their corpses. In passing he noticed that the owner of the stomach he'd buried his face in was Captain Tybar.

The enemy looked up from their looting in shock to see him amongst them. Nikhael pushed himself to his feet and ran. As the arrows flew past him, or carved through his cloak, he spotted three still standing warhorses being guarded by a scout. Not even breaking step he drew his sword and rammed it into the surprised man's gut. The look on his tattooed and pitted face was one pain and surprise as he collapsed to the ground and released the tangle of reigns.

Leaving his blade jammed in the man's guts, Nikhael vaulted onto the horse. Pain lanced through him as an arrow pierced his forearm and immediately after, a second one slammed into his shoulder. A third arrow stuck into the meat of his panicked horse's flank and it tried to throw him. Using all of his strength he desperately held onto the reins as it galloped back the way they had come.

The small frontier town of Archenon Creek sat on the Gall side of a shallow twenty-foot wide creek, the plain that reached into the Black Lands stretching out opposite. Dirt roads were lined with poorly built huts and a single long hall. The few hundred villagers capable of heavy work were desperately pushing any barricade, be it a wooden carriage, a barrel, or a pile of rubbish, to the edge of the creek bed to create a wall. Men furiously shovelling dirt filled gaps in the line. Women and children streamed back from the town away from the plain, clutching babes and what little personal belongings they could to their chests.

As the work continued at the lip of the creek, the scouting party from the Secundan Fifth army along with their general arrived and after looking out over the plain to see the enemy slowly creeping across the far horizon, General Stern called over his scout leaders and had them immediately set to planning out the positions of their regiments along the line constructed by the townsfolk.

A creek to hold for the young *general. An easy task even one of my* inexperience *can handle,* Stern sneered to himself. *A general by skill and victory, not by right and all of a sudden age is a problem. Were I a son of Mirator I would have command of the fortress by this age of thirty summers.* Stern took a deep breath. *No point wasting time whinging. Best get on with it, as my father always said.*

"Genar, go get me a regiment. We need more men to work the defences," he ordered. "Arms and armour to be left behind. Brawn and digging tools welcome."

The scout saluted and ran back. Within the hour a full regiment of a thousand soldiers crested the small rise behind the town, devoid of their mail shirts and weapons. They set to with fervour along the line, relieving the townsfolk of their backbreaking efforts as the army's engineers directed the effort.

Stern watched impassively, the efficiency and work ethic drilled into his men chipping away at his sour mood. *I may not be the most respected of His Majesty's generals, but I'll be damned if my men aren't the best who wear Secunda's colours.*

Two hours later, the main body of the Secundan Fifth crested the hill and moved in to rank. Six thousand men stood in glittering ring mail armour covered in tabards sporting the king's family crest. Open faced conical helmets sat atop their heads and a forest of spear tips created a canopy of steel above them. Six captains strode forward to receive orders from their general.

Stern was short and blunt with them, his words as efficient as his men. Each captain nodded at the end of his briefing as he checked their understanding of his orders.

"Go, captains," said Stern. "You are Secunda's defence. You are the stone cut from her mountains, the steel dug from her mines, and the courage sent down from her skies. Do your duty, and we shall carry this day. Win me this battle, and we shall carry this war."

Having taken on their orders, each of the six captains met with their lieutenants and in a painfully slow manner the thousand strong regiments began to move to their positions on the line.

Three hours later, still only four of the six regiments were in place along the mile-long front. The roads and tails cut into the grass were a slurry of mud and animal excrement. Captains and lieutenants roared with anger and frustration. Men were stretchered away by comrades for twisted ankles and exhaustion.

Stern leaned over to one of his runners. "Go over there and start pulling companies out, one-by-one and move them around the greater body of men."

"Could I not just pull them all out? Get them out of the sludge, sir?" said the runner.

Stern's gaze narrowed, the man must have been twice his age. A grizzled veteran by the looks of him. "Was that my order?"

The runner's head dropped. "No, general. As you say."

Stern glared after him. *Must every order be questioned? Every standard practice queried before carried out? Will I be remembered as Stern the Uncertain? Stern the Unsure? Stern the Hapless General Who Knows Nothing Of Soldiering and Needs His Runners to Advise Him How to Unclog Military Traffic Because He is -*

His internal rampaging stopped as the baggage trains and his eight hundred archers finally arrived. He watched as a company moved around the column of slow moving men and jogged across unspoilt grass towards the end of the line. A second broke off soon over. Sending down more runners, Stern soon had his men spreading out and moving again. *Men moving with order. No randomness. Exactly as I wanted.*

General Stern turned his back on the movement of his regiments and rode to the highest point he could find, commanding a view for miles. It was the best place for him to see the battle. By his side, twenty swordsmen formed up ready as both his bodyguard and his messengers. He surveyed his men as each regiment continued to work on their positions to finish the hardy work of the seventh regiment. Six hours after he had arrived, he felt positive he and his men could hold this line along Archenon creek.

In his mind's eye, he watched the water and dip in the land of the creek slowing down the enemy and bunching them. Clouds of arrows would fall as the enemy charge compressed and slowed and the spearmen on the front line should be fresh with the advantage of the high ground when a tired and soaking wet enemy finally reached them.

We can hold them. The ground is on our side. Victory can be earned here. My name can be earned here.

The thundering of marching men caught his attention. Turning from the line he looked back behind him to see over two hundred knights in full plate mail moving towards him from the fortress. Ten knights on horseback rode ahead of the column to his position. Atop the front horse sat a tall captain in the livery of the Knights Aggressor. The man patted a fist against his chest in greeting and dipped his head in recognition of the general's rank.

"General Stern, I am Captain Unamor," said the man in a gravelly voice. "I have two hundred and fifty knights. We are at your disposal."

"Well met captain," replied Stern. "Stay here a moment, we have time to consider the best deployment for you while we await the arrival of the Gall Reserve army. We should be expecting ten thousand of their men before tonight."

Unamor's eyes swept out over the plan. "They'll be here before the sun sets on the morrow."

I recognise that fact, thank you Captain, his mind snapped venomously. Stern licked his lips as he watched a veritable flood of the enemy slowly swarm past forests, made tiny by distance, towards the line. *There are so many.*

"We'll do well to hold them here, general," said Unamor, his voice taking on a harder set.

Stern blew out his cheeks. "If we can hold for a couple of weeks, it'll give the king time to bring the full force of our nation forward to join with Gall and we'll destroy them there."

Unamor snorted, locking hard and confident eyes with Stern. "We'll hold them here. Not at Gall. Here. Glory and Armenius await, general."

There was a long moment of silence between the men. *Best get on with it.*

"Captain. You'll split your men into five groups of fifty and place them equally along the line at weak points. Places where the wall is small or hindered by nature, where there are easy crossings for the enemy along the creek bed, and one group at the end of the line with the fifth regiment," continued Stern. "Let the spearmen do their work at the wall but make sure your men are in the line and not behind it. If we get surrounded, have the knights on the end of the line fold the line back, do not let them get behind us or we are lost. The Sixth Regiment will go with you in reserve should they get in a position to flank you."

"General," nodded Unamor, and waved his men in behind him. As they moved off, the Sixth regiment fell into step behind them.

Kael smiled a smile full of filed sharp teeth. He tongued the points as he watched the barbarians he was using as a scouting party pull the black-feathered arrows from the bodies of the two Secundan messengers. *If only I could afford to have more of my brothers with me. Being so close to this disgusting race insults me.* The tattooed scouts, armed with axes and armoured in dirty leathers, sliced the dead messengers open from ear to ear to make sure their message never reached its destination. Kael spat as he glared malevolently at the scouts. *A necessary evil for the greater victory, I suppose.*

Four bold warhorses stood placidly near their deceased riders, awaiting somebody to mount them and direct them further. With a slash of his hand Kael ordered their throats slit and the beasts put down. One of the men flashed a look of dismal unhappiness at the order. Kael needed only lock eyes with the man for a fraction of a heartbeat to show his displeasure at the craven's weakness. He shook his head in annoyance as the barbarian ran off towards the warhorse like a whipped dog, blade in one shaking hand.

With the sun cresting the curve of the world behind his shoulder, Kael warily looked to the horizon to make sure he and his scouts were alone. The scouts dragged the dead bodies into the ditches on the side of the road and covered the cadavers with dirt and brushes. The horses were also dragged into the ditches and hacked into smaller chunks, making them easier to cover.

Kael brushed his greasy, pitch-black hair from his eyes, wiping his hand on his pants in a pointless effort to clean the palm of his own filth. His eyes were tired and sore, and he imagined his blue irises were surrounded with red-veined spider webs. One of the scouts looked up to him and started in fear as he found Kael's gaze narrowed upon him. Kael smiled inwardly, his teeth, his glare, and the scars upon his battered face having the exact desired effect upon the barbarian.

Brushing a couple of fleshy chunks and dirty clumps from his close-fitting and dark coloured steel plate armour, Kael waved the tribesmen over to him. A translator arrived first and in low whispers and vigorous hand gestures the dark metal clad warrior almost beat his message into the scrawny translator. With a disgusted sniff and turn, Kael moved away from the men in their tattered and filthy furs and leathers. The translator moved to the small group of scouts and passed on their leader's words in the guttural tones of one of the hundreds of guttural languages of the Black Lands.

The scouts split onto four groups and disappeared into the countryside, awaiting any further attempts by the White Frontier to pass word of the assault onto their kings. Kael smiled again, the skin of his face drawing tight across his high cheekbones as he envisioned the great slaughter to come.

A slaughter well overdue, he thought, nonchalantly bending his arm up to run a finger along the dented tall inner collar of his pauldron. His gaze went back to where the four groups of scouts had gone and he grinned viciously at what he and his brothers had planned. Ten years of meticulous strategy and sacrifice was about to pay off. It had been so long since they had last set foot on this side of the White Frontier, ten long years since the bloody schism that had seen him slay so many of his own brothers, only to be undone at the last moment. Kael snarled at the decade old memory of fleeing into the Black Lands.

Faces and names of those he and his men had betrayed raced through his mind and stoked the fires of his rage. *How could they have all been so blind? How could none of them have seen the power they could wield? How could they have drawn blade and raised shields against me to remain as meek slaves to a meek god?*

Kael's fists clenched so hard his knuckles cracked loudly. *They all could have been gods! Fools!*

The tall warrior hawked and spat upon the ground, and took a deep breath. There was a time to channel the rage he had been gifted, to unleash the bloodlust within and bring the wrath of his new god upon the Lands of the Light. That time was not now. Now was the time for cutting off messengers and raiding supply lines. Now was the time to sow fear of the unknown in the frontier towns, and for spies hidden in these lands for a decade to make their presence known.

Now was the time to make sure his enemy had as little time as possible to prepare for when the barbarian warlord, the man he and his fellow Black Wolves had raised above all the petty tribal squabbles that kept the Black Lands from wielding true power, opened the dam and let a million axes loose. A million wicked, half moon axes wielded by a million screaming tribesmen would destroy all in their path on a front hundreds of miles wide. Kael lifted at the thought, his singular focus and leadership and the culmination of ten years of dedication firing his blood.

A face came to mind. Young, stern, honourable. Storm. Kael's memory flashed to life.

"First Captain Kael! What in the name of Armenius are you doing?"

"Showing you a new world, my brother. A world where we are Gods amongst men. Where the Lands of Light and Blackness

bow to one supreme Order. Where the world bows to me and my Wolves."

"And who do you bow to? You are no god!"

"Contempt does not become you, brother."

"Traitor! Treasonous filth! You have betrayed the Eternal Lord, you've betrayed the King, you've betrayed your Order, you've betrayed our people, and you've betrayed me. Already you daub the traitor's black over your glorious grey! Draw your blades, cur, and let us see if you can bleed without a soul."

"Gladly, brother."

Their blades had met only three or four times before they had been pushed to other areas of the battle by their raging brothers. Kael's mind swam through the faces of those who chose to remain in the grey of the traditional Order and some in the black stain who had sided with him. A swirling melee of fratricide around him, unrivalled in savage hatred.

Kael could remember the duel as if he had fought it yesterday. His movements had been perfectly balanced and delivered with the power and ferocity expected of a knight first captain. Storm had fought with skill and the gusto of youth but Kael knew his man. Had watched him train for countless hours, advised him on how to use sword and shield and knife and his body to defeat almost any given foe. Had called him brother and sworn sacred vows to him and those like him. Kael allowed himself a brief smile as he remembered the tenacity of the young man. Such promise. Such a waste.

Kael snarled as he remembered the blow that had felled him. The bone-jarring impact of a kite shield as a lord slammed bodily into him. His feet desperately trying to keep him up. Tripping on a corpse unseen behind him and falling upon his back. His armour weighing him down just long enough for that lord's blade to come scything down and hammer into the join between his cuirass and gorget. The join had not been able to completely deflect the blade and Kael had bled his strength upon the ground.

His fading sight had rested firstly on the face of his assailant, and then seen the look of smug satisfaction on Storm's face as he stood over him. Battle had swept them up again, giving them only a moment to savour this false victory, and Kael had risen unsteadily and seen that this fight was lost. He and his brothers had failed to sacrifice enough of their erstwhile brethren, and they had suffered defeat.

This time, I will have my sacrifice, and my Wolves will rule as we were meant to.

Lord Field Marshall Loghan Faramon stood atop his bastion on the White Frontier. In front of him, hundreds of thousands of the enemy advanced upon Archenon Creek, like a black flood forging towards them. It was only a matter of hours until the flood would hit the dam. Looking to the right of the walls, he observed as the Secundan Fifth finished moving into their prepared positions, the late morning sun glinting off the long rows of metal armoured, and spear armed, men.

With pride he watched as the two hundred and fifty of his brother knights separated and moved to five different points in the mile long line. With two regiments in reserve and the creek to the fore, he felt quietly confident that the line would hold long enough for the messengers to reach the two kings to the rear of the line. His gaze settled on the small group surrounding the army general on the rise behind the line and the reserve regiments. Lord Faramon whispered a small and urgent prayer to Armenius that those eight thousand men could hold. *Their general is young, but sound. The line will hold there.*

Running a leather-gloved hand through his hair he turned in the opposite direction to gauge the progress of the Secundan Third army to the fortress's left. Without the protection of the creek bed that the Fifth enjoyed, they would be hard pressed to hold the line against the oncoming enemy. Like the Fifth, the Third had made the best use of the natural barricades to supplement the earth of their defensive line. Their eight thousand men stood proud and ready to receive the charge. The Third's general had held only one regiment in reserve, the additional men and the knights allocated to them pressed into the potential weak points of the line.

A tall knight garbed in polished plate armour and a spotless white tabard moved to stand beside the lord field marshal. Loghan noted the burning desire for glory in those deep blue eyes. There was a hunger beyond that of the rank and file knight in them. The tall knight sneered as his eyes swept out over the plane and seemed to drink in the sight of the foe.

"Lord Ambar," said Loghan, turning to his friend. "I look forward to locking shields with you my brother. This foe shall both test us and define us in the annals of history."

Lord Ambar's eyes remained locked on the approaching horde until he slowly dragged them away to look at Loghan. "Define us they will, lord field marshal. Define us they will."

Loghan noted the finality in the man's voice. He didn't like the tone, nor the look on the face of the man he had fought beside for the last twenty-five years. There was something in the lord's eyes that had changed. *Fatalism perhaps? No, there was too much strength there for fatalism. Too much self-belief in our coming victory.*

Before he could ponder his brother's demeanour further an aide to Lord Ambar approached and whispered into Ambar's ear. The lord listened intently, never breaking the king's brother's stare. The aide finished, spared Loghan a cautious nod of respect, and then departed. Loghan frowned at this casual slight from one of his men. Before he could speak further, Ambar excused himself.

"I must away lord field marshal. I am required," was all he said before turning and walking away.

Angry now, Loghan called out to the departing lord. Ambar turned, his face like a mask over the man Loghan had once known.

"My friend, are you alright?" he asked, reeling in his raging ego. An argument with one of his closest friends and leaders prior to the greatest battle of his life just would not do.

The Lord Ambar paused for an eerie moment, his face leering and cracking into an odd smile. "When they are here I will be, my lord general."

Loghan nodded to nobody in particular as the lord had already once more turned away.

Loghan hadn't noticed the Lord Irill approach until he appeared by his side. Loghan smiled as he regarded his brother. Trusted friend and stalwart leader of men, the Lord Irill was a man to follow into battle like few others could claim to be. He was a charismatic leader and solid fighter. Men would follow him into the front garden of Death herself if it meant a chance to lock shields with him.

"Well met, brother," said Loghan.

"Probably just itching for a fight, my lord field marshal," said Irill amiably.

"What?" asked Loghan.

"The Lord Ambar," Irill responded. "He seems a bit off, I know. I believe it is just the excitement of getting to grips with the great enemy in a front on battle instead of all these minor skirmishes we've been involved in over the last few years. It is about time those bastards came at us with some decent numbers."

Loghan slowly agreed, more to himself that to Irill. "It's a fair point. Unfortunate that they could not wait a month or two until we had more men at the frontier. Then we could crush them here in one decisive battle and begin the crusade to take back Mother Secunda in the one year."

"Fortunate, however, for us," smiled Irill.

"How so?" asked Loghan.

"All the more glory for our blades," said Irill cheerily. "The Lands of the Light shall never forget the days when the warriors of the Knights Aggressor met the beasts from the Black Lands."

Loghan smiled, won over by his friend's words.

"Have you ever seen such fine men?" asked Irill, changing the subject and sweeping his arm out over in the direction of the men of the Secundan Fifth.

"They do me proud, my friend," responded Loghan. "The enemy are almost here."

Lord Irill drew his lips thin. "They are many. And we are few. But such are the beginnings of legend! I will return to my men. If Armenius calls you to His side before I see you again, make sure you keep a spot beside you in His shield wall for me."

"Armenius guide your blade, my friend," responded Loghan sombrely as his gaze returned to his deployed men. Their finery and preparedness warred within him with the sight of so many thousands opposing him. He lost himself for a while as he watched them come.

Hours had passed as he had observed his men fall into line and the enemy slowly make its way across the plain. The pivotal moment of his life was about to come to pass. Years of training and politicking and making war in far smaller theatres to get to his brother to give him this position had led him to this point. *By the shining armour of Armenius I will not let my king or my country down. I will not fail!*

Confident in the prowess of his brother knights and the soldiers they stood amongst, one final question plagued his mind.

Where are my scouting parties and where are the men of Gall?

Nikhael's vision slithered through shades of grey and black as his exhausted horse pushed him and itself ever closer to the Archenon Creek fortress on the White Frontier. Stumbling over small divots and branches, the horse's strength eventually gave out leaving the wounded knight to tumble to the ground with its soured body.

The young Knight Aggressor used his uninjured arm to push himself to his feet and continued towards the fortress, his footsteps faltering but certain in their direction. The black feathered arrows stuck in his body quivered and pulled moans of pain from him as he moved. He looked up and pleaded for help from his brothers. At more than a mile he doubted they could see him.

Shredded by branches, his tabard hung on his stricken form. Tearing it off with his good hand, he held it aloft to gain the attention of his brother knights. He dragged his exhausted body across the plain until he saw the forward gates open. A troop of four armoured knights galloped towards him and the waves of relief washing over him finally collapsed him to the group's arms, his energy spent.

Nikhael Rokarn had finally been defeated, his body useless as he allowed himself to be picked up by his brothers and taken back to his lords.

Within the hour he stood wavering upon the fortress ramparts before the lord field marshal of all of Armenia's armies, wearily recounting the death of his brothers, the slaying of the enemy, the push to get home before he was caught and killed. Nikhael looked out to the west to watch the solid black mass of the great foe rolling ever closer to them. He almost allowed himself to despair at the thought of their waste. He and his brothers had been sent out to gauge the strength and distance away of the enemy. They had achieved nothing but the death of many much-needed knights.

As the lord field marshal dismissed his presence a surgeon approached him. He looked at the arrows jutting from his flesh, their pain now a dull agony in his exhausted form. The surgeon sat him down and told him how lucky he was that the barbarians did not use barbed headed arrows. Nikhael summoned a searing remark and was about to let fly when the surgeon gripped one of the shafts. His touch alone brought the pain scorching back. Nikhael closed his almost black eyes and clenched his jaw.

Armenius, steel my soul.

CHAPTER FIVE

Hours later, Lord Field Marshal Loghan Faramon still stood atop the fortress walls, watching the enemy finally close to within a mile of his lines. A veritable flood of barbarian humanity plastered the plain in front of him. The very foulness of their being stained the soul of the land. Their filthy battle chants flowed over the fortress like a tide of invisible ants flowing over a corpse. Lord Faramon felt, and exercised, the need to spit to cleanse his mouth of the foulness before him.

Come on! Come here so I can slay you! Come here so I can carve my name into the annals of glory! The wait frustrated him to no end. Deep calming breaths and solemn prayers to the Eternal Lord were all that stood between him and ordering, and leading, a glorious charge to defeat the disgusting barbarians. Some of the knights immediately around him looked to him with stealthily worrisome gazes. Any that he caught he visually burned with the courage of his conviction.

It was beyond his doubt that they would hold. Here, on the White Frontier, his name would forever be burned into the histories as the general who held the line against not tens but hundreds of thousands. *Maybe more than a million. Who can say? When victors write the histories, who can deny we stood against the entire barbarian race?*

Irrespective, his name would be marinated in glory for once, instead of his brother's.

One thousand feet. The enemy started to move more quickly.

Five hundred feet. Come on. The soldiers manning the White Frontier began calling to each other. He could hear their voices floating upon the wind.

"Hold!"

"Hold the line, brothers!"

"Spears to the fore lads! Show them some Secundan steel!"

"For the King! For the Eternal Lord!"

Three hundred feet and Lord Faramon's vision centred on the Fifth army to his right as the archers drew their bows and loosed. While the shafts still flew towards their apex, a second volley was loosed. Before the first volley struck a third was in the air. Close to two and a half thousand arrows lazily cut their way through the sky before striking home with devastating effects. The cramped conditions of the approaching horde saw a horrific number of casualties as the first volley of steel-tipped doom struck. Hundreds fell to the ground with the dark wood shafts of Armenian hatred jutting from their bodies.

Those brought down slowed the men behind them and in moments the dead were almost doubled as the second volley struck home, carving through the tightly packed barbarians like a scythe through a wheat field. The enemy died in bloodied droves but despite over a thousand fallen dead or wounded this was like a pinprick to the wild boar.

Loghan saw hundreds of small acts of horror and heroism in those moments. A man was slain trying to pull his wounded barbarian comrade away from where the arrows were falling. Both were trampled to death by another charging horde. Someone caved in the head of a mortally wounded barbarian with the back of his axe in a mercy-kill. Another barbarian picked up a dead body and used him as a meat-shield to advance under. Many continued forwards with shafts jutting from their limbs. Archers pulled arrows from the dead, and some not so dead, whilst more flitted down amongst their number. *Almost enough to see them as men, and not pure evil. Almost.*

With the swift speed of the battle the great enemy's minions struck their fur and dirty leather booted feet into the sluggish wet dirt of the creek bed and finally met the forest of steel and hardy souls that made the White Frontier.

Captain Unamor's steely gaze narrowed and his jaw clenched as the clamour of flesh meeting steel rendered him almost deaf. Holding a central part of the Fifth's line he and his fifty knights struck out as one, their bright blades stabbing amongst the long spears of the Fifth to skewer and pierce the mighty foes that affronted the White Frontier. Around him men roared in hatred and screamed in pain.

Someone died next to him and soaked his tabard red. An axe hammered in to his shield and jarred his shoulder. He was shoved sideways as he swung his blade, his strike going wide of the head he was aiming for, and sinking into another barbarian's shoulder. Feet slipping and sliding in the mud, catching on the dead and wounded below, Unamor steadied himself, doing his best to keep his shield up.

As the enemy forged their way in closer and closer, the knights truly came to their forte, hacking and stabbing a heavy and bloody toll through the ocean of men before them. Limbs flew and men collapsed as the creek quickly turned to red sludge and then disappeared beneath the weight of bodies that fell within it. Even as Unamor cried out the glory of his god and king to the heathen before him, he watched helplessly as his brothers were grabbed and dragged into the frothing mass before him by bare, muscular, tattooed arms and brutally hacked to death.

Roaring loud enough that his ancestors might hear him, Unamor drew back his arm and struck the forearm of a beast of a man grappling with one of his brothers. The tattooed arm came apart at the wrist. So loud was the battle around him the pain scream of the owner was lost long before it ever reached his ears. Looking upon his men he came close to despair as his swift estimate brought only thirty of his brothers to his eyes.

With the renewed vigour of revenge his sword hacked at the enemy. An axe clanged from his armour, tearing away a chunk of his Knights Aggressor tabard, soaked red in the crimson of the enemy.

Someone grabbed his tabard from behind and Unamor turned to see a young soldier of the Fifth with lieutenant markings on his garb. The man had lost his helm and a deep gash ran back from his forehead and into his hair, spilling blood over his fair features. He was yelling something but the knight could not make out his words. With a few quick steps Unamor grabbed the soldier and dragged the lieutenant behind the front few rows and leant in to hear the man.

"My lord! We're killing them five to one but they're starting to get a fair few of us!" yelled the lieutenant.

Beneath his helm Unamor's eyes narrowed. *Coward.* Reaching up he pulled his helm off and grabbed the soldier by his tabard to lock eyes with him.

"You and your men hold the line. You hold this bastard creek," said Unamor, shouting to be heard over the clamour of battle. "Make no mistake, we hold or we die, there is nowhere to go if we lose. No withdrawal. No quarter. Death or glory."

The lieutenant's eyes flicked up to the fortress that loomed over them. Unamor read the gaze.

"Don't even think it, lieutenant. I see you run and I promise you an arrow or blade in the back and Armenius's scorn in the afterlife," growled Unamor.

The lieutenant writhed a little under his gaze. Unamor shoved the young man back towards the line and slammed his helmet back onto his head in frustration. *When did the men of the Secundan Fifth start leaving their balls at home next to their wives' wash buckets?*

To his right, where few of his brothers stood with the more stalwart of the Armenian Fifth, Unamor felt more than saw the line start to give. He watched breathlessly as the almost black metal of a brutal serrated sword erupted out the back of one of his brothers, clean through his glorious plate. Within seconds the same sword had split its way through three of the Fifth, their ring mail providing almost no protection against the brute strength behind the blade.

The sounds of the dark metal carving the air, armour and flesh alike attacked Unamor's mind as it slew his brothers. The steel wailed like a banshee craving the lifeblood and souls of the innocent. A few seconds more and the armoured beast wielding the serrated dark blade had climbed over the earth wall and had hacked a small beachhead around himself to allow the fur and leather clad barbarians to stream in behind him as he smote Secundan after Secundan into bloody ruin.

A monster. A creature of slaughter. I can't kill him, he's too - A moment of fear and doubt enveloped the captain as he saw the beast, easily seven feet tall and rendered almost unbelievably massive by the thick dark plate covering his chest and shoulders, causing havoc before him. Chunky large pauldrons of unpolished, darkened metal with a dented and split high inner collar sat atop the man's patchy fur pelt coated cuirass. They moved fluidly as his immensely muscled and scarred bare arms swung the sword powerfully into the mass of tightly packed Secundans. The giant's head was covered in a horned bucket helm which had sharp, vicious sight and breathing holes cut into it in the shape of a demonic wolf face. It looked at Unamor for a moment and unleashed a terrible roar of guttural hatred at all those before him. Men visibly cowered before the giant and were cut down mercilessly as fans of their blood soaked those around them. *Armenius give me strength.*

His courage quickly returned as Unamor recognised the armour pattern. Under those mottled black pelts and gory trophies was a dark burnished version of his own armour. *Our armour. Stolen from the dead. Turned black with their filth. It shall not stand. By my blood, it shall not stand.*

A snarl of surprise and hate passed his lips as Unamor raised his sword and dropped his shoulder behind his shield. Charging into the fray surrounding the plate armoured beast, he forced his way through the bodies until he reached the front line of the fighting.

Determined to straighten the line, he clambered over the butchered soldiers of the Fifth, his feet struggling for purchase in the mud, blood and bodies. Taking advantage of the surprise of his approach, Unamor swung his blade with all the strength gifted to him by Armenius at his chosen foe. His blade struck at the join between the pauldrons and the cuirass with an almighty crack of metal breaking asunder. He yelled with furious joy as he watched a spray of dark crimson explode skywards and felt the snapping of a collarbone beneath the plate armour. A roar of pain jetted steam from the twisted helmet's faceplate.

With savage glee Unamor drew back his pure Secundan steel for a killing stroke. He never saw the foot long blade driven up into his head through his throat by the wounded foe. He never felt the tip of the blade erupt through the top of his helm just as he never shared the elation of the knights and soldiers around him as they took advantage of his assault and pushed the dark plated man off balance, back through the hole in the line with his foul minions.

Unamor's sightless gaze fell upon the line he had helped straighten one last time as his body fell onto the men already departed for Armenius's halls. His stern jaw finally unclenched from the effort as his life's last breath flowed past his lips and took his spirit to join his brothers.

Captain Dorn of the Knights Aggressor clenched his fists in agitation on the leather reins of his mighty warhorse. As second captain of the Knights Aggressor Order he demanded the respect of the soldiers and knights under his command. His men looked to him and in their eyes he saw both their fear and their belief in his utterly fearlessness. They saw him as unwaveringly heroic. *Something I have earned through blood and sweat and tears. Something Armenius has gifted me.*

Unconsciously his bare fingers ran over his plate-covered shoulder, the pauldron engraved with a message from the King himself in reward for his gallantry. *Fifteen years of service. I've been a captain for ten, promoted young, but a captain nonetheless.* Moments like this, rare as they were, brought back memories of the men he had joined with in his youth. They were mostly gone now, having dedicated their lives and deaths to the Knights Aggressor and the Eternal Lord. Only his friend Kambok remained as his lieutenant by his side, the grizzled veteran having been both a stalwart of the Order and a true friend and confidant.

The finest two hundred and fifty men I ever knew. The finest men Secunda has.

But now, standing with his two hundred and fifty brothers, Dorn would have given all of his title and heroics away to have the strength of the ten thousand strong reserve army of Gall by his side. Ten thousand men that were meant to be holding the line at his back as they stood in the mile wide gap between the lines of Secundans. The ten thousand sons of Gall that had not arrived. *Bastards. Where in Armenius' name are you?*

Looking at the stern faces of his brother knights, he knew they had prepared themselves for the glorious passage to meet the Eternal Lord. Short of turning their backs and retreating there was no way out of this now. As the Lord Armenius had done when they sacrificed themselves to give time to the refugees of their homeland, so would Dorn and his brave men sacrifice themselves. Looking to his old friend he placed a hand on Kambok's shoulder.

"Brother, it's been good life," he said solemnly.

"It's been my life's honour to serve with you, my friend," returned Kambok.

As the great enemy pulled within two hundred feet of them, Captain Dorn put heel to his mount and waved the column on after him. As he gained speed, the thundering of hooves filling his ears, they formed behind him into a tightly packed fighting wedge. Two hundred and fifty of the Knights Aggressor's most valiant men formed up in all of their glory, white tabards flowing in the slipstream of their brother's courage. With a shout to echo through the ages they crashed into the horde before them.

The momentum of their charge carried them through the first mass of the enemy. The weight of fully clad knights on battle mounts made a mockery of the barbarian's ramshackle lines. Dorn struck out again and again, as the point of the wedge, slaying whichever foe came in reach of his blade.

Behind him his brothers carried the charge through, slaying many, but losing many in return as they were dragged from horseback or their mounts tripped over the dead or were slain with spear. Above, one of the Order's centuries old banners flapped in the wind vigorously, as if the holy material yearned to fight alongside those that carried it.

It was with great shock and surprise that Dorn found he and over one hundred of his brothers had burst through the first mass of the enemy and into the clear space between hordes. With an almost savage glee he rounded his brothers up into a second, much smaller wedge and looked for something worthy of his life. One last laudable foe to smite before the end. His eyes found one target and narrowed.

A tall man in what looked undoubtedly like a befouled apparition of Secundan battle plate sat gesturing to barbarian leaders and runners from atop a black horse. Dorn heeled his destrier and raised his sword, crying out for the blessing of Armenius in this last battle. Behind him his brothers raised first their swords and then their voices. More details of the man became obvious as they galloped closer. The armoured man looked unlike any of the barbarians he had seen previously. Matted pitch-black hair on pale skin made him look more like a horrible imitation of a man of Secunda. *All he needs are our Secundan blues and -*

Dorn never got to finish that thought as a mass of filthy armed men streamed forward past the man in armour and charged at Dorn's wedge of brothers. Once more the impact was brutal and the wedge's momentum carried Dorn to within twenty paces of his goal before he was unhorsed, his mount slain by a thrown axe beneath him. His brothers tried to pull him up onto another horse but it was too late and momentum was lost.

Everywhere Dorn looked he saw his brothers fighting desperate and hopeless last battles amongst an ocean of filthy, bearded faces with deep-set dark eyes unhinged with bloodlust. Beside him, Kambok fell as a wave of barbarians unstoppably ploughed forward and over the knights like an avalanche. Through the mass of men, one of the last memories Dorn took with him was the sickly evil grin of his intended target just twenty short feet away.

As they were quickly enveloped and hacked up by the thousands they had charged in to, one drawn out last cry went up to the heavens to precede their souls.

"For Armenius!"

And within a few short gore filled moments, they were gone.

The Lord Field Marshal Loghan Faramon clenched his jaw as, three miles to the north, he watched the seemingly unstoppable tide of the enemy stream through the massive gap in his defensive line like water through a break in a dam. Two hundred and fifty of his brother knights had charged into them and been swallowed in a moment of self sacrificial glory. Second Captain Dorn and the heroic men of his company were now just more names for the quickly growing honour roll of the battle. *If anybody survived to write one.*

He watched with approval as one of the reserve units of the Secundan Fifth smoothly moved in to corner off the end of the Secundan battle line. Despite the enemy's superiority in numbers, the Fifth had defended the line valiantly and had now held for over an hour. But their time was short-lived and without the creek bed as a natural defence the casualty rate would elevate alarmingly until they broke or died to the man. As he watched, the reserve impacted the enemy brutally. Behind the line he could see the young General Stern standing with his final reserve and the archers who had fired their full compliment of arrows and drawn their short blades.

As a group of thirty or forty foul barbarians burst through the line a two hundred strong section of the last reserve unit smoothly ran down the rise and butchered them in short order before pushing the beasts back into the creek bed. Loghan could just see the small figure of Stern make a quick flurry of hand gestures to send part of the last reserve moving into weak points and the remaining five hundred marching off towards the end of line. Stern remained in his place with his small personal retinue and the eight hundred archers, waiting for

Armenius to call him and his four thousand remaining men to His side. *Hold, by Armenius, hold the line. Give me more time. Gall will come. They have to.*

Looking down to the base of the castle wall, Loghan watched with the detachment of a tried and proven general as the enemy brought their siege ladders to the front. The barbarians tried to start raising them up the incline as the Knights Aggressor waited to push them back while they poured volley after volley of arrows, crossbow bolts, rocks and burning tar into in the blanket of foul flesh below them.

A few of the archers fell as return volleys of arrows started to stream back and clatter against stone, metal, or thud into flesh. Loghan was momentarily blinded as a shield was raised up to protect him. An arrow thudded heavily into it, the sound ringing in his ears. Without even looking to his saviour he then strode quickly over to look at the left side of the line where the Third was almost in full rout towards the forthcoming lines of the Fourth. *Damn it.* Barely a thousand men remained, with a loose spattering of knights in amongst them as backward step by blood soaked backward step they slowed the enemy advance.

Arrows cast a shadow across their sacrifice as the Fourth's archers unleashed their first volley with devastating effect. Some two hundred dark clad warriors were smashed to the ground. A second and then a third volley and the massed enemy were falling in a constant wave of death towards the formed up ranks of the Fourth. The Third finally broke and streamed through their lines and caused some consternation as they made their way to the back.

Lord Faramon clenched his fists in anger as he watched fully half of the remaining Third continue to run in panic. Twenty or thirty of the Knights Aggressor, having survived the initial battle, ran around attempting to rally those that were still fleeing. To his intense shame, he was sure one or two of his brothers ran with them. Those who stood true to their vows and courage lashed out with bloodied swords at those who would not listen but few fell to the knights' frustration. Lord Faramon shook his head as he watched over three hundred desperately needed men fleeing for their lives back towards the Fourth's camp. His heavy heart was alleviated somewhat as he watched the other three to four hundred men and his brave brothers re-form behind the Fourth next to the army general as a reserve unit.

Then came the impact. Bright Secundan steel met filthy barbarian iron in the south with the sound of hundreds of men's worlds ending in one brutal moment. The horizontal forest of spears of the Secundan's front two rows reaped a high toll amongst the oncoming enemy but soon the spears were spent and the hack and stab of true close combat began. Taking stock of the situation he felt confident those men would hold for an hour or so.

As he walked back across the battlement to view the progress of the northern battle, three knights fell into step with him.

"Still no sign of the Gall armies my lord," said one knight.

"Food stores have been calculated my lord," said the second. "We've enough to last a week or two with the food and water rationed. Arrows, we have plenty of and should last us a month long siege."

"Lord, we've brought in the latest group of initiates. They've been armed, armoured and are ready to fight. I've placed them within the walls of the keep for now, awaiting your orders," finished the third.

Lord Faramon absorbed the information with a small nod and without breaking his stride. All of a sudden his dreams of glory were on the verge of becoming a nightmare of defeat. *Gall, where are your soldiers?*

CHAPTER SIX

Uthiel's heart nearly beat itself out of his chest in excitement. Sweat glistened on his skin in the oven heat of the smithy. His first deployment had been announced for a month's time and now he stood before the blacksmith having his personal suit of armour engraved with his name. *No more beaten and dented training armour.*

He already had the chainmail and padded leather undergarment on and had settled comfortably, despite the cloying heat. His powerful body filled out the leather and chain easily. Uthiel moved his arms and swayed his hips, testing the weight. The weight was almost naught to his strength.

The light and consistent tapping of the blacksmith engraving his cuirass was music to his ears as Uthiel looked over to the armour stand that held all but the chest plate. The large pauldrons with their thick inner crests sat the most predominant in their shining glory as they reflected the bellow's fire. Down the right pauldron a prayer to Armenius had been engraved into the metal in tiny, delicate handwriting. Between the pauldrons hung a gorget and to either side of the stand hung his vambrances and goussets. Below his upper body armour his mail skirt hung above the plain greaves. All up, many pounds of Secundan steel would sit proudly upon his strong shoulders, ready to defy the blades of the enemy and allow him to cleave more of the hated foe. *Such a heavy burden of history and expectation to sit upon my shoulders.*

Atop the stand sat the bucket helm; another item passed down to him from another slain knight. *I shall do that fallen brother proud.* A single horizontal slit spanned the eyes with a clustered peppering of breathing holes in a fist-sized square on the left cheek. Uthiel couldn't contain his smile. He had been amongst the last of his brothers to have this work done and he didn't mind admitting seeing Branor and his friends standing in their new armour while he waited for his name to be called made him green with envy.

The blacksmith stood straight and stretched his back, huge shoulders shrugging up around his ears. He turned with the cuirass held aloft in both of his blackened meaty hands and began to walk towards Uthiel. Unclasping the leather straps on the side, he opened up the cuirass and beckoned the young knight to raise his arms so he could be put into the case of metal. Within moments Uthiel was standing tall with the chest plate being fastened. He looked down at the left side of the plate where his name now sat above two other names.

The blacksmith noticed him looking and, upon finishing doing up the buckles on his side, smiled a harsh smile and turned away to get the gousset.

"Make no mistake boy," grated the blacksmith's deep voice. "That be a young cuirass. Both of its former owners were killed less than three years into service."

Uthiel's mood dulled only slightly before his grin once again broadened.

"You shan't be getting this back off me for some time, master blacksmith," said Uthiel.

The blacksmith's face scrunched in some form of silent acknowledgement as he attached the gorget to the cuirass and then buckled on the vambrances and goussets. The mail skirt was then added, clipping in to the inside of the cuirass and tied on to his padded undergarment for extra security. The two large pauldrons were then buckled on and finally Uthiel stepped into his greaves. With a motion from the blacksmith he moved around and gauged the difference from his training amour. *Flexible, but surprisingly light.*

"Master blacksmith, this armour is lighter than that I have worn this last year – "

"Training armour," grunted the smith.

Uthiel's face must not have registered the correct level of understanding.

"Weighted. Your training armour is made heavier."

Uthiel chuckled. *Storm probably saw to that.*

The blacksmith ignored him and continued to check his work, pushing and pulling at the plates to make sure they held securely. With a nod to himself and a satisfied grunt, the blacksmith gave him a light shove towards the door. Before Uthiel could voice his thanks the burly metal worker was bellowing for the next initiate.

Before he could leave the blacksmith's room, the solid man called and threw a sack to him with a long, thin leather shoulder strap. Uthiel reached for it and missed clumsily. He reached down awkwardly, and then had to kneel to retrieve the small sack. *Not* that *flexible.*

"In there are your polishing cloths and cleaning tools. Best you look after your armour, lest she fails to look after you," said the blacksmith before turning away once again.

Uthiel smiled as he walked away, his eyes still sweeping over his armour in awe. "I'll love her like a beautiful maiden, friend."

Uthiel felt twenty foot tall in his resplendent armour as he entered the armourer's room. His eyes widened a little as he saw row upon row of swords, axes, polearms, lances, crossbows and shields. A tall, skinny man with a fat book resting in the crook of his forearm looked up from his scrawling to rest his blue eyes on him.

"Name?"

"Uthiel Caellar," responded Uthiel, still looking around the room in wonder.

"Number thirteen," said the armourer as a matter of fact, his eyes not wavering from his book. "One shield. One sword. One knife. One whetstone. That is all. Come with me."

The armourer scurried away across the stone floor, with Uthiel lumbering behind in tow, still moving around and testing and adjusting to his personal suit of armour. The man pulled down three swords from the wall and had Uthiel test each one. Uthiel swung, parried and stabbed, moving about the floor with each one until he found one that felt right for him.

Next were the shields. There was far less choice here as each one was the same shape and size for the knight brothers on foot. Most were dark red and had bronze emblems bolted to their front and centre. Uthiel picked a dark crimson shield with a brass 'Armenius' bolted on to the front, hefting it on his left arm with a smile.

As he walked back on to the packed parade ground, sword and forearm length knife scabbarded on either hip and his shield on a carry strap across his shoulder, he was greeted by Branor, Keldon, Linton, Lokhi and Tobias from amongst the other sixty odd brothers.

"Look at our brother!" called Branor. "Almost as pretty as the dusk on a cloudy night!"

"Jealousy does not become you, Bran! Do not hate me because you were born with a face like a horse's arse," retorted Uthiel.

Branor bent down and picked up a clod of earth and threw it at his childhood friend. With a laugh Uthiel dodged and bent down to return the volley but stopped as he saw Captain Phyrus walking down from the battlements into the parade ground. His brothers spotted his line of sight and immediately began to form up into rank as Uthiel rushed to join them. Captain Phyrus strode out to them as the last of the freshly elevated knights came out in their new armour and hurried to the end of the line of thirteen brothers.

Phyrus scowled at the last young knight as he fell into line and then continued to inspect his new recruits. His face remained stoic as he examined each man and each suit of armour. He straightened a pauldron here, and brushed some dirt off there. Ghurkar Storm came down from the battlement a moment later, a broad open smile almost an impossibility across his weathered face.

"Little brothers!" he called. "How handsome we all look this morning! I hope you're ready to give that shining metal a nice coat of barbarian blood!"

The thirteen brothers, as one, all looked at their captain and raised their fists with a cheer. Phyrus just smiled.

"You carry great honour upon your bodies," said Phyrus solemnly. "When a knight of the Grey Wolves dies, most of his soul goes to join Armenius is the Shield Wall in the Sky. However a little piece of him remains within his armour. A little piece of every brother that has worn every piece of your suit of armour lends strength to your sword arm and his force of will to your body's defence."

Singling out Branor, Phyrus stepped forwards and placed a hand upon the young knight's cuirass, nostalgia gleaning his eyes. "A great brother wore this cuirass before you, Branor. A friend of mine named Fulm. A club smashed his helm from his head and then brained him while we were at the frontier way up north near Imonetia."

Branor licked his lips and looked to Uthiel. Uthiel shrugged almost imperceptibly, unsure of how to react to a man who had treated them with such coldness and harshness but now revealed a far more human side of himself to them.

Phyrus sniffed, and took a step away from his men. "This armour and I will always remember him as a brother and a friend who stood by me from when we were young boys fist fighting the richer children in the alleys of lower Secunda, to the men we became slaying the great foe on the White Frontier."

Phyrus backed up a few steps further, his eyes once again hardening.

"My brothers," he said. "Gather your gear. Our first departure has been brought forward. We leave on the dawn of the morrow. Ensure your arms and armour are all accounted for before we leave. We won't be coming back for some time. Lieutenant Storm will fill you in on the rest. I'll see you in the morning."

With that he turned and marched towards the fortress keep. All the knights focussed on Ghurkar Storm, their anticipation and eagerness almost palpable.

"My brothers," began the lieutenant, pausing for effect. "Tomorrow we leave for the White Frontier. We'll be escorting a baggage train travelling three miles behind a column made up of two hundred knights of the White Rose, one thousand foot soldiers of the king, and one hundred of our brothers. Those brothers are led by First Captain Solanthur Verutus."

That was it, the fourteen young men could not hold in their excitement anymore. Branor whooped out loud at the prospect of following one of the most decorated Grey Wolf captains of the last four hundred years to the White Frontier. They would march to the line where good met, and conquered, evil: the line where heroes were blooded and plied their glorious trade.

"As far as we know," continued the lieutenant, "the section of the frontier we're travelling to has been quiet for some months now so don't go getting pictures of glory in your pretty little heads. The column of knights will be relieving a large regiment of the Knights Aggressor, some two thousand knights led by the king's brother."

Uthiel nearly exploded with happiness. *Battles or no, not only will I be travelling in the same column as the legendary first captain of the Grey Wolves but I will be seeing the king's brother! The greatest general of all the lords in Secunda!* Branor gave him a nudge with his elbow and flashed him an excited grin.

"To your arms, armour, and supplies little brothers!" bellowed Storm. "Tomorrow is a grand new day for you. Come sun up, we march."

As the sun was just beginning to make its way up to the horizon, turning the morning clouds a beautiful orange, Uthiel stood in a line of ten of his brothers on the right hand side of a horse drawn carriage stacked high with sacks of grain. On the other side of the two long rows of carriages the other ten men of his company stood on the left hand side, spaced out by three strides. At the head of the column, Captain Phyrus sat atop a tall warhorse, speaking with the lead carriage's driver.

Uthiel looked down at himself. A broad smile erupted onto his face again as he looked at the dark grey tabard that now sat atop his polished plate armour. *I am a knight. A Grey Wolf. A defender of Secunda!* Looking back over his shoulder he nodded to Branor behind him. Branor looked almost exactly the same as Uthiel, his grey tabard flowing in the wind.

Branor flashed him a grin and a wink. Uthiel turned around to face the back of the brother in front of him. Beyond Lokhi Dorn's broad shoulders, Uthiel could just make out the three hundred knights beyond them. Half were mounted and the remainder stood by one thousand soldiers of the king, the morning light glinting off their chain mail shirts and their horizontal spear tips.

A few hundred feet away, First Captain Solanthur Verutus sat atop a strong looking brown warhorse. The first captain was addressing a general of the Knights of the White Rose and a captain of the Secundan soldiery. With a salute to the general, the first captain turned his horse and rode back to his brother knights. The ninety mounted knights under his command hastily drew in to a column, followed by another formation of dismounted knights, and prepared to lead the guarded baggage train at the rear of the army. With a wave of his arm, the first captain sent the mounted knights to the rear of the baggage train and in a thundering of hooves and a spraying rain of earth clods they galloped past Uthiel and his brothers.

Uthiel leaned out to try to get a better look at the first captain as he trotted over to speak with Captain Phyrus. The man looked every inch the hero of Secunda that his legend made him out to be. Atop his warhorse, he looked absolutely glorious with the morning light reflecting from armour polished to almost a mirror sheen. Scripting had been delicately cut into his vambrances and the wolf inscribed into his gorget had been painted a bright red to stand out from his dark grey tabard. His mail hood hung back between his shoulders and his helm sat over the pommel of his saddle leaving his hard face open. Uthiel was disappointed as the great man turned his mount away to take his position at the head of the dismounted knights. *He is all that I aspire to be.*

A loud trumpet blast signalled the start of the march and the knights of the White Rose departed first.

"Word has it the general and his brothers intend to lead the column the entire three day march to the frontier," said Branor.

"I'd expect no less from the mightiest knights in the land," responded Uthiel.

The morning dragged on as slowly but surely, the column began to move. Uthiel stood patiently and although he was excited, he couldn't help but feel the day so far had been a bit of an anti-climax in comparison to his boyhood dreams of charging off on horseback to the White Frontier for a lengthy session of barbarian slaying.

It was almost another hour before the baggage train received its order to move off. Uthiel smiled to himself. *Years of hard and brutal training. The initiation. I've not seen my family for almost two years. I've been bruised, beaten spilt some blood. I've been exhausted, cold, tired, weary beyond words. All of it to earn this moment. I am going to serve Secunda. To serve my Eternal Lord. To earn glory for myself, my family, my Order, and my king.* Uthiel's chest swelled with pride. *I'd do it ten times over.*

Four hours into the slow march and Uthiel was already feeling the weight of his armour, despite the built up strength of his body. Without the rush of combat, or training combat in his experience, he felt somewhat less able to carry the beautiful burden. It had even crossed his mind that perhaps he and his brothers on foot should have stored away their armour for the march. He'd taken to watching the feet of Lokhi, after having tripped twice in small holes already much to the amusement of Branor.

His boot caught on a half buried root and Uthiel stumbled for a step. He caught his balance quickly, cursing severely under his breath.

"Do you intend on tripping in every hole and root we walk over?"

Uthiel quickly looked over his shoulder and was about to give Branor one of his more choice insults when he tripped again. His friend snorted with laughter, spittle flying from his lips. The brothers around them chortled. Uthiel couldn't help himself and let out a little chuckle. *Any reprieve from the tedium.*

Once again lost in his own thoughts as the column pushed ever westwards, he barely noticed the thudding of horses' shod hooves on the earth beside him until the first captain loomed right over him, Captain Phyrus by his side.

"Get your chin up, brother," came Solanthur's deep gravelly voice. "Armenius watches us from above, how can he see your face if you've not the pride to walk tall?"

"My apologies first captain," stammered Uthiel, straightening his neck and head instantly and keeping his eyes to the fore.

"Good lad," continued the first captain. "Captain Phyrus has been telling me promising things about you."

With that he kicked his horse into a trot and headed on up the column. Phyrus waited a moment, nodded at his charge and then galloped away to catch up the first captain.

"Promising things?" mused Branor. "What, like he looks so pretty in armour? Can march almost two hundred feet without tripping over?"

"I heard this promising young lad can even wipe his own arse," chimed in Lokhi.

"Gah, obviously he hasn't yet seen my martial prowess!" proclaimed Keldon, jinking around and swinging an imaginary sword. "For if he had, well, I'm not sure I could physically handle all of the backslapping that would come my way..."

"Brothers," growled an older voice from behind. "Stop mocking your betters or I'll stop you."

Lieutenant Storm glared at them, anger set deep on his hard features.

"The first captain is an unparalleled warrior and judge of fighting men," continued the lieutenant. "If he believes that one of you polished cow turds has promise as a knight, then I'm just going to have to beat you into something worthy of his praise while we are on the frontier."

Another six hours later, with the dusk beginning to darken the sky, the baggage train arrived at the camp that had been set up in a farmer's large grazing field. Uthiel could still hear the farmer's objections as a small herd of steers were being butchered before him. Huge parts of his grazing pasture had already been turned to a mud slush by the hooves and boots of the column. *You owe it to us. Our blood protects these fields. The least you can do is feed us.*

Hundreds of canvas tents had been set up and many of the knights had already fed on the fire-cooked beef and retired for the night after the day's march. The soldiery would, for the greater part not including their officers, be sleeping under the stars for the night.

Not two hours ago they had crossed the friendly border of Gall and passed through one of the towns this farm bordered. The locals not working their fields had come out to cheer them on. Uthiel smiled to himself as carnal thoughts crossed his mind about some of the beautiful young Gallite maidens.

One in particular had stood out to him. She had been a beautiful young brunette girl, perhaps a year or two younger than he with the most beautiful face he had ever seen. Her heavy working dress had not done the best job of hiding her arousing form and Uthiel felt his face flush at the memory of her locking eyes with him and then walking over to lightly touch his vambrance and brush her supple lips against his cheek in a light and welcoming kiss.

She had whispered a name into his ear. *Emilia.*

"You are a knight? Of Secunda?" she had asked, her voice soft and with an almost imperceptible lisp.

He had nodded, dumbstruck by her beauty.

"And you are off to the White Frontier?"

"I cannot say, lady," he had responded; still staring at her and not at where he was going.

"And what awaits you where you go?" she asked.

The question threw Uthiel a little, but in his heart he knew the answer. "Glory."

"You men, you all claim glory in the killing of our fellow man," she had mused a little harshly.

"We protect the Lands of the Light from the darkness without!" he had protested almost too fiercely.

"Did you ever question why the barbarians are our foe? At what point in history did our nations each decide to carve out our own little kingdoms at the cost of whoever was there first? Who is here, now, to say that we are not the foreigners to these lands and the barbarians had it taken from them?"

Uthiel's mouth worked soundlessly for a moment as he was wrong footed by the thought before his gaze hardened. "It matters not, when they took Mother Secunda from her people and butchered hundreds of thousands of innocents who were trying to escape the war, they surrendered any due pity their ancestors may have had."

"And this is what you believe? Who is to say we did not do the same?" she asked.

"It is where Armenius was marked as our God. It is by His word and honour that our history is written," responded Uthiel matter-of-factly.

"Have you ever heard a saying about history being written by the victors? That truth is a matter of perspective?"

Her question hit him like a punch. In a heartbeat he went from angry, to disbelieving, to hurt, and then straight back to angry. *How could she say that!? She may as well say the sky is the ground and the ground is the sky and we are all flying! She is calling Him a liar!* He'd looked around at his brothers, almost hoping for their support in this argument. Some were munching on food passed to them by the villagers, others spoke to young women or local men, while some openly ogled village whores. His jaw clenched to the point of hurting in his disbelief.

In that moment of rage, barely held in check, Uthiel noticed an almost imperceptible gleam of mischief in her eyes. He took a deep breath.

"What would you believe?" he asked, actually having to make a conscious effort to unclench his jaw.

She cocked her head a little and smiled. Immediately that angelic face placed a soothing balm on his anger. *Sweetest thing I've ever seen.*

"You divert away from my question because it makes you mad?" Emilia continued.

Uthiel forced a smile. "I'm not at ease, lady. You cloud my mind."

Emilia feigned anger, pouting her lips and raising her eyebrows. "Why! I never! You are very forward, knight. Were my father here he might take to you with the broom!"

Uthiel looked to the ground, embarrassed. "If you are only going to make fun of me, girl, please go away, for I am busy."

For a heartbeat a look of hurt had flashed over her face and she withdrew her hand from his arm. Immediately Uthiel regretted his harsh tone. "I am sorry Emilia, I spoke harshly. Please, walk with me once more."

She began to walk beside him, but to his disappointment the beautiful brown haired girl did not take his arm. They walked in silence and again Uthiel found himself staring.

"Did your mother never teach you not to stare?" she had asked as she glanced at him, laughing a little, though more guarded this time.

Uthiel had blinked as if awaking from a dream and snapped his gaze forwards, displeased by his own rudeness and her manner of constantly teasing him. He shook his head and took a deep breath. The temptation to retrieve his helm and cover his face was almost overwhelming and he felt his cheeks flush harder and harder as she linked arms with him once more and giggled.

"It matters not, young knight, for I like your gaze," Emilia had continued, completely ignoring his embarrassment with her large and honest smile. "what is your name?"

"Uthiel," he had managed to spurt out. "Uthiel Caellar of the Order of the Grey Wolf."

"I am Bran," called out Branor from a few feet behind, craning his neck to see her better having listened to most of their conversation. "Pleased to..."

"Uthiel," she had said thoughtfully, completely ignoring Branor. "You have kind eyes and I think a gentle spirit despite your vocation. I shall remember the name. As I hope you shall remember mine. Should you ever need the hospitality of my village, you had but mention you are my friend. I hope to see you again soon."

She raised the back of her hand and Uthiel took it and kissed the soft, milky white skin. With a coy smile she ran off.

Uthiel continued walking on, playing the discussion over again in his head. Emilia had made him feel slow witted and clumsy, but had aroused something in him that that told him he had met someone special. *Someone worth remembering.* Uthiel smiled and turned to Branor.

"Bran, are women just the most confusing and wonderful things? I think she may have liked me!"

Branor snorted at this, complaining that he was by far the better looking, undoubtedly the better endowed of the two brothers, and therefore Emilia was undoubtedly speaking with the inadequate Uthiel in order to try to make him jealous. His mood quickly changed when two of the local whores leaned out of their rooms atop the towns and called out their wares to the group of knights. Branor had called back to them, but was swiftly silenced by the crack of a well-thrown pebble against the back of his head. Swearing out loud he'd looked back to find the steely gaze of their lieutenant focussed squarely on him.

That night, sitting around a campfire on the outskirts of the camp, Uthiel contemplated the chances of being caught. He could try to sneak out of the camp after curfew and see the Emilia as his brothers sat eating their small allocations of smoked meat and bread. Looking around at their faces in the firelight, he smiled as he watched them talk, jokingly insult, and laugh. *Such a fine brotherhood*, he thought.

At this moment he and his brothers were happily indestructible. They were knights of the Order of the Grey Wolf. They were on their way to test themselves and all they had trained for since boyhood against the great foe, and by Armenius they were going to conquer those barbarous fiends and cut such great swathes of glory through history that their names would be spoken of for a thousand years through uncountable generations of Secundans.

Branor caught Uthiel's eye, a look of sheer mischief twinkling in his own. With the slightest motion of his head the message was clear and he'd got up.

"Brothers," said Branor. "I'm off to see if I can scrounge up some more food. Uthiel, your almightiness, favoured of the first captain, would you please lower yourself for this unworthy task and assist me?"

Uthiel took the meaning right away. With a laugh he tossed a chewed rib bone at his friend and rose to follow him away from the jeers and hoots of his brothers. The two snaked their way through the tightly knotted groups of knights and soldiers sitting around their campfires and finally made it to the edge of the field. With little effort they snuck past the two sentries sitting on the farmer's fence who were engaged in a game of dice and paying no attention to their surroundings. Out in the dark they quickly made their way back to the town, young hearts beating for the hours they envisioned were in front of them.

CHAPTER SEVEN

The morning sky had barely turned a shade less than black when, bleary eyed, Uthiel stumbled out of his tent with a slack-jawed smile on his face as the memory of the night before came back to him. Emilia had met him by the outskirts of the town. This had surprised Uthiel, as he didn't think he'd made the best impression on the young lady. She had been even more beautiful than he had remembered. In hushed tones they had suggestively whispered and laughed for hours until finally she had shyly slipped out of her dress, her pale skin prickling with goose bumps under his exploring touch. The memory of his fingertips against her flushed cheek as he leaned in for the first kiss broadened his smile.

Upon the straw they had begun fulfilling their youthful desires. That was until her father had been woken by an unbidden cry from her beautiful lips as she straddled him and come to investigate what he thought to be a cry of alarm. Uthiel rubbed his shoulder and then the right cheek of his bottom where his tabard and padded cloth clothing covered the two painful welts that the large man had dealt him with a length of hardwood as he tried to escape while pulling his trousers up, Emilia screaming and crying at her father in the background.

He laughed as he looked back at his tent to see Branor, as always far more bright eyed than Uthiel despite the night's excesses, giggling like a schoolgirl. He'd come running out of a whore's room to heed Uthiel's calls of their need to flee the town. Slapping Uthiel hard on the back, knowing full well the beating his brother had taken the night before, Branor shook his head and laughed some more.

"My brother," he snorted, "did you even manage to loose the arrow or is it still sitting in your quiver?"

Uthiel grimaced, rubbing his buttocks gingerly.

"I mean," continued Branor, "did the horse erupt from the paddock or did it run into the gate? Did you mount the..."

Uthiel waved him quiet as his laughter began to hurt his ribs, pulling odd looks from the other brothers coming from their tents and already beginning to don their armour.

"Brothers!" called Branor to those of Phyrus' knights around him. "If you are in front of Uthiel in the line today be sure to check your three feet distance else you risk being speared in the back!"

Looks of confusion were all he got.

Smiling a brilliant smile, Branor turned back to Uthiel and motioned to their tent. "Come, my friend, let us get pretty for the captain before he makes his rounds."

New as they were to their armour, it still took them some time to get fully prepared and when captain Phyrus came by, the two brothers were still strapping on their sword belts. Phyrus looked at both the stragglers disapprovingly before returning his attention the other brothers who were prepared and waiting in formation. As Uthiel and Branor joined the end of the line, Phyrus opened his mouth to address his men. The words never made it out.

Shouts come from the far end of the camp, a great commotion with hundreds of bodies moving to investigate. A sharp look from Phyrus was all his men needed to realise that they would not be joining the rush to the other side of the camp.

Phyrus looked to his lieutenant. "Have the men pack away the tents and prepare for departure. I shall be back presently."

The twenty knights were at attention in their positions either side of the baggage train and ready to march by the time their captain made it back to them. His stern features did not betray what he had found out. Uthiel and Branor exchanged nervous looks as they awaited their orders. Being at the far end of the rear of the Secundan camp had meant that news had not even travelled to them by word of mouth yet.

"My brothers," started Phyrus. "The White Frontier has fallen."

Uthiel's world ground to a halt. The White Frontier, bastion of all that was holy against the darkness, had fallen. *It cannot be.*

"Which fortress, my captain?" asked Carn, one of the veterans.

"So far, from what we can tell, there is a large hole in the frontier directly in front of Gall. We must assume that at least one of the fortresses has either fallen, or is under siege," continued Phyrus. "The filthy barbarians are miles inside the frontier and running rampant throughout the land. Herein, we are in contested territory."

The men around Uthiel straightened a little, the veteran's faces hardening while the more youthful knights' faces lit up in excitement or fear.

"My brothers," said Phyrus. "We are no longer a relief and resupply force for the White Frontier. We are now Gall's only hope of assistance within four days march."

Branor spoke up. "My Captain?"

Phyrus nodded to him to continue.

"How did this news come to us?"

Phyrus licked his lips and then pointed to the edge of the field, a short distance away, indicating that Branor should go. Uthiel watched his friend jog to the edge of the field and look down on to the road from the embankment on the edge of the field. His friend froze, hands gripping the rotted wooden rails of the fence. Uthiel watched Branor's head turn slowly up and down the length of road that ran parallel to the fence and he said something to someone down there before turning and trudging back, a horrified look on his young face.

"Thousands of them," he said. "There are thousands of them. Some are wounded, some are sick, some have little babes. What can we do?"

Phyrus replied, "What we have trained to do, Branor. Their only hope is that Gall holds until they can reach Secunda. Riders have already left to notify the king. While he organises the army and the remaining Orders into a force and marches, we are their only hope. We leave in an hour."

For the next hour, the camp was in complete organised chaos. Every knight with a horse, including Captain Phyrus, immediately took a small bag of provisions from the baggage train and thundered west in one large column of mounted steel. A short time later, all of the dismounted knights remaining, excluding Phyrus' men, marched off, also taking their provisions. One hundred of the Secundan soldiers were broken off from their main force to join the guard of the baggage train before the remaining nine hundred soldiers departed.

It seemed like an age before Lieutenant Storm, having been given command of the train, ordered the five carriages that had been emptied to be abandoned and led the last part of the Secundan army west. With Uthiel and his eighteen brothers to the fore, and the soldiers split in half and in single column down the lengths of the train, they trudged through the churned-up earth left by the advance.

As Uthiel and his brothers continued, the signs of full-scale war began to trickle through at a greater rate. More small groups of refugees streamed back past them. Desperate people trudged doggedly, their tear-streaked faces speaking the words of loss and sadness their mouths were too tired to voice. Despite their obvious hunger, only a frantic few asked the soldiers for anything. One young boy reached out to Uthiel. Another fleeing man grabbed the boy.

"Do not take food from these brave men," berated the man. "They walk tall into the jaws of a meat-grinding beast."

Uthiel cringed. The man bared his broken, yellow teeth in an attempt at a smile. Uthiel returned one half-heartedly, fear touching him as he saw the man had a wooden leg and no arm below the bicep.

The man caught his stare. "March well, lad. May you come back a whole man, and not in pieces."

Uthiel walked on. *May you come back whole.* The thought and the image of the man's ruined body stuck with him.

Early in the afternoon, as Uthiel willed his leaden legs to continue to pull themselves from the earth and push him forward, it began to rain. The sound of the downpour impacting the knights' pauldrons was almost deafening. Very quickly their road became treacherous, the carriages getting bogged in the mud.

As they pushed further into the mire, well beyond the point of exhaustion, they saw the first signs of the enemy raiding parties. Bodies of men, women, and children littered the ground in the small village. They had been there for days, and in the damp conditions their unfortunate corpses had ripened. Uthiel covered his lips, doing his best to stem the wave of saliva filling his mouth, demanding he throw up. The lieutenant looked back at his men.

"Those bastards were smart," he growled. "Didn't set anything on fire so the surrounding towns wouldn't see the smoke."

As they walked past, Uthiel found himself torn between outright hatred, and the stomach turning nausea that came from seeing rotting bodies lying in puddles of water, excrement and blood. Behind him he heard some men loose the contents of their stomach to the smell. Not wanting to look back, he hoped that none of those men with weak constitutions were his brother knights. Now, if ever, they needed to set an example for the soldiers they were with.

They were Knights; *we are bloody Grey Wolves, by Armenius!* The citizens of Secunda and Gall needed their valour and example of strength now more than ever. Uthiel felt fresh strength lend itself to his wavering legs. They'd not be found wanting in the eyes of the common soldiery or the people they were sworn to protect.

As they topped the next rise, the lieutenant called a halt to the column. Below them, the previous contingent of soldiers had stopped their march and had pulled into a defensive formation. Uthiel spotted groups of ten or so men scouting out and away from the main group. He pointed them out to Storm.

"Brother, scouts. Ours."

Storm shielded his eyes. "I can see them. What the bloody hell do they think they are doing?"

"I think there are some officers down there, brother," said Branor.

Some men were milling about in a group around something.

"Reckon they're arguing about something," ventured Branor.

Lieutenant Storm turned back to his brothers.

"Uthiel, Branor, Carn, Tobias, with me," he ordered, already starting to march down to the group of officers. "The rest of you I need on guard. Something is amiss."

As, behind them, the baggage train guard took up defensive positions, the five knights briskly walked through the outer defensive line of the soldiers and marched straight up to the officers. As they heard them approaching, the five captains took a couple of steps back to allow the knights to see what lay on the ground.

They're scared. Uthiel could see it in the set of their shoulders before he even spied their faces. He'd seen it a hundred times in his youth: The stance of bullied, beaten men, defeated before anyone laid a hand upon them.

Seven soldiers lay bloodied and cleaved, often into many pieces, on the ground. The remains of their faces showed sheer terror in their last moments, a terror that still hung in the air around them. Uthiel forced himself to look at them. *Armenius give me strength. Let the butchery stoke my anger and righteousness.* His teeth, throat, and stomach began to hurt from the effort of keeping his food in his guts.

"I am Lieutenant Ghurkar Storm of the Order of the Grey Wolf. I demand to know why you have stopped," snarled the lieutenant as Uthiel and his brothers formed up behind him menacingly. "Every moment wasted here is a moment when my brothers up at the forefront of the column do not have the support of your soldiers."

One of the captains sneered. "I believe we out-rank you, *Lieutenant*. You will show the correct manners when – "

Storm took a step forwards. The captain shrunk back, suddenly very interested in the mud under his boots.

"I am a knight of the Grey Wolves. Your rank means nothing to me. Tell me what is happening, before I am forced to kill one of you."

The captains all started to speak at once, renewing their argument. The lieutenant's patience cracked. "Cease your babbling!" he roared.

He pointed at one of the captains. "You. Name, rank, and then for the love of Armenius tell me what is going on here!"

The captain straightened himself out quickly as Storm grew more and more impatient.

"Captain Trovel of the Twelfth, sir," he said, regaining his composure as he spoke. "This was one of our scouting parties. They've been slain by a raiding party nearby. We've an opportunity here to track down that party and capture them. Perhaps we can find out..."

Uthiel watched Storm's jaw begin to clench and unclench at an increased rate.

"...from the raiding party where more of their parties have gone..."

Storm's fist began to clench as the veins in his neck bulged. Instinctively Uthiel put his hand on his sword.

"...we can help the other towns nearby. Captain Kell of the Fourteenth thinks we need to move on but - "

Uthiel barely saw the punch that laid Trovel on his back.

"Fools!" spat Ghurkar Storm. "You bunch of wet nurses! There isn't a pair of balls between the lot of you! We are at war. Men will die. Women, and children will die. The only thing we can hope to have semblance of control over is how many that final tally will be! Now get these bodies, throw them off the road so my men don't have to walk through them, pick up that miserable little piece of cow shit, and get your men moving towards Gall!"

The captains' jaws worked but no sounds came out. Ghurkar moved forward as if to strike another one and instantly they began to move. Captain Trovel had woken by this point and was being helped to his feet by two of his men. His murderous stare locked squarely on Lieutenant Storm. Rubbing his jaw and wiping the blood from his lip, he shoved one of the men who had helped him away.

"I will have satisfaction for that cowardly strike," he said to Storm.

Lieutenant Storm turned, bemusement written across his face. "There will be enough bloodshed to sate your thirst for glory and honour over the next few months. Secunda needs her sons killing the enemy, not each other."

"Nevertheless," continued Trovel. "I shall bury you for that insult. Military law stipulates officers serving the king and Secunda may call out an equal to draw blood over an insult. I demand satisfaction once the battle for Gall is over."

Lieutenant Ghurkar Storm smiled, and with a gruff laugh of contempt said, "You are not my equal. If you survive the next few days I promise to send you to your ancestors."

Then he turned and marched back up to his column. Uthiel fell into step behind him, in awe of the big lieutenant and seeing him in a slightly different light. *A true leader. A man worth following.*

"Brothers and soldiers! Up you get, we move onwards!" bellowed Storm to his men.

Over the next hour or so, the nine hundred Secundan soldiers formed up and began their march towards Gall. Beneath their feet the soggy ground had become slurry of mud and grass until finally the way for the baggage train was left clear, a dark streak through green rolling plains and the foliage of light forests. The knights of Storm's command stood once more in formation to the fore of the train with the hundred soldiers behind split equally down each side of the train.

With a wave of his arm, Ghurkar Storm ordered the column forward. Before Uthiel could take a single step, the sound of desperate footsteps heading towards them turned him around. His hand leapt to his sheathed sword. Around him, the rasp of polished metal on treated leather acknowledged those knights quicker on the draw than their brothers as they turned to the perceived threat. A soldier, breathing hard and stooped low as his legs powered him forward, pulled up short in surprise as he saw swords and crossbows levelled at him.

"Soldier!" yelled Storm. "Get back in formation! What..."

"My lord, be quiet..." gasped the soldier.

Storm took one aggressive step forward, his face storming over in anger again. "You would quiet me, whelp? You dare..."

The soldier's eyes widened as he realised his own audacity and he took a step back. At the same moment Branor reached forward and grabbed Storm's pauldron.

"Brother, quiet," he hissed, his eyes looking back behind the column and his other hand signalling for the quiet of the rest of those around them.

Ghurkar's face remained as hard as stone but with the rest of the men he held his breath. Quiet reigned as horses were calmed and armour was pressed down to soothe the sounds of ruffling. A light breeze blew through the group. On it carried what could be a sound. Perhaps the notion of sound. Uthiel struggled internally, trying to discern between what he could hear and what noises his imagination created to torture a sense being stretched to the limits of human possibility.

Finally, a whisper carried to them on the breeze.

The men around Uthiel had but to breathe and they would have missed it.

Then it came again. Louder this time. *A sound. A female. Panic. Fear. Pain.*

Then again, slightly louder, still a mile or so away. A scream. *Terror.* This time it discernibly cut out prematurely and then a new voice took up its siren sound. Then two more voices. Then ten more voices. Men, women, children.

Uthiel's eyes flicked from his lieutenant to his brothers, to the direction of the sound back the way they had come. They had passed the outskirts of a town yet untouched by the bands of cutthroats roaming the lands. A light smudge of smoke had started to make its way to the heavens. Uthiel looked once more to Ghurkar Storm. The veteran's jaw was clenched tight and his eyes were locked on the smoke. Not one hour after knocking out a captain of the Secundan army for thinking the same, Uthiel could see his lieutenant was warring with his own decision. Storm met Uthiel's eyes for the barest of moments. Those cold and hard eyes burdened with leadership told Uthiel all he needed to know.

"The column continues to Gall!" Ghurkar called out.

Keldon was bold enough to begin to object before the lieutenant cut him off.

"Brothers, with me," he began. "Keldon, Lokhi, Linton; crossbows from the carriages. Now. The rest of you; shields and helms on the carriages. Swords and knives only. Follow me."

As the knights began to follow Ghurkar Storm, the veteran stopped and turned, ushering his brothers forward, but stopping Carn.

"Not you, old friend," Uthiel heard him say sombrely. "I need someone with half a brain leading these men to Gall."

Carn's chest puffed out in defiance and his face clouded over, his body language every inch the objection his soundlessly working mouth could not exclaim. With a look from Ghurkar, his face softened and his shoulders slumped in recognition for the need of him to do the duty asked of him. Carn blew out his cheeks and bobbed his head once dejectedly, but spoke no words as he turned back to the baggage train, finally finding his voice as he called them onwards.

As the last of the knights was placing their helms and shields on the carriages, Ghurkar Storm called out to Uthiel and Branor. Uthiel jogged over, his friend in tow, excitement and fear warring inside.

"Brothers," Storm said sternly. "You will both be out front scouting. One hundred paces to the fore and not a foot farther. You will not engage the enemy until we get there, understood?"

Uthiel nodded so hard he felt his neck rattle.

Storm sighed. "Go, brothers. Armenius be with you."

Uthiel and Branor turned and with a look to each other started off at a steady lope down the muddy road from whence they had come, back towards the smoke.

"You will wait for me to fight the enemy!" called out Storm.

Uthiel acknowledged him with a curt hand wave over his pauldron. As they rounded the bend, feet pounding the dirt, Uthiel could barely hear the remainder of the knights beginning to give chase.

Far down the road, Uthiel and Branor continued their way towards the sound of slaughter, revelling in the possibility of going into battle for the first time. Their blood was up and their confidence sky high. Uthiel could sense it in his friend as much as he could feel it within himself. The running helped hide the excited shaking of his hands and the slightly nauseating swirling in his guts. *Excitement for glory. Not fear. I am a knight. It will never be fear.*

Above the trees on their right, Uthiel could see the smoke had moved ever closer and become thicker as whatever was burning caught fully alight. The screams of the dying were starting to be punctuated by the cruel laughter and guttural language of the great foe. Uthiel started as a loud, close by, high-pitched scream to their right brought them both to an immediate halt. In a heartbeat both swords were drawn and the Uthiel had cut into the underbrush in the direction of the scream, Branor right on his heels.

As they moved through the brush they crouched low, using the dense foliage to cover their approach. With no further sounds or signs of fighting in the immediate vicinity, Uthiel signalled a halt with a raised hand. He and Branor dropped to a crouch behind a large tree.

Uthiel was the first to pick out the hulking shape in the shadows of the canopy. *Pure luck not to blunder on into the clearing. Armenius is with us.* Uthiel squinted as he tried to see into the shadows. As his sight adjusted he spied two silhouettes. The first was obviously a woman, laying splayed face down in the on the ground. The second was a hulking figure, kneeled over her.

Uthiel's eyes continued to adjust to the dark quickly and it started to become apparent just how large the barbarian before them was. He was broad across the shoulders with dark furs hanging limply from his massive, dark metal pauldrons, and then half way down his back. Even though the beast was hanging his head as if inspecting the woman closely, Uthiel could see the back of a great helm not too far different in general shape to his own. His inspection of the barbarian stopped immediately as a thick bare arm reached down with a knife held in a meaty fist. With a flick of the blade the woman's skirt was thrown up towards her head and her soiled undergarments were laid bare above pale skinny legs.

Uthiel felt Branor's hand upon his vambrance. Even though he could not tear his eyes from the scene the message from his brother's touch was clear. *Do not engage the enemy.* Uthiel knew, however, that there was only so much he could take. This foul beast was desecrating the corpse of a young maiden. Emilia flashed to his mind. She was a beautiful young girl; he shuddered to think what could happen to such a stunning young woman if a monster such as the one before him got a hold of her.

Uthiel flinched, thankfully not making a sound, as the beast drove the knife halfway up to its hilt into the dirt next to her head with apparent ease. His dark reddened hand reached down once more and gripped the woman's inner thigh, swiftly running up between her legs to finish in a position painful enough to bring a squeal from the lady.

Her ploy at playing dead in tatters, she squirmed and tried to get away. The beast's fist casually rose above his head and in a vicious lightning chop rendered her unconscious once more. With a self-satisfied laugh the beast stood, hands reaching to his belt buckle from which hung two shorter swords in black leather sheaths. The movements and sounds of moulded metal on moulded metal let the brothers know what was going to happen next.

Before he even knew what he was doing Uthiel was already standing, brushing off Branor's desperate grasps at him. The sound of his sheath bouncing off his greave was enough to gain his foe's undiluted attention. In a movement that almost belied what a man in armour should be capable of, the buckle had been redone and a bright sword had leapt into each of his hands. The man was fully six and a half feet tall, and now Uthiel was finally able to appreciate the sheer power of the man as the dark warrior slowly began to cover the thirty pace distance between them.

Thick rippling muscle bulged under dirty tattooed skin, the abundant cords of tendons smoothly constricting and stretching as the warrior began a series of shoulder loosening movements. *Not unlike those I was been taught as an initiate.* As the monster moved closer towards them, twenty-five feet now, he strode through a small patch of sunlight. Mud covered boots and greaves. A slightly damaged knee length chain mail skirt over red stained cloth pants. A pitted and gore dotted plate metal cuirass with three finger length rows of what might be text on the left breast. Large pauldrons with an inner collar. *He looks like -*

Uthiel felt, more than saw or heard, Branor move to his right and take up a fighting stance as the horror of the beast before them began to take full form. Uthiel's mind churned first with a moment of confusion, and then anger as he recognised what this barbarian filth wore. *He wears our armour!*

The sheer nauseating disgust at the once glorious symbol of Secundan knightly strength sullied with the blood of the innocent made Uthiel want to spit on the ground. Secundan metal, pulled from the bosom of the rebuilt nation and beaten into armour most holy with which Secunda's sons defended her people, corrupted and turned back on its mother.

Uthiel froze as the great helm came into the light for the slightest of moments, its ugly visage a parody of the glory a Grey Wolf helm held. An ugly, blood spattered monstrosity sat on the head of a barbarian foul enough to have desecrated the visage held in such awe by the people of Secunda. A growl of anger left Uthiel's lips. A sharp intake of breath to his right told him that Branor had seen the same thing.

"Filthy bastard. He's wearing our bloody armour! That's Wolves armour!" hissed Branor beside him.

Uthiel found no words, only action. In unison they strode forward, swords raised to strike, long bladed knives forward to both counter balance and parry. *Armenius, you are with me. You are with me. Give me strength for victory.*

At ten paces the beast quickened the movements of his blades, their pattern becoming more and more complex until coming to a halt. For the barest of moments Uthiel and Branor hesitated. This was all the beast needed as his muscles bunched for the blink of an eye and he sprung forward with a roar. Uthiel and Branor leapt forward to meet the charge. Uthiel's sword rushed down at the beast as he met him first, Branor a pace or so behind him. His gleaming blade sliced through the air at the helm of his foe with all the strength and speed he could muster.

At the last possible moment the dark figure sidestepped to Uthiel's right, taking Branor momentarily out of the equation. His first sword darted up and deflected Uthiel's blade. Uthiel barely had time to register the move before the second sword followed through, the fist holding it delivering a powerful chopping blow that snapped his head back and broke his nose. Had he not been put so off balance and thrown backwards by the deliverance of the punch, the returning blade that cleaved through his cheek and some of the bridge of his nose would have surely split his face horizontally in two.

As Uthiel hit the ground, his vision a mix of white pain and red spots from the blood spraying from his broken nose, he heard Branor yell. Two heavy clangs of sword on sword followed by the cracking sound of sword on cuirass followed immediately after. A heavy impact close by told Uthiel that Branor had also been put to the ground. His vision quickly clearing he scrambled to his feet and yelled out to call the beast's attention away from his fallen brother, fear beginning to run its cold fingers down his spine.

As his eyes fell on his enemy, Uthiel knew there had been no need. With the confidence of a mountain wolf circling its already wounded prey, the barbarian had allowed the momentum of his move to carry him a few paces away from each of the hastily standing young knights. Fear's fingertips traced their way into his chest and wrapped cold clammy hands around his heart. *I can beat him. He's so fast. I can beat him. He's stronger. I can beat him. Armenius help me, I can beat him.*

In each hand the beast flicked his sword through a full circle and then gripped it again, the muscles in his forearm tensing and loosening rhythmically. With Branor to his right and a groggy Uthiel to his left, he spun both swords around together in a show of complete and utter contempt for whatever martial prowess the two young knights may have.

In a moment of almost novice like foolishness, Branor took his eyes off his foe, looking for his brother's lead. Like a striking snake the barbarian stabbed out at Branor, the shining blade neatly slipping between the cuirass and gorget then withdrawing quickly pulling a thin string of blood with it. Branor was almost in too much shock at the sheer speed of the blow to even cry out in pain as his knees gave below him and he collapsed to the ground on his back, fingers clutching at his gorget and neck. The warrior's sword hurtled down at Branor's face.

Uthiel dove in when he saw the blade penetrate his friend's armour, lunging beyond his ability to balance with his sword held out. His gleaming blade intercepted the downward stroke of the beast's that surely would have finished Branor. His blade broke in two as the edge of the foe's sword met the flat of his but it was enough to deflect the blow onto Branor's pauldron.

With a snarl the beast's elbow sped up and once more Uthiel heard his nose crunch and felt his neck snap backwards as the full strength of the strike flung him onto his back again. All around him black fog spotted his vision, earnestly trying to take him from the pain of his reality into the sweet sedative sleep of unconsciousness. But to black out in a battle was to invite death on oneself. Uthiel fought back the fog and tried to sit up. He was instantly rewarded for his efforts with a savage kick to the gorget that left him gasping for air.

As he felt another couple of half-hearted impacts to the side of his head, he tried to swing back a couple of his own. Gloved fist met metal plate in knuckle-cracking pain. Another heavier blow rocked him. He felt a hand grasp the inside of his gorget and pull him halfway towards sitting up. The steel kiss of a blade met, and sliced into, his cheek, splitting the skin as it went down and over his jaw towards his neck. More and more of his precious lifeblood flowed down over his face, over his chin and down his throat.

Something burned the skin between his collarbones, a heat that both scorched and breathed life. Uthiel had not noticed when it started, and its pain was dull in comparison to his face and neck, but it gave him a focus away from his other agony.

Uthiel felt a strange calm come over his fog-abused mind. The cutting still hurt, but the edge was taken away. He realised at that moment that it was time to heed Armenius' call to the eternal battle in the sky. A fear gripped him in that moment. *What if I'm not good enough to be chosen to fight at His side?* He was about to be slain by the first enemy he had faced. He was about to suffer the ignominy of being part of two men, two knights, killed by a single foe who had desecrated the beautiful armour of a Secundan Grey Wolf. *What if the Eternal Lord turns his back on me?*

Before his eyes one last thing passed his vision as he registered the tip of the blade clip his jawbone. Three rows of text on the breastplate before him. The lettering was filled with mud and gore but the first name on the upmost row could just be read.

Kael.

Uthiel closed his eyes and prepared himself to pass from this world. *Eternal Lord, forgive me my failure.*

Half desperate scream, half battle cry, a dark figure impacted the beast. The sounds of two fully armoured bodies in the thick plate mail of Secunda colliding reverberated in Uthiel's head. His head lolled to the side, the darkening vision of his conscious mind slowly losing out to the battering it had received, focussing just in time to see Branor put to ground once more with a vicious strike of the beast's fist. There would be no getting up now for the young knight. In the background seven leather and fur covered barbarians emerged from the undergrowth. One pulled a screaming young woman, stripped to the waist, along the ground by her blonde hair behind him. A look of surprise registered on that barbarian's face as the thick haft of a crossbow bolt was suddenly jutting from his chest.

Two sharp twangs sounded from the opposite direction. Something impacted the beast on his pauldron and knocked him backwards. Behind the beast a second barbarian went down with a bolt passing straight through his throat and burying itself in the shoulder of the filthy, axe wielding man behind him. A cry of anger and recognition erupted from behind Uthiel. *Brother Storm?* Uthiel craned his neck but couldn't see anything behind him past the inner collar of his armour.

The shock gone, the barbarian warriors raised their axes and charged to come forward to the stricken form of their leader, whose pillaged armour had deflected a second bolt but was now on one knee from the impact.

The beast's helm had fallen clear and red-rimmed, veiny blue eyes shot a look of pure hatred back over Uthiel's prone form. A mouth full of sharp, filed teeth opened and unleashed a scream of rage and dismay. The warrior turned and fled with his barbarian brothers into the thick forest behind, stopping one last time on the edge of the clearing to glower balefully at the Secundans. In a show of preternatural speed, the beast swayed backwards as a crossbow twanged from right behind Uthiel's head, and flashed by the foe into the forest.

Uthiel watched them go. *Not dead. I'm alive. I'm alive.*

Armoured forms ran past him to give chase to the barbarians. One man, in polished metal Secundan plate, knelt over him, loosing a final bolt in the direction of the barbarians. Uthiel felt a hand press down on his cuirass and saw the owner's blurry face look down on him.

"Stay with us brother. You're not done yet."

CHAPTER EIGHT

Uthiel's dry, bloodshot eyes slowly wavered open. Thick, blurry bars of golden light carved their way through myriad shades of black shadow before him. His head swam as garbled voices floated around his fog. The taste of blood spiced his tongue and coated his dry teeth and cracked lips. As his befuddled mind attempted to make sense of his surroundings, his sight first began to improve, with shapes beginning to coalesce, and then the pain of his severely beaten head and broken nose quickly sharpened his world back to throbbing consciousness.

"He wakes!" yelled a voice. "Skull shod from iron and a brain cut from rock!"

Eventually the faces of Linton and Keldon swam into clarity before, *no*, above him as they looked down at him. Uthiel could feel the tight pulling of fresh stitches in his face and winced. He murmured a small thanks that Armenius had seen fit to keep him unconscious until the needle had pierced and pulled his skin.

"See, little brother," said one of the veterans, Calus, walking over and kneeling beside Keldon. "I told you that you weren't done yet. There is an enemy to slay and while you still draw breath you will pursue him with us."

Keldon smiled and offered his hand. "Brother, you used to be so pretty."

The start of a wounded smile began to creep to the side of Uthiel's mouth but was quickly suppressed by the alarming memory of his brother's fate. Despite the instant sharp pounding in his head he jerked himself to a sitting up position, frantically twisting around to find Branor. Cold, nauseating, brutal fear swam through him and wrapped around his chest like a massive constricting snake. His eyes widened and his breath left him entirely as he saw his friend, pauldrons and cuirass on the ground beside his prone form, lying unmoving against a tree trunk with eyes closed and a dirty crimson stain running down his front.

In a moment that could have lasted forever Uthiel's throat constricted at the thought of losing a friend born not twenty feet and two months after him. The horror of losing a friend he had gone through every trial and tribulation in life with, struck him like a fist to the stomach. In his short life Branor had been the one constant besides his parents and his drive to become a knight. As a lone tear fought its way through the blood covering his cheek and settled upon a raw stitch, Branor moved.

Firstly it was just a slight wince. But as Ghurkar pushed a needle and thread into the torn flesh near his collarbone, Branor bared his teeth and let out a low growl of suppressed agony. Uthiel grasped Keldon's still outstretched hand and rose to his feet unsteadily. Feeling unbalanced as he moved, Uthiel stumbled over to his brother and dropped down to one knee in front of him. He grasped Branor's free hand while the other hand grabbed the back of his neck and pulled their blood and sweat covered, pain-etched foreheads together. Branor's eyes locked on Uthiel's as another cry of pain was barely smothered by cracked and split lips.

"My friend, you live!"

Branor grimaced. "I do. The blade got in under my gorget. Apparently I am very lucky to be alive. You had a nice little sleep over there, didn't you? Relaxing while I did all the work as usual. Suppose some lord or other will want to give you a castle for staying out cold for longer than me."

Uthiel just smiled, and immediately winced as his stitches pulled tight.

"My friend," said Uthiel, his voice serious and his stare hard and meaningful. "My brother. My life for yours, whenever you require it. You need only ask."

Branor's response was cut off as Storm roughly pulled the last stitch tight and tied it off the raw wound. Storm's face mirrored his surname, his brow creased deeply in thought, as he stood and turned away from his injured brothers. As the leader stood, his big gloved fist clenched and unclenched. He walked away towards where the remainder of Uthiel's brothers had picketed the clearing, twice half-turning back to Uthiel and Branor only to growl or clench his jaw before snapping back to the other direction and continuing away, lost once more in his own thoughts. Uthiel watched him go nervously before helping Branor back in to his armour, a wary eye surveying Storm's mood from afar.

Finally, as Storm reached the other side of the clearing, the big lieutenant squared his shoulders and stormed back to the two young knights, pure anger burning in the baleful glare that fixed the two young knights. Uthiel saw him coming and finished tying off Branor's pauldron. Linton and Keldon stood to intercept him Storm, hands out in conciliatory motions.

"Brother..." started Linton, but a raised finger, and look so filled with rage it took the Uthiel aback, stopped Linton's reconciliatory speech in its infancy.

Ghurkar stopped before Uthiel and Branor, locking them each with his baleful eyes, muscles on the side of his face writhing as he searched for the right words. A long moment passed with the only things moving being those angry blue eyes.

"Do not engage the enemy," growled the lieutenant. "You stupid whoresons, is that not what I said!?"

Spittle flew as Storm's last couple of words came out as a shout. Again he stared down the two young brothers, both of whom dropped their pained gazes to the soft ground in shame.

"The woman..." began Uthiel, stopping as Ghurkar's meaty palm clapped like a thunderbolt into the side of his face.

A long string of blood mixed with mucus slowly spooled out from Uthiel's nose as his injuries were reopened. His watering eyes flashed with anger but he still avoided his leader's gaze. Ghurkar aggressively pushed himself to his feet and turned his back on them.

"You've no idea how close you both came to being killed, little brothers," he said.

Uthiel couldn't stop himself from staring at his leader. The anger was beginning to seep from the lieutenant's anvil-like face.

"By Armenius, by all rights you should both already be bloody dead."

What?

Uthiel never had a chance to voice his thought as, with that half heard last comment, Storm made his way back to the picket line. Just audible above the sounds of the forest and the crying of the two young women, the lieutenant could be heard mumbling to himself in his guttural voice.

Uthiel looked to Branor. "What was that?"

Branor just shook his head.

"Everyone up!" Ghurkar yelled as he got to the brothers at the edge of the clearing. "We move out in pursuit immediately. This foe cannot be let loose in our lands."

A couple of the knights looked at each other warily and questioningly but none uttered a word as they stood and began to follow their leader. Lokhi and Keldon helped the badly beaten Uthiel and Branor to their feet. Almost forgotten by the knights, the half-naked woman who had been dragged by the barbarian into the clearing reached out from her shielding embrace with the other stricken young lady and gripped Lokhi's tabard.

"Please..." she mumbled, her pleading look begging for her saviour to do something, anything to make the situation better.

Lokhi hesitated for a moment.

Without even turning Ghurkar called out. "If you stop to help that woman, Lokhi Dorn, I'll hit you so hard your ancestors will feel it."

119

Lokhi's face fell.

"I'm sorry, lady," was all he could whisper. Her sobbing continued and intensified.

It was only a short run before they came to the edge of the town that had been attacked. By this point the raiders had left, with only three or four of their number lying prone upon the ground. The bloody, mangled forms of the villagers lay everywhere. Men, women and children; none had been shown mercy or given quarter. Most sickening of all were the naked, filthy forms of women of all ages, abused and then murdered in a brutal end to their lives. Some of the knights held their gloved hands up over their noses to avert the burning stink of death. Uthiel felt no shame to be amongst those men.

One of the veteran knights picked up a pail of water and threw it at a burning hut. *As pointless as trying to spit out a campfire.* Here and there were signs of people hanging on to life. The pale pallor of their blood-drained bodies against the stark red of their heinous wounds was an obvious statement of their impending death. Some asked for the sweet mercy of death while others mewled for a miracle of life. Ghurkar nodded to Uthiel, who had picked up a short, one handed axe with a wicked quarter moon blade on one side and a thick steel spike on the other from a fallen barbarian. The two halves of his Secundan blade were held securely in the scabbard at his side.

Uthiel's eyes looked at his lieutenant questioningly. *What does he —*

"It's your foolishness that meant we could not arrive in time to save any," said Ghurkar. "You will give these people the mercy of death they need."

Uthiel's jaw dropped. *Is he serious? Does he really expect me to —* Storm narrowed his eyes at him. Uthiel vomited into his mouth and then swallowed it back down, raw bile and hard edged chunks burning his tongue. His shoulders slumped and he trudged over to Calus, who waved him over to a young boy who lay on the ground.

As Uthiel arrived, Calus lightly clapped him on the shoulder, wincing in understanding before walking away. The young boy, who could not be a day over eight, had been struck in the chest with an axe. Parts of his ribs had been torn back through his skin by the departing blade and the pink flesh of his burst lung was visible in the rent. Uthiel could barely bring himself to look at the child. *Too young. This cannot be. He is too young. Too young.*

Uthiel looked back over to Storm, knowing his own face openly begged the lieutenant to call him away, but too horrified to feel the shame of it. *Don't make me. Please.* Storm's stare remained, unwavering in its hardness. Uthiel looked back down to the boy.

The child's eyes, delirious with pain, rolled around in his head and his skinny muddied legs weakly pushed his own blood through the sludge in shallow grisly trenches. Uthiel allowed one wet sob to come out, the pressure in his mouth reopening some of the stitches in his cheek. His eyes reddened as he twisted the haft of the blade and raised the axe into the air. In that moment the young boy's eyes locked on his in grim clarity. Tears began to roll down the youth's cheeks.

"I... don't... want..." crunch.

The boy never finished his sentence as Uthiel sent his soul to meet Armenius with a swift, vicious chop of the spike to the top of his skull. Uthiel knelt down on one knee and closed the boy's eyes with his thumb and forefinger. Tears welled up in his eyes as he took in a face too early in years to know the cold peace of death. *Armenius, take this young boy to protection behind the Shield Wall.* Uthiel looked to the sky, closing his eyes and swallowing hard and often to keep himself from being sick. *Armenius, steel my -*

"Uthiel!"

Keldon knelt over a young woman and turned to wave Uthiel over with a solemn expression on his face. Uthiel took a deep, shuddering breath and trudged over to him.

Twelve times Uthiel repeated this process, the axe's spike now thick with brain matter and gore and his eyes hollow and hooded. Finally finished, he walked up to Ghurkar and without breaking eye lock, hurled the blade into the ground beside him, burying the quarter moon almost up to the haft in the mud. He hawked the taste of bile onto his tongue and on the ground next to the blade.

"I apologise for my disobedience and will ensure I follow orders correctly in the future," he said clearly, and then turned away to fall into line with his brothers.

"Uthiel!" called Ghurkar, tossing a scabbarded shorter sword to him before Uthiel had completely finished turning back around. "One of the townsfolk had this strapped to his waist when we found him. It looks like Secundan steel, best you use it."

Uthiel caught the weapon by the dark brown leather scabbard and swiftly drew the four-foot blade of shining, unblemished steel for inspection. The blade was well looked after and without a single notch in its edge. Uthiel untied the scabbard of his blade and looped it over his back with the pommel rising above his right shoulder and then clipped the new blade to his left hip without much ceremony.

The Secundans moved out into the forest behind Lieutenant Storm, spreading out in the hope of finding the enemy's trail once more. Uthiel glanced once at the town name engraved in the trunk of a beautiful tall tree. *Tadel. I shall never forget your horrors.*

Half a day in to their search, sweat rolled down Calus Tern's neck at the hard going through the forest. They had gone some time without even the faintest suggestion of the group of marauders they followed and his suspicious internal worrying was starting to get the best of him. Ten feet to his right was a brother he had fought beside for five long years: a brother who was a veteran of the White Frontier where almost half of the Order of the Grey Wolf had disappeared over a decade ago. This brother was a tried and tested veteran of many battles and arguably one of the best rank and file knights in the Order.

A knight Calus was beginning to have a niggling doubt about.

Ghurkar Storm.

Giving a low whistle to the brother on his left to show him his intentions he began to angle his advance towards the lieutenant at the centre of the line. From his position he could see the side of the leader's face. See the jaw clench and then unclench again, see cracked lips mouth words to himself, see his hard stare trained out to the fore with a master engraver's intensity. Getting ever closer he could start to make out some of the words coming from his brother.

"Murderer..."

Calus strained to hear more.

"I saw you fall..."

"...dead like so many betrayed..."

"My brother..."

"Cannot be so..."

"...how?"

Calus reached out his gloved hand to touch his rambling lieutenant. Almost faster than his eye could see Ghurkar whirled and grabbed his wrist. A knife's blade flashed in the light and before he could put up an arm to defend himself it was at his throat with Ghurkar's fierce gaze staring down its razor-edged length. Clarity quickly cleared the confusion and the blade dropped away from his throat and was sheathed. This all happened in the space of four racing heartbeats.

"Apologies, brother," murmured Ghurkar. "You should not sneak up on me like that."

Calus held his tongue for a moment. His hammering chest urged him to some sort of verbal riposte or reprimand. With a deep calming breath he slowed the thumping of his heart enough to think clearly enough to realise that now was not the time. He had to choose his words carefully.

"No matter, brother," replied Calus. "I would speak to you for a moment, Ghurkar."

Storm's eyes narrowed and flicked to Calus for a moment before returning to looking back to where they were going.

"Yes brother?" growled Ghurkar.

Calus swallowed hard before continuing. "I have known you five long years of service, Ghurkar. We have marched hundreds upon hundreds of miles side by side. We have killed and we have seen brothers killed. You have stitched me back together more times than I can remember. I know you.

Something is troubling you this day; I've never seen you in such a fell mood before..."

Calus trailed off before continuing. "... and I've never known you to disobey an order before."

Ghurkar said nothing. Calus continued.

"We are disobeying Captain Phyrus' orders to remain with the baggage train. I can understand the quick sortie to the town to drive the marauders away but this chase? This fruitless squander of our brothers' strength and possibly lives to chase some piece of filth who thinks he looks pretty in our armour - "

With a snarl of rage Ghurkar's hand was all of a sudden clenched around Calus' throat and choking him. The man's strength was phenomenal and his face a map of fury.

Spittle flying into Calus' face, Ghurkar spoke through clenched teeth. "You know not what you speak of... little brother."

This exchange finally brought the attention of some of the knights nearby and Calus could hear low whistles and whispers going up the line to halt the advance. *Shit, shit, choking me!*

One of the remaining veterans, Hult, ran over to the two and quickly got between them. Air rushed into Calus' lungs like the sweetest nectar running over razor blades. Ghurkar stormed away further down the line of brothers. Throat still burning with the intense friction of Storm's hold, Calus watched the lieutenant he passed Keldon and barked at him to find a camp for the night. Keldon looked to his two closest friends, Branor and Uthiel, and they began the search for a likely spot. *What is the matter with you, Ghurkar?*

The look of shock quickly hardened on Calus' face as Hult stood beside him, waving the line of knights behind them to come in and form up. Hult looked at Calus questioningly.

"Brother, what in the name of Armenius is going on!?" he hissed.

"Something is wrong," whispered Calus, almost to himself. "Something is very wrong and Ghurkar knows something about it."

**

As the sun made its way down and the forest once again darkened, the knights sat and listened, their backs to the campfire they had made and their attention on the darkness outside the circle of light. Some of them picked warily at pieces of dried meat or local fruit, carefully ensuring their attention was never drawn away from their sentry duty for more than a moment. Around the fire, in the centre, lay the seven prone forms of sleeping knights. Uthiel and Branor were both amongst them.

Calus lay awake, staring at Ghurkar Storm from the shadows of the fire. He stirred and slid himself towards the sleeping lieutenant. Reaching out, he nudged him awake. Ghurkar sat up with a start, the shining blade of his knife once again in his hand and ready to stab out at the foe. Seeing Calus, he frowned.

"Calus? What is it?" he asked impatiently.

Calus started again. "My lieutenant, you need to tell your brothers what is going on."

"Brother, you need to sleep the hours I assign you else you will be more useless tomorrow than you were today," retorted Ghurkar.

Calus ignored the barbed comment for the deflection attempt that it was and pressed on.

"How are your brothers supposed to trust you if you keep secrets from us?" whispered Calus. "Secrets seemingly paramount to the nature of the men we follow?"

Ghurkar rolled over and turned his back on Calus. Calus waited for a time and was about to press on when Ghurkar spoke.

"That beast, I have seen and fought him before," rumbled Ghurkar. "On the White Frontier. There are very few warriors in the land that I know of that could match him one on one. If you see him, call for me, lest you find yourself before Armenius' feasting hall that night."

Calus rolled that information around in his head. It wasn't enough for the full picture.

"When I walked up to you earlier you were saying something to yourself. Betrayal. Seeing a brother fall. What did you mean? Who betrayed you? Which brothers did you see fall?"

Once again Ghurkar was slow to respond. When he did, his voice seemed resigned and tired.

"Sleep brother. We all need the rest."

That night, Ghurkar dreamt fitfully. Seeing the betrayer had set his soul afire with rage but something inside of him quailed as he looked down upon the fallen form of Kael. The man's face was no longer the handsome young first captain that had been his commander, no longer the very image of honour and glory that he had looked up to as a young knight.

Now his face was coated thickly in the blood of yet more of Ghurkar's brothers, his teeth filed and sneering as a forked tongue licked out over bright red lips. A blade swung at Ghurkar and he raised his pauldron to deflect it without urgency, having dreamed of this battle a hundred times in the last ten years. The heavy blade clanged from his thick pauldron and stopped against the tall inner collar. A slashing riposte hammered into a traitor's cuirass and sent the man reeling to the ground before a loyal brother drove a sword into the man's throat.

Already knowing that a crossbow bolt would slam into that loyal brother's back a heartbeat later, Ghurkar turned back to Kael, hoping something could tell him how the fell creature had survived a blow that had sliced into his neck. Only a pool of dark black blood remained. He put a toe in the liquid and it came away sticky and congealed as if it were tar.

With a snarl of anger, Ghurkar turned away and back to the battle he already knew he would win. Only, there was no battle raging behind him. No brothers and traitors butchered each other. No lords and captains and brothers alike lay on the ground soaked in their own blood. Just one soul.

One gore-coated soul stood in the centre of a clean battlefield. Ghurkar's lip raised in a scowl. Kael?

Kael grinned, his forked tongue flicking in amongst his filed teeth. Contempt does not become you, brother.

Before Ghurkar could move, a Secundan blade had been driven in through his stomach and had erupted out between his shoulders. A forked tongue licked his face as blood began to rain from the dark sky. Torches guttered and went out in quick succession. Kael's face grew darker and darker.

"Until the morrow, brother."

Ghurkar woke with a cry as his mind tried to pull him back to reality, hands scrabbling for the dreamed hole in his body and finding nothing, as Kael twisted the blade and wrenched it out into the darkness.

The next day brought more of the same. They walked until midday, passing through another devastated town. On the border of the town, a weather-worn piece of wood had the name "Tarm" burned into it.

The atrocities had escalated. Dismembered bodies were found nailed to the wooden walls of buildings, their innards pooled below them from empty rib cages. The town well was full to the brim with the blue bodies of drowned children. Some ten people had been herded into a house and burned alive, their bodies still crackling embers. A small pile of decapitated female bodies lay naked in the mud, their heads tied by their hair to the leafless tree that shadowed their place of horrid demise.

There were none in need of the executioner's mercy this time. Not a soul lived. Even all of the wildlife had fled the hell the small farming community had become. Uthiel and Branor picked their way through the corpse-strewn town centre. Uthiel couldn't speak, and Branor offered up no conversation either. The horror was simply on too large a scale for their collective years to comprehend. Uthiel walked into the open door of a small hut and rebounded out, gagging.

Entire families had been butchered and hacked well beyond death until only a gruesome slurry of bone and meat remained. Women and young girls were in piles, their abused bodies always naked and decapitated with their heads hanging by their hair somewhere above. Babies had not escaped the murder, dashed against the wall over and over again until the only thing recognisable as human was the stump of a foot or leg. Family pets had been skinned and disembowelled.

Uthiel vomited loudly, unable to keep his stomach under control. The greater majority of the knights vomited more than once. *Can't think any less of my brothers for it.*

As Uthiel left Branor to his dry retching outside one of the last houses they had checked, he reported back to Storm.

"More of the same, brother," he said sombrely, flecks of vomit still in his stubble.

Ghurkar nodded but did not speak. His jaw was clamped solidly shut and his face was rage incarnate. As Uthiel walked away a thought struck him and he turned back.

"There must be fifteen families here," he started. "and they have all been butchered in ways that go far beyond killing. That's over a hundred people."

"That much is obvious, brother," snapped Ghurkar.

"The first village numbered less people and had been less badly destroyed," continued Uthiel. "We did not give them much of a lead... perhaps half a day at most...

"...How did they have time to do it all, and then withdraw to move on before we got here this time?"

Ghurkar didn't move. He worked his young brother's words around and tried to think it out in his head. *They've even taken the time to skin the animals.*

Ghurkar looked around at what his brothers were seeing. *Most have thrown up their breakfasts; they'll be weakened.*

Ghurkar looked around at the disposition of his men. *They are spread out with no formation and they're distracted by what they're seeing.*

Ghurkar took in his surroundings. *Lots of small buildings. We're in a crossroad at the centre of the village with four directions to defend and no reinforcements.*

Ghurkar's eyebrows lifted, his mouth opening and sucking in a deep breath to shout. *The whole town is an ambush.*

They haven't left.

"Ambush!" he yelled.

To his right he heard the thud of a body falling to the ground. Hult lay on dirt, weakly grasping an arrow with only the feathers at the back of the haft jutting from his throat. His wide eyes blinked a couple more times before he bled out into his lungs and drowned within his own body. Dark crimson splashed from his vermillion lips as he died, lifeless eyes staring to the sky. Ears deaf to the cries of his brothers as they fought and died around him.

Ghurkar screamed at his men to rally to him but it was already too late. A half dozen melees already had formed. Two more Secundans already lay prone on the ground, their blood adding to the gallons of Gall blood already soaking the earth.

Then he spotted the beast. *Kael.* He watched as young Tobias was skilfully and brutally cut to pieces by the traitor knight. Uthiel had been not six feet from him when the arrow had struck. He was now sprinting back the way from whence he had left Branor.

Branor stood, back to a wall, alone facing three black fur and leather-clad barbarians. Already one filthy beast lay slain upon the ground, his axe wielding hand separated from his body half way up the forearm and Branor's knife buried to its hilt in his heart. Without further thought Ghurkar launched himself after Uthiel. *Unify the battle. Get my brothers together. Strength in numbers.*

As Branor's sword parried and struck deep into his attacker's ribs an axe found a home in his pauldron, splitting the plate and cutting shallowly into his left shoulder. The plate took the majority of the force but the brutal axe still drove the young knight to a knee. Ghurkar bellowed a battle cry to draw the attention of the barbarians away from his young charges. *Faster, old man! Run! Your brothers need you!*

The third attacker was poised with axe raised to split his skull asunder but without warning two feet of beautiful, glorious, red stained Secundan steel erupted from his chest and hastily withdrew only to slice through the throat of the barbarian with his axe still buried in Branor's shoulder. Ghurkar breathlessly cried out to Uthiel as another tattooed warrior ran at him.

Uthiel swirled around and got his blade up. His sword deflected the axe down to the right and then swept back up and over his left shoulder leaving a red gouge out of the barbarian's chest. Ghurkar Storm arrived a heartbeat later. He reached down yanked the axe wedged in Branor's pauldron free. Tossing the axe he grabbed the youth by the vambrance and pull him to his feet.

"On your feet brother!" yelled Ghurkar. "Battle awaits and your brothers need you!"

CHAPTER NINE

The sun had moved over to the other side of the battlefield as the hours had passed, casting long shadows through the town. In the sky, crows circled above the deathly quiet crossroads, waiting for the living to depart before they swooped down to feast on the corpses thickly littering the dirt streets.

At the centre of the crossroads, Uthiel was on his knees, his gloved hand holding on to Ghurkar Storm's blood spattered pale fist. Ghurkar lay on his back amongst the carnage of his last battle. A flap of red flesh hung loose from the remnants of his cheek just below where his left eye used to be. His cuirass and pauldrons were dented and rent in many places, visible only due to his blood soaked tabard having been torn from his body in his berserk assault.

The beast in Secundan plate had reared his head again. Single handedly he had accounted for the deaths of Calus, Tobias, and another of the younger knights. Each dazzling display of swordsmanship had been well beyond the skill of Uthiel or any of his brother knights to have dealt with one on one. Each contest with this monster in Secundan plate had ended with a brother dying to a series of precise stabs or brutally accurate cuts.

Ghurkar had spotted him first and with a wordless snarl had leapt at the group of marauders blocking his path to the beast. Branor and Uthiel had sprinted to create the arrowhead formation either side of their lieutenant, acting more like shields for Ghurkar's insane attack as they desperately struck out to glance away blows or strike at the attacker's bodies before they could strike at Ghurkar. Uthiel counted three marauders that fell to his blade before they closed in behind Ghurkar as their leader reached and challenged his chosen foe.

As Uthiel and Branor fought shoulder to shoulder, Ghurkar attacked the beast with fury unbridled. Only one word on his snarling lips.

"Kael!" he had screamed as his sword met the beast's time and time again.

As the Secundan's superior arms, armour and training started to take its toll on the barbarian marauders they began to take control of the battle. Uthiel looked around at his brothers still breathing. *No veterans. Ghurkar sorely wounded. A sorry state indeed.*

Six of his brother initiates had stood by him. The bodies of the barbarians had begun to pile up before their feet as the flow of the enemy began to ebb and slow before eventually grinding to a halt. At Uthiel's order, three of the six brothers turned towards where their leader duelled with the beast. Behind them the three others had stepped forward and started stabbing down at the wounded enemy.

Ghurkar and the beast flowed around each other like a pair of whirlwinds. Their blade work was almost mystifying to Uthiel. He didn't even see the strike that cleaved through the side of Ghurkar's face and destroyed his eye. Ghurkar didn't even seem to notice, his blade stabbing deep into the beast's forearm in response.

The two had broken apart, each measuring the other's strengths, wounds, weaknesses, and remaining stamina. Both men slouched, their big chests labouring hard. Ghurkar struck out with a lightning lunge. Kael seemed to not read the move but just before the blade struck he darted aside and struck Ghurkar's blade in an arrogant show of contempt. Uthiel remembered feeling fear and despair in that moment, almost like he imagined watching an infallible fortress fall would feel.

Kael's form had straightened, hidden strength visibly lending itself to his limbs. A whisper of doubt crept across Ghurkar's face as he stared at the black eye slits in the leering wolf helm of his foe.

"I saw you fall," stated Ghurkar, his words coming amongst rasping breaths. Uthiel had barely heard the words.

The beast did not respond. Instead he darted high with his sword and then, in a move almost unbelievable in its brilliance and speed, reversed the angle and stabbed deep into Ghurkar's thigh. The chain mail had been dragged up Ghurkar's thigh as his weight went down with the intention of blocking high and then striking low leaving only his cloth leggings to protect him. The blade pierced this like a sheaf of paper, twisted viciously and then withdrew from the inner thigh as Ghurkar's wounded leg failed him and sat him on the ground.

The man named Kael had backed away, never once making a sound as the three initiates rushed forwards and got between their stricken leader and the beast. One crossbow bolt buried itself in his sword side black pauldron and another glanced off his helm as he reeled further and further back from them. Keldon and Lokhi ran up beside their brothers, reloading their crossbows with urgency as Kael turned and started to run. Lokhi finished first, dropped to one knee and fired but his bolt flew just wide, burying itself in a wooden wall some fifty paces beyond the fleeing beast.

Keldon took his time, tracking the beast's side-winding run and loosing his bolt. It flew straight and true but glanced away with a loud clang, sending the armoured man sprawling behind a stable out of sight. Four of the knights, led by Branor, sprinted to the place where he fell. Uthiel was already kneeling by Ghurkar, whose face had started to turn towards a deathly paleness.

"Brother," he said as he grabbed his leader's hand. "We have chased him off, he is wounded. We must dress your wound so we can pursue."

Ghurkar smiled weakly. "There is no point, little brother, I am undone."

Uthiel shook his head, a little panic fluttering within. "Come, brother, the wound is deep but you will live."

Ghurkar winced as he lifted his ruined face. "Remember your training, little brother; see how the blood pumps instead of flows? I am not long for this world."

Ghurkar coughed, his cheek flap blowing out to reveal his bloodstained teeth and gums. His eyes rolled back in his head and with a rumbling, sickening groan Ghurkar's eyes closed. Uthiel removed his glove and held his bare hand over Ghurkar's mouth. Relief washed over him as he felt the faint push of Ghurkar's breathing against his palm. He turned to look up his brothers.

"Lokhi, hold his feet."

"Keldon, Linton, his arms."

Uthiel drew his knife and split Ghurkar's legging to reveal the wound, still pumping weakly. Pulling out a needle and thread he started to try to press the sides of the wound together to start the repair. The torn flesh was slippery with blood. The needle pierced the skin anyway and Uthiel pushed it into the pulped meat on the other side of the gaping wound. Ghurkar immediately awoke and began crying out, his eyes wide open with shock and his mouth agape as he struggled against those holding him with a mewling, pitiful example of the strength that bestowed such a veteran warrior.

Uthiel finished two stiches, then the skin tore as he tried to carefully pull the stiches tight. Ghurkar had stopped making any sound louder than a rambling moan or mumble. Keldon reached out and put a hand on Uthiel's vambrance as he was lining up a second attempt at the stitches.

"Uthiel," said Keldon. "Uthiel. My brother; my friend. Let him go. Armenius will be welcoming him with open arms, brother to brother, very soon."

No. No! It cannot be so! Who will lead us? Who will guide me?

Uthiel reached forward for a moment, his hand quivering with indecision as his gaze flicked between Ghurkar's face,

Keldon, and the wound. Eventually, Uthiel bade the others release the dying lieutenant and re-gripped Ghurkar's hand. The veteran's eyes fluttered open, unfocussed and wide. For a moment he looked at Uthiel, his remaining strength gripping his brother's fist harder.

"Uthiel," he rasped. "The Black Wolves are here."

"The Black Wolves, brother?" asked Uthiel, leaning down to put his ear next to Ghurkar's mouth.

"The Black Wolves," repeated Ghurkar with more urgency. "The master of our Order must know. Kael has slain me. Speak to none other. The Black Wolves, Uthiel... we thought we had slain them... our brothers fell on both sides of the sword... they came back for us like demons in the darkness... Like demons in the..."

Ghurkar's eyes glazed over as his free arm clasped his sword for a brief moment to his chest, and then pushed the blade to Uthiel. Uthiel grabbed the blade just below Ghurkar's hand and looked back to his leader's face, only to see life had left him. Uthiel's head bowed as the excited terror-surge of battle began to subside and a great weariness swept over him.

He looked up as the pounding of feet broke him from his short moment of reverie. It was Branor.

"Uthiel," he said between gasping breaths. "I found where the beast's body fell. But there is no corpse. He is gone."

Branor sighed as he looked at the dead form of Lieutenant Ghurkar Storm. His eyes then looked back to Uthiel.

"Do we pursue?"

Uthiel hesitated for a moment. All the eyes of his seven remaining brothers were locked on him. Branor, his pauldron tinged red through the rent in it and his face scrunched in barely suppressed pain. Keldon, his strong jaw and stereotypical Secundan features intent on Uthiel. Linton, as usual with his ears sticking right out from his usually meek expression now turned sour. Lokhi, spattered from head to toe more so than the rest in gore both from a long split in his forehead and that which had been shed by his blade, wore an expression of absolute resolute exhaustion.

Tarren was the only one not looking at him, his attention focussed on his bare right arm as he tied a torn piece of cloth around his bicep to stem a wound from an axe that had split his gousset. Eliem and Umbar, Eliem as always looking like he was wearing his father's armour and Umbar the polar opposite looking like he would burst from his any moment, both had looks of expectation on their blood spattered features.

No, I can't do it. Not me.

Tarren completed his bandaging and in a heartbeat all eyes were on him. *Why are they all looking to me?* He placed a finger and thumb either side of his still lightly throbbing nose and lightly squeezed. *What can I do?* Uthiel knew doubt for a moment; knew hesitation. They were waiting.

They're waiting for a decision.

Lord Field Marshal Loghan Faramon peered over the battlement to look at the siege works below his position on the White Frontier. The enemy camp stretched for many miles around, with hundreds of campfires filling the air with a smoky haze. Their filthy, ramshackle tents were everywhere and seemed to be bunched into small communities. Fields had been cleared and forests hacked to the ground for the construction of siege ladders, towers, rams and catapults.

Crude, hastily built, arrow screens formed a wooden ring around the frontier bastion. Dark shapes would swing around from the side to loose an arrow at the defenders from time to time. In their haste they more often than not aimed too low and the arrow head struck stone. In response archers and knight crossbowmen waited for those enemy archers to come out and then return a volley. Many barbarian archers lay dead on the ground already. Very few defenders had been slain or wounded.

To the right of the fortress, at the small frontier town of Archenon Creek, the river that supplied Loghan's men had been soured by the bodies of tens of thousands of barbarians and Secundans. The Secundan Fifth army, some eight thousand men strong had fought valiantly there with two hundred and fifty of Loghan's brothers, slaying easily three times their number before being routed back to the castle. The river upon which they had made their stand had run low, thick and red into the castle walls. The well had been stopped to prevent people from falling sick to the foul water. Loghan well knew his people had maybe enough water stored for a day or two more.

The Secundan Third army had been assumed completely destroyed, apart from the few men who had completely lost their nerve and fled to the lands beyond, along with the entirety of the Secundan Fourth. Sixteen thousand men and two hundred and fifty of his brothers were dead, almost to the man. A scant hundred or so of the Fifth were now on the fortresses walls, General Stern among them.

Now they were an island in the storm, cut off from the remainder of the Lands of the Light, and the king of Secunda's younger brother was finding himself and his men put to the ultimate test. Loghan's dream of glory had been ruined when Gall's reserve armies had not shown up to plug the holes in the line. The twenty four thousand soldiers and his brother knights had not been enough to create a defensible line against the horde that assailed them. A large piece of Secunda's standing army lay slain upon the grounds or hopelessly trapped in the fortress. Loghan swore to himself as his mind worked through the horrible necessities of this war.

His brother would have to draw on untried reserve armies and ageing retired veterans from the populace to field a sizeable force against the oncoming torrent of death. Men who were untrained or grey beards would march out and do battle with the warmongering barbarians. The real soldiers lay slain upon the field or unreachable in distant theatres of battle. The king would be at a severe disadvantage with his true strength squandered at Archenon Creek. *We are lost. As our forefathers fell, so shall we. There is no Gall to save us now. No saviour nation to come to our aid. Nothing. Secunda shall be lost.*

In that moment, exasperation took Loghan over. Both hands rose to his face and covered his royal features. His strength forsook his limbs and, for a heartbeat, he felt his knees bend. It lasted only a moment. As a single tear made its way down his stubbled cheek his jaw set and his mind hardened like ice. *I am the king's brother. I am a descendant of Armenius himself.*

I am a son of Secunda.

Standing to his full height he roared to the foe on the fields before him.

"I am a son of Secunda and you shall not have this fortress!"

Around him his men raised their fists and screamed their defiance. Tired, thirsty, hungry, resolute souls basked and fed from their lord field marshal's defiance. Men with little to no hope of survival were buoyed by one moment of Faramon zeal. It was glorious. *If there is anyone left of the Lands of the Light at the end of this war, somebody will one day tell our tale of when a resolute few boldly stood in the face of the barbarous many.*

As the din died down, some voices did not. Looking around he tried to find the source of the vehement yelling. Some of his men started to do the same. Without a second thought he started walking around the battlement and then down the stairs to the wall of the fortress. His bodyguards and runners followed him. Down another set of stairs and he was on the stone ground and walking briskly towards the rear facing wall of the fortress. The yelling was becoming louder. All of a sudden a great cheer rose from the battlement. Hundreds of voices raised in a cry of hope. *Hope. I could do with a flagon of it.* Loghan quickened his step and started running to the stairs that led up to the rear facing wall.

As he crested the wall he immediately saw what his men were cheering on. Atop a green hill's crest burst the brilliant white rose on a red background flag of the Order of the White Rose. Next to it was the dull grey banner of the Grey Wolves. Loghan smiled but did not yet allow himself to cheer with his men. He drew his sword and lifted it to Armenius in salute of the brave generals some miles distant. Surprisingly, the grey and red figures at the spear tip of the column did likewise and raised their swords, the sun reflecting brilliantly from the polished steel.

The barbarians had spotted them by this point and a few large figures in furs had started to rally their troops to counter the knights. The knights upon the hill charged, the spear tip broadening as they gained speed and started smashing through the more sparse region of the barbarian camps. *Come on, brothers. Break them.* The thunder of their hooves would be heard for miles. Hundreds of knights in all of their Secundan glory hammered through more and more of their foul foe like a freshly honed blade through supple flesh.

Break them. Armenius let them break the foe.

The wedge swam through the barbarians, not yet losing its momentum as it closed the gap to less than two miles. Soldiers on the battlements still cried out but like flies to rotting meat the barbarians began to swarm in greater and greater numbers towards the spear tip. *They shall not to make it.* Loghan knew how this would play out and his head dropped once more for a moment. But still the spear tip refused to completely flounder.

Finally the crush of the foe became too much and the spear tip swarmed in a circle hacked in barbarian blood around the two generals. Once more the general raised his sword to Loghan. Then the man in the red tabard turned and called to his men to retreat. *Armenius, no. Don't abandon us.*

Please.

With some cries of dismay the defenders of the tower watched the knights turn and orderly flee the field of battle, leaving behind hundreds of slain barbarians and, to Loghan's dismay, many slain knights. Only a half to two thirds of the knights who had charged onto the field managed to retreat off it, many of the dead leaving their beautiful war horses to undoubtedly become meat for the bellies of the barbarians.

Loghan instantly recognised the despair on his men's face. Moving quickly he used a thick wooden flagpole to steady himself and stood upon an empty oil cauldron.

"My brothers!" he called at the top of his lungs. "See how our brother Orders smite the foe! They will be back! The holders of this keep will forever be held in glory when my brother arrives. You will all be heroes spoken of through the ages as the island of light in the darkness."

He jumped down and started moving amongst the men, grabbing some by the arm, locking iron stares, and gripping forearms in warrior's handshakes.

"Brave stalwarts of the mighty Secundan Fifth alongside the men of my Order! The Knights Aggressor and the mighty Fifth!"

And with one final roar "Glory to Secunda!"

Men, lifted once more, punched the air. "Glory to Secunda! Glory to Secunda! The mighty Fifth! The Knights Aggressor! Glory to Secunda!"

Loghan smiled, but it was only on the surface. *Men's morale is measured in very short spans of time. I have scant days of morale, at best.* Even now, amongst the cheering, he could see some small clutches of men speaking warily to each other. He was saddened to see some high-ranking knights amongst them. He sighed; *even I am distraught. Who could not be when they know the setting as well as I? It should not surprise me that lesser men fear the siege. It shall be wasteful and bloody.*

For a moment he locked eyes with Lord Ambar. Again he saw in that stare something other than fear. Something other than courage.

Ambition.

Loghan huffed and looked to the sky as he whispered to himself. "Father, watch over me as I guide these men through these troubling times."

CHAPTER TEN

An exhausted messenger lying prone beside a lame horse was the first sign of trouble in the lands of Secunda. A knight patrol of Grey Wolves picked him up, clad in filthy and sweat soaked Secundan army clothes. He spoke in the mad tongues of food and water starved delirium. It would be almost half a desperately needed day before he was able to regain consciousness long enough to pass on his message. Tucked into his horses rucksack, it was written in hasty handwriting on a piece of torn parchment carrying the seals of General Colle Gill of the Order of the White Rose and First Captain Solanthur Verutus of the Order of the Grey Wolves.

The knight column immediately abandoned the soldier to the farmers nearby and charged at all possible speed to the gates of the city of Secunda. Seven knights broke off and made for the home fortresses of the seven knightly Orders. War had come to the Lands of the Light. The king needed to know.

It was close to dusk before they made it to the gates of Secunda, their headlong charge through the cobblestone streets of the city drawing many retiring citizens from their homes. Within a few short hours, town criers were everywhere. Small crowds quickly swelled to large ones throughout all the quarters of the city, both rich and poor. The criers' loud and clear voices cut through the hubbub very quickly.

The White Frontier has fallen.

Barbarians ravage the lands of Gall.

Over twenty thousand men at Archenon Creek considered lost.

Tanin Caellar, walking home from the market with a small sack of potatoes over his shoulder was one of the first people to hear the town crier who came to their area. From down the street Antony and Argo spotted him quickly and ran to join him. Looks of concern were plastered across their faces. Tanin was well aware that both had sons serving in the Fifth.

"General," Argo called out the old rank to get Tanin's attention. "Has there been word on the Fifth? Do you know which order Uthiel was accepted in to?"

Tanin turned and spotted them quickly, their tabards making them easy to pick out, and waved them over with one hand and bade them be quiet with the other as he strained to listen to the crier begin his message again. Antony and Argo ran over and joined Tanin amongst the press of bodies.

There were cries of disbelief, despair, and anger. Pointless calls for news on individual regiments within the Fifth rang out to be lost in the tumult. Many in the area had sons who served with the Fifth. Fewer had sons amongst the Orders but all were obviously concerned, some to the point of hysteria.

It took the crier a frustratingly long amount of time to get the crowd settled enough to get his message across.

"People of Secunda!" he called out, his voice clear and crisp. "I beg of you, please quieten yourselves so I may portray our king's message!"

"Citizens of Secunda, today I have the sad duty of bringing ill tidings to your quarter. News, quite possibly, of the most terrifying nature that generations to come are likely to ever hear of. Citizens; the White Frontier has fallen. Hordes from the Black Lands run rife in the lands of Gall. They butcher, murder, rape and pillage. They befoul the land of the very people whom fought with our Eternal Lord Armenius over four centuries ago to save us!

"General Colle Gill, of the Order of the White Rose, and the legendary First Captain Solanthur Verutus of the Order of the Grey Wolf, leading their brave knights and a thousand soldiers of the Secundan Twelfth and Fourteenth, encountered the fleeing citizens four days past. Their horrifying stories spoke of the fall of the frontier fortress."

Uthiel. Is that where my boy is?

"There was a mighty battle at Archenon Creek, where over twenty five thousand brave Secundan souls of the Secundan Third, Fourth, and Fifth are now assumed utterly destroyed."

Tanin could not help but feel his soul a little crushed. The Fifth had been his for so many years. Either side of him, Argo and Antony's heads both went down. Argo let one wet sob escape before clamping down on himself in a grunt of pain. His reaction was mirrored and surpassed in grief by many, many more parents.

"Of the men of the Order of the Knights Aggressor, nothing is known. Some two hundred and fifty were spotted in Archenon Creek and are also assumed lost. The rest are assumed either lost further south or besieged within the fortress. News from the front is scant but with almost half of the standing army strength of Secunda now assumed lost, our mighty king, direct descendant of our Eternal Lord, Kentigern Faramon calls all able men to the field of battle."

Antony strode forward, pulling his Tabard from his body and holding it in the air, and roared to the crowd. "The fathers of the mighty Fifth stand ready to fight once more! For Armenius and the glorious dead!"

His declaration was met with a general roar of approval. Oaths were sworn. Fists pumped the air. Men recognised Tanin and called out to the old general. When the din died down somewhat, the crier raised his voice once more.

"Aye! And the mighty Fifth shall fight again! Soldiers will be here in the morning to take names and to once again raise the glorious Fifth army.

"I ask that you steel yourselves, and pray to Armenius for strength in the days to come - for they shall be bloody."

"And glorious!" called another voice. "We shall avenge our sons!"

"We shall avenge Archenon Creek!"

With that the town crier took a cup of water offered to him. Draining it quickly he turned and moved on to the next area on his route.

My son. Where is my Uthiel? Is he alive or fallen in some charge or hopeless last stand?

Immediately the group of almost two hundred people devolved into a rabble. They were angry, grief stricken, directionless people with a desperate need of a leader.

My son needs me. He still lives. I know it. I can feel it. Hold strong Uthiel, for I am coming.

Tanin took the podium where the crier had stood moments before. Very quickly, the attention of the mob turned to him. Argo and Antony stood before him, their king's tabards proudly displaying the number five on their right breast.

"People!" called Tanin. "We have suffered a loss most horrible this day. Many of our sons lie slain at Archenon Creek."

"Not yours!" called out a female voice from the back. "I know for a fact that your son is a glory hound knight!"

Many voices called out to berate the lady but Tannin raised a hand for quiet.

He slowly nodded, sticking out his bottom lip. "You are right, my only remaining son is a knight, though I know not which Order he has joined and have little idea where he is."

"My son is also a knight," called out Camen, Branor's father. "What of it? Are we less entitled to fight if our sons did not die with the Fifth?"

"I am Tanin Caellar," stated Tanin, stopping all argument or debate before it gained momentum. "General of the Secundan Fifth, now retired. Formerly I led eight thousand soldiers into five major battles and over twenty minor ones and the Fifth were always victorious. Many of you know me, many have served with me, and many of you have simply heard of me, I ask now that the men of this quarter follow me once more. When the soldiers come to take the names of those

144

brave enough to march out and face the barbarians, I pray to Armenius that you will put your mark beside mine."

Hold strong, Uthiel. I am coming for you.

On the dawn of the next day, Tanin stood at the front of a queue over six hundred men deep. The officers who had arrived to take names set up a desk and with parchment and quill began to take the names of the re-formed Fifth. One of the officers had been a junior officer in the Fifth almost ten years prior, before being advanced to the Seventh after receiving his promotion. Having served under Tanin he recognised the grizzled veteran immediately.

"General Tanin," said the officer with a smile, offering his hand. "It gladdens my heart in these dark days to see you join us in our hour of most need."

Tanin reached out and took to officer's proffered grip. "It saddens mine that we must meet once more under these circumstances."

Tanin took a moment before continuing. "At last count, we have six hundred and thirty-three men for you, captain. Around two hundred are veterans who have served under me in the Fifth and I can personally vouch for. A further hundred or so served in the First, Sixth or Twelfth armies. There are few ranks left amongst them that I know of and I will point them out to you as they make their mark. The remainder are stout men looking to defend their country and avenge their sons."

"We're going to need every Secundan capable of bearing arms, general. The king wants to march with as close to fifty thousand men as we can muster in less than a week," replied the captain, before his gaze was pulled over Tanin's shoulder.

Tanin turned to see the burly figure of Lonetta Hulfur, followed by Antony, as they bustled through the crowd. Antony carried a thick wooden pole that stood two and a half times his height. At the top was a horizontal pole six feet in length and from this hung a black banner. In the centre of the banner a large white canvas "S" had been stitched into the fabric. A smaller black canvas number five had then been stitched into the lowest curve of the two-foot tall letter. Two thinner pieces of canvas had been also attached on either side of the black banner. Vertically they were as long as the black banner but they were only a hand span wide. Names had been hand stitched into the canvas in thin black thread.

What in the name of...

Tanin squinted and as the Hulfurs came closer. He realised they were the names of the young men presumed killed at Archenon Creek. Lonetta's cheeks were red with exertion and her eyes were deep set and had dark underlying bags.

"General," she said addressing Tanin. "The Fifth will have lost their colours. I've made new ones."

Tanin nodded, his throat tightening at the gesture.

Lonetta continued. "I stayed up all night but I could not come close to finishing the honour rolls for all the boys we have lost. I'm sorry."

Her head bowed and tears streamed down her cheeks. Tanin once more glanced at the white banners and saw her two sons' names on there, amongst what must have been almost a hundred others. When he looked down, Antony had his wife in his big arms, speaking soothing words into her ear. He looked up at Tanin. Tanin turned and got a quick nod of approval from the captain.

"Lonetta Hulfar," he said, raising his voice for the benefit of those around them. "You do the Fifth a great honour by making our colours. I swear it shall fly high over our victories until we are able to place it over the graves of our fallen."

A rousing cry went up from amongst the hundreds of men. Lonetta's red, teary face emerged from her husband's big chest. She mouthed a thank you to Tanin.

As the day wore on, more and more men arrived. Another two hundred retired veterans of the Fifth, having heard of the banner, came specifically to Tanin's recruitment post to ask their sons' names be entered onto the honour roll as they made their mark. Some had come by from the closer farms. Even some with missing limbs put their mark down to fight. Lonetta and six other women worked hard to get as many names onto the honour rolls as possible before the day ran out. When no more could fit, they started to try to make room for two more honour strips either side.

Those who came from the outside described the muster of armour and arms occurring at the city gate. Great wagon trains of grain were being loaded up from the granaries in front of the city and the standing armies had begun to picket their tents in farmers' fields. Tanin listened intently. Supposedly, the full sixteen thousand men of the First and Second armies would be there by the third day of muster. And the much smaller armies of the Seventh, Ninth, Twelfth, and Thirteenth would bring the standing army to almost thirty thousand men by the end of the week. The king obviously hoped to gain a further twenty thousand fighting men from the general populace of the city Secunda and the surrounding communities by the fifth or sixth day, and within eight days they should be meeting up with the knight Orders closer to the border of Gall and Secunda. *Biggest muster I've ever seen. The King might get his fifty thousand after all.*

If Gall could raise a similar army, the two nations should be able to field a formidable force. With almost every able and available male short of the Bastion Guard and city watch committed to the battle it was an all or nothing fight. Should they fail to stop the barbarians, then first Gall would fall. And then the barabrians would finally finish the war they'd started over four centuries ago against the Secundans. *With only her disabled, mothers, children and elderly left to defend her, city Secunda will fall and the hundreds of thousands living in the towns and communities more than five days march away throughout the land will burn with her.*

By the end of the day, Tanin and the captain had well over a thousand names. The banner fluttered in the wind over them. Hundreds of names now crammed tidily into the four white honour rolls either side of the black banner. The captain looked up at him and nodded.

"A good day's work general," he said.

"Agreed, captain," responded Tanin. "Though with only five hundred having soldiering experience, we are going to have to hope that what we can teach them in the next four or five days will be enough. Can we have them armed and picketed by tomorrow?"

The captain licked his lips nervously. "As to arms and armament I am unsure. I was given the specific duty to recruit only, not to manage their deployment."

Tanin frowned. "Then who do I speak to in order to get these men ready for the greatest battle of the age?"

The captain looked through some notes at the top of one of the recruitment sheets.

"The Lord Pomen of the Order of the Grey Wolves will take command of the reformed Fifth. He'll not be here for at least four days, however."

Tanin began to get frustrated. "Four days! Captain, I need you to get me immediately reinstated to my rank, or even with a captain's rank so I can get these men picketed and training! I have five days at the very most in which to turn sturdy hearts and raw courage into a useful tool of war!"

The captain paused and then nodded. "I agree. Take control, have the men down at the gate to be armed and armoured at sunrise tomorrow morning. I will handle your rank."

The captain stood and offered his hand and forearm in a warrior's hand shake. Tanin took it.

"Tell the men to enjoy their last night with their wives and families," the captain said gravely. "For most of us, I would expect it to be our last."

The captain was true to his word and by the late afternoon of the next day, Tanin and his men were picketed with tents and a training field at a local farm. Each man had been given a knee-length shirt of mail armour, helm, wooden shield and a spear. Only one in every three men had also been given a sword due to a shortage of blades.

The ragged old farmer had looked on exasperated as thirty of his cows were slaughtered to feed the men of the Fifth. While a small group of men saw to the butchering and cooking, Tanin picked out the two hundred veterans known to him and had them help him begin to drill the men of the Fifth, whose number had been bolstered to almost three thousand. Tanin ordered them into companies of one hundred men apiece and began with marching drills, learning the direction calls. *Forward, left, right, halt, stand firm, charge, withdraw. Words more natural to me than the "I love you" I say to my wife.*

As the night time brought the smell of meat wafting over the men, some tried to peel off towards the cook fires before the final drill had been finished. Tanin punished them harshly, enforcing full military discipline upon them without remorse. *For the barbarian shall show no remorse. He'll allow no time for cook fires and meat. I'll beat the softness from these men, or I'll hang it out of them.*

The next day and the day after brought more of the same as the men continued to be hastily turned into working units. Phalanx drills were introduced, shields locked and spears stabbing over them as they half-step marched steadily forward or backwards. They were awkward and unruly at first but by the time the Lord Pomen arrived with four knight bodyguards on the eve of the fourth day after the Fifth was raised, Tanin and his men were starting to find some cohesion.

As the Lord Pomen approached, Tanin bowed to the noble. Behind him, almost three thousand men drilled in their hundred-strong units. Pomen nodded for him to rise and Tanin immediately drank in the man's sheer presence.

Well into his fifties or sixties, perhaps seventies, the lord knight stood tall and straight as he observed the soldiers going through their drills, his brilliant blue eyes housing a fierce intelligence. His wiry frame sat comfortably in his plate armour, the tall inner collars of his pauldrons, polished to a sheen, reflected his wrinkled leathery skin and white hair. Seven names had been etched into his cuirass, of which his was the latest. His thick black cloak was clasped beneath his chin and hung to the ground from behind his pauldrons. A helm was clutched under his right arm. The right side of the face had a short verse inscribed into it. Pomen caught him looking at it.

"As long as I fight in his name,

And draw the blood of those that would sully Mother
 Secunda, for Him,
The Eternal Lord shall be my blade.

As long as I fight in His name,
And protect those that cannot protect themselves,
The Eternal Lord shall be my shield.

As long as I fight in His name,
I shall fear not the blade's kiss,
For the Eternal Lord watches over my body.

As long as I fight in His name,
I fear not the pain of glorious death,
For to die in His name,
Is to be welcomed into His arms.

First Captain Uthiel Pomen,
Order of the Grey Wolf."

The knight lord's recitation was delivered in a deep, baritone voice. Tanin did not know how to respond.

Lord Pomen allowed the discomfort to continue a moment before speaking. "A family prayer penned by one of my ancestors some two hundred and fifty years ago, general."

Tanin was a little taken aback by the lord's use of his old rank.

"My lord?"

"I have fought beside you once before, General Caellar," responded Pomen. "A pitched battle at the frontier town of Delit. I was quite impressed with you and your men."

"Thank you, lord," said Tanin.

"Please advise me on our current strength and readiness," continued Pomen.

Tanin cleared his throat.

"My lord, you have two thousand, nine hundred and fifty-five fighting men at your command. Approximately eight hundred of these men have military experience. Around five hundred have fought under my banner, the remainder under various other Secundan generals.

"I have taken the liberty of organising them into three regiments. The first two regiments have ten companies of one hundred men apiece. The third has nine companies of one hundred men. The remaining fifty-five men have been made auxiliaries who will provide drivers for the supply carriages, cooks, and so forth with the civilians and servants. The least able of the men were, of course, selected for these roles.

"The veterans have been spread amongst all of the regiments to help with the speed of the training. Out of the twenty-nine captains required, I could only find three previous captains and twelve lieutenants. The other fourteen captains and the full twenty nine lieutenants had to be promoted from those myself or the other captains could vouch for but are as yet untried as battlefield commanders."

Lord Pomen nodded, scratching his chin. "Continue."

"Yes, my lord. Each man has been appropriately armoured and given a spear and shield. Only one in three men could be afforded a sword however, due to a blade shortage. The men are well fed from the farm's livestock and local granaries but we are yet to be designated supply wagons.

"This is the fourth day we have been able to train and drill the men since their arming. Their training is coming along well. With the use of the veterans, I have managed to squeeze weeks worth of training into days. However, we could of course use more time. Four days of marching and phalanx training is not going to equate to a unit completely capable of a cohesive battle."

"Deserters, disobedience or dissenters?"

"No deserters, nor dissenters. The first day did bring forth some disobedience but since they have discovered military punishment there has been no further. Many of these men have lost their sons on the White Frontier. I'm hoping the constant drilling will help focus their grief."

"I would expect no less," said Pomen. "What of our supplies and support?"

Tanin waved towards the cook fires and private wagons. "There are around three hundred folk who've joined us. Three surgeons have been assigned to us. We've a blacksmith and his four apprentices, many elderly men, women, and boys for use as stretcher-bearers or nurses, water runners, and cooks. A couple of whores have latched on to the army but I suspect their skills with their hands will make them good with needle and thread.

"We've enough food to last us until a few days after we march: bread, honey, grain that we can roll into oats for watered porridge and a small amount of dried meats. I've already got the men on rations to make sure it lasts. We'll need to send out foragers each day to try and keep up a supply of meat. The farmers may not like it but we need to keep the boys' bellies full if we want to get the best out of them come a pitched battle."

Pomen nodded again. "Therefore, our three main problems at the moment are a shortage of swords, a lack of designated supply wagons, and a lack of training... commendable though your efforts thus far may be.

"We can increase the number of swords when we pass my Order's fortress on the way to Gall, but I doubt we can put a sword on every belt. There is a war council with the king, the other generals, and the lords tonight. I'll find out about the carriages then. Training however is a concern. I expect them trained in individual combat by torch and firelight tonight and up with the sun for more drills in the morning. Five hours sleep should be enough. Should we not depart tomorrow, I expect much the same."

Both men stood silent for a time, watching the Fifth move through a full spread phalanx advance with the third regiment in reserve. The Fifth's new black banner was held aloft at the centre of the line, five rows back from the front. Companies were then designated "Dead" and lay down on the ground as the advance continued, half step by half step. Portions of the third regiment, at the call of a trumpet jogged forward, and moved into place.

"All so easy on the practice field," said Pomen to nobody in particular.

Tanin waited before bothering the lord. "Lord Pomen?"

Pomen turned and motioned for him to continue. "Where would you have me?" asked Tanin.

Without hesitation Pomen stopped him from going further. "General, once we march for Gall, as my chief advisor you will be no more than six feet away from me, thank you."

Tanin nodded as Lord Pomen walked away towards where the king had set up camp. Inwardly he smiled. *Feels good to be in charge of my brother Secundans once more.* Though he hated to admit it, he knew this was where he belonged, standing beside a lord of one of the knightly orders. There was nothing in this world he was better at than training his men so they could be an efficient tool in a pitched battle in defence of Secunda, fighting for his god, his king, his people, and his son. Tanin breathed in the fresh air of Mother Secunda. It was like Armenius himself had blown new life into him.

He looked to the darkening sky.

Uthiel, my boy. Hold strong. I'm coming. And I'm bringing Secunda's purest fury with me.

Loghan Faramon sat within the keep of the fortress at Archenon Creek, sipping a goblet of wine. The feel of the cool silver against his lips was a pleasant replacement for the sweaty sword grip he had been hefting for the last few days. The goblet was a simple thing with no majestic adornment or design. There were no pieces of inscribed holy scripture, nor inlaid gems, just a simple silver goblet filled with a smooth, deep red wine. *I wish life could imitate this simplicity at times like this.*

He rolled the drink around within the goblet and watched as some of it stuck to the sides and slowly slid back down to the vermillion surface. *Such a simple thing,* he thought. Then he laughed to himself. What he would have given for the ten thousand simple soldiers he had been promised from Gall. His battle plan had been perfect. *It was simple and it should have worked. Funny how the simple things can often be the most treacherous.*

He raised the goblet to his lips and sipped. The wine was a little grainy but tasted rich and bold. It smelled of the deep red grapes it was made from and also slightly woody. Swishing the room-temperature liquid around in his mouth he decided it was as fine a drop as he could expect in these circumstances and swallowed, relishing the feeling of his sliding down his throat.

Taking a deep, almost resigned breath he looked around at the lords gathered to him in his keep. The lords Ambar, Irill, and Rolm stood out the most. They were speaking. Rolm was urging him to approve night time sorties into the siege works to get food and supplies. Irill was arguing against it and Ambar... *That look in his eyes again...* was keeping silent. They were all looking to him for something. To get them out of this with glory and honour intact. *Or just their lives.*

He looked past them and saw his armour on its rack, having been polished just that afternoon by one of the keep servants. Eight-foot tall tapestries hung from the solid stone walls behind it. They depicted scenes of glorious battle from centuries past. Some of them were over two hundred years old. His eyes flittered back to the gaggle of lords around him.

All of a sudden, Loghan felt the weight of command upon his shoulders like never before. It was as if it was almost physically restricting his breathing, the pressure was so strong. He licked his lips and wiped a hand across his forehead. His lips were damp but cracked and his forehead was coated in a cold, feverish sweat. He tried to speak but his head was pounding and his lips refused to obey him.

Am I ill?

Again he raised a hand to wipe his forehead. His hand almost made it up and then lost its strength and flopped back to the arm of the chair. Something warm began to dribble from his nose as he felt his headache deepen and his throat constrict. All conversation stopped around him. The lords Irill and Rolm leapt towards him, Rolm dabbing at his face with a white piece of material which came away red with royal blood.

Loghan frowned. *Just what is going on?*

Without warning his airway closed and he found himself on the ground choking for breath. Ambar was pointing and yelling urgently, though it did seem strange to Loghan that the urgency in the lord's voice did not match those eyes, which burned brighter than ever as they stared down and locked with his own.

Loghan's vision blacked out as his pain became too much to bear. He heard the voice of a surgeon he knew, though he could not recall his name. There were other voices too, some he recognised and some he didn't.

"What happened, my lords?" said one voice urgently.

"The king's brother has fallen ill!"

"Shut up Ambar, you know as well as I he has been poisoned!"

"How is that possible? The foe cannot get into our keep, it must be a plague sent by the enemy to befall us!"

"Ambar! Stop it! If it were a plague then there would be more of us showing symptoms. There must be a traitor!"

"We must toss his body from the wall."

There was a scuffle and Loghan felt hands grab at his body. Some pulled him up while others pushed him down.

"This is the king's brother! Direct descendant of the Eternal Lord and you would toss his body to the carrion birds!?"

"It is either that or we all die!"

"My lords!" said the first voice. "You must leave me with him. Get me a mattress, quilt, pillows, water and my medical bag. Now, lords! He may not have much more time!"

Then Loghan Faramon slept. Painful dreams filled with hallucinations of the most horrible kind filled his pounding head. A city with a pillar of fire. Skinny, pale, tattooed limbs moving like flesh puppets around hollowed-out bodies. Forests of blood fed to a god. Brothers rising to slay their sword-kin. Treachery most foul and a pair of eyes, one almost translucent blue and clear with a pupil shaped like a wolf's head, the other a darker blue and burning with terrible ambition and hate.

Something washed the pain away from his mind and his soul. A bright light cascaded over his fever-wracked body like a cool bucket of water after a hot day's work. Refreshing and relaxing. Loghan Faramon opened his eyes and there stood a peerless warrior in unmarked armour. He wore no tabard and his face looked just like Loghan's brother. He smiled and called out, but his voice was silent. The golden figure smiled back and reached out a hand, which Loghan took and allowed himself to be lightly pulled to his feet.

Cool grass met his toes as he stood, and he wiggled them gleefully. He looked down and to his surprise saw shiny new leather boots sitting under a pair of polished greaves where bare feet should have been. Looking up his body he saw armour polished so bright that the field around him was reflected in its mirror sheen. By his side hung a sword with a thick cross-piece inscribed with the words of Armenius. In his gloved hand was a helm.

He felt hands grabbing his own in welcome and looked up. He was surrounded by knights. Some he noticed wore the white tabards of his Order. Some wore tabards from the other Orders. Many wore no tabards at all and he squinted to see their names. He looked back to the golden figure and saw a knight holding a tall standard pole with a lightly flapping banner hanging from it standing next to him.

Without speaking to him, he knew the banner bearer's name was Archenon.

Very quickly he realised he knew all of their names; Polan Toren, Nestor Pomen, Uthiel Pomen, Elym Omas, so many men he didn't know by face or reputation. And then he saw two faces he did know: Second Captain Dorn and his lieutenant, Kambok. Loghan's heart fell.

The golden figure held out something to him as a loud horn blast silenced everything. He felt his left arm and vambrance slip through a leather loop. His gloved hand gripped a wooden handle. The familiar weight of a shield nestled to him like an old friend.

"Come, my descendant," said the golden figure. "I need you by my side in the battle to come. Will you lock shields with me?"

Loghan took a deep, unrestricted, breath and in a moment he felt his spirit soar.

"Yes, my lord, I think I shall."

CHAPTER ELEVEN

Ice cold water burnt Uthiel's skin red. His hands wetly ground and scraped down his face and rubbed into his short and scruffy beard. Pinching the lightly throbbing crease in his nose, he took a deep breath in and opened his eyes.

In the calming water below him, he could see red rimmed eyes. Fair, yet raw skin with deep scars coated his brow and cheeks. His cheeks were sunken and the bone of his jaw more prominent than he'd expected. His eyes closed once more as he scooped handfuls of water over his lank hair, doing his best to wash out some of the sweat, soot and dust. The last three months had been extremely hard on Uthiel Caellar and his young band of Grey Wolves.

Uthiel stood, looking to the sky as a light sleet began to fall. With a slight shiver he brought his thick, bloodstained and torn cloak closer around him and turned away from the river and back to the brothers watching the tree line to his rear and the opposite shore. A sword cross-piece and handle jutted out over his right shoulder from the deep folds of the dark grey cloak. A small buckler, hung from a brown leather strap that looped over Uthiel's shoulder, bounced off the dark sheath of a second sword hanging from his left hip. A light gust of wind revealed darkened, unpolished armour beneath his thick garment.

Six young Secundans stood loosely around Uthiel with their eyes outward, looking relaxed, but on guard. Each bore a thick cloak of one colour or another that had been scavenged from the enemy or the slaughtered people they came across. Uthiel laid eyes on each one, almost as a way of reassuring himself. Branor and Keldon still shouldered crossbows, though their few remaining bolts were now almost as precious as gold. The rent in Branor's pauldron could still be seen under the cloak he wore, the jagged metal revealing a thick cloth he had stuffed inside.

At the tree line, Linton and Lokhi knelt hunched down, clouds of steam visible over their shoulders as the cold tried to steal the heat from their young bodies. Both had looted bucklers looped over their shoulders. Tarren stood not far from Lokhi, his bare bicep showing an angry purple scar where an axe had split his armour three months prior. Sitting on a stump, further away from Uthiel than any of his other brothers, was Eliem. With extended hard living, he looked even slighter and his filthy armour even more ill fitting.

Uthiel's gaze shifted to the empty space next to Eliem, where Umbar would normally have been. He almost laughed in anticipation at the thought of the portly Umbar sitting in his usual place next to his skinny friend. *Almost.*

Umbar had been lost to them for near on two weeks. A wicked half moon axe had hacked a ragged gash in Uthiel's brother's neck. Horrid memories of pumping bright vermillion splashing onto pale skin and filthy armour coupled with the sounds of their large friend very quickly choking and bleeding to death were a constant in Uthiel's mind. Though his fingers and palms were now white with cold, he could vividly see them slippery with crimson as he desperately tried to stem the flow. The others oft tried levity to remember his more cheerful side, but to Uthiel it was always blood and choking, a good young knight under his command slain. *A brother dead under my orders.*

For three, long, brutal, exhausting months Uthiel had tried to get he and his brothers back to the lands of their home. Four times they had tried to sneak through the mass of barbarians that had advanced through Gall and into the lands of Secunda. Four times they had failed. *Wounds a plenty on all four attacks. I must have thought we were invincible, to try time and time again. And now, a brother dead. Umbar. Fat Umbar. Brother Umbar. I cried with our brothers at your loss. But none of us could cry enough tears for the life you've lost.*

Uthiel licked his teeth and pinched the bridge of his nose to hide his moistening eyes. Three months of skirmishes and scavenging from the raped countryside had seen the eight brothers forge a friendship in the fires of hardship. Umbar's loss had been sorely felt by the seven he left behind in the cruel lands of Gall. Uthiel took a deep breath, calming the anguish battling to breach his new inner defences.

They will never see this of me again. I will show no softness of character. Their lives are in my hands and they need a leader, not a friend to mourn loss with. Uthiel's eyes narrowed at Eliem's back. Already, in a fit of bereaved rage, his brother knight had all but accused his leadership to be the cause of Umbar's death. *It pains me that you would think it so. Though I know it to be true, it still pains me.*

Taking a deep breath, Uthiel, the last to have refreshed himself from the river, called softly to his men and they moved to the cover of the tree line and crouched down. Eliem took watch without a word, his turned back a statement Uthiel was sure was not lost on his brothers.

Branor broke the silence. "We're trapped between the rear of the horde and the Black lands, brothers."

The knights nodded their agreement.

"Glorious death or drawn-out starvation through the winter?" questioned Keldon, his preferred option clear.

"I agree, brother," added Tarren. "Best we die in a glorious charge than waste away through winter and be slain by the first band of children with axes that find us."

Lokhi held his tongue.

Linton looked to Uthiel. "Lokhi and I will follow your decision, brother."

Lokhi flashed Linton a look but did not speak.

"As will I," said Branor. "Uthiel?"

Uthiel took a moment to think before speaking.

"Brothers, we have fought to get home and get Ghurkar Storm's message to the lord or our order for three months," he started. "We've bled. We've slain. We've lost and we've seen things no man should see."

Uthiel let the last part sink in. They'd seen thousands upon thousands of slain and mutilated corpses through many townships and small battlefields. The decapitated heads of Gall women hung from tree limbs by their hair above piles of their desecrated naked bodies stuck with him like a knife in the gut. *Babes and young children...* Uthiel saw his brothers frown and clench their jaws as each young man went through his own horrors in his mind's eye.

"After all this, would you allow them so light and selfish a victory as one last glorious charge?" asked Uthiel, his voice hard and resolute as his scarred features. His brothers did not respond.

"Would you allow them to continue to slay our kinsmen and butcher our lands while we rot on the ground, the armour of our Order's forefathers grafted onto some filthy barbarian?" he continued, his voice raising and his hope of action resting on his brothers increasing choler.

"No, my brothers," said Uthiel, raising his voice. "By Armenius, no."

His brothers mirrored his conviction. Looking up he could see the back of Eliem's head moving from side to side in silent disagreement. Uthiel continued, noting Eliem but not allowing one to slow down his plan. They'd been moving about with only the thought of survival keeping them alive but as the plan started to form more clearly in his mind, Uthiel felt his confidence rise as he pictured in his head what they would do. Getting through the enemy and back home was very unlikely to happen, but there was another way.

"I say we live and I say we fight."

His brothers nodded their agreement. Eliem could take no more and turned, his face screwed up with anger.

"And do what? Should we slowly allow ourselves to fall one by one in failed attempt after failed attempt to get home to deliver some mysterious message you will not tell us the content of?" he snarled.

Uthiel locked eyes with Eliem and stood to his full height.

Not breaking eye contact, Uthiel continued solemnly. "My brothers, we're not going home."

There were frowns of confusion. Uthiel had everyone's full attention now, including Eliem's.

Tarren was the first to speak. "So, you would keep us from pitched battle and glorious death and keep us from home. Are we to stay in the wild and knit woollen blankets to survive?"

There were a few nerve-wracked sniggers and stifled laughs at the half joking comment. Uthiel smiled a devious, cracked lipped smile.

"In all these months of moving among and fighting the bands of foul barbarians, have you not noticed anything?" asked Uthiel.

Blank looks met his gaze.

"Tribes. Warbands. Many of them in this one region. All with a leader," said Uthiel.

Branor caught on quickly. "Like our captains."

Uthiel nodded, blowing warm breath into his cupped hands. "Should we remove enough captains by bolt and blade, I'll wager someone higher up will come out this way when they start to lose control of the region's warriors. There, my brothers, is our first real target."

Keldon chimed in. "Take the head of the beast and the body will fall."

Uthiel reached over and patted Keldon on the shoulder. "Then we will avenge our fallen brothers."

The young Gallite girl was running hard. Her legs and her lungs were burning as they powered her away through the forest. Her long brunette hair flowed wildly behind her as she hitched up her heavy blue working dress and pushed herself even harder.

She dared not look back. One lapse in concentration and she would trip or run into something and then they would have her. Those filthy beasts would have her. She tried to push such thoughts out from her mind.

In her peripheral vision she saw another young woman, Palia, perhaps a few years older than her, running in the same direction. Palia spotted her and in that moment, as the older girl took her eyes from her path, tripped over a rock with a scream of pain and fear. The young Palia reached out from the ground and called to her as the fur clad barbarians reached her, one already undoing the leather drawstring on its dirty britches.

No. Be quiet. Don't let them know where I am.

"Emilia!" cried Palia, and was quickly silenced by a fist crunching into her face.

Emilia stifled a sob and coughed as her lungs screamed for air and rest. Her body begged her to surrender. She had seen her family and friends slaughtered and raped. Choking smoke had burned her eyes as she watched men burn and screams had torn at her ears as the women were stripped of their clothes. *I didn't want to leave them. I had to. Someone has to get out. Someone has to get help.*

The memory of her father trying to defend her with his broom, only to have a massive man in plate armour ram two short swords through his chest simultaneously, would haunt her to her dying day. *That might not be too far away for me.*

Quickly she culled that side of her thinking as she rounded a tree and sprinted for a thicket of bushes. Behind her she could still hear them chasing and it spurred her pounding heart to further fuel her limbs with abject terror. She could still hear Palia's defeated screams and pleas as her bare feet carried her further and further away from the horror of the day.

The roars and whoops of the barbarians also followed her. Foul men hardened by war, they were bigger and far stronger and every moment brought their heavy pounding footsteps ever closer. One was so close she could even hear his labouring breaths. *No no no no no no no! Please, no -*

She risked a look back. He was right there, not ten paces behind her. He and five or six of his heathen countrymen. *Shitshitshitshit – Gods, let me live! I want to live!*

Her limbs burned like never before but the knowledge of what would happen to her should she stop or stumble kept her going. Palia's screams still echoed in the bushes around her. She spotted a trail leading into thicker underbrush. Somewhere she could perhaps hide and lose them, if only to let her catch her breath and think of a way to escape. She risked another look back, and completely missed seeing the huge clenched fist that snaked out from behind a tree and cannoned into her chest, stopping her dead in her tracks and crunching her to the ground.

Emilia's breath exploded from her as she heard her ribs crack under the power of the strike and then the impact. Scrabbling in the dirt and desperately trying to breathe again she looked around through wide, pain filled eyes. Above her, standing over her like a statue of some horrible god, she saw him.

No no no no no no. Please, no.

The barbarian was easily six foot of pure, lean muscle covered firstly in barbarous tattoos and then in some horrible plagiarism of the Secundan knight's armour. His face was covered by a helm showing a sneering wolf. As a heavy boot slammed into her side and laid her out once more, her mind took her away from her pain as she blacked out. She floated within herself, wistfully moving from memory to memory, trying to find one that had not been destroyed by the ruination of her home, until her mind's eye rested on Uthiel.

The young knight she had fallen for the moment she saw the man behind the knightly mask. The moment she had delved into those almost translucent blue eyes and lost herself, she had known that he would be hers. The moment she had seen him and that oaf of a friend walking back to the town, having snuck away from their camp. The retrospectively funny moment of her father chasing him away with his broom. She groaned. *My father.*

The beast who reached down and grabbed a fistful of her hair and dragged her back to reality was the polar opposite of the young man she had firstly teased and then, later that night, lay with. Where Uthiel was a kind and brave young man, with deep seeded religious and social mores and a boyishly handsome face to go with it, the man who began dragging her back towards her town by her dark brown locks was the leader of a raving pack of brutal murdering rapists. Everything about him radiated evil and raw physical power. There was nothing she could do to defend herself as he dragged her further and further towards her doom. *Nothing but try not to die of terror, before they rape and murder me like Palia.*

Then she saw what had become of the men and children of her town.

Emilia screamed. She screamed and struggled hysterically, losing herself in a fit of blind fear as the horror of the barbarian's method of war assaulted her from all angles. Her eyes felt almost detached from her mind as they reeled to take in what she saw. Her hands and legs ground themselves against the gravel until they were bloody and raw. Nothing she did slowed her plight as the huge barbarian kept on pulling her towards the centre of her beloved town.

Eventually, her energy spent, she allowed herself to be dragged without struggling. She was dragged through the pools of blood of her family and those she had known and loved for her short life. Spittle rolled down her chin as she sobbed at the pain in her scalp and body and mind. She cried out as some of her hair was wrenched from her head but could not will her body to do anything further.

Finally, they stopped. Massive, unbelievably strong hands gripped her arms and pulled her to her feet. A blade rasped from its sheath and Emilia closed her eyes, imagining the razor edge cutting across her throat and her lifeblood bubbling down her chest and staining the cloth of her dress dark. She would welcome it, fearful of death as she might be. She felt the cold steel touch the skin at the back of her neck, just above where the thick cloth covered her back. It slid down until the tip rested under the material and then pulled tight against her dress and swiftly cut down until it passed her bottom.

She felt the cold air kiss the bruised skin of her back for a moment before a hand roughly grabbed the garment at the neckline above her breasts and tore it down. She staggered forward in shock, her arms quickly whipping up in a vain attempt to cover herself and therefore not arresting her fall. Another set of hands roughly grabbed her under leggings as she lay on the ground and in a heartbeat they were also cut away, leaving her scratched and bruised body bare to the elements and the jeers of the men around her.

She heard screaming, women calling her name. She recognised their voices as she was once again hauled to her feet. She looked up and saw faces she knew looking out of one of the tavern windows. She saw her mother in there, and two of her cousins. She could see they were in a state much the same as her own, crammed in like cattle at a slaughterhouse muster.

Before her a guard opened the door, and she was roughly tossed into the darkness of the room inside, crashing into white skinned legs and sliding on the sawdust layering the floor. For a moment light streamed over the bruised and beaten bodies of the women around her, glinted from the tears flowing from fearful and mourning eyes, and then there was darkness as the door slammed shut and the press of bodies by the window cut out the cold afternoon sun.

Emilia could hear the fearful rasping breaths of the women around her. She could smell their dank sweat and the excrement of those who had soiled themselves in fear. She could taste their terror and feel their hopelessness in the shaking hands of her mother and cousins as they reached for her to pull her into their embrace. In that moment she knew, with absolute certainty, she had only seen the beginning of the horror. Once more she thought of Uthiel. Her heart fluttered in hope and then fell into sadness. *He won't come for me. Nobody can.* Tears of hopelessness began to well in the corners of her eyes.

Emilia sobbed; there was no waking from this nightmare.

**

By dusk of the next day Uthiel and his brothers had searched almost ten square miles of what they assumed were still the lands of Gall. They'd passed three townships. Two had been abandoned in time and only the buildings had suffered the wrath of the advancing horde. The third had not been so lucky. That was an hour ago and only now did the young Grey Wolf pull out the two small pieces of cloth he had stuffed up his nose out and bury them in the dirt. His face hardened as his eyes locked on their target.

With a quick look to his brothers he waved Keldon and Tarren to move through the bush. They moved quietly, faces darkened with charcoal from the last village, until they were barely visible almost forty feet away. Lokhi, Linton and Eliem took their cue and moved backwards to ensure their escape route remained clear. Uthiel placed a hand on Branor's pauldron. Branor had the stock of his crossbow level with his eye, looking down the dark timber bolt and past its iron tip at the six foot tall, fur and leather clad beast who had just finished caving in a shorter barbarian's head with a wicked looking spiked mace.

With pieces of skull and mushy brain matter hanging from the mace, the heavily tattooed barbarian held his weapon pointed at the remaining thirty of forty warriors who surrounded him. He bellowed his challenge at them in their guttural language. Some looked like they were ready to attack him, barely held in check by their fear of the gore-spattered mace levelled at them. Their eyes flicked to the warriors around them for support that didn't, to Uthiel, seem to be there. Those men obviously more loyal to the leader began to move over to him, weapons low in a clear sign of supplication. Finally only three or four were left opposing them. Eventually, they began to move over.

Their shoulders were slumped with defeat and they were jeered by those opposite them. One was struck and reeled backwards until he stumbled and fell. The warriors rushed forward in a yelling tide of fists and leather boots, leaving their leader standing back watching the mob beat the screaming man to death.

Uthiel, his voice barely a whisper and his eyes never leaving the target, dropped his arm to signal Tarren and spoke the leader's death sentence. "Now."

Branor's crossbow unleashed the bolt. Less than a heartbeat later it punched clean through the leader's leather armour and chest, exploding in a fine mist of blood out of his back. Before the leader could even register what had happened a second bolt slid cleanly between his ribs and skewered his heart. The leader dropped without more than the wheeze of his last breath, long dead before his body finally came to rest upon the ground. The four Grey Wolves made it almost ten feet before a cry went up from the tribe. By the time the tribe had found where the bolts had come from it was too late, all seven knights were gone.

Three flawless assassinations, and a week later Uthiel and his brothers finally got their chance. Kneeling amongst the thinning bush upon the top of a twenty-foot cliff, the seven brothers looked down at hundreds, if not thousands, of fur and leather clad barbarians. For the last few days, the invaders numbers had been growing and growing, the sounds of far off battle getting ever closer with smoke consistently on the horizon. Above them, angry storm clouds hung low, as if the Lands of Light were themselves finally rejecting the sickness engulfing their body, began to spew forth sleet and snow.

On the white plain before them a colossal muster had continued through the night with great fires being lit to keep the warriors warm as winter began to fully assert itself on the land. With the lands having been so sorely raped and pillaged of all stock and food as the flood of barbarians surged through the lands on their way to Secunda, starving barbarians had resorted to eating grass and bark and in some horrific cases, each other.

Chewing on a raw piece of rat, Uthiel remained almost motionless, and as the sun dipped down behind them, his eyes had begun to droop through lack of movement. All of a sudden his eyes snapped open and focussed. Turning to his left he saw Branor's intense stare, fingers sliding to his hip to reach for crossbow bolts that no longer existed. Uthiel silently moved his hand to rest on his friend's vambrance.

The huge barbarian was seven foot tall if not more, and easily one of the largest, fiercest looking men Uthiel had ever laid eyes upon. A long shaggy mane and beard hung lank down onto the dark furs of a wolf clasped onto massive brass strap pauldrons. Hanging down over his chest, the shaggy heads of the wolves clamped down on an adjoining chain to give the impression the two wolf pelts made a cloak. Arms and thighs like tree trunks, covered in half healed battle wounds, were bare to the cold and fat animal skin boots left huge foot prints in the snow as he moved through his forces. The sheer barbaric majesty of the man left no doubt in Uthiel's mind who had led this massive incursion into the Lands of the Light.

That wasn't all that grabbed Uthiel's attention. He felt his gorge rise as he spotted no less than thirty barbarians fully clad in one variant of Secundan knight plate or another. Uthiel almost had to physically stop himself from rising to bellow out a challenge. Rooted to the spot, Uthiel realised what a high value target he and his brothers had been presented. Now it was just a question of how to get to him from behind the thousands of barbarians and the personal bodyguard of plate armour clad men. *I need a diversion, or one massive stroke of luck sent to the by the Eternal Lord himself.*

Uthiel used hand signals to get Keldon to keep his eyes on the massive warrior and his bodyguards and then turned to convene with the other six brothers that remained of his group.

"My brothers," whispered Uthiel. "Armenius himself stands with us today. Almost four months of bloody sacrifice finally rewarded with one golden opportunity."

The men around him smiled gaunt, white-lipped smiles.

"All we need," continued Uthiel, "is one moment. We stick to and track this beast like a wolfhound, and when the opportunity presents itself, we strike."

"We avenge Umbar," said Eliem, vicious relish coating every word. "I'll cut his name into that bastard's heart."

"I'll hold his arms for you, brother," said Branor.

Tarren reached out and placed a hand on Eliem's pauldron, sharing his brother's loss with a heartfelt glance. His gaze turned to Uthiel, and an almost imperceptible nod showed his begrudging approval.

Uthiel licked his dry lips excitedly. "By Armenius this is our chance, my brothers. We strike at the heart. Two brothers will keep watch at all times while we rest. We shall need our strength for when our opportunity arises."

It took almost three days for that opportunity to arise. In that time they had almost been undone five times, the dirt they had smudged all over their cloaks and armour saving them from being spotted against the sparse foliage of the winter. On the morning of the third day, there came a long horn call, not a mile distant. It was a Secundan war horn. Uthiel almost could not believe his ears as he hurried to Branor's side on the cliff. A smile almost split his face in half and a tear worked its way down his cheek as he saw a line of men in glinting armour emerge from the trees. A tall grey banner with the sigil of the Order of the Grey Wolf fluttered in the wind.

There were hundreds of knights in glittering plate. Uthiel heard Branor stifle a sob as banners of the Secundan Fifth and Secundan Seventh armies appeared, to the knights' right and left, followed by thousands of soldiers. Never had a sight been so glorious to Uthiel's eyes as they watched the orderly assembling of the Secundan line. Below them, the tribes rushed around in chaos, the seven-foot tall war leader waving twin axes in the air and bellowing as he attempted to stall the barbarians already storming towards the Secundan lines and call, or threaten, back those trying to flee.

As the Secundan line slowly advanced, easily ten thousand barbarians milled about the war leader until finally the seven-foot monster roared his assent at the charge and sent the horde forward across the snow. The leader did not move, and in a momentary lapse of judgement his bodyguard began to disperse, some staying by the leaders side, some wandering to higher vantage points to watch the battle, and some already storming off away from the battle. All of a sudden, as if the

Eternal Lord himself had taken personal interest in his sons' plight, the mighty warlord stood unprotected but for a spattering of barbarians and his Secundan plate-shod personal guard. *Our chance. Right now. Armenius be with us.*

Uthiel rounded up his brothers and they carefully traversed the cliff paths down to the plain. Uthiel's eyes kept moving over to the battle lines where the barbarians had arrow-headed their attack into the centre of the Secundan line, directly into the massed ranks of Secundan knights. The sound of the impact was immense, even from almost seven hundred feet away.

First, the clash of steel - and then the screaming began. Screams of rage and anger and of bloodlust very quickly changed to screams of fear and pain as the Secundan Fifth and Seventh swung around and closed in the barbarians on three sides.

As Uthiel and his brothers began to move over the plain, seven hunched and dark figures carving though the churned mud ground towards the leader of the barbarian horde, barbarian stragglers began to notice them. Gleaming steel lashed out as they moved, blades always aimed at throats to keep their swift advance secret for as long as possible. Far off in the distance, Uthiel heard the sounds of thundering hooves as a large unit of knights bearing a deep purple banner impacted the rear of the barbarians. He returned his attention to their target. *Forty feet.*

With Ghurkar's blade in his right hand and the Tadel blade in his left Uthiel was like a harsh gusting wind of death sliding through the sparsely forested lands, felling all that came within his reach without breaking stride. *Twenty feet.*

A plate armoured barbarian spotted Uthiel and cried out in alarm. Branor raced forward with Keldon and plunged into combat with the man. Branor's gleaming blade met a dark, serrated sword in a loud clang of metal on metal as the rest of the Grey Wolves streamed past. *Ten feet.*

More and more barbarians came at them now and their advance slowed as Uthiel moved and struck, parried and dodged. Blows began to ring on his armour but their momentum carried them on to within five feet of the leader, who was brandishing his axes with a grin. With a roar Tarren leapt into the barbarians and bodyguards attempting to block Uthiel. A blade pierced deep into his thigh and Tarren fell, dragging two down and knocking three more barbarians off balance, giving Uthiel one chance. A clear line across the last four feet to the leader.

One chance he fully intended to take. Eyes narrowed, Uthiel charged forward.

CHAPTER TWELVE

Tanin Caellar stood tall amongst the men of the Fifth as they emerged from the forests. With Lord Pomen, and under the leadership of the king of Secunda, the last three months had seen them fight three major battles. The first had been a brutal loss on the borders of Gall. They had given the barbarians a real bloodied nose, easily killing three men to every lost Secundan. An orderly retreat had followed as the barbarians had consolidated their close victory and rebuilt their numbers for another surge towards Secunda.

The second battle had been deep within the bosom of Secunda herself. The line had formed up before the walls of the Order of the Grey Wolves' fortress. They had fought for almost a day. The battle had hung on a knife's edge as the discipline of the Secundans waged vicious war with the unbridled berserk fury of the barbarians. Tanin felt a shiver of cold run down his spine as he remembered the slaughter.

Shields had held for an hour, and then been split asunder by a renewed charge, only to have the line straighten again as a fresher company moved forward a half step at a time. Tanin had nearly died three times, once falling to the ground to be overrun, only to see the tabards of his men shove the foe back over him moments later. He wasn't ashamed to say he'd come close to filling his britches more than a couple of times that day.

The battle was almost lost when the barbarians' leader, after months of not revealing himself, had finally brought the true face of savagery to battle. He brought with him men armoured and armed like Secundan knights. These men would have been out of place were it not for their bestial cries and darkened, gore coated plate armour.

Of the first company those thirty odd men of the leader's bodyguard charged into, not a single man survived. The dark figures in plate armour had fought with barely restrained fury, forming a thick wedge behind the berserk warlord, who wielded two massive axes that by the end of the battle were so clogged with blood they were almost blunt. The two adjoining companies suffered losses of almost half their men before the Grey Wolves made their charge and pushed them back. With the king and his bodyguard carving the horde's flanks to pieces, the invaders had finally broken.

Tanin could not remember ever having seen so many slain and wounded men in one place. There was nothing as sobering to a soldier as the aftermath of a battle. Easily a hundred thousand lay upon the field, never to stand again. But they had held. They had pushed the enemy back and not allowed him a foothold in Secunda. The Lord Pomen and the other Grey Wolf lords had hastily ordered the tainted armour of their Order, and the filth that had it worn into battle against the men it had once protected, burned in a massive pit and then covered. The Grey Wolves were almost aggressive in their refusal of help from the other army units, barking at them to look to their own. They'd left the other bodies to rot after that and marched off in pursuit.

And finally, now, he stood with a little over two thousand of the Secundan Fifth and two thousand more of the Secundan Seventh on the left flank of almost a thousand Grey Wolves and four thousand more of the Seventh army on the right flank. To their rear, the king himself and his household guard, almost three hundred cavalry, sat mounted and ready to encircle the enemy. Across the plain, not a mile distant, milled thousands of barbarians in apparent disorder. Amongst them Tanin could see the dark hulking shapes of the leader and what remained of his plate-armoured bodyguard.

To the left, atop a low cliff that rounded the edge of the plain he thought he saw a glimmer of movement, perhaps a shrub swaying in the wind. He paid it no further heed as, at a call from the king, he and seven thousand hardy Secundan souls began to march across their field. Miles to their north and south, tens of thousands of Secundans were split into several armies of between five and ten thousand and moved to regain the ground lost after their first defeat on the border of Gall. Each army moved in pursuit of a large sub-horde of the fleeing enemy. The purge of the disease of barbarism had begun, with the purity of Secunda being regained once more through blood and fire.

Something drew Tanin's eye to the cliff once again, lower down this time, his sight drawn to the fore as the horde was unleashed in their direction with a fell cry. Beside him Lord Pomen looked haggard and tired, his depth of character shining through only in his eyes, which remained alert as ever. Tanin looked to him and as the barbarians reached just over a few hundred feet, Pomen nodded and Tanin turned to his men.

"Halt!" he called. "Archers to the fore!"

A ragged group of archers rushed forward and dug a small bundle of arrows into the dirt before them. Bows already strung, they each drew an arrow and raised their sights to the sky. A captain in dirty leathers and torn chainmail looked to Tanin. Tanin called out his assent to action and with a curt nod the archer captain released a loose storm of death into the sky. Before they had reached the pinnacle of their flight path a second volley was notched and released. Before they reached their targets a third volley was in the air.

Finally, like the scythe of Death herself, the steel tipped rain cut into the mess of warriors. Men toppled, staggered, rolled, and tripped up their followers. A few heartbeats later, the second volley struck, then the third. By the time the arrows had stopped falling, bodies littered the snow like leaves during autumn behind the advancing mass.

Tanin frowned as he saw the massed sides compress towards the middle of the advance. He turned to Lord Pomen.

"My lord, they are going to hit the centre of the line. We should prepare to fold in and hit them from the side."

"I concur, general," he responded. "Prepare the men to move. We await the impact and then crush in. Send a runner to inform the king of the battle plan."

Before Tanin could call over a runner, one of the king's household guards galloped up to them, deep purple cloak billowing out behind him. As he pulled up before them Tanin took in the sight of the man. A sixteen-hand steed beneath him with shining steel war plate set him high above Tanin and Lord Pomen. Glorious plate armour with gold detail, beautiful in comparison to the armour of the Order like a stunning young maiden in comparison to an aged, handsome woman. Crested helm on his thigh he pulled up before them and addressed Lord Pomen, ignoring Tanin completely.

"Lord Pomen," said the man. "The king would have you pivot and encircle the enemy's left flank once they impact the Grey Wolves line. He shall then lead the charge around the flank and into the rear of the enemy. We shall destroy them utterly there."

Pomen nodded his acknowledgement. "For the king."

The rider heeled his steed and galloped back to the king's position as the barbarians began their final sprint to the Grey Wolf's line. Tanin called to his men and their spears thrust forward like a thicket of knifebush. Another guttural yell erupted from the barbarians as they impacted the line in a crash of metal and flesh on metal as barbarian axes and bodies slammed in to the heavy shield wall of the Grey Wolves. The Wolves bowed in as they took the crush and as the bloody first exchanges quickly turned into a quagmire press of stabbing bodies. With the first captain at the centre of the line, the Grey Wolf's line straightened.

The Secundan Fifth, their black banner flowing in the wind five rows back from the front, had begun their move the second the first wicked half moon axe had struck the glorious shield wall of the Grey Wolves. The inner companies pivoted first and held their position until the outer companies had run in to make the new line. Very quickly they began their march forward to enclose the horde. The barbarians turned to face them, too late realising their bloodlust would cost them their lives as the well drilled, and now battle hardened, Secundan Fifth began moving forward a half step at a time.

Tanin watched them from the rear of the line, a fierce mixture of hatred and horror, righteousness and revolt, spiralling in his gut as he called out commands. Tattooed faces screamed in pain, fear, and anger. Spears split and men shattered around their points. More of the filthy, half starved, fur and leather clad men charged at them, while others backed away in fear.

"Third company, hold them! Hold them!" *Sometimes, it is easy to forget that these barbarians are still men.*

"Runner! Move the Seventh in to reinforce the third." *As barbaric as they are, they are still men with dreams and loved ones.*

"Ninth company holding strong!" called out a returning runner.

"First company, someone get me news on first company, damn it! They hold our flank!" *They still feel the gut wrenching fear of charging a wall of steel.*

"You! What? Pulling back? No! Get back there and tell those bastards to hold! Take a reserve company with you. I don't care which one, just take one!" *They still have the moment of horror when a blade rips your guts out and your worst nightmares come true. Despite all that we hate them, it is hard to put aside that they are still men.*

In a moment, the chaos of command became the voyeuristic horror of watching a rout from behind the lines. Some tried to flee as they began to see more and more of their fellows impaled on Secundan spears. They turned and dropped their weapons and ran, only to discover the last blow of the king's plan come to fruition as a wedge headed by the liege of Secunda speared into their fleeing forms and brutally ran down or cleaved their way through the barbarians.

Tanin took in a deep breath and worked his sore jaw wide open in a yawn. *Better to be on the victorious side of a rout, no matter what virtues I believe the foe to posses. Armenius save me, I've been on the other end of them before and I'm too old to survive another.*

A scant few hundred of the enemy managed to flee, many covered in the gore of their brothers as they tried to make good their escape. The Grey Wolves moved forward at a lope, crimson coated steel lashing down at any wounded. The Fifth and the Seventh rolled back their pivot and soon the Secundan line stood renewed, the Grey Wolves and the king at the line's centre watching the remaining enemy flee. It was only at this point that anybody noticed the melee occurring away from the main battlefield.

On a small rise, many hundreds of feet away, a swirling battle could be seen: half moon axes meeting bright steel visible amongst armoured warriors centred around one very large barbarian, easily a foot taller than a cloaked assailant with two swords. The cloaked man ducked and weaved, looking horribly outmatched in every way as the large barbarian struck with blistering speed, sending him tumbling to the ground. That this fight would not last much longer was evident, even from this distance.

The Lord Pomen squinted and stuck his chin out. "They..." he started.

"...they move... like us..." he finished, almost to himself.

And then, over the pounding of the feet of the retreating forces heading directly for the skirmish, over the deathly moans of the mortally wounded, ever so lightly on the wind like it had been whispered to them by the Eternal Lord himself, Tanin heard it.

"... for Armenius!"

Pomen had turned and was running to the king, but it was a wasted effort. The king and his men were already galloping away over the battlefield.

Uthiel's left arm was numb and his fingers barely gripped the Tadel blade. He bled from three ruptures in his cuirass and the bent steel was lightly crushing his side. His left pauldron was a mess as the fierce bite of the war leader's axe had cut through it twice in a flurry of unbelievably powerful half chops. Only a mangled piece of metal hanging limply from its join to the cuirass remained. His foe's speed and power were supernatural. Always in balance, he was a warrior born whom Uthiel knew was well beyond the match of his ability.

His focus had only strayed twice as he had lashed out to protect himself from other assailants. Both times he had been almost killed as the warlord had leapt upon any advantage that Uthiel presented him with brutal efficiency. His own wheezing, panting breaths were all Uthiel could hear as he backed away from the cruelly smiling warlord, trying to catch his breath and desperately trying to think of how he would slay this monster. His strength, speed and reach were inferior. He was wounded and weak, exhausted beyond reckoning.

Uthiel didn't even notice the forearm length knife that seared past his back end embedded itself in the throat of the plate-armoured bodyguard that had been bearing down on him. The thunderous sound of hooves and the screams of the vicious running retreat heading his way mixed with the battle surrounding him were like the sounds of a stricken bird amongst a hurricane of fear and focus. In the eye of the storm were Uthiel and the warlord. Uthiel feigned forward with Ghurkar's sword, trying to buy time and room more than anything. The haft of an axe swiping sideways battered the flat of his sword out of the way and then cut back at him with the speed of a striking snake.

Uthiel's leaden feet couldn't move in time, the tall collar on the inside of his right pauldron caught the brunt of the blow and sent the young Grey Wolf sprawling. Seeing the other axe flashing down at his head, he raised the Tadel blade in weak defence as his strength finally came to its end. A shard of white pain sliced his left wrist, and he cried in despair as the blade fell to the ground. Ghurkar's blade rested on the ground submissively, the leather bound handle held loosely in his open hand.

In a last move of defiance Uthiel raised it to swing at his foe. The beast barked out a laugh and struck out with his foot. Uthiel's fingers cracked loudly, the blade spinning from his grip. Uthiel was defenceless and on his knees. A wicked, brown-toothed grin leered down at him from seven thickly muscled feet up. Uthiel's chest burned with exertion. The poison of weakness pumped through his leaden body. Crisp, cold air stung his sweat-coated face. Above him a massive axe rose into the air in a wicked arc.

His numb left fingers sat by his side, the tips brushing against leather. Uthiel's vision sharpened as pale fingers wrapped around the handle of his dagger. The very last of his will poured through his legs and forced them to move, propelling himself forward. With a snarl of defiance, Uthiel lanced the dull steel upwards, burying it up to the hilt in the warlord's groin. With a second cry of rage Uthiel twisted his blade and hoarsely shouted out in victory as he felt hot, thick wetness stream down his arm. The warlord crumpled, both axes falling to the ground as he squealed in pain and fell on to his back.

Uthiel fell with the warlord, his face plunging into the mud. Rolling on to his back he reached over and picked up Ghurkar's sword before pushing himself first to his knees, and eventually managed to get a foot back flat onto the soft ground beneath him. Every inch of his battered body ached and hurt. He was cut, gouged and bruised in more places than he could have counted. Forcing his other foot beneath him he slowly, painfully pushed himself up. By Armenius, he'd never felt so alive! *And never so bloody sore.*

He staggered one step, and then two, until he finally planted his boot on the barbarian's shuddering chest. Around him, he could begin to hear blades clash and men cry out as his brothers continued their own duels. With all the effort remaining in him he raised the four feet of shining Secundan steel in his right hand and struck down. His first cut made it three quarters of the way through the warlord's neck, and almost sent him tumbling to the ground as he overbalanced when the blade finally cut clean through. Rich crimson pumped into the snow and on to Uthiel in a quickly weakening staccato rhythm as the warlord's tongue lolled from his gaping mouth and his eyes rolled back behind his drooping lids. His second, carefully aimed blow severed the head in a spray of gore.

Wrapping the head's hair around the palm of his free hand, wincing when he bumped his badly bruised wrist, Uthiel stood with Ghurkar's sword raised in salute to the Eternal Lord in one hand and the head raised above the field of battle in the other. Painfully filling his lungs within his beaten cuirass he looked to the storm clouds above and roared.

"Secunda, victor!"

Around him his surviving brothers raised their weapons and echoed his cry as the remaining bodyguard and barbarians fled the field with all haste. He could see Branor, Keldon, and Lokhi; blood covered brothers of battle one and all. His friends from childhood were now men of war with bonds so thick that only death could separate their brotherhood. He smiled for a moment as he locked eyes with their wounded and exhausted forms, until a pang of pain struck him as he realised those who were missing.

With a last and final mournful cry to his god he yelled hard enough to bring spikes of painful pressure from his wounded chest, and send thin streaks of tears down his dirt and soot covered cheeks. His voice one moment cracked with pain and grief and the next struck out the harder with vindication. "For Armenius and our glorious dead! Secunda, victor!"

Cries of, "Victory for Mother Secunda!" echoed his. Hundreds of voices rose above the din of the final rout. *A more beautiful sound I am never like to hear again.* Uthiel turned to see hundreds of plate armoured men with deep purple cloaks billowing out behind them as they galloped towards him on glorious steeds. At the head of them was the king. The man was beautiful in his royal glory, armed in the most resplendent plate; stout, tall, regal, and wielding a blade that shone brilliantly despite the darkness of the cloud cover and its crimson coating.

Sitting tall upon a magnificent white steed the king of Secunda struck out; once, twice, three times and each time the perfectly aimed blade dealt a perfectly vicious blow to a fleeing barbarian that the only hardest training wrought from an unparalleled warrior. Uthiel was dumbstruck by his liege, second only to the Eternal Lord in majesty, and he once more fell to his knees and sunk into the mixture of snow and blood and mud. Uthiel wiped tears and blood from his eyes, with mud-blackened hands, as he watched his king stop his mount not five feet away.

Uthiel struggled to tear his eyes away as a small group of the king's household guard stopped by as the remainder continued to chase the barbarians to the far side of the plain. Finally managing to show his supplication to his king, Uthiel averted his eyes and looked to his painfully throbbing hands lying in his lap. Some of his fingers were swollen and despite the ridiculousness of the thought, considering the situation, Uthiel cursed himself for his dishevelled appearance. *By Armenius I am about to meet the king of Secunda! Tanin would have my hide for this.*

"I would have your name, Secundan," came a voice deep like thunder but smooth like an expensive spirit.

Uthiel was so dumbstruck to be in the presence of the king he forgot to speak in reply.

"I have a war to fight, do not waste my time," continued the king, a hint of anger beginning to stem from his impatience.

Uthiel stammered, "My king, Uthiel Caellar, son of Tanin Caellar, retired general of the Secundan Fifth."

"You wear the armour of our knight Orders. Explain," said the king, his hard stare flicking over Uthiel's form and then out to his men in the field.

Stupid bastard, can't even introduce yourself properly!

"I am with the Order of the Grey Wolf under Captain Phyrus. We are all that remains of his company sent to accompany a supply train to the White Frontier some four months ago," said Uthiel.

The king seemed to think on this for a moment before replying.

"And you are the one we saw slay the warlord in single combat?"

"Yes, my king."

"By honour he should have been mine."

Uthiel's mouth worked soundlessly and his eyes darted around looking for answers amongst the fallen. Nothing came, there was no answer. Then, he heard the chuckling. It started as a deep rumble, and then spread through many deep pitches as the king's household guard took up their lord's laughter. Uthiel looked to his right and saw Branor. Branor's mouth was slack and his form wracked with exhaustion. Uthiel watched, speechless as his friend's mouth began to twist up into his trademark smile.

It took a little while of staring at his friend for Uthiel to register he was being made fun of. With a chuckle that sounded alien to himself he rocked back on his haunches and looked his king in the face.

"I jest, young knight," said the king. "You fought well and slew an impressive foe. Would you do me the honour of gifting me the warlord's axes for my trophy room?"

It was not a question. Despite the dull ache in his limbs, Uthiel moved with as much dignity as he could and stood, an axe in each hand, the hafts still lukewarm from their previous owner's grip. Holding both hafts in his good hand he held them up to his king. One of the king's guards moved forward and grabbed the hafts with a nod of quiet thanks.

"Uthiel Caellar, son of Tanin Caellar, knight of the Order of the Grey Wolf," said the king, seemingly to himself. "I shall remember the name."

With that he turned and cantered his horse back in the direction of the approaching Secundan battle line. Looking back over his shoulder the king called back one final thing.

"Caellar. Your father, he is not as retired as you might think. He is not two hundred feet from you at this very moment. Praise Armenius!"

To Uthiel, this last statement did not sink in immediately as he stood and joined his brothers looking for the fallen forms of their friends. The first was found by Branor. Linton's face was the image of peace. There was no pain in his visage. His eyes were closed and his brow unfurrowed. His thin lips were almost grinning. He looked to have fallen defending Uthiel's back not seven feet from where the duel with the warlord had whirled. If it weren't for the dagger that had found its way through a gouge in his armour and sunk into the side of his chest, the young knight would have looked as if he was sleeping pleasantly.

Three bodies of the enemy lay at his feet, and two more beyond that. His armour was rent in many a place but for the most had held firm. Uthiel's chest constricted sickeningly, already feeling the intense emptiness of Linton's departure. Clenching his jaw to stop it from shaking he stood and turned to Keldon's call. He had found the other two.

Uthiel stumbled over in Keldon's direction, his gait quickly turning into a forced jog as he heard Keldon's excitement at having found one of their brothers alive.

"It's Tarren! He still lives!" called Keldon.

Uthiel ran over, his excitement all but washing away his pains for a brief moment until he saw the unconscious form of Tarren. Keldon was kneeling beside him, probing the wound in Tarren's thigh as he fumbled in his pockets for a needle and thread. He smiled as Uthiel approached.

"He lives, Uthiel," said Keldon, the joy on his face vivid. "Best we patch him up while he sleeps. He struck something when he fell from the looks of it and spent most of the fight unconscious. The wound on his leg is shallow and has missed anything vital. Lazy bastard probably spent the whole time have a right lovely sleep!"

Uthiel laughed for a moment, but the laugh caught in his throat when he saw the hacked up body of Eliem laying disfigured at Tarren's feet. His sword was shattered on the ground next to his hand, on which only two fingers remained. His body was rent with many deep sword gashes including two to either side of his neck and one that had almost split his forearm in two along its length. Eliem's face was one of anger and hate, his eyes open and his face locked in a scowl.

Tarren groaned as Keldon slid the needle through his flesh and pulled the stitch tight. His eyes groggily opened long enough for him to speak once.

"He... he stood over me..." murmured Tarren. "He stood over me to the end... his life for mine... my brother... "

Uthiel knelt down next to Tarren and gripped his friend's hand. "He watches us from Armenius' side, my brother. Rest, now."

For a moment Tarren tried to sit up, his eyes wide with anger. "They wear... our armour... bastard!" he spat. "Killed... Eliem... bastard..."

Tarren's eyes closed as he fell back to the ground, his grip slack. His chest still rhythmically moved beneath his cuirass. Uthiel didn't move and didn't release his brother's hand. He looked to the sky. *Armenius, if you love your sons, please do not let this one die.*

Behind him he could hear the stomping of the advancing Secundan line as it rolled ever closer. A gloved hand rested on his ruined pauldron. Uthiel turned and his eyes met two blue, yet almost translucent eyes looking back at him like a mirror.

"Father."

"Uthiel. My son." Tanin dropped to his knees and wrapped his big arms around Uthiel, barely holding his relief in check.

"My boy, I thought I'd lost you."

CHAPTER THIRTEEN

How they had survived this long was well beyond Nikhael's comprehension. Surrounded by tens of thousands of foes, the Knights Aggressor had watched as the men of the Secundan armies and their knight brothers were slaughtered by the invaders on the battlefields of the White Frontier. Without the support of Gall's armies the line had not even lasted a day.

The Fifth had used Archenon creek to their advantage and still, four months later, its waters lay choked with rotting corpses. Nikhael sniffled, but smelled nothing. The rank odour no longer affected him as it had in the first month, his senses long since having overloaded on death and decay. His swollen, dry tongue licked his painfully cracked lips. Nikhael's stomach rumbled hungrily. The last thing he had eaten had been some tree bark from a dead stump in the forecourt of the fortress two days prior.

For all we know, these few hundred men at Archenon Creek are all that remained of the glory of Secunda.

For the first month they had repelled assault after furious assault. Twice they had lost walls or guard towers and twice they had won them back, hurling the barbarians from their sacred stone through sheer grit and determination. Their food had run out at some point. The horses were the first to be slaughtered and carved up for food. Most of their mounts had been ridden to the open field battles, however, and so the few that were consumed didn't last long. Nikhael's mouth began to fill up with sour spit at the thought of the seared flesh.

Nikhael shuddered at the memory of the brave sorties that had charged out under the cover of night, targeting the food stores of the enemy. The first two or three were successful with few losses. He'd even charged out with his brothers in one. He'd thanked Armenius when he and his brothers had made it back alive, leaving only three men behind to the chaos of the barbarian camp.

It had not taken the barbarians long to work out what the Secundans were doing and a trap was set. Over a hundred were lost. That had been a month ago. Nikhael had tasted rat for the first time weeks past. Some had chosen to starve. That's when the first delegation of the enemy had walked forward, surprisingly, under a white flag of truce.

The Lord Ambar had gone out to meet them. Nikhael's inquisitive nature had led him to the battlement above the gate where the meeting had occurred. He had been almost bowled over in shock as he had seen the men who had come to meet with the Secundans were armed and armoured in the same style as he and his brothers. Six tall, well built and brutal looking men had stood in a solemn rank with a massed horde of barbarians not twenty feet behind them.

Around him he had heard his brothers and the soldiers whispering fearfully. Those six barbarians, clad in Secundan plate, had sent a ripple of fear through the ranks. These men were not mere barbarians; they resembled the foe in almost no way at all.

A shiver of trepidation had made its way down Nikhael's spine, a feeling he was most unaccustomed to. Ambar had fronted them on foot with five of his personal bodyguard. In the custom of warrior lords, they had exchanged flagons in a show of trust. The lord had seemed hesitant but accepted the drink. A long exchange had finished, with Ambar and his men turning away and marching back to the fortress. Nikhael had been unable to find out anything on the discussion. He'd even approached Amorn, who'd been his usual sullen self. Weeks had passed and the lords of the Order had spent a great deal of their time in the fortress' war room. Nikhael couldn't even remember the last time he had seen the king's brother.

Sporadic attacks or attempts at night time subterfuge had come from the barbarians but nothing that had been successful or cost more than a few lives. They were at stalemate; and they were starving. It would not be long until they were all too weak to defend the walls and the enemy walked in and killed those that survived at their leisure.

Nikhael slumped down next to another one of his brothers.

"I would give my left testicle to know what was spoken between Lord Ambar and their leaders," said Nikhael.

His brother frowned at him. "That is for our lords to know, brother. Our duty is to enforce and uphold their decisions."

"Are you not even curious?" pushed Nikhael.

"No," was all the response he received.

"So you care nothing for our fate? What if they surrender?" said Nikhael.

The knight next to him barked out a short laugh. "Not on your life, young Nikhael. Lord Ambar probably just wanted to make sure he could mark the face of the leader so he could challenge him in single combat when we give them their next bloody nose."

I'm not convinced, brother. Something is not right. Does the Lord Ambar even speak barbarian?

Seeing a question on Nikhael's face, the knight continued. "Stop being a bloody fool. Ambar is a chosen family of Armenius. Do you think for a moment he would allow us to leave this field with anything but victory? You mark my words; the lords will get us through this. Have faith in them and Armenius, little brother. Now, get you gone, you're depressing me."

Annoyed now, Nikhael pushed himself to his feet and moved on down the battlement. He looked out over the surrounding plain as he moved. The ground was white with snow, but littered with camps of barbarians. Their numbers had been steadily thinning as the temperature had dropped and the snows moved in from over the mountains. Groups trickled, and soon began to stream, back through the lines towards their homelands. Large gaps could be seen in the encirclement. The enemy were now concentrated around the main gates of the fortress.

A thought struck Nikhael. *With around three hundred knights and soldiers we should be able the break out and move for the Lands of Light.* He quashed the thought quickly and savagely. For all he knew this was the last piece of land being defended by Secundan men. *This may as well* be *Secunda, right here in the stone under my feet and the blood running through my body.*

Nikhael sighed, a feeling of hopelessness overwhelming him as he walked down from the battlements and towards the keep of the fortress. *I need a new whetstone anyway, and a walk to the armoury might calm my mind.* He arrived just in time to see one of the lords of the Order storm into the forecourt. Shining armour, as if fresh from the armourer, flashed past him as Nikhael pulled up and bowed his head in supplication. Before he could move a second lord followed him out.

The first lord turned on his heel and faced the second. Nikhael would have sworn the first was going to strike the second. Instinctively he crept backwards to stand behind the corner of a wooden storehouse.

"Would you have their lives wasted?" the lord stormed. "Thousands, hundreds of thousands, maybe millions, and you would allow this to stand?"

The second lord moved forward and grabbed the first by the arm. "Would you betray your lord? Would you betray your bond of brotherhood?"

"What!?" snarled the first lord. "He is not king. He is not who demands your fealty, brother!"

"Lord Faulken is in command," said the second lord, his voice transferring smoothly from stern to conciliatory. "The decision is his. This is for the survival of Secunda, what other choice do we have my brother? Rolm? What choice do we have?"

"We saw knights, Ambar! They almost made it to the wall..." said Rolm, his voice now less sure of its own conviction.

"We saw knights four months ago!" exploded Lord Ambar. "And then four months of nothing. Four months of starvation. Four months of watching our men fight and die and suffer! Men drop from disease every day and still we do not see the king. Armenius rest his soul but the king, and the people he lords over, have gone to join the Eternal Lord. We are all that is left!"

"How can you know this?" asked Rolm, his voice a defeated whine. "We see the smoke of battle on the horizon at least once a week."

"No, my brother, what you see are the funeral pyres of Gall."

Ambar allowed this to sink in for a moment and then continued, his voice lowered conspiratorially. "And if our king is alive, then he is the last of his line, and undoubtedly has abandoned us while he sits safe behind Secunda's walls."

Nikhael's heart jumped into his mouth. It was all he could to stop himself from striding forward with his blade drawn. *How could Lord Rolm allow that insult to stand?*

The Lord Rolm stood, his mouth working soundlessly, his tired eyes hardening with anger.

"Lord Ambar," he snarled. "Insult my king's honour again and I promise my blade will ensure you never live long enough to see our saviours."

Finally, some spine. But what is going on?

Ambar moved in close, and Nikhael strained to hear him. "Would you stand against your brother lords for a king you will never see again?"

"Yes."

"We are abandoned by our allies, surrounded by the enemy, and the last of our kind." said Ambar, his face moving closer to Lord Rolm's. "Would you stand against all of us, and be cut down as a traitor to be discarded over our bastions in bloody pieces, for a nation that is all but destroyed?"

"I..."

Ambar moved even closer, his teeth clenched and his voice hissing. "Would you throw away the only chance our people have of surviving and rebuilding for some sick and stupid sense of honour to a dead king who cares not for us? His one meagre, pathetic, attempt at rescue failed so miserably it sickens my stomach to think of it."

Rolm did not speak.

"One thing I promise you, Rolm," sneered Ambar, backing away from the lord's slumping form. "If you and your men side against us, each and every one of you will be cut down, hacked into as many pieces as we can manage and then handed to the cook fires of the barbarians. Your life and your honour is your own, but your men..."

Bastard.

Rolm seemed to slump further at the implication, his eyes falling to the ground as if the enormity of the world lay on his shoulders. It was only at this point that Ambar noticed Nikhael. Before he could move the lord turned to Nikhael and stormed over to him.

"How much did you hear?" he barked. "You would eavesdrop on the conversations of your betters? Show some respect, boy!"

Nikhael dropped to a knee. "I heard nothing my lord, I swear."

The Lord Ambar loomed over him and placed a hand under his stubbled chin and lifted his gaze. Nikhael's face did not change, his dark eyes emotionless and empty as usual. If he was honest with himself, it was forced. He could feel sweat dribbling down the inside of his collar. The lord nodded to himself, his composure regained.

"You speak of this to anyone, and I will gut you and hang you from the walls. Away with you, back to the wall," he ordered.

Nikhael turned and hurried away. A glance over his shoulder showed the two lords speak further and head back into the keep, their initial rage spent but the tension between them so thick it could be cut with a knife. Nikhael's head swam like never before. In his short years as a warrior and a knight, he had always been happy to be a brother warrior and nothing more. Standing in the battle line, or back to back with his friends was what he had always wanted, despite the visage of nonchalance he always presented.

He replayed the two lords' discussion over and over again in his head, completely forgetting the need of a whetstone. Something began to pick at his mind. Something about that discussion, that smack in the face of a discussion of betrayal and treachery and hopelessness and defeat, it didn't sit right beyond the obvious with him. He walked, without really seeing where he was going, towards the tower stairs that led up to the battlement of the keep.

Abandoned by our allies...

Nikhael reached the base of the stairs and stopped. Slowly he began to step up the long flight, dragging his hand on the inner wall to guide his way as his eyes were clouded over, lost in the world of thought.

Would you stand against all of us...

They are infighting? Over what? Is there a divide amongst the lords? Ridiculous. Unbelievable. Not possible. No, that wasn't it. Nikhael continued, his mind jumping from sentence to sentence, from word to word, desperately attempting to remember each piece as it was before his memory began to round the edges and lose the details and exact wording.

Then he is the last of...

A desperate scream followed by a wet thud broke his line of thought. He looked back down the stairs he had half climbed.

Shining armour, splashed in mud and blood.

He looked up to the windows of the keep. And for a moment; one brief, horrifying moment saw the look of sick satisfaction on the Lord Ambar's face. In that one moment he knew who had fallen and began to sprint down the stairs.

Nikhael needn't have bothered. The Lord Rolm had struck the cobblestone ground face first from three storeys up and his head had flattened like a stepped on egg. He looked up once more to where the Lord Ambar had been, but the window now stood empty and dark beyond. A crowd quickly gathered, inclusive of the lords whom they had not seen for some time.

His direct commander, Lord Irill, saw him and came directly towards Nikhael.

Youthful in comparison to some of the other lords, Irill was a tall and well built man well at the latter end of his thirties. His stained white tabard was snug over his battle-damaged armour. A shock of white hair hung unruly and unkempt from around a weary face but his blue eyes flickered with full alertness between the mess of Rolm's head and Nikhael. Nikhael bowed his head in respect of one of the few lords he had seen on the battlements fighting alongside his men during these last months.

"Brother Nikhael," said Irill. "Did you see it? What in the name of Armenius just happened?"

"I apologise, my lord," responded Nikhael. "But I did not see how it happened. I only saw what you see here now."

Irill cursed under his breath. "Such a waste," he said to himself.

"My lord?" asked Nikhael.

"Nothing. Nothing."

There was a moment's silence as the two stared down at the ruined form of Rolm. Nikhael cleared his throat before daring to speak once more.

"My lord, should the Lord Field Marshal Faramon know of this?" questioned Nikhael.

In a moment that passed so quickly Nikhael wasn't even sure it happened, his lord's face showed the briefest pang of mixed emotion. While he awaited a response, Nikhael tried to work out what he had just seen. *Is it pain? Sadness? Anger? Regret? Guilt? Some unhappy mixture of all?*

"The lord field marshal is..." Lord Irill stalled for a heartbeat, "...detained."

Irill stared for a moment longer as if in a trance before turning to Nikhael.

Nikhael made to begin speaking again. There was too much coincidence here. He had to say something. His mouth was open and drawing in breath when he looked up to see Ambar's eyes locked on him. Quickly, he closed his mouth and returned his stare to the ground.

"Nothing further? Back to your post, brother," said Irill dismissively.

"My lord," replied Nikhael, his curiosity now melding itself into outright concern and worry and possibly fear as he paced back to the stairs that led to his post.

Something was going on. Something to do with the lords and the lord field marshal. Of who had killed Rolm, he had no doubt. Ambar was a part of what was happening. The temptation to speak out of turn to his lord Irill had been immense. Never had he felt so nervous and never had he had such a feeling of outright fear constrict itself around his chest than when he had momentarily locked eyes with Ambar.

In those eyes he saw such coolly masked hatred. Such well veiled anger. Nikhael shivered a little at the thought. Very few people or things unmanned him anymore but something about the Lord Ambar had begun to unravel his courage. Sitting back at his post, Nikhael kept himself awake well into the night despite his exhaustion, trying to work out what was going on. The illusion of the simplicity of being a rank and file knight had been shattered today. Nikhael was embroiled in something. What it was he knew not but as he fell asleep, back against the wall and next to a brother on guard duty for the night, he couldn't help but feel overwhelmed by a sense of dark foreboding.

Screams of battle tore Nikhael from his slumber. Next to him, the brother who had been on guard duty lay slumped at his feet with a crossbow bolt through his throat. Nikhael was up and into a crouch with sword drawn in a heartbeat. Grabbing his shield from its lean against the wall, he rammed on his helmet and rose to look over the battlement to see where the enemy had come from. His senses still swimming in sleep, it took longer than a moment for him to realise the inaction of the barbarian camp. It took a much quicker moment for him to turn and see the fierce battle occurring below him in the courtyard.

"Men of Irill!" came the loud voice of his lord. "Men of Irill! Form up on me! We are betrayed!"

Without thinking Nikhael slammed on his helm and moved down the stairs, still not quite grasping what was going on. It wasn't until he put together what had happened the previous day with the call of his lord below in the courtyard and the crossbow bolt in the guard he had fallen asleep beside that some clarity began to dawn on his mind. *The enemy don't use crossbows.*

The thought hit him like a hammer. It rang around his very soul. He had heard about different knight factions having honour duels, despite the disapproval of the king, but this was insane. Below him, three hundred of his brothers and their lords butchered each other with a brutality he had never seen before. Below him he could already see scores of dead bodies, mostly from the Secundan Fifth. From where they lay, it looked like the majority had been knifed while asleep, their armour next to them to help rest their bodies. The few who had rose to fight had stood little chance.

Nikhael reached the ground and was nearly thrown from his feet by the slamming impact of a crossbow bolt on his shield. He did not bother looking for the wielder but instead charged into the melee. Not knowing friend from foe he made as quickly as possible for Irill, only stopping to protect himself from those who tried to attack him. Twenty feet before he made it to the circle of brother knights protecting his lord, his name was called with booming clarity. Nikhael searched the surrounding battle, still dumbfounded by what he was witnessing.

Then he saw him. Blood spattered and battered with his sword gleaming red in the firelight held pointed directly at Nikhael, Amorn looked the very image of vengeance. For a moment Nikhael dropped his guard at seeing someone familiar and from his past. Someone, who despite their historic differences, he knew he could trust as a brother.

"Amorn!" he called, walking forwards. "What is..."

He never got to finish his sentence. Amorn roared wordlessly and sprinted forward, shield up before him and gore spattered sword releasing an arc of crimson above his head as he swung it back to strike at Nikhael. In shock, Nikhael almost forgot to raise his shield or sword in his own defence. Amorn's first blow glanced from his pauldron. The blow put Amorn off balance. Nikhael saw his opening to land a strike on his estranged brother but something held him back.

Amorn turned before Nikhael could speak and snarled. "Are you incapable of defending yourself, traitor?"

The next ten heartbeats went by so quickly that Nikhael couldn't remember how he found himself without his shield, looking up at Amorn from his knees. A rent in his cuirass and side let him know that one of Amorn's cuts had split his armour and flesh. A swollen and closed eye gave him the realisation his helm had been removed by a vicious blow to its faceplate. Above him, Amorn's face was that of the berserker; fury so raw and unleashed that he was more beast than man.

"Wha? Why? Brother?" was all Nikhael could manage through his aching mouth. Blood and part of a tooth dribbled over his lips.

For a moment, Amorn seemed to channel his anger away from the beast and into the man. His jaw clenched and unclenched with such force Nikhael found himself surprised his brother's teeth did not crack.

"You would betray us?" spat Amorn. "For them you would throw away your oaths and the vengeance due for a million souls butchered!"

Before Nikhael could speak, Amorn was once more lost to his inner beast and raised his sword, raging red fury burning from his eyes. Nikhael closed his own and prepared to meet Armenius. The blow never landed. Nikhael opened his near black eyes and saw Amorn staring in shock at the stump of his right hand. The hand, still clenching his blade, lay on the blood drenched cobblestones below him. A second later, a flash of cold steel separated the top of big man's head from its lower half, just above the high inner collar of his pauldrons.

As Amorn's body fell to the ground, a gloved hand reached down to him and grabbed his. Nikhael looked up at his saviour.

"Come on my brother, if we are to survive this great betrayal, I'll need my loyal men by my side!" said the Lord Irill.

Nikhael rose to his feet with his lord's help and joined his brothers in the fighting.

Armenius let me survive this so I can at least know why we are dying. Armenius, let me see out this madness.

CHAPTER FOURTEEN

As the sun rose above the battlement, the final traitor was slain. Around him Nikhael saw his brothers in a mixture of elation and disbelief. *Have we really just killed over a hundred of the men we had fought and suffered beside for the last four months? Had the brotherhood of years of service to the Order of the Knights Aggressor just been washed away in a torrent of blood?* Nikhael's thoughts suddenly were filled with the horrid memory of Amorn. What had happened to his brother that had led him to betray them all? Amorn, a brother he had fought with and against since boyhood, had turned on his king, his country and his god in one fell night.

Nikhael felt his stomach churn as he thought of the brothers he had killed that night. Two he remembered laying killing strokes upon. A further three or four more he was certain he had badly wounded, but his recount of the hours between the betrayal and dawn were no more than a blur to his memory. Lords, captains, lieutenants, and good brothers all lay strewn throughout the courtyard. Death; she had been indiscriminate this night in her reaping of the treacherous and the loyal.

Many of his brothers had begun picking through the dead, some moaning or crying out when they found a friend or brother, some of the seemingly morally challenged crying out in raucous victory when they found an enemy their hand had slain. Nikhael felt nothing. This last assault on his soul had destroyed a little piece of him. He turned to find the Lord Irill looking at him.

"You fought well, brother," he said.

Nikhael could only nod dumbly.

He looked around to see who else he could recognise. Only about sixty of his brothers remained alive after the night's fighting, sixty blood-soaked white tabards from the two thousand that had held the White Frontier posting not four months ago.

"My Lord Irill!" sang a clear, happy voice. "Your men have done the Lord Faulken proud!"

"My thanks, Lord Ambar," called back Irill, his voice far less jovial.

The Lord Ambar walked past Nikhael and grabbed Irill's hand in a warrior's handshake.

"Finally, we have cut the traitorous cancer from the body of Mother Secunda. No longer are we the lap dogs of the fallen king! Finally we are the true lords the men of the Order of the Knights Aggressor were born to be!"

What?

Cold fear stabbed into his chest as many of his brothers punched the air and began cheering. Forgetting himself, but unable to hold back, Nikhael walked forward.

"What has happened here?" he called out, the men around him almost simultaneously falling quiet at his outburst. "We have slain our brothers! Our fortress shall fall in hours to those outside! What have we done?"

For a moment there was no answer. Nikhael, incredulous at what had happened but slowly coming to the realisation of his situation, sank to his knees. In one grim, gut-wrenching moment he realised what had happened. These men, his brothers, were the traitors. And then in a moment that nearly saw his stomach come out of his mouth he realised.

I am a traitor.

A hand rested upon his pauldron. He looked up, his eyes travelling over filthy Secundan knight armour. Any pieces missing showed weathered pale skin covered in barbarous tattoos taut over lean muscle stitched with battle scars. A mottled, ragged wolf fur hung from the man's shoulders and there on the cuirass he saw a name. Only a single name could be seen for the second name had been so filled with blood and filth it could not be read.

"Brother, I think you'll find that the men outside will no longer be a problem," said Kael.

"We march for Gall!"

Inside the king's command tent, Thomak stood over a large map upon a table surrounded by the other generals of Secundan host and the lords of the knight orders. Thomak watched the king as he looked around at the many faces in the room, his intelligent eyes pausing for a brief moment on each of his commanders. The king lifted a small glass of wine to his lips, sipped, and spoke.

"Lords, generals, we have fought well and hard and cleansed our home of the filth that had assailed it before winter wrapped its cold embrace around us."

To this, his generals and lords roused a cry of celebration at their efforts. Thomak forced his own cry into the symphony of loyalty.

"But I must ask you this one last thing."

The cries died.

The king cleared his throat before continuing.

"Four centuries ago, Mother Secunda fell and our people, led by my ancestor and our Eternal Lord, sought the refuge of the king of Gall. Refuge was provided and our forebears were able to rebuild Secunda as we now love and cherish it.

"The people of Gall spilled their blood in the defence of their allies. Were it not for their allegiance I would not be here speaking to you now. Were it not for the selfless charity of their actions, none of us would be here right now."

The king cleared his throat.

"It is time to repay that debt."

Some of the generals and lords voiced their agreement. Others did not. The king continued.

"I understand the trepidations some of you may have about a winter campaign into Gall, but understand this; Gall has fallen. Of that there can be no doubt. Their armies have not been seen on the field of battle since we had knowledge of the incursion. We have had no messages from King Grenhel, nor did they manage to make any impact on the enemy before they entered Secundan lands. We must assume the worst."

"Is it not possible they simply withdrew behind their city walls?" interrupted a general.

"And allowed their lands and their people to be completely ravaged? I think not," said Lord Pomen.

"Then how do you explain a standing army twenty five thousand strong just disappearing? How do you explain hundreds of thousands of people gone?" said the other.

"We have had many refugees..." began lord Pomen.

"Some few thousands, lord," interrupted the general once more. "A scant few in comparison the many hundreds of thousands that made up Gall and her lands."

The king held up his hands for silence. All attention returned to him.

"I would not have my countrymen bicker at a time like this. We must be of one voice or we shall fail in the winter campaign. If the barbarians gain a winter foothold in the lands of Gall and bring in reinforcements come the spring, we shall be besieged once more. We must push them back past the frontier. We must keep them on the run, ever using our cavalry to turn retreats into bloody routs. The more we slay in the cold, the less we will need to defend against come the warmth of summer.

"Their leader is slain, their force is in disarray. This, my countrymen, is our chance to strike at them like never before. This could be the catalyst for our return to Mother Secunda."

A few sharp intakes of breath showed the importance of that statement.

"An update on our strength; now please," said the king, addressing the knight lords.

The Lord General Thomak strode forwards.

"My king, the Order of the Grey Wolf has three hundred and thirty-nine knights fit for battle. A further sixty-three are wounded and under the care of the apothecaries and healers. With us march those of the Secundan Fifth and Seventh armies. With the latest reinforcements from Secunda, the Fifth has a standing strength of almost two regiments – nineteen companies in total, plus auxiliaries. The Seventh has a standing strength of four and a half regiments plus auxiliaries. All sick and wounded from the Seventh and Fifth have been rolled into the Twelfth, who have marched for home. I have almost seven thousand men for you to command.

"We are short on swords, food, and medical supplies. The men we have are tired but dogged. They are knights and old soldiers and citizens fighting for their homes. Most have lost sons or brothers or friends from the original founding of the Fifth. We are resolute in our duty and ready to strike for Gall."

The king nodded. "You have taken some heavy losses. That you are so keen for further service does your order honour. My thanks, lord general."

Thomak nodded, proud but also painfully well aware of the casualties amongst his Order. For the second time in a decade, the Order of the Grey Wolf had lost half of its strength defending the Lands of the Light. The king turned to address the next member of the war council.

"My king?" jumped in Thomak.

The king turned back to him. "Yes, my friend?"

"It would be our honour if the Grey Wolves could lead the attack to push the taint from the lands of our ancestral allies. We shall not fail you," said Thomak, allowing the fervour of the coming glory to light his eyes to hide his true purpose.

The king considered for a moment, before nodding his ascent. "The purge of the city will be yours."

Thomak nodded his thanks. Inwardly he simultaneously released a long sigh of relief and steeled his soul for the scouring of their Order's hidden treacherous past. *This is my one opportunity to remove the taint of the Black Wolves from our history. In secret.*

"My household guard and I shall accompany you," said the king almost as an afterthought.

Damn. The lord general of the Grey Wolves heart sank as he nodded his acknowledgement and did his upmost best to hide his disappointment.

Well over two hours later, Thomak still stood amongst the war council as the king finished detailing the great push back to the White Frontier. All of the knight Orders had vital roles and would be sorely tested in the coming months at the forefront of the advancing Secundan line. This line would stretch for almost twenty-five miles as its separate knight and army groups advanced through the lands of Gall and pushed for the White Frontier. Thinking of his own Order, he imagined that the anticipated skirmish style fighting in the city of Gall would suit some of his knights more than others.

Brothers like the Lords Pomen and Ryan were brilliantly suited to open field advance and command. They were the match of almost any foe when in charge of a cavalry wing and several large units of footslogging warriors, but their style of fighting would not suit the closed in streets of a major city like Gall where they had no time or space to manoeuvre. The brilliant First Captain Solanthur Verutus would be a perfect leader with small groups of skirmishers.

Thinking of skirmishers made him instantly think of the young knights who had somehow infiltrated the barbarian horde and slain the warlord amongst the retreating foes. A small spark of jealousy had sparked for a moment as he thought of the young man standing aloft a small rise with a blade in one hand and the warlord's head in the other, right in front of the king. The young Grey Wolf had had the honour of handing his battle trophies to the direct descendant of the Eternal Lord. Thomak smiled to himself ruefully. Such glories were for the young.

Thomak's knowledge of his prime having passed him was sometimes hard to bear. At fifty-two he was not some mewling, wrinkled, toothless old fop incapable of wiping his own arse. He was still a formidable swordsman and a brilliant military strategist, but it had been many years since he had been amongst the most capable duellers in the Order. He looked over to the Lord Pomen who was intently listening to the king's plan. He pitied the old lord in a way. Undoubtedly this would be his last glory in life. One last campaign before his body rendered him too weak to don the glorious plate armour of the Order.

The Lord Pomen turned to meet his gaze and nodded. Those eyes were made of the very pure steel of the old lord's soul. They spoke of hardship, glory, pain, sacrifice, experience and loss. They spoke of a life lived in servitude and they spoke of the honour of that servitude. Thomak nodded back to his brother in recognition of a man who had given his life to Secunda and loved every moment of it.

The king finished his directives and stood solemnly for a moment, his face the picture of loss for a brief moment before he addressed them once more.

"My friends, my countrymen, my brothers," the king paused for a long instant, contemplating his next words carefully before continuing. "Let us take stock for one moment. Not of our situation but of brothers lost and absent. Of those who, at this very moment, watch over us and advise our souls quietly in the campaign we are about to embark on. Let us, for a moment, turn our prayers to our lost brothers of the order of the Knights Aggressor. Pray with me, this moment, my brothers.

My Eternal Lord,
May you watch over our lost brothers,
And welcome them to your battle line..."

The prayer was long and heartfelt. The king finished with a moment's silence and then personally shook the hand of each member of the war council. He paused for a moment, firm grip around Thomak's forearm in a warrior's greeting, locking eyes for a brief moment with the lord general of the Grey Wolves. The meaning in that look was clear. The king felt no need to share words on the matter and released his grip and moved on.

Hard resolve formed in Thomak's chest. He would never allow himself or his order to let Secunda down again.

Gall will be ours or we will die to a man taking it.

Thomak's eyes closed for a moment as he recited a quick prayer and swore an oath to Armenius.

"We shall re-take Gall for the Lands of the Light and in doing so purge the taint from the Grey Wolves in His sight..."

Thomak paused for a deep breath.

"...by the blood gifted to me by Armenius, I swear this oath," murmured Thomak.

He turned and walked from the command tent. Pomen fell into step beside him without word and they both began threading their way through the tent city that had risen around them. The king had given them a month to get their forces in order before the march into Gall. There was much to do.

Their forces had to be reorganised. Lost leaders had to be replaced. The scant reinforcements for the Orders and Secundan army units had to be marched in. Men had to be trained specifically for what they were about to go into. His forces had to be rearmed and fed. Ruined armour needed replacing or mending. He needed to start his paperwork on their losses for later entry into the Order's records. His head began to spin at the sheer volume of what he needed to achieve in the next seven days.

"My lord general," said Pomen, interrupting his thoughts. "I may be old but I am far from useless. If you need my help with the reorganisation of our forces you need only order it and I will be there."

Momentarily, Thomak smarted at the offer of assistance. *Does the old man think I can't run the Order myself?* Quickly he backhanded his ego to the rear of his thinking. *This is no time for petty squabbles about who is in command here.* The Eternal Lord had given him Pomen for a reason, and this was it. Pomen might not be useful in a swordfight in the streets of Gall, but by Armenius he was brilliant when it came to ensuring his men were armed, armoured and fed. That would leave him the important purpose of the restructure.

If the Lord Pomen noticed the brief moment flash across Thomak's features he did not say anything.

"The assistance would be greatly appreciated, old friend," said Thomak, half forcing a warm smile onto his face.

Lord Pomen nodded. "What would you have me do, lord general?"

"My Lord General Thomak!" called a voice, young by the sounds of it.

Thomak and Pomen both turned to see a young knight, his armour clean but damaged, with open rents still visible in places, standing just out of their way. Thomak thought to reprimand him but the face struck a memory to the fore of his mind.

The young knight bowed his head. "My lord, please, I pray you give me but a moment of your time. In private."

"You would interrupt a lord of your order, young man?" questioned Thomak.

"For this, my lord, I would interrupt you both a hundred times over," countered the youth.

Thomak thought a moment. "Your name?"

"Uthiel Caellar, of Captain Phyrus' company, my lord general," said Uthiel, and then hesitated, his almost translucent blue eyes flicking to the Lord Pomen.

Pomen's eyebrow lifted. "Phyrus never returned from the frontier. Is there a problem?"

Uthiel wavered but a short moment, and in that moment Thomak was unsure if the youth would continue. "I... my lord general... I was instructed by our brother Ghurkar Storm to pass this on to you in person... privately, my lord general."

Thomak suppressed a chuckle. Pomen smarted. "You would excuse my presence, young whelp?"

Uthiel's eyes hardened, much to Thomak's surprise, as they levelled at the Lord Pomen. *The young brother has fire to him.*

"My lord, please accept my apologies if I offend you," he said. "These were the last instructions of my dying lieutenant and I will not sour my last memory of him by breaking my word."

Pomen looked to Thomak. Thomak nodded ever so slowly.

"I shall attend to our food and arms shortage, lord general," said Pomen curtly, and then took his leave.

Thomak turned to Uthiel. "What would you have to tell me that is more important that attending to my duty?"

"Black Wolves, lord general. Kael," said Uthiel.

Thomak's blood turned cold. "Come with me."

He escorted the young knight away from the large groups of men in the centre of the camp. Thomak watched Uthiel carefully, this young man knew about his Order's greatest secret. This boy knew about the greatest betrayer Secunda and the Grey Wolves had ever known. For him to know of them, at all, means he must have seen or even spoken to them. He directed their fast paced walk towards the Order's billet.

As they walked further and further through the camp, eventually bypassing their Order's tents and campfires and heading for the outer areas of the army's camp, Thomak found his concern steadily growing like a rancid piece of meat in his stomach. Just the name Kael made him feel sick. *The finest swordsman the Order had ever seen betraying his brothers and taking near a third of the Order with him across the White Frontier and into the Black Lands after a pitched battle with the loyal.* It was a pitched battle that the Lord General Thomak remembered with horrible clarity in a red haze of hate and disbelief.

He and his men had given chase a few miles into the Black Lands. Kael had teased them from afar, decapitating women he had taken from an outlying settlement and hanging their heads by their hair from trees to torment the pursuit. He had dared Thomak to chase him, challenged the lord general to follow him deeper and deeper into the uncharted Black Lands. Eventually, Thomak had had to pull his men back to safety. Men like Ghurkar Storm had railed at the pulling back of his leash at the time. Men like the Lord Pomen had counselled in agreement with his action.

Shaking away the memory with a quick flick of his head, Thomak found himself and the youth out near some of the latrine pits. The stench was quickly growing more sickly as they approached, and the youth gave him a questioning sideways look, but few men ventured here voluntarily and hence he felt a more open style of speaking may be possible. He measured up the young man before him.

Uthiel had sandy blonde hair and eyes that were young but hard and did not attempt to avoid his gaze. His face was a mess of battle; an obviously broken nose and a host of tiny nicks and cuts, almost healed, on his face. Two ugly purple scars marred his obviously once handsome features. A horizontal one ran from his nose and back through his cheek while the other began at his eyebrow, intersected the first scar and then ran down to his neck. He was well built but looked half-starved and tired.

His armour was in desperate need of the blacksmith's hammer and he wore two swords in an unorthodox manner; one pommel over his right shoulder and the other blade hanging from his left hip. A dirty dark grey cloak was wrapped over his pauldrons to protect against the icy wind blowing through the camp.

In the moment it took him to take in the appearance of Uthiel, the knight grew impatient and spoke.

"My lord general, I have waited three months to give you this message. It could not wait another moment," he started.

"I understand, young brother. You must learn patience," interrupted Thomak. "There is a place and time to discuss such things. The news you carry is not for ears apart from mine."

Uthiel's face presented a momentary modicum of confusion. *Might the lad not know the import of the knowledge he carries?* For a moment, Thomak thought about how best to approach this delicate situation.

"Who else knows of this message?" asked Thomak.

"None, lord general. The message was for your ears alone," responded Uthiel.

Thomak took this on with a nod, warily grateful. "Good. Brother, I will have your word of honour that it will stay that way. Now."

Uthiel nodded. "You have it, on my honour and my family's."

Thomak was silent for a moment. He took a deep breath before continuing.

"Tell me. Explain to me how it came to be that you and your brothers were so far behind the enemy's lines. Tell me how it came to be that it was your sword that found the warlord's throat."

"It is a long story, my lord general," responded Uthiel. "Though I shall recount it as best I can."

Thomak stood for some time listening to the youth's story. Sometimes he asked clarifying questions or had the lad repeat a series of events not so much as he didn't understand, but more so to see if Uthiel recounted it in the same way. At times he was inwardly amazed at what the survivors of Phyrus' company had managed. Sometimes he questioned whether the young knight's age may have led him to increase the individual heroics of he and his brothers. Looking into Uthiel's eyes, however, he doubted that was happening.

By the time the story had finished Thomak had reached his decision. His first thought had been hard and ugly, feeling a little piece of his life-long accumulation of honour die within him as he considered making the young knight disappear, but with the understanding of what the boy had done to bring him this message he had decided otherwise. It was obvious the youth knew nothing of the import of his message. There was an opportunity here; one to raise the hopes of the seven thousand men under his command and more, a chance to give them a heroic and glorious young man to focus on, while the Lord General Thomak went about the grisly business of cutting the Order's cancerous past from its body. All he needed was to start spreading the story quietly and soon it would take hold. *The young knight who slew the monster.*

A plan quickly formed in his mind as he looked at the expectantly waiting face of his subordinate. He managed to catch the scarcest hint of a smile as it played across his face before he forced his features into a well practiced look of authority.

"Brother," he started. "What you and your men have done reminds me of the legends of old, of legendary knights who stood against impossible odds and emerged victorious."

The youth reddened under such aggrandisement of his actions. *The modest warriors are the most loved.*

"You and your brothers shall be rewarded."

They are also the easiest ones to make into heroes.

CHAPTER FIFTEEN

Uthiel strode forward alongside Branor, Lokhi, Keldon, and a still physically weak Tarren from their camp. Before them stood the assembly of Grey Wolves being issued their new captains and lords under the restructure of the force for the push on Gall. It had come as an immense shock, to all five of them, that they were to be honoured with fighting in First Captain Solanthur Verutus' small company of elite veterans.

The men they moved to stand amongst were all grizzled warriors. They were some of the best and most experienced men in the Order; some of the stoutest in Secunda. All sixty of the brothers under the first captain had been broken down into small groups of skirmishers, their role to move ahead of the main force as it marched through and cleaned the city. Uthiel couldn't help a stab of excitement to know he would be among the men who delved into towns and homes to burn out the barbarians from where they squatted. He would be with the men who fought in the harshest, fiercest, least ordered places to return light to where the darkness had consumed it. This was everything he'd trained for. They were the vanguard.

Uthiel couldn't help but feel naked without the armour he had spent the last four months wearing. Many of the Grey

Wolves were today without their armour or weapons. The steady staccato ring of the Order's blacksmiths could be heard in the background as they tried to beat some of the heavily abused pieces of holy metal back into service.

As the group of knights stood at ease in front of their captain, Solanthur moved amongst them. He shook a knight's hand in a warriors grip here, and shared a quiet word with another there. The knights who were lucky enough to have those brief moments of attention from the revered first captain seemed to stand taller for it. Uthiel felt a small pang of disappointment as the great man strode by he and his brothers, barely laying an eye upon them.

Uthiel looked to Branor, who seemed distant but shrugged and opened his palms. All thoughts stopped, however, as the Lord General Thomak stood atop a wooden step placed in front of the knights. This elevated him above their eye level by a good two feet. His armour had obviously had the chief blacksmith's attention for the past day or two, as it was perfect in every detail. His helmet was held against his hip by his gloved hand and his hard lined face looked over his knights. He waited for the men around Uthiel to be quiet before he began speaking.

"My brothers!" he called, his voice clear and loud above the outside din of the camp. "For three days we have sat stagnant upon this field as our wounds healed and our holy armour is looked to. This is three days too long!"

The Grey Wolves unleashed one loud cheer and then fell silent.

"This campaign will be like none you have ever fought before," continued Thomak. "There will be no open field battles, very few glorious cavalry charges, and little room for our shield walls to form up. Were we any less than the Grey Wolves we may have faltered at a task that presents such a challenge. But, my brothers, I have a plan that will see the Grey Wolves emerge victorious!"

Again, the Grey Wolves voiced their agreement in a single cry. Thomak's face grey solemn.

"Brothers, Armenius has sent us a test so difficult it will challenge the very fibre of your beings. Your mettle shall be tried again, and again, and again. When your brothers fall around you and all hope seems lost, simply remember."

Thomak held the quiet for a moment. The only sound was the wind playfully toying with Thomak's cloak.

"Remember that you are a Grey Wolf!" he yelled. "You are Secunda's finest warriors chosen by our Eternal Lord and you shall not fail!"

A roar of approval far louder than the last erupted from the Grey Wolves. Uthiel almost yelled himself hoarse adding his voice to the tumult. Thomak allowed this to continue a short while before raising his hands to quieten his order once more with a smile. Uthiel stared in anticipation, eagerly awaiting his lord general's next words.

"We are to be sorely tested during winter's chill touch. Foul things await us in the city of Gall. Warfare like neither you nor I have witnessed before will be waged between good and evil. In times of hardship, look to your brothers," said Thomak. "Look to men like First Captain Solanthur Verutus, hero of many battlefields and the greatest combatant this Order possesses."

A roar of support and cheers went up from the Order for the first captain.

"Look to men like Carn Kolen, a veteran of our Order who does his fallen brothers honour with every step he takes towards the enemy."

Carn received a like show of support to the first captain.

"Look to men like our young brother Uthiel Caellar, the boy..." Thomak stopped for a moment once more and locked eyes with Uthiel. "No. The *knight* who slew the barbarian warlord in single combat!"

Despite the shock at being named amongst such gloried men as Solanthur and Carn, Uthiel couldn't help a sheepish smile as he received a great cry from his fellow Grey Wolves, including some back slaps from the veterans he and his brothers now stood amongst. Looking up at the Lord General Thomak, he saw a look of smug satisfaction on the man's face as he looked over his Order and raised his hands to quieten them once more.

In the corner of Uthiel's eye, he saw a look of hurt exclusion on his closest friend, Branor's, face. Keldon and Tarren clapped Branor on the back in support, but hadn't seen the expression. *Bran?* Uthiel's view was blocked for a moment. When Branor came in to view again he was smiling and clapping, eyes locked on the lord general. Uthiel stared a moment, hoping to catch his brother's gaze. His friend ignored him.

"We have a little over three weeks to be prepared for the march on Gall," continued Thomak. "Your captains shall begin your training this very moment. Look to your arms and armour and ensure you are ready to depart this camp in three weeks' time. Some of you may be used as parts of scouting parties before then. That is all, brothers. For the king and the Eternal Lord!"

"For the king and the Eternal Lord!" echoed the Grey Wolves before turning their attention to their captains as the lord general and his lords began to retreat from the camp on their own business.

Uthiel and his brothers turned to face Solanthur. With a wave he bade them follow him and led them towards a section of open fields with a covered cart standing in it. A section had been picketed off for them and in surrounding picketed areas men were training hard with blunted swords and shields. Uthiel rolled his shoulders as he relished the opportunity to shake off the monotony of the last few days in camp.

The large cart was uncovered to show blunted swords, battered practice shields and training armour. Immediately the first captain called Uthiel and his friends over to the cart. Knights handed them swords and bucklers. When Uthiel was handed a buckler he offered it back and requested a second sword. The veteran knight looked at him with a smirk, but gave him a second sword anyway.

Uthiel hefted both weapons and tried to accustom himself to their weight as quickly as possible by going through a series of practice swings and movements he had been using during his three months behind enemy lines. The first captain came before them, armed only with a single sword. Seeing Uthiel's choices of weapons he smiled cruelly and motioned to the knight standing by the cart with his free left hand. Instantly the warrior in Uthiel identified the first captain's dominant hand as his right one. That was until Solanthur caught the thrown practice sword in his left hand with a skilful and coordinated flourish which finished in a fighting stance most unlike the one Uthiel had become used to.

"You first," said Solanthur, pointing his dulled blade at Uthiel. "The cocky one."

Uthiel frowned at the comment as he pulled on a practice cuirass and pauldrons. Solanthur had on his battle armour without his helm. As Uthiel finished tying on his goussets and vambrances, the first captain began to move towards him, one sword at his hip and the other above shoulder height with the tips of each blade pointing at Uthiel's face. Uthiel took his practiced stance quickly, one blade forward and horizontal and the other back and ready to strike.

"Fighting with two swords is not an easy discipline, little brother," said Solanthur.

Uthiel started to reply but before he could open his mouth he had desperately fended off three attacks. The two knights circled each other. Uthiel licked his dry lips. Those first three strikes had been unbelievably fast and powerful, yet he had the distinct impression that Solanthur was toying with him. Uthiel clenched his jaw in anger at the insult.

"First captain, you pull your strikes. You insult me," grated Uthiel, lancing his left blade forward and then cutting down with his right blade.

Both blows were turned aside easily and then returned with interest. Uthiel blocked the first two strikes but as he blocked a strike across his body with the left blade to keep his right free for a riposte, his left pauldron was hammered with a full force blow from the first captain. Pain rang through his shoulder and Uthiel dropped to a knee, holding a blade up to protect himself but not getting it up in time to stop Solanthur's boot from connecting with his chest and fiercely kicking him on to his back.

Uthiel landed harshly and felt his breath leave him. Above him Solanthur brought his blade down towards Uthiel's chest. Uthiel reached up with both blades in a cross and blocked the strike.

Instead of pressing his attack Solanthur stepped back, his face unreadable. Uthiel surged to his feet but the first captain held up his hand to stop the fight.

"Little brother," said Solanthur. "With both of your swords committed to the block, just what were you intending on using to stop my next strike? Do you think I am some meat headed warlord who doesn't know how to put down a little pup like you?"

There were a few harsh laughs from the veterans watching the duel, but Solanthur's face remained stoic. Uthiel felt his cheeks redden and he re-took his stance, refusing to rise to the barb and provide a retort of any kind. Solanthur raised his eyebrow before slowly taking a fighting stance, this time with both swords at hip level and the blades again pointing to Uthiel's face. Uthiel attacked.

Their blades met and met again, each time ringing out as the dull edges crashed together. Solanthur moved with grace and smoothly transitioned from attack to offensive defence. It was like watching a dancer. Nothing Uthiel did seemed to surprise the first captain. It was like fighting someone who knew what you were going to do three heartbeats before you did.

Uthiel desperately tried to keep a cool mind. As the duel wore on, Solanthur began to land more and more harsh blows against his armour until Uthiel finally snapped, surging forward with a roar and putting his weight and strength behind his pauldron as he shoulder barged the first captain. Solanthur swivelled away at the last moment, taking only a glancing hit, and cracked the flat of his blade against the back of Uthiel's unprotected head. Uthiel saw stars and fought to keep his consciousness and feet.

His vision blacked out for the briefest of moments and he awoke to find himself on his knees. Putting his hand on the ground for balance he pushed himself back to his feet. Solanthur moved towards him once more. Uthiel snarled and lashed out but it was a wasted effort. The strike missed Solanthur altogether. A dull blade thudded heavily into the back of Uthiel's knee, which collapsed his leg, and he found himself upon his back once more.

Solanthur turned away and pointed his blade at Branor. "You next. Come here and let me get your measure."

"Not yet... first captain."

Uthiel stood wavering on his feet once more. He was in a stance that imitated Solanthur's first stance, the two rounded points of his practice blades levelled at the first captain's face. The briefest grin crossed Solanthur's face as he moved in. It wasn't the cruel grin he shown at the start of the fight, but one of a slowly growing respect.

This respect did not show in his dispatching of the young knight however. Uthiel stabbed out dumbly and in a move that was both fluid like water and fast like a lightning strike Solanthur dropped both his swords, blocked Uthiel's blade with his vambrance, and knocked the youth out cold with a vicious punch that drew a spray of blood from his cheek. Uthiel's feet left the ground and his consciousness momentarily left his body.

"Did I win?" Uthiel's pounding headache was made all the worse by the roaring flood of laughter that rolled over him. He opened his aching eyes to see a circle of faces staring down at him. Some he knew, some he didn't. One of his hands still gripped the handle of a blade, but he couldn't work out which one it was yet. Looking down his body he could see he was on the ground. Somebody had removed his gorget and he could feel warm wetness drooling down his cheek.

Branor's face came in to view, a smile on all of it except for his eyes. "And you used to be so pretty, brother."

More laughter.

Uthiel frowned as he was helped into a sitting position. The world around him swayed for a brief moment until he properly reattached himself to his surroundings. At his feet he saw the first captain looking over the shoulder of one of the men. Solanthur gave him a brief nod and then turned away, calling over his shoulder for Keldon to bear arms and face him.

Uthiel was helped up and leaned heavily on Branor as they watched Keldon face off against Solanthur. "By Armenius Uthiel, you used to be a lot lighter also," complained Branor sourly.

Keldon fought with blade and buckler and gave a good account of himself before being bested. Lokhi was next. Branor was called out last. He passed Uthiel on to the nearby Carn and strode out with his buckler and sword. Three sword clashes later, Branor found himself on his back. He made to get up to continue the duel but Solanthur rested the tip of his blade on the top edge of Branor's gorget, just below his chin, to signal an end to the training bout.

"That will be all, brother," said Solanthur. "I tire and we must look to training the whole company, not just you five. I have the measure of you now."

Solanthur offered his hand to Branor and helped the young knight to his feet. Branor moved back into the ranks of Grey Wolves, away from where Uthiel stood under his own power now, his face sullen and stormy. Keldon couldn't help himself.

"Ah, brother Branor!" he called out. "Three strokes and you're done, no wonder the camp whores charge you so little. They could fit in ten sessions with you in the time it takes to please the mighty Keldon!"

Branor laughed with the others but it was only Uthiel that saw the intense hurt and embarrassment beneath his friend's façade. After the day's training was complete Uthiel approached Branor.

"My friend," started Uthiel. "Not much better than a hard day's training with your brothers under Armenius' gaze!"

Branor did not respond, his angry eyes not meeting Uthiel's.

"Bran?" continued Uthiel. "What is the matter? Was it the practice duel this morning?"

Branor's eyes rose at this. There were red thunderhead storm clouds in those eyes.

Uthiel took the opportunity Branor's silence gave him to keep going and try to soothe his friend with levity. "You saw the first captain beat all of us. There was no shame in being bested by the greatest swordsman in the Order. Look, he even gave me a new scar to impress the camp whores!"

Branor still did not respond, instead turning and walking away without a word. Uthiel chased after him, laughing and reaching out to put his arm around him. Branor turned and shoved him away.

"Get off me!" he spat.

Uthiel let the force of the shove take him a few paces away from his friend with shock written all over his freshly stitched face. "Bran? What was that for? What is your problem, brother?"

Branor turned on his heel and face Uthiel.

"My problem?" he snarled. "You! You are my problem! *Uthiel* slew the warlord in single combat. *Uthiel* manages to land a shoulder on the first captain and gain his respect. *Uthiel, Uthiel, Uthiel!*"

Uthiel was instantly taken aback by the poison on his friend's tongue.

"Bran?" was all he could manage in the storm of Branor's rage.

"Do you know how many times I saved your life while we fought that warlord? Do you?"

Uthiel shook his head dumbly.

"Do you have any idea how many times we all saved your life? Linton died at your back and you didn't even bloody notice! Your cloak was dragged through his blood as you gallivanted around with that bastard with your precious two bloody swords!" by this point Branor was shouting and had drawn the eye of some of the other veterans nearby.

Keldon rushed over. "If my barb earlier offended you, I apologise Bran, but this is unbecoming!"

Branor fixed him with his raging gaze. "I don't care about your barb! What I care about is this bloody glory hound pretending like he is bloody Armenius reincarnated! What about us!? What about Linton? And what about Eliem and Umbar? Did they die just so this buffoon could make a name for himself?"

Uthiel still couldn't believe what he was hearing. His mouth worked but nothing came out. Branor's eyes narrowed.

"Nothing to say for yourself? Waiting for me to say something funny and make it all better?" snarled Branor.

Uthiel didn't respond. He couldn't. Even Keldon backed away, such was the ferocity in Branor's words.

"You are no longer my friend. You are no longer my brother. You are nothing!" shouted Branor, the last few words coming out in a scream.

Uthiel's eyes dropped to the earth and he remained unmoved for some time while all around him was still and silent. With a dumbfounded nod to himself he turned and began to walk away.

"Not even the courage to speak up for yourself. Even bloody Keldon said something," then Branor's eyes narrowed once again with intent. "Coward."

Uthiel stopped dead, his hand reaching to his waist for a sword that wasn't there. When the hand felt no purchase his other hand reached for a sword over his right shoulder and once again groped at air. Branor felt his face twist into a smirk as he stared at Uthiel's back. He watched as his childhood friend took a deep breath. Then another. And the tall form of the man he'd known since birth disappeared into the crowd that had gathered around them. The first captain stood there staring at him.

Branor's face fell as he realised what he had done. Inside he recognised his righteous rage for what it really was. Jealousy. Uthiel had bested a foe that would surely have seen him with an axe buried up to its haft in his chest. Uthiel had led them to glory for three months. Shame filled him. He couldn't meet anyone's gaze for fear of what he might see there.

I am the coward. Too afraid to meet the stares of my brothers. Is that what it is? Am I?

No, it wasn't for fear of what he might see in those awkward stares. Branor knew what he would find. He knew there would be scorn from his brethren. He knew they would shun him. But they didn't know what he and his brothers had been through. They judged without truly knowing him. They would all take Uthiel's side, as usual. Head and shoulders low, he moved through and away from the crowd, the embers of his jealous anger still smouldering within.

CHAPTER SIXTEEN

A young knight stormed through the Secundan camp like a lone thunderhead through clear sky. Soldiers, knights, auxiliaries, and slaves nearby snapped their heads around for a moment as his seething rage grasped their attention for a fleeting moment. One of those watchers turned away before turning back quickly, surprise across his aged but handsome face. Two almost translucent blue eyes flashed with a father's recognition.

Uthiel fumed like never before in his young life. His heart and his head pounded. His fists clenched and unclenched, dirty nails leaving a line of small red half moons on his palm. He stopped, turned, stormed a few steps, stopped, turned in another direction and continued. His clenching jaw quivered with rage. *How could he call me that? After all we have been through as brothers, how could he call me that?*

With a sharp growl Uthiel struck out, his fist connecting with a solid crack against a tree trunk. The pain in his knuckles didn't even register as his vision went red and he cocked back his fist to strike the wood once again. A hand grabbed his wrist in a grip of iron. Uthiel whirled around, and with the base of the palm of his free hand, smashed the hand away.

Immediately a look of clarity crossed his features and Uthiel dipped his head. "Father."

Tanin Caellar stood before his son, ignoring the pain the strike had caused his wrist. Before him his boy was a picture of barely suppressed anger. He could almost see Uthiel's broad and well muscled physique shaking with rage and those eyes, a mirror version of his own, were locked on his with such intensity he feared he may have wilted were it not for the knowledge his own blood would never knowingly strike him.

"Uthiel, my boy," soothed Tanin, as he reached out and put a hand on his son's shoulder and felt the muscles under the grey tabard bunched like a predator a moment before striking.

Moving forwards, he brought Uthiel into a warm embrace. Uthiel resisted for a moment but Tanin persisted and gradually felt the tension begin to recede from his son. A smile cracked Tanin's face as he felt his son's arms reciprocate the embrace.

"My boy," said Tanin. "Come, it looks like you need to get something off your chest. Let us go enjoy the clear air and speak of what troubles you."

He pulled back from Uthiel. The boy had relaxed somewhat but there was still something in his eyes that raged or hurt with burning intensity. He put his arm over Uthiel's shoulders and led him away from the massive crowds of soldiers starting up campfires, eating, laughing or carousing with the camp whores. It was a long time before a further word was spoken between the two. Tanin led them to a tipped-over baggage carriage with a snapped axle and they both sat down with their backs to the wooden vertical tray.

They sat a while, just watching the thousands of men move about their duties or using their free time as they pleased. Tanin turned to Uthiel. The rage in his eyes seemed to have dimmed and the boy appeared fine just to sit there and stare, but it was not Tanin's nature to leave the hurt he had seen in his boy's eyes go.

"Uthiel, there are times when it is best to hold yourself in check and there are times when it is best to seek out someone you trust and gain their council. I am here to listen and help if you would like mine."

For a while it looked like Uthiel had decided to ignore him. Tanin opened his mouth to try a different approach when Uthiel's head dropped and his eyes closed.

"Father," came Uthiel's voice, quiet and soft, "have you ever been... blamed for something you knew you did not do?"

Tanin thought for a moment.

"There are always the friends and families of the men lost under my command," he responded. "Despite the assumed glory of winning a battle, their eyes always accuse you of what their voices do not. I lost their son. I sent him to his death. It is the burden of command any man must deal with when his men are lost."

"That's... that's not exactly what I mean," said Uthiel, working the words out slowly and purposefully. "Have you ever been blamed by someone you loved as a brother? By someone, though not your kin, who may as well have your father's blood flowing through his veins?"

Then it made sense to Tanin in one clear instant. "Is this person Bran?"

Uthiel's face hardened for a moment. "Yes, father."

"Tell me."

Uthiel paused again, for a far longer moment this time before he launched into his story. He told Tanin of the fight in which he and Branor were bested by a superior swordsman. Of the horrors they had seen in the towns while tracking the foe. Of the ambush they had survived and fought through. Of the three months of hard living and of the brothers they had lost in that time and finally Uthiel spoke of the fight with the barbarian warlord.

How did I let this happen to my boy?

Tanin kept finding himself having to close his mouth. In the months of campaigning with the Lord Pomen, at times he had forgotten that there was a good chance his son was at the forefront of the fighting. He'd forgotten that his son was a knight and had been training for many years for just such a war to assail Secunda.

Some father I turned out to be.

He noticed Uthiel trying to speak of the part his brothers had played in the battle without adding any real detail to their plights or deaths. He saw a tear run down his son's face as he told of the two friends he had lost on that rise, brothers who had died defending his back so that he may kill the warlord. And then finally he got to the crux of the problem. Branor.

"Father, I don't understand," said Uthiel. "Bran and I have been brothers since birth! We ran the same streets as children, competed in the same trials as young men, and went through the same fights over the last four months. And yet he insults me! Calls me a coward and a glory hound! How can he say that!?"

Seeing Uthiel's ire begin to rise, once more Tanin interrupted.

"My boy, what happened after you killed the Warlord? Put yourself in Bran's shoes for a moment."

Uthiel stopped for a moment and thought, rubbing a calloused hand over his eyes and face and then his light beard. He looked up to his father.

"I know what the problem is."

Tanin nodded, already knowing what Uthiel would say next. "Tell me."

"I was credited with the victory. I have been called a hero. I am receiving a gift from the lords of my Order. My brothers aren't. Branor is mad because he thinks he and I are no longer the same. He believes I have put myself above him."

Tanin nodded. "I think you are right."

Uthiel made to stand, but Tanin stopped him. "Let him cool off, son. Do you remember when your mother hit me with a rolling pin just before you went into one of your first trials as a boy?"

Uthiel raised his eyebrow questioningly.

"Indulge your old man," said Tanin.

"Yes, I guess so," responded Uthiel.

"Do you remember Lonetta? Antony's wife?"

"Yes, what is..."

Tanin cut him off again, chuckling to himself as his eyes went to the sky nostalgically. "Well, a few hours before that she had seen me talking to Lonetta, not yet knowing that she was Antony's wife.

"We had a disagreement, and when your mother wouldn't listen to me, I told her that she had a skull thicker than a bull's arse cheek."

Uthiel snorted and laughed, the sound music to Tanin's ears.

"As you can imagine, despite me being right, your wonderful mother was more than a little upset at this and stormed off. Instead of letting her anger simmer out and apologising later I chased her straight away and received this for it," chuckled Tanin, fingering a scar on his eyebrow.

Father and son sat and laughed for some time, reminiscing about happier days gone by when their lives had not been turned upside down by war. They spoke of times when Uthiel did not wear the tabard of the Grey Wolves and Tanin did not stand at the head of thousands of soldiers. Tanin's heart lifted as he watched some of the hurt and anger wash away from his son. He very carefully ensured any conversation was steered away from mentioning Branor, which was incredibly difficult as the young man was as much his son as Uthiel was.

Listening to his son speak of his youth as a part of his family swelled Tanin's breast with so much pride and happiness he thought he would burst. He had long resigned himself to accepting there would be many times in life when Uthiel would have no recollection of a moment that Tanin looked back on with such affection but now, he realised that Uthiel held many of those same memories close to his heart. Obviously being covered in six-month-old Uthiel's regurgitated breast milk was a bit beyond the lad, but playing Armenius versus some evil monster as they both charged around the house and wrestled was there. Tanin felt a dampness in his eyes and faked a cough to excuse wiping it away. He had not known such happiness for many years.

Just as he felt he could almost forget they sat on the fringe of a massive war camp a figure strode through the tents and groups of men, garbed in full plate armour covered by a grey tabard. The plate was freshly repaired and polished, and looked glorious on the bareheaded veteran who wore it. He stopped before Uthiel.

"Brother Uthiel, the first captain has requested we attend him," said the man. "We are to scout forward to Gall. Best you get your armour, lad."

Tanin chest clenched. *No! He can't go with you!*

Uthiel sucked his teeth and nodded. "Brother Carn, this is my father, Tanin Caellar. general of the Secundan Fifth."

Carn nodded in respect to Tanin. "I have heard of you, general. It is my honour to fight alongside you and your son."

Tanin stood and offered his hand in a warrior's handshake. Carn took his outstretched forearm in a strong grip and Tanin could see the measured respect in the knight's eyes. Carn looked once more to Uthiel.

"Brother, we must away. It is not wise to keep the first captain waiting."

Then turning to Tanin, Carn continued. "Armenius watch over you in the days to come, general."

"And you, Carn," responded Tanin.

Carn turned and left back into the thick of the camp. Uthiel stood beside Tanin. Tanin turned to face his son and placed a hand on each of Uthiel's shoulders.

"My son, may Armenius shield you. Share a word with the Eternal Lord with your old man?" said Tanin, dropping to one knee.

Uthiel dropped to his knee also and pressed his forehead to his father's as they closed their eyes and faced the earth. "My soul, my blood, my life for you my Eternal Lord. Praise be to you Armenius, for my life and my family's I thank you."

Both men stood and embraced, one last time. With a nod and without further word, Uthiel turned and was soon lost from his father's sight. *No. Please don't go, my son. How can I protect you when our duties call us apart? What sort of father am I to allow duty to pull me from my last remaining son?*

Tanin sighed, already missing his son. With a deep breath he steadied himself and began the walk back to his men. In a whisper meant only to be heard by his Eternal Lord, he prayed once more that Armenius would watch over his son.

Nikhael stood, aghast at what he was seeing. Brothers he had fought beside and thought to be the very best of men were laughing as they herded three young women to a stable. Three young women they had sworn to protect stood mud – and blood – covered and bare to the winter cold. They screamed in fear, begged to know what was happening, why they were about to be raped by men they had up until a few days ago viewed as valiant saviours.

Nikhael began to walk forward but stopped himself, much to his own disgust and shame, as the realisation of what would happen should he speak out sunk in. Already six of the treacherous Knights Aggressor had been beheaded for speaking out against their lord's actions, caught on the wrong side of treason most foul. Nikhael gritted his teeth and inwardly cursed his weakness as one of the women locked eyes on him and latched on to the sympathy there.

She was young, and under different circumstances Nikhael would have found her very beautiful. Light skin, dark long flowing hair and light blue eyes. She had a slim, curvy and attractive body with long lean legs and large breasts that Nikhael should have found arousing. But that skin was covered in mud and filth and blood, that hair was matted and tangled, those eyes were red rimmed and desperate, and that body was bruised and beaten. *And my cowardice is as much a cause as my brothers' fists.*

She ran towards him, one arm reaching out to him and one holding back her bouncing chest, trying to break the circle of knights around her but she was brutally struck and sprawled to the mud in a flurry of pale white limbs and dark hair. She screamed as she desperately scrambled backwards and away from the knight who had struck her. Blood streaked over her lips from a broken nose as once more she locked her eyes on Nikhael.

All the young man could do was avert his eyes in disgrace as two of the knights pinned her to the ground while a third dropped his pants and hefted up his mail skirt.

"I'm sorry," whispered Nikhael. "Armenius burn my soul, I'm sorry."

He turned away from the sight and the sounds of screams as the other two women were set upon in kind by those he had once known as brothers. Walking through the town, he stepped swiftly as he moved to its outskirts and avoided the atrocities being committed within its borders. Everywhere he went, he ran into small bands of barbarian warriors, some of whom eyed him warily while others stared at him with downright hostility.

All around him as he moved, there were people being forced into slavery. They were raped, tortured, beaten, and humiliated in a hundred different ways. How these people had survived this long Nikhael would never know. It pulled at what remained of his soul the hardest when he saw people of the same pedigree as himself, people who had relied on him and his brothers to protect them.

Turning again, he looked up to the White Frontier fortress. The village of Archenon Creek, in which he now stood, would never be the same again. If by some miracle he survived all this, Nikhael promised whatever god may still listen to him that he would come back here and salt the ground so that such evil may never find souls walking its earth to feast upon again.

How have I become so lost? Nikhael, for the first time since he was a boy, barely old enough to remember being alive, wept. Fat tears rolled down his cheeks and spittle dribbled onto his ragged beard. Remembering where he was, he slammed his helmet on. Weakness would not do. If a barbarian saw a chink in his metaphorical armour he would be challenged. Knight training and armour or not, if a few of that barbarian's friends joined him, Nikhael would die.

For the first time in months, his thoughts moved back to his friends. He thought of the often dour Uthiel, the ever laughing and playful Branor, Linton with those oversized ears, and the ever boastful Keldon. The thought of his childhood friends made him smile for a moment. He chuckled to himself as he remembered the fights Uthiel and Amorn used to get in to. For a moment he forgot himself and chuckled sadly at the memory of when Amorn had found out Uthiel had deflowered his little sister.

A scream followed by a solid and wet crunch broke his reverie. More screaming; two voices. Then another wet crunch. Then a third. Then silence. Nikhael knew what had happened before his legs had got him back into the centre of Archenon Creek.

When he made it to the town square he felt his gorge rise as he saw the warrior Kael pointing up and directing one of his dark brothers in the tying up, by the hair to a leafless tree, of three decapitated female heads. Nikhael bit his tongue as he saw the beautiful blue eyes and dark hair of the girl who had reached out to him swaying dully from a low branch. Those accusing eyes seemed to lock on his, even in horrific death, and he felt his shame peak.

He turned once more to leave and almost walked straight into Lord Irill. The lord stood watching the proceedings and Nikhael made to pass him by. The lord reached out and grabbed him by the pauldron.

"Brother, stay a while. Remove your helm," he said in a low voice.

"As you wish, lord."

He took off his helm, tactfully swiping a dirty hand over his face in an attempt to cover up any tear streaks on his cheeks.

"It has been noticed, young brother, that you do not partake in the frivolities of our Order as we march on Gall," said the lord, aloof in his manner.

Nikhael could find no response. To speak in agreement of what he saw going on around him would see the final shred of his morality and the remaining whisper of his soul torn from him. To speak his mind and utter the words of disgust that caught in his mouth would see him dragged before Kael and beheaded.

The Lord Irill continued. "Secunda is gone. Our home is no more. All of its people are slain and all those you once held dear are gone. Gone is our king, too cowardly to come support us or too pathetic to defend his people. Gone are the oaths that bound us to a deity long passed. Gone is the notion of honour we once had forced upon us. Gone are the shackles of restraint that stopped us from waging war as real men should."

Despite the horror of the last few days, Nikhael still could not believe what he was hearing. How could they all betray everything they had believed in for centuries? How could this lord of Secunda be so carefree about the atrocities his men were committing? Not for the first time since the betrayal, Nikhael wished Amorn had slain him. Cursed with this life, his usually unflappable demeanour and his faithful soul had deserted him, *and rightfully so.*

"You can live and fight as you want, Nikhael. What more could a knight ask for in life?" asked Irill, his delivery gathering enthusiasm and momentum.

"Tomorrow, we leave the frontier to go start a new kingdom within the almighty walls of Gall. Lord Kael has promised that the city is all but cleansed of its previous occupiers and we can start afresh there.

We'll breed a new race of knights with the women captured and enslaved there. We'll have thousands of slaves for the mines left in the mountains of our previous homeland. And we'll be the rulers of a land that stretches from the lands of the barbarians all the way through the four nations of the Lands of the Light! We'll be like gods walking the land lording over a warrior people far stronger than any race we have ever been a part of!"

By this point Lord Irill had grabbed Nikhael by the pauldrons and his eyes, burning brightly with ambition, were locked on the young knight's. Nikhael forced his face to feign his usual nonchalance, lined with a light coating of false excitement at the prospect he'd been presented with. He knew, with absolute certainty, that to allow his facade to slip for one moment would see his lifeless body thrown atop the pile of men he had once called brothers.

Inwardly Nikhael raged at himself. Where and when he had lost the courage to face his convictions with his life he was unsure, but standing here as a lord of his once proud Order spoke treasonous words turned his stomach. But what truly disgusted Nikhael was the knowledge that, after the visage he had maintained all the way from youth to his adult life, his courage was no better than the next man's. It had a breaking point. The Black Wolves and the betrayal of his lords had taken him past his.

"Are you with me, brother?" asked Irill.

Nikhael paused a moment until he finally felt himself fall into the great abyss within him.

"Lord, I am with you."

CHAPTER SEVENTEEN

Two days hard march through the outskirts of Gall in full plate armour had left Uthiel and his brothers tired and on edge. They were in enemy held territory and every moment they risked being caught or ambushed. Uthiel felt calm, despite being physically tired, the experience of having lived and fought behind enemy lines for three months serving him well. As they moved, every now and then Uthiel allowed his thoughts to float back to his father.

The chance meeting with Tanin had done his spirits good. To speak of older, happier times when life was far simpler and less violent had allowed the sun to shine upon his heart once again. Then his mind turned to Branor as the man's armoured back passed his field of vision. Uthiel had tried to apologise to his estranged friend the day before they left camp.

Branor had said he'd accepted the apology, but offered none of his own as he normally would when the two had fought as youths. Uthiel could still see the hurt and anger in his eyes and knew that the schism between them was not over. It would come to a head one day and Uthiel dreaded it already but there was nothing more he could do about it right now.

Twenty paces ahead, he saw the leather-gloved fist of First Captain Solanthur Verutus as it rose into the air. Uthiel stopped and dropped into a crouch. He rested his hand on the pommel of Ghurkar's sword on his hip and smiled for a moment as he looked at his new vambrances, a gift from the Lord General Thomak. The shining pieces of armour had an outer ridge that ran from his elbow to the base of his palm farthest from his thumb.

The thick ridges allowed him to use his vambrances like a reinforced shield and block strikes, allowing him to get rid of his scavenged buckler. Along the shining metal ridges 'Shield of Secunda' had been painstakingly scribed by one of the Order's armourers. Uthiel grinned as he remembered the Lord Thomak explaining how the vambrances had belonged to a famous first captain with the same first name as he, a distant ancestor of the Lord Pomen. The Lord Pomen himself had supposedly approved Uthiel to wear his ancestor's pauldrons. Uthiel had been honoured beyond words.

A whisper came back through the knights of the first captain's command, calling him and Keldon forward. Uthiel looked to Keldon, who had his crossbow drawn and ready to shoot. In unison the two brothers ran forward at a crouch to kneel by the first captain. Solanthur turned to them and waved them forwards.

"Brothers, move forward and see what lies over that rise ahead. There should be a large town and I need to know if friend or foe occupies it," said the first captain.

With a nod, both the brothers moved out. Uthiel drew Ghurkar's blade but kept his other hand free as he pumped his legs forward. Keldon kept pace, his crossbow at the ready, as they cut through some low-lying scrub and crossed a dirt road on their way to the rise. As the two came to the top of the rise, they both dropped to their bellies and wriggled forward, the action made difficult by the bulk of their armour.

Their helmetless heads crested the rise and looked down to see the burnt-out remnants of yet another Gall town. The town must have held perhaps ten thousand citizens once. Instantly Uthiel knew what he and his brothers would find. He was about to stand and wave an all clear to the first captain when he spotted movement.

A small child, probably no older the six or seven, stumbled through the ruins. His mouth was agape and screaming in the way that only the pure terror of the innocent can. Without thinking Uthiel made to stand, but was pushed roughly to the ground by Keldon. Uthiel looked at him questioningly until he saw Keldon's eyes locked on something down there.

Uthiel turned back to the scene below him and stared hard at the buildings surrounding the child. Blackened husks of wood and stone stood like the still upright corpses of a butchered people. He stared a few moments more, trying to catch movement, but saw nothing. A rustle behind him alerted Uthiel to someone else's presence. He rolled on to his side, ready to spring forward with his blade, and saw the first captain crawling to them.

Uthiel turned to look at Keldon, whose eyes had not moved an iota, and then looked back down to the town. The child still sat there, screaming like his flesh were aflame. Keldon reached out an arm and pointed as the first captain came to rest beside Uthiel.

"Seven buildings up the main street, right hand side, second floor," he whispered. "Look for the shape of an arm."

Uthiel squinted hard, his eyes beginning to hurt with effort. Then finally, he saw it. A lighter piece of skin stood out against the burnt-out backdrop in which it hid. For a long agonising moment it didn't move and then with a slight flinch Uthiel saw it was a part of a greater whole as the barbarian shifted his weight. He turned to the first captain.

"Ambush," rumbled Solanthur.

"Agreed, first captain," said Keldon. "Looks like a small one though, I can only see a few other signs of people."

"Clustered around the child?" asked Solanthur.

"Yes, first captain. That I can see. That boy must have been sitting out there for hours waiting for us," responded Keldon.

Solanthur licked his lips, staring hard ahead. "I'll send some more brothers to you soon. When they get here, skirt the

234

town and come in from an angle to avoid the trap. We'll ensnare their ambush and slaughter them all. Leave none alive."

Uthiel and Keldon nodded as Solanthur ran back to the main column. Keldon was still looking into the buildings around the child, but Uthiel now tried to look for an area where they could cross the twenty pace gap between the first buildings and the cover of the rise. Tapping Keldon on the pauldron he pointed to a place some two hundred feet to the right. Keldon looked over and nodded his agreement.

Behind them they heard men moving through the soft grass towards them and they turned to see Branor, Tarren, and Linton, being led by Carn. Uthiel put up a hand to stop them and he and Keldon made their way back down to their brothers.

"Have you found a way in, brothers?" asked Carn.

"Yes brother," said Keldon. "If we skirt this rise about two hundred feet to the right, we can move into town under the cover of some bushes. It'll take us a little while to cut through the town and get into position but we'll catch them unawares."

Carn grinned. "Then let's go."

The six men loped off at a steady run as they made their way to their entry point. Each knight held down scabbards and swaying bucklers to keep their noise to a minimum. Soon they were all looking to the short run they had to make over open space into the town. The risk was not being shot at by archers, as they would only be in the open for mere heartbeats. No, the risk was being seen and having the forces waiting in ambush for them change tactics.

Carn looked to Uthiel and gestured with his head. *You first.* Uthiel drew his Tadel blade from over his shoulder and, in a heart-hammering burst of speed, powered his way over the short clearing and came to rest against the single remaining black wooden wall of a demolished house. His heart pounding in his ears, he listened desperately for any sign that he had been seen. After a few deep, calming breaths he turned and waved to the next brother to run over.

Branor was next. The knight sat next to Uthiel for but a brief moment before moving away with a quiet shuffle to the opposite end of the wall without looking at Uthiel once. Uthiel smarted for a moment before getting his mind back on the job, his head racing to remember his training not long past. Spinning on his heel, he ran in a crouch towards the end of the wall and peered around.

Before him, the desolation of yet another large town spread out. The sight of the murdered bodies of the Gall citizens didn't even cause the flicker of an eyelid anymore and he stared across them with the same indifference as he looked past piles of rubble from charred buildings or barricades. Seeing nothing moving, he turned and signalled to his brothers and in a single file stream they quickly moved across to him.

In an arrowhead formation, the brothers then began to move quietly through the destroyed buildings towards their targets. As they moved, Uthiel drew his second sword. As his heart began to pick up speed at the exertion of their movement and the thrill of the battle to come, Uthiel began to smile. To not be in command and responsible for people's lives let him revel in the simple excitement of impending combat.

They cut through gutted buildings filled with the bodies of entire families. Uthiel noted, almost without thinking, that he saw no women with their decapitated heads hanging above their naked bodies by their hair. The women had either been taken or had been slain in the same manner as their rest of the population.

Carn's fist rose in the motion for them all to stop. Uthiel checked his last steps to ensure they would not fall on something that might alert their prey to their presence before returning his gaze to the ruination around him. Nothing moved before them but still Carn stood motionless. With a few quick hand signals he split the group in half and sent them into a two-storeyed building.

Uthiel, Keldon and Branor moved together to the stairs as they watched Carn lead the rest into the ground floor. Uthiel went first, his swords pointing up from either hip as Solanthur had so harshly taught him. Keldon came second with his crossbow and Branor brought up the rear. Stepping as lightly as their armour allowed them, they moved up the wooden stairs. Uthiel cringed at any sound they made.

After what seemed like an age had passed, the three reached the summit of the stairs and began to look into the rooms to find their quarry. The first two rooms were empty. As Uthiel slowly peered around the doorframe of the third and final room, he saw his foe.

With his fur covered back towards them, a barbarian warrior stood in the shadow of the window. In his hands he held an un-drawn bow. The heavy head of an armour-piercing arrow was clearly visible in the wan light of the room. Leather armour with pieces of scavenged Secundan army mail hung from his well muscled form. Uthiel's lips drew back in a silent snarl.

Turning to Keldon and Branor, he handed each one of his swords before drawing his forearm length knife blade. Moving as silently as possible he stalked up behind the barbarian, doing his best to keep his arms and shoulders still to prevent his pauldrons from scraping on his gorget or cuirass. His steps were small and slow to prevent the rasp of his chainmail skirt from becoming audible His breathing was low and quiet.

Uthiel stopped dead as the barbarian grunted a moment and shifted his stance, only five steps away from Uthiel's drawn blade. The young knight waited a moment and then moved forward another step. A lone bead of sweat rolled down his nose and dripped to the floor. The barbarian did not notice. Uthiel took another step, and then one more. Finally, he struck.

With a strike that could only be likened to that of a snake, Uthiel drove the tip of his blade through the side of the barbarian's neck from behind, cutting the windpipe in half. Using the momentum of the blade, he cut the edge forward out the front of the throat, creating a clean cut from the spine forward and more than half decapitating the barbarian.

Uthiel grabbed the man quickly as his lifeblood pumped out, and lowered him to the floor. No sooner had he done that he heard the familiar twang of a crossbow as Keldon came to his shoulder and loosed a bolt in the one movement. Across the road a barbarian who had drawn his bow, with intent to fire on

Uthiel, fell backwards clutching at a crossbow bolt through his throat.

Almost as if that had been the trigger, the buildings around them exploded into life as the Grey Wolves' first company engaged the ambush. The battle was over in moments. As he heard the groups of knights call out their successes it pumped Uthiel's chest out when he heard no casualties amongst the knights. Some had taken wounds but none had suffered seriously.

Uthiel heard Carn call out to them. Branor called back, affirming their kill and absence of injury. Uthiel looked out the window onto the road that had been intended to be a killing ground for the knights. The first captain now stood there, looking up at his men. With a brief nod to some of those he could see, he called out to them.

"Come down, brothers. The army approaches. We move out before them and must clear the way to the city."

"What of the boy?" called out Uthiel.

Solanthur shrugged. "Gone. Duty dictates we move on."

Nikhael gritted his teeth as his heart threatened to hammer its way out of his chest. Before him the gruesome ritual that was unfolding was beyond that which he had ever seen before. Earlier in the day, Kael had come to them and proclaimed how tonight would see the Knights Aggressor Order inducted into the Black Wolves. He'd spoken of how they would rule the land with an iron fist and glory under the gaze of new gods.

The young knight had aged a lifetime in the last week or so, and he felt what little was left of himself inwardly writhe and whither at what Kael was saying and at what he was seeing. He had clenched his jaw even harder as those brothers around him had fallen to their knees at the mention of a new deity dedicated to the blooding of the earth. *Zhar T'hur demands purity of the land through blood,* he'd said. *Purity through blood,* his brothers had echoed.

Nikhael's soul railed weakly at the thought of what he was about to do. Before them, Kael spoke in a powerful and wicked voice. Behind Kael, the Black Wolves had teams of barbarians erect seven-foot tall trestles and tie young captive women horizontally to the top of the dark timber, bare to the elements and their faces screaming at the dark earth below them.

"My soon to be brothers," said Kael. "To purify the land we must first purify our souls, our bodies, and our armour. To purify these things that make us be, we need blood. Blood for and from our god. Blood is the blessing of Zhar T'hur. Blood, and the strength to spill it, is the gift Zhar T'hur offers: a strength to rule the land as He is brought forth for the Great Cleansing."

Kael drew a forearm-length blade and walked casually over to one of the trestles. Atop the trestle a girl Nikhael guessed to be no more that twelve fought her ropes desperately. She screamed and yelled and sobbed, spittle dripping from her lips in long lines, and her skin reddened and bled as the ropes ground against her flesh. Kael didn't pause for ceremony. He didn't stretch out her unavoidable fate with speeches or sermons.

The Black Wolf reached up with the blade and slit the girl's pale white throat. Her face lifted in shock for a moment, her eyes wide and her mouth open in a soundless scream as her lifeblood pumped out the gouge in her flesh. Kael stood below the wound as a hammering rain of blood sprayed over his bare face and his pauldrons, long rivers of red running down all over to eventually soak into the ground.

Mercifully, the girl bled out quickly and soon her even paler face hung limp and lifeless. Nikhael felt numb. He closed his eyes resignedly. There was no victory against evil such as the Black Wolves. There was no victory against what Nikhael himself was becoming. This was it. Either he made a stand and killed one or two traitors before he was slain, or he walked under a scared young innocent and finally accepted the full scope of his fate.

Nikhael opened his eyes. Before him was a blood-soaked aberration of mankind, a man whose soul had so succumbed to evil that Nikhael briefly wondered if there was in fact a soul within his crimson soaked Secundan armour. Kael offered him the handle of the blade he had used to snuff out the life of a twelve-year-old girl. The intent was obvious.

"Come, brother," said Kael. "It's time to join us. You have promise. A blank slate. My god could make you magnificent if you would but whet his appetite a little with your servitude."

Nikhael took the offered blade mechanically. The remnants of his soul stood on a knife edge. In one flash of movement he could drive the blade up to its hilt into Kael's throat. Just one flick of movement that could perhaps take some of the stain from him when he met Armenius. Would that be enough when he met the Eternal Lord? Could Armenius forgive him for what he'd done?

Nikhael gripped the knife handle hard, his knuckles cracking painfully. His eyes narrowed and his muscles bunched. He'd made his decision. As if in slow motion he felt his leg take a pace forward, towards Kael. His weight shifted forwards as it had countless times before in life. This was it. A single moment at a fork in his road to die for those he could not save or to embrace oblivion. In his mind he saw how his father and friends would react, saw his mother with tears in her eyes. It wasn't until a moment later that Nikhael could imagine if they were tears of grief stricken pride, or ashamed horror.

A second step took him straight past Kael towards the hundred or so whimpering young women who had been tied to the seven-foot tall trestles.

Some of them screamed. Some of them sobbed and moaned or prayed as they looked at the dead girl's slashed throat slowly dripping what was left of her to the dirt below. Some looked at him or other knights in disbelief, their faces agog. Few begged to be let free, promising what they could with their bodies or riches from families now burned to ashes. One or two screamed at him with hate, their eyes raging with baleful fire at their betrayal.

Nikhael looked at each one in turn, his eyes nonchalant and uncaring. For the first time in his life it wasn't a facade. Whatever good had been in the Secundan youth, in the face of such wholesale evil, had buried itself so far down in Nikhael it would never be found again. His cold eyes looked for a worthy sacrifice as a signifier of his new allegiance and the shedding of his previous self.

Each girl or woman he looked at locked eyes back with him for a moment. Some were pleading, some were challenging, some had surrendered. None fitted his need. Finally, a few rows into the small forest of waiting sacrifices, he found her. She was his age, perhaps a few years younger at most. She avoided his gaze and trembled. She was beautiful, perhaps the most beautiful girl Nikhael had ever set eyes upon.

Long pitch-black hair hung down the side of her face in a tight ponytail. She was lean and her skin was pure, albeit reddened where the ropes had been pulled tight to her flesh. Nikhael walked under her and looked up into her eyes, seeing the intense fear of the innocent there, and then walked down and looked over her body like a butcher sizing up a cut of beef. He noticed her redden with shame under his scrutiny. *Why am I smiling?*

He flicked the forearm-length blade in a carefree but well practiced twirl and walked back under her face to lock eyes with her again. A word bubbled from her lips. Nikhael didn't understand what she said. He cocked his head slightly as her eyes pleaded with him in a way her words could not. Again she tried to speak.

"Pl.. please... you're our protectors... help us..."

Nikhael's gaze switched from her eyes to the furiously pulsing vein in her neck. His arm moved like a lightning strike, cutting her plea short. Nikhael held his arms outstretched, his face to the sky and his eyes closed, the blade in his right hand trailing a short string of viscera through the air. He got one short, last, Armenius worshipping breath before the flood hit him.

It was hot and it gushed over his face, onto and into his armour, and finally spread to the shredded and dark remnants of what little soul he had left. He felt the sheer glory of what he'd just done. He revelled in the destruction of the girl and himself he'd wrought. He spread his lips and smiled, vermillion staining his teeth and the taste of sweet metallic blood coating his tongue.

Finally he understood the betrayal. He understood why he and many other of his brothers stood in the armour of Secunda, but not for any of the ideals the now undoubtedly destroyed city represented. As the blood flow began to falter and spit and spatter, Nikhael licked his lips and embraced freedom for the first time in his life.

He was free of the mores and rules of Secunda. He revelled in the gift of freedom from anything he'd willingly learned or been forcefully taught from the small amount of schooling from his youth to the hard training yards of the Order. Freedom to enact any facet of his will or whim upon others without mercy or compassion. Freedom to rule as they saw fit.

Nikhael's black soul matched his black eyes as they opened and looked into the dead stare of the beautiful girl that had been the giver of a new life of freedom for him. Nikhael smiled and cocked his head once more, a single name on his lips.

"Zhar T'hur," he said, specks of blood spitting from his lips. "My soul, my blood, my life for you, Zhar T'hur."

Behind him Kael smiled, his tongue flicking over his filed teeth.

"Oh yes, my brother," he said with sickening relish. "You most certainly do have promise."

Emilia tried to push the flecks of vomit from her messy dark hair with almost blue, shivering hands. Tears of rage and horror streamed down her face and dripped from her chin and nose to the churned up ground. Around her hundreds of naked women whimpered and screamed and cried in terror, as the barbarians bayed and laughed in their guttural tongue at the scene around them.

The young Gallite gritted her teeth and choked back further expulsion of what little food she had eaten in the last few days as her gorge rose again. Hot and bitter and fetid it still smelt better than the small town they were walking through. She wiped the tears from her eyes and faced what she was certain would be their immediate future.

Their bodies at least two days cold, forty young women had been brutally tied to trestles and drained through the throat. The muddy ground was still sticky with their leavings and the smell was abhorrent. The crows had had their feast already and many of the now swollen creatures basked their filthy black feathers in the dull sun.

Some of the young women around her fell to their knees and begged their captors to take them as slaves. Sex, cooking, sons; whatever they could possibly want. Emilia snapped at one older girl, the tension and fear inside her unleashing at the pathetic scene.

"You would beg these filth to be their bitch slaves?" she yelled, pointing at a group of leather – and fur – bound men. "You would spend your life being beaten on to your back to pop out little bastards to keep our people enslaved? Where is your dignity, woman?"

The girl looked up at her through red veined eyes, surging up to her knees. "What would you have us do? Be strung up and sacrificed like them? Be raped and then gutted like pigs? I want to live!"

There were some assenting voices amongst the women. The barbarians just looked on in bemusement. One of them, clad in disgusting heavy Secundan plate armour, leered at Emilia's young body. She ignored him, the last few days having leeched her of embarrassment.

"You fight with all you are worth to protect your dignity, as the gods would demand, not welcome their foul seed! If we are to die, we should take the blade's sweet release as women of Gall, not as willing barbarian whores," she responded icily, surprising herself with her own angry words.

There were a few murmurs of agreement. The girl stood up from her knees and came to eye level with her. "Easy for you to say. You've no honour left between your legs anyway. I heard about you and the Secundan. Slut."

The sound of Emilia's hand meeting the girl's cheek rang out across the camp. Emilia's eyes burned with such fury the girl visibly quailed before her, despite being the older of the two. The crowd of women around them stood in a silent circle.

Taking a moment to calm herself just enough to speak, Emilia stood straight and flicked the hair from her eyes. "When the barbarians tie me to a stake and send me to the gods, I will go as a woman of Gall who knew love, albeit for a short day. A woman who looked into a young man's eyes and saw someone worth my honour. I'll accept any ill will the gods may hold against me for that in the afterlife. You on the other hand... I'd like to say it saddens me to think of what the gods would do to you, but then that would suppose I had sympathy for a traitor to Gall."

The women around her let out a mixture of gasps of shock and shouts of agreement. There were curses hurled at the barbarians and the women who had been willing to surrender themselves. Black Lands leather and steel was spat upon and spattered with thrown mud as the crowd began to fight their oppressors. More than one girl or woman paid the price for their resistance with fresh bruises and breaks, and Emilia was among them, her eye swelling heavily after the barbarian in plate armour punched her in the face.

Dazed and upon the ground, tears of pain streaking down her cheeks and sobs bursting from her lips, Emilia found herself looking into her mother's eyes. Twice, the elderly face tried to speak to her and twice a sob cut her short. Emilia reached up, her soft, young hands touching the side of her mother's face, calming the woman enough to speak.

"My child, my beautiful child," she said. "I've never been so proud of you in my life. Never been so proud to be a woman of Gall."

Emilia smiled. There was a long moment's silence between the two as the chaotic scene around them continued with the women of Gall kicking and punching out at the laughing and taunting foe.

"However, what is this about you giving away your honour to some Secundan?"

Emilia's smile vanished. "Let us not discuss it, mother. Now is not the time."

"Whist, child, take my mind from this horror and tell me of the happiness of your first love."

"Father caught us. He beat him with a broom," Emilia let out a sharp laugh, the memory bright in her mind of her enraged father trying to beat up the powerful young knight. "Father beat a young knight of Secunda with a broom..."

Emilia stopped as she saw the ashen look of loss smash into her mother's face sure as if she had struck her with a fist. The young Gallite's head looked away as her mother tried to regain some sort of composure.

"Mother, I..." she stammered.

She looked up to see a sad smile on those familiar lips. "A young knight you say? Is he handsome?"

Emilia smiled, grimacing as her dry lips cracked and then wincing as salty tears flowed onto them. Wincing, she reached up her arms to hug her mother.

CHAPTER EIGHTEEN

Tanin Caellar felt his breast swell with pride as he marched at the head of his men beside the Lord Pomen. Just behind him, the black banner of the Secundan Fifth fluttered in the wind, the thinner white pieces of cloth with the names of their fallen rippled and curled at its side. His men marched in perfect rank, beaten and bloodied by the crucible of battle but straight backed and stern in the face of the greatest war of the last four hundred years.

But this was only a small part of the pride that Tanin felt, for before him, sitting atop a tall majestic horse and surrounded by hundreds of his personal bodyguard, was the king of Secunda. It took all of Tanin's self control to not run up to get a closer look like a fool-headed youth. From the fifty or so feet away that he was, he caught brief glimpses of shining silver and gold armour covered in scripture and stamped images through the masses of purple cloaks and tall horses.

Above the mass of bodyguards fluttered the king's golden banner. Golden weave upon a white background shone brilliantly in the light and Tanin felt himself and his men stand taller at the mere sight of the banner that the men who fought beside the Eternal Lord had carried. That banner, and the ancient last king of Mother Secunda had seen four centuries of Secundan armed might and every man who looked upon it felt the weight of ancestral responsibility that fighting beneath it brought.

They were a few days march from Gall at most and had met no resistance. They'd passed many signs of the progress of the Grey Wolves' first company in which his son fought. Small piles of barbarian bodies, emaciated and weakened by the winter and a lack of food, looked half starved and seemed to have offered little resistance for the knights scouting ahead of them. They had found two or three knights reverently lain to rest in graves with their swords stuck into the earth above their heads and their bucklers or shields leaning against the blades.

At the sight of these, Tanin had felt his heart miss a beat as he thought of Uthiel and hoped the brave souls sent to Armenius before him were not his beloved boy. There was absolutely nothing he could do to act on his paternal instinct to protect his last son. He took a deep breath, needing his mind in the here and now and focussed on the task of his men.

As he walked, he looked around him and took in the landscape. Much of it had been ruined and the Gall he had once marched through on his way to the White Frontier was no more. Towns still smouldered and stank of death. Bodies of Gall's citizens choked rivers and roadside ditches. In some places women had been butchered in a manner that Tanin struggled to comprehend, their rotting heads hanging by their hair from trees above their decomposing bare bodies.

Tanin took a deep breath and looked back to his king. Having never spoken to, or even been close to his king, it was amazing how the sheer presence of the man could lift his spirits. Tanin looked to the Lord Pomen who marched beside him, never seeming to tire despite his age. Pomen also had his eyes locked onto his king. Pomen caught him looking and turned to him with a smile on his face.

"A magnificent sight, is he not, my friend?" asked the lord.

Tanin smiled back and nodded. "The sight of him lifts my very soul, lord."

Tanin and Pomen's friendship had grown as they had commanded and fought side by side throughout the campaign. It had been a moment that Tanin hoped would last his lifetime when the Lord Pomen had offered him a small book as a gift one evening as they made camp. It was simple and leather bound and held many of the prayers he already knew by heart but on one of the spare pages at the very back of the book was the Lord Pomen's family prayer to Armenius.

He thought of one of the stanzas, the one he loved most, and prayed for his men;

> "As long as I fight in His name,
> And protect those that cannot protect themselves,
> The Eternal Lord shall be my shield."

"You like the prayer, then?" asked Pomen.

Tanin's eyebrows rose. "Apologies lord, I did not realise I spoke out loud."

Pomen rubbed his chin thoughtfully, pushing the folds of his skin around. "You know, no matter the situation, that prayer steadies my heart and soul. As long as I can draw a sword and heft a shield and fight the enemies of my land and the lands of our allies, I shall have purpose and I shall revel in life."

Tanin nodded. "I swear, lord, when we are done with this war and we have but a moment's respite, I shall have these words printed onto my skin. This will become my family's prayer in honour of you."

The Lord Pomen smiled again, despite the audaciousness of Tanin. "General Tanin, my friend, it makes me happy to hear that. They are fine words."

There was a long moment's comfortable silence as the two continued at the head of their column of brave Secundan souls.

"I have no sons, Tanin," said Pomen, all of a sudden. "No daughters, no family. No one to carry on my name."

Tanin was a bit taken aback by his friend's openness. He recovered quickly, sensing the great man beside him and his need to feel like his line would continue in some manner.

"My lord, you may consider me your brother, if I may be so bold," said Tanin in a heartfelt outburst. "And through me you have a nephew who will pass on your stories of glory and honour to his children and they on to theirs. It has been my life's honour to command at your side and to be counted amongst your friends. Allow me this gift."

Pomen allowed his last couple of steps to take him out of the line of marching troops and Tanin followed. Pomen turned and stood face to face. Tanin could see the glisten of a tear in the corner of the lord's eye.

"You have brought a ray of light into the darkness of this campaign," said Pomen. "And a little bit of hope to an old knight. I thank you, brother."

Tanin smiled and nodded, but offered nothing further.

"Now, my brother, let us make war," finished the Lord Pomen, indicating that Tanin should kneel as he himself was doing.

Lord Pomen led their prayer.

"As long as I fight in his name,
And draw the blood of those that would sully Mother
Secunda, for Him,
The Eternal Lord shall be my blade..."

Tanin's attention was distracted for a moment as a pair of well worn boots came to stand before him and a throat was cleared. Pomen and Tanin ignored the interrupter and finished their prayer before looking up as the man cleared his throat to gain their attention again.

"For to die in His name,
Is to be welcomed into His arms."

Tanin looked up and saw a captain of the army looking down at him. He stood up to his full height and the man saluted him. Pomen then stood beside him, his previous happiness gone with a flash of annoyance. The man shrank a little under the lord's well practiced withering gaze. Lord Pomen let the mood hang for a moment to allow the captain to understand his complete displeasure at the interruption.

"You would interrupt a family in personal prayer to our Eternal Lord?" asked Pomen rhetorically.

The captain made to respond but Pomen raised his hand for silence and was obeyed.

"I am disappointed. Who are you and what army are you from? You are not of the Fifth or the Seventh."

"Captain Trovel. Of the Twelfth, lord," said the man, straightening and obviously trying to harden his voice to sound more sure of himself than he was.

"Why are you here? You should be some ten miles away from here on the way home with the wounded," responded Pomen.

"I was given... special leave for the day to find a knight for... a personal matter," said the captain.

Tanin narrowed his eyes. *What are you hiding, captain?*

"Do you think me old and foolish?" asked Pomen casually.

"No, lord."

"Do you think I am bereft of any form of intelligence above that of a mule?" continued Pomen, his voice becoming even more hostile in its coolness.

"N... no, lord! I would not!" stammered the captain, realising his mistake.

"Then you have one more chance to be honest before I have you stripped of rank and flogged until I can see your ribs white through the flesh of your back," finished Pomen, moving forward a step to impose his presence further on the captain.

Captain Trovel licked his lips as his eyes darted around, as if he might find the right answers written in the dirt of the road upon which they stood. Finally he sighed and looked up to the lord.

"I am looking for the knight known as Ghurkar Storm. He travelled with the Twelfth with twenty of his men and a baggage train. We have a matter of honour to settle and as we are days from Gall, I would settle it now."

Tanin shook his head in disappointment. Pomen laughed dryly in the captain's face. The captain flashed red with anger and he opened his mouth but once again Pomen silenced him with a stern look and a raised hand.

"You forget yourself, captain," was all he said, but kept his hand up in the captain's face as he turned to Tanin.

"General Tanin, you will inform this piece of filth that even if he was enough of a man to not shit in his britches as soon as the mighty Ghurkar Storm drew his blade and took one stride in anger towards him, he will not be able to face him today, nor upon any other day.

"You will inform him that, like a true Secundan should, Ghurkar Storm gave his life in battle over three months ago. Like a true Secundan he put aside all petty squabbles and did his duty to the sacrifice of his own life. In fact, if I am not mistaken, he saved your son's life as his leader just before dying without fear and with the fire of the Eternal Lord in his heart.

"And finally, you will inform him that if I should ever, ever, lay eyes on his pathetic form again he had better be ready to challenge me and every other Grey Wolf who still stands after this bloody war is finished for to spit on one of our names is to spit on us all.

"Best he dies in some battle with the Twelfth and save me the effort of having to blunt my sword on his neck."

With that Pomen nodded to Tanin. "Good day, general, I shall see you at the front of our men once you have cleared this roadside of the waste upon it."

Pomen walked away and left Tanin with the agog captain. The captain's eyes were fit to burst with rampant fear mixing with anger at the insults of the lord. Tanin felt a sliver of rage run up his spine at the captain's sheer stupidity. Secunda needed her sons fighting together, not against each other. Tanin spoke his next words slowly and forcefully.

"I'll be having a word with your general once this is done, captain. You may take your leave."

The captain made to speak.

"You. May. Take. Your. Leave. Captain. Now."

The captain turned without further word and stormed away. Tanin rubbed his chin in annoyance, his heady mood from earlier gone. He quickened his step to a jog as he made his

251

way back to the front. He heard mutterings of approval at Pomen and his actions from some of the soldiers as he made his way back past them.

Soon he was back at the front of his men where he belonged. Again he glimpsed the king and he felt his spirits lift a bit. A water bearer came by and he accepted a long draught from the copper cup and then offered the cup to Pomen, who took it and drank gracefully. Before them they could see a small forest and on the other side a thin clearing around a burnt out town. A figure in the armour of a knight, a long distance away, stood upon the road waiting for them.

He had two swords, one on his left hip, and the pommel of the other coming over his right shoulder. Tanin's heart soared to see that young knight once more.

Uthiel stood upon the road, his patience wearing thin, waiting for the column of soldiers and knights to catch up to him, but his excitement at who was at the head of that column almost caused him to explode. He drank in the three hundred strong mounted group at the front of the column, resplendent in their beautifully worked armour and deep purple riding cloaks.

For the second time in as little as a month, he was about to meet the king of Secunda. As he drew closer, Uthiel dropped to a knee in the centre of the road and lowered his head in supplication. He could feel the very earth beneath him tremble at the beat of hundreds of hooves and thousands of boots that approached him. Inwardly he grinned, but on the outside he held his face firm, refusing to sully the order's honour in front of the king by being anything but professional.

A shadow cast over him. *This is it.*

"Report," said a deep voice, majestic and glorious.

Uthiel stood and faced his king, chest out, shoulders back and face proud.

"My king, we have cleared the town ahead. There was light resistance."

"Losses?"

Uthiel beamed under the gaze of the king and revelled in the glorious sight of the man closest to the Eternal Lord of them all.

"None slain and no wounded. We killed perhaps twenty of their number who laid in ambush either side of the main road," said Uthiel in a matter-of-fact manner to match his king's way of speaking.

"Well done. Please report to the first captain that he is free to continue. We shall do one last sweep of the town and its borders and follow with all haste. Next stop is Gall, Uthiel Caellar. The first captain is to find the army a point of entry and signal for us."

Uthiel couldn't believe the king remembered his name. He almost forgot to respond.

"Yes, my king," was all he could manage to stammer.

He looked past the king before turning away in the hope of seeing Tanin and smiled as he spotted the old general. Tanin waved. Uthiel waved back and whispered under his breath. "Armenius be with you, father."

The young knight turned and loped back up the road at a fast jog, eager to re-join the first captain and move on to Gall. They were only a day or so away from Gall and then they would discover what had caused the disappearance of their usually staunch ally. Uthiel wandered through the possibilities of what could have happened to such a great nation for it to sit and slumber when the land around it burned.

How could they have no show of force when their people were pillaged, raped and slaughtered on such a massive scale? How could the king of Gall just allow that? All those women and children; the barbarians had shown no mercy to any they had come across. Uthiel did his best to push the images of a murdered populace from his mind, of pale and bloodless heads swinging by their long hair lazily in the breeze, as he came upon the clearing and saw Branor and Keldon waiting for him.

They waved him over and he jogged to them, his chest puffing hard at the exertion of the run but his battle-bred and natural fitness countered it quickly.

"Brothers, you would not believe it! The king and his retinue are still with us. I made my report to him!" he exclaimed, his excitement prevalent.

Keldon smiled for him and clapped him on the pauldron. Uthiel barely caught the flash of annoyance that crossed Branor's face before he forced a smile on and grasped Uthiel's vambrance in a warriors handshake.

"Congratulations, brother."

Uthiel smiled at the support from his two best friends and laughed. "Come my brothers, we are to find and designate the entry point for the army at Gall. We go to see the city that saved our forefathers!"

Keldon smiled.

Branor didn't. "We also get to find out what happened to them that an entire army of barbarians was able to cross their lands unharried."

That broke the mood of levity quickly.

"By Armenius, Bran, I think I'd rather spend a night with death herself than you. I'm sure she'd be less gloomy!" said Keldon, laughing.

Branor shot him a look.

Uthiel put a hand on both his friend's pauldrons. "No Keldon, Bran is right. Gall had the largest armies of us all. Where are her soldiers? Where are the hundreds and hundreds of thousands of her refugees? We've heard of scant few from the others around the camp who marched from Secunda while we were in the wild. How do so many people just... disappear?"

Two days later Uthiel and his brothers strode in a spaced out arrowhead with Carn at its tip as they moved through a long grassed, but well trodden, field. The last two days had seen little action as they marched past the lands and townships surrounding the city of Gall. They had passed through ruined and burnt out towns that would have held anything from a few hundred people to tens of thousands.

Death had been everywhere but the danger of that death had long passed, leaving only a stench of human rot and burnt wood. This was a smell that Uthiel and his brothers in the first company were by now well accustomed to, a sad fact of the nature of the war they fought in and the sheer brutality and evilness of the enemy they faced.

If anything, each slaughtered town they passed through hardened them further. Uthiel found himself feeling less and less guilt at previous slayings of unarmed barbarians as they lay wounded on the ground after battle. The young knight began to feel the hot fires of hatred build within his breast, fires that were being fuelled every five or ten miles by the lingering forms of the massacred people of Gall.

Uthiel looked across the field to his right and spotted the small group of knights on their flank. He did not yet know their names but knowing they were knights of the first company and had trained and fought with the first captain for many years gave him confidence and put a smile of anticipation on his face. Soon they would be in Gall. Soon they would be in their element.

Before them, Carn stopped and dropped to his knee, bringing the tall grass clumps up to chest height. Uthiel and his brothers copied and their eyes started to scan their surrounding area for the cause of alarm. To their right, the veterans on their flank spotted them and also dropped to their knees.

Keldon had the stock of his crossbow at eye level and was panning from left to right methodically searching for targets. The veterans on their flank also had a single crossbowman searching the horizon. They knelt still for what seemed like hours to Uthiel. The sound of their small movements were almost lost in the rustling of the grass as the wind caressed it lovingly, creating light waves of movement through the yellow pasture.

Uthiel was momentarily struck by the beauty of what he was looking at. Here was nature in all of its glorious beauty. There were no bodies that he could see, no burnt out buildings, no smoke billowing into the low lying grey clouds in the sky, and most of all there was quiet. Screams of battle and pain and terror did not assault his senses in this place. Uthiel, for a short moment in his violent young life, felt the purity of serenity and peace.

He drew in a deep breath and smiled, licking his lips and almost wishing he could taste the sweet smell of spring on the horizon. He looked to his five brothers and in this moment he could truly feel the breadth of kinship he shared with these men. Most in his group were men he'd grown up with. They'd gone from playing at being knights with large pieces of bark stripped from trees and long sticks to being blooded on the proving grounds of battle over and over again.

A couple of feet to his right was Branor, a man who was so much more than a brother knight to him. As far as Uthiel was concerned, Branor was his brother by blood and their friendship had got him through the trials and tribulations of his life to this point. Branor didn't unleash his wide, cheeky grin as much anymore and his usually jovial demeanour had matured into something a bit quicker to anger and somewhat surly, but Uthiel still loved him like the true brother he was.

His view then shifted to Keldon as the knight continued to scan the horizon down the shaft of a crossbow bolt. Those stereotypical Secundan features usually so quick to boast and joke were now calm and concentrated, his breathing slow and rhythmical as he kept his mind clear and his eyes open for an opportunity. Uthiel turned away to the rest of his brothers.

The long white scar across Lokhi's forehead had served to harden his young face and Tarren's usually sour expression seemed almost tranquil. Kneeling at the front of them with eyes to the fore was Carn. Being many years their senior, he was well built and fit in well with the other brothers in the first company. His grey cloak covered his polished armour and since their elevation to the command of the first captain, his stride had found a new spring in it.

Uthiel knew that this was where Carn belonged. He was made to lead young knights into combat and they would do very well by his leadership. Uthiel smiled to himself as his eyes gazed back out to the windswept grassy field. He rested his left hand upon the pommel of the Tadel blade.

Right here, right now, at the spear tip of his king's forces, he knew he was exactly where he should be.

CHAPTER NINETEEN

Nikhael Rokarn strode towards the immense outer city wall of Gall. His armour was dark with unwashed dried blood and dirt, and an abhorrent version of the shining glory it had once epitomised. A thin leather loop hung from his hip, a ball of hair knotted on to it and the rotting head of the young lady he had slain atop the trestle some days ago bouncing around on the outside of his thigh and bearing witness to his plunge into darkness. His pitch-black hair hung lank down to his shoulders and his cloak was tattered and flowed stiffly in his wake.

They had marched for almost half a day through the outlying town that surrounded the wall. Through these areas he had seen and done things that his soul should have railed against. But Nikhael felt no remorse and cared nothing for the lack of it. He only cared for one thing. He only lived for one thing; the taking of life. For that brief heartbeat when the soul of the vanquished went screaming into the darkness, a light of savage glory sparked within him, fleetingly, and then it was gone.

He stopped for a moment and turned back to look over the gathered force advancing with him. Immediately behind him were Kael, the Black Wolves and the rest of his brothers.

He no longer cared for them beyond their ability to take him to the core of the fighting where he may take the highest tally for his new god. The more he took and the more brutally he took them, the more often Zhar T'hur would reward him with that heartbeat of life that he so craved, that flash that lit the darkness within.

Behind them came the thousands of barbarians, filthy meat shields and unworthy scum under Zhar T'hur's heels. Nikhael's lip rose in a snarl and then he laughed to himself. *They will serve their purpose.* Within the walls of Gall would see the Black Wolves' greatest offering to their god yet. Within those walls, Kael had promised, men like Nikhael would be touched by Zhar T'hur, blessed by their own terrible Red Father.

Within these walls, Kael had told them, was the Black Wolves' greatest work. Such worship, he said, had never been seen on such a scale. Such a sacrifice had never been made and such an opportunity for their god to manifest in the world of man may never come again. Nikhael usually put no stock in ritual and witchery, but his world had changed of late.

Since the lifeblood of the young maiden, which still clung to his body and armour, had flowed over him and the last vestiges of his old life had been banished to the far reaches of his mind, he felt a purity of purpose. There was nothing stopping him in the slaughter. Where some might baulk, he would charge in with his shield up and his sword ready to flay life from body. Where once notions of honour and decency held him back, he was no longer shackled.

Nikhael knew what it was to be truly free of the trappings of his abandoned people. Nikhael smiled to himself; the days ahead were going to be gloriously blood-soaked as he led the final push against Gall. Soon they would be the lords of Gall, and they had a host of captured Gall women to drench the ground red and bring Him down to lead His chosen warriors and build their empire, which would take the Lands of the Light and dark and unify them under the crimson banner of Zhar T'hur.

Uthiel and his brothers had met scant resistance as the first company continued their push into the heart of Gall. Keldon had managed to slay one fleeing barbarian with his crossbow, but that was the only foe they had seen. The sun was high in the sky, and shone dully through the clouds. The next day they expected to reach the outer townships of the capital city of Gall, and then the real work would begin.

Both of Uthiel's swords were sheathed as he walked forward along a heavily pitted dirt road towards the small town of Rouen. The town sat in a wide plain and, despite its dirt roads, was constructed mostly of well built stone and timber buildings. Some of the communal buildings had dark slate roofs but the remainder looked to be thatch. Were it not for the complete lack of life, the little town would have looked almost picturesque.

Uthiel glanced down at the inscription that ran along the thick outside of his vambrances and smiled. To know these had belonged to a glorious first captain and one of the Lord Pomen's ancestors made him beam with pride. Up ahead, Carn raised a hand and they dropped to a knee. As a precaution, Uthiel reached to his left hip and drew one of his blades.

Carn was looking to another small skirmish group about fifty feet to their left, one which First Captain Solanthur Verutus led. Verutus waved them forward. Carn stood and his brothers stood with him. Together they advanced warily, those with bucklers or shields moving to the fore and Keldon with his crossbow ever traversing the first line of buildings, looking for a target.

As they moved forward at a crouch, the hackles on the back of Uthiel's neck rose. *We're being watched.* Looking to his brothers, he could see their unease at being in the open was shared. The buildings they moved towards looked abandoned and seemed to have escaped the worst of the ravaging barbarians, but reminded Uthiel of a person without a soul. *Or a corpse without life.* For a fleeting moment the image of Nikhael's face came to the forefront of his mind.

Dark windows were stark against weather-stained pale walls. Empty lamps swung from their posts. The very wind, like the breath of Death herself ghosting through a graveyard, licked Uthiel's face.

"Caution, brothers," said Carn. "Something is not right here."

Nobody responded but Uthiel could feel the tension in the group become more taut as every knight focussed that little bit more. They were only ten feet away when Uthiel heard a faint and rhythmic thudding coming from the far end of town. It quickly faded away.

"Did anyone else hear that?" he asked in a harsh whisper.

Carn's eyes didn't leave the forefront of their advance. "Yes brother, I heard it, though I'm not sure what it was."

The heavens above opened, and rain began to patter upon their armour.

Keldon turned his head to Uthiel. "I'm getting pretty bloody sick of the – "

Branor swore under his breath. "Armenius damn me for simpleton son of a regiment whore! Bloody horse! That was a bloody horse! They're off to warn someone!"

He stood to his full height immediately and strode forwards, an impulsive and rash move that undoubtedly saved his life. The first arrow glanced off his gorget, at the level where but a moment ago his head had been. Uthiel looked to Carn for direction as he raised up one of his vambrances in front of his head to provide some protection.

Carn was on his knees. An arrow had cut through his cheek, mouth, and throat. The steel barbed tip of the arrowhead poked out the back of his neck right next to his spine. His eyes wide, the veteran clawed weakly and desperately at the shaft as he choked on his own blood.

Uthiel summed up their situation in a moment. They were easily a few hundred feet away from the safety of the main advance. They were only ten feet away from the black unknown of an ajar door into a large, two storeyed house. An arrow slammed into his pauldron, and then another bruisingly hammered into his chainmail-protected thigh, breaking both the skin and his moment's pause.

"Branor! Help me!" he cried out as he reached down and grabbed Carn by his rim of his pauldron on the left hand side.

Branor obeyed instantly and reached down. Together they began to drag the dying veteran towards the door. Keldon, Lokhi and Tarren charged forward, already knowing their roles. As soon as Keldon was in, Uthiel heard the twang of his crossbow and a scream of pain followed by Keldon's unmistakable roar as he charged into combat. Lokhi was in next, but Tarren was too slow. Four arrows simultaneously hit him. Three were deflected by his armour but the fourth got between his greave and his chainmail skirt and put him to the ground.

"Bran, get Tarren in! Go!" yelled Uthiel and Branor obeyed immediately as more and more arrows thudded into the ground or glanced off their armour.

Branor quickly bundled Tarren into the doorway, despite a loud cry of pain from the young knight, and looked back. Uthiel followed through quickly, dragging Carn behind him. Once inside Uthiel slammed the door behind him and turned to face the room, drawing his second blade from over his shoulder. In the moment it took him to adjust and get his bearings he could see there was no immediate danger.

Lokhi stood over a gurgling barbarian, his sword still dripping with his blood. Keldon was kneeling by a window reloading his crossbow. Tarren sat leaning against a wall, trying to muffle his cries as he built up the nerve to push the arrow through and out of the side of his thigh. Branor was against the wall, looking out another window, trying to spy who had shot at them.

This main room was mainly empty, devoid of life apart from the knights and a single corpse. Some ruined chairs lay splintered about, and the remains of clay crockery was scattered sparsely across the floor.

With a quick look down, Uthiel could see that Carn was dead. *Make that two corpses.* The veteran's eyes were open and his mouth filled with a pool of his own lifeblood. Uthiel clenched his jaw and then moved over to Tarren. He knelt down in front of his brother and put his hand on the wooden shaft of the arrow. Looking where it passed through the meat of

Tarren's thigh and out the other side he could see the barbed tip. He looked into Tarren's eyes.

"Brother, this is going to hurt, but you must not cry out. They must not know we bleed or they will think us weak and attack all the sooner," he said.

Tarren nodded and looked up as a crossbow bolt landed lightly in his lap.

"Bite down on the shaft, brother," said Keldon, not taking his eyes from their surroundings.

"Best make it quick Uthiel," whispered Branor. "I see ten... no, twelve barbarians approaching the house from the centre of town."

"I count twenty from this side!" hissed Lokhi. "Less than thirty feet away!"

"About the same from this side," called back Keldon, his voice followed by the twang of his crossbow.

"One less, but we're still in trouble if Solanthur doesn't get here soon!"

"Get it done, brother," snarled Tarren, steeling himself for the pain and placing the shaft of the bolt between his teeth.

Uthiel drew his lips back across his teeth, and then without a moment's hesitation shoved the shaft the rest of the way through. The crossbow bolt muffled Tarren's scream but every muscle in his body snapped taut, wracked with the moment's agony. Ripping a piece of cloth from his tabard, Uthiel quickly wrapped it tightly around the wound.

Arrows had begun to thud into the walls of the building and mixed in with the cries of battle from outside as the rest of first company advanced. *I hope that is the sound of my brothers and not more of the foe.* Uthiel stood and dragged Tarren to his feet. An arrow plunged through one of the windows and skittered across the floor. Uthiel ran to the door and opened it slightly to see where the rest of his brothers were. He watched in horror as he saw his brothers forced into a fighting retreat, centred on the first captain, back the way they had come.

No, no, no, no.

Uthiel and his brothers were behind enemy lines, again. Uthiel's breath caught in his chest for a moment as a spike of fear drove itself into his heart. He turned to look back at his brothers. Branor and Tarren were locked in combat as barbarians tried to force their way through the window they stood at. Lokhi was likewise entangled as he drew his sword back from stabbing it through an attacker's chest and wildly parried an axe swing, stumbling back as his feet caught on each other.

Keldon had somehow bought himself some room and fired a point blank bolt into a man's stomach as he reached the window. The bolt punched through the first man and felled the one behind him. With a second's glance back to Uthiel, Keldon drew his blade and with a roar began to hack and stab at those surrounding his window. That look was all it took to reignite Uthiel's courage. That look said it all. *We need you to lead us, brother.*

Uthiel knew that he had two simple choices. They could possibly break out through the door and risk the archers of their hated foe with no cover, or they could stay and hope they lived long enough that the king may rescue them. Uthiel looked to the stairs that led to the second storey and realisation struck him. "Brothers of the first! Pull back to the stairs!"

He darted forward to Lokhi's side and with two quick stabs of his blade had cleared enough time to allow his brother to pull back. A quick turn left and right and he saw his other brothers pulling back quickly, Tarren limping badly. As he ran back to the stairs he called out, "Up, brothers, up!"

Before he climbed up the stairs he looked back at Carn's body once more. It grieved Uthiel to see a veteran of many battles, and as good a Secundan as you were ever likely to meet, laid low in such a manner. It was made all the more heartbreaking to know he could not take his fallen leader with him. They would need to leave his body to the bloody whims of the barbarians.

A scrawny-looking shape slipping through one of the abandoned windows grabbed his attention for a fleeting moment. The figure only wore a fur loincloth and his bony physique was heavily tattooed and elongated. In his right hand he held a long staff well endowed with bone totems both animal and human. His face was covered with long matted hair and his attention was undoubtedly upon Uthiel's fallen brother. Uthiel fought the urge to attack the scrawny man. His righteous rage screamed at him to stride forward and smite this odd foe. He turned away from the scene, knowing that to stride forwards would be to add his body to the fallen.

With barbarians beginning to pour through the windows and door, Uthiel backed up the stairs, the last Grey Wolf out of the room. He was halfway up before the first filthy, leather and fur clad, axe wielding warrior arrived at the bottom of the stairs, glaring up at him. The beast roared through broken, yellow teeth and leapt up the first three stairs. His first boot never landed as one of Keldon's bolts whipped over Uthiel's shoulder and slammed through the barbarian's bare forehead, snapping his head back and sending him tumbling back to the floor.

Quickly Uthiel turned and ran back up the stairs as more warriors formed down at the bottom of the stairs and started running up en masse. Uthiel could see Keldon at the top of the stairs, desperately but methodically trying to reload another bolt to his crossbow. Seeing he wasn't going to make it in time, Keldon tossed his weapon to the side and drew his sword, standing just to the side of the opening in the floor to allow Uthiel past him.

Uthiel made it just in time as Keldon stabbed out behind him and a squeal of pain let Uthiel know just how close he had been to getting an axe through the back of his head. As he swept past Keldon, Branor pushed next to Keldon and with his buckler to the fore started hacking and stabbing at the tide of warriors forging up the stairs. Lokhi joined in quickly, stabbing over Branor's shoulder and reaping a bloody tally as the barbarians kept trying to get past the doorway so they could make use of their numbers against the young knights.

The floorboards were soon slick with sticky and slippery blood as yet more bodies began to pile up at the doorframe and on the stairs. Uthiel turned his attention to the two windows that both looked out over the plains approaching the town where his brothers of the first battled desperately to get back to the main army. Uthiel felt another moment's pang of fear as he tried to find some advantage to keep his brothers alive. *They're relying on me to have made the right decision. Armenius, let me have made the right decision.*

Through the sheer luck of having looked out the windows and into the sheeting rain, he was there when the first barbarian clambered up the roof and tried to climb in through the cavity. With a cry Uthiel launched himself at the surprised warrior. The man had no time to react before Uthiel's blade buried itself in his stomach. With a garbled cry he slumped backwards, rolled down the roof and off. Uthiel could see more barbarians levering their lithe forms up on to the roof and looked back for support.

Tarren was already by his side and together, for what seemed an age they battled to hold the two windows against what felt like an inexhaustible foe. Uthiel quickly lost count of those he killed. His armour was scratched, scored and dented and he bled from many cuts and gashes to his face and hands but his cuirass and pauldrons held true.

And then, like the sudden death of a raging storm, it was over. One moment the room had been filled with screams and clashing metal and the next all Uthiel could hear were the soft moans of the wounded and dying and the heavy breathing of the surviving knights. He locked eyes with the white faced Tarren. Tarren was on the point of passing out and reached out a crimson hand to lean against the window frame. Uthiel looked down to see his brother still held his sword with a strong grip. Putting a hand on Tarren's shoulder to help support him, he looked to the rest of his brothers.

Branor sat on the floor, a massive rent in the front of his cuirass and his chest heaving. By some miracle the blow that had cut his metal skin had not passed into his ribcage. His face was scrunched up in pain. Lokhi leant against the door, his armour in one piece but a small chunk of his scalp and one of his fingers missing. His face was soaked in a mix of his and others' blood and his eyes screamed exhaustion. Leaning on the other side of the door was Keldon. One of his pauldrons had been torn from his armour but otherwise he seemed largely unharmed.

Uthiel looked past them and saw the bloody destruction they had wreaked. Bodies lay strewn through the staircase so thickly it was impossible to see the stairs, or the floor beyond, underneath them. Lines of sprayed arterial blood and explosive clouds of red viscera thickly peppered the ceiling and wetly coated the walls and the floor. From the top of the stairs, the three Grey Wolf knights had used their superior elevation, superior armour, superior training, and superior strength of faith to stab three blades into the chest of every barbarian who had charged up the stairs.

Uthiel let out a short laugh and smiled broadly to his brothers, some of whom mustered the strength to return the gesture. They had looked Death in the eye and they had stared her down again. They were victorious. Uthiel laughed again.

Branor looked up. "So, we spit in her eye again, eh?"

Uthiel offered his hand to help Branor up. "We do, my brother."

Branor stood and then stopped, a look of confusion overcoming his features. "Can you hear that?"

Uthiel held out a hand for absolute quiet. Everyone stood still, the only sound the whispering of the breeze through the windows. Uthiel was about to laugh again and devise some light insult at his lifelong friend when he heard the solid impact of a well-weighted boot against a hardwood floor. One loud impact that rang through the building like a thunderclap as it smashed the silence. A second followed it and then a third, coming to the bottom of the stairs.

Uthiel squinted down to see a large dark silhouette at the base. In the darkness he could see two cloud white eyes looking up at him. Either side of the rough outline of a face sat two large armour plates with an inner collar. Uthiel squinted harder, and his breath caught in his chest as the shape began to become more familiar to him. It was only when he saw the dark outline of an arrow shaft jutting out from the warrior's cheek did the true horror of what he was looking at dawn on him.

CHAPTER TWENTY

Tanin Caellar stood tall next to Lord Pomen as he looked out at the fleeing forms of the first company led by Solanthur Verutus. They fought a desperate retreat in the face of overwhelming odds. Verutus mustered his men with the mastery expected of a knight first captain and fought like a cornered wolf. His men were falling at a rate that saw less than half their original number left.

The king and his personal guard were over a mile to the south with the Seventh, and the rest of the Grey Wolves were somewhere in between. This fight would be the Fifth's.

Pomen nodded to Tanin and drew his sword, already marching forwards before Tanin had had time to issue orders to the his men.

"Secundan Fifth! On the double!" he cried out. "Second and third companies follow me! First and fourth companies on our flanks!"

Behind him hundreds of men ran to form ranks by his side and by the time he and Pomen had raised their swords to strike at the enemy, the black banner of the Fifth flew tall and proud. The fight was short lived and bloody, the spears of the Fifth stabbing the life from the barbarians quickly and with few casualties. Of the Grey Wolves' first company, only twenty-five men remained.

Tanin's knees nearly buckled under him as he realised his son was not among them. Forgetting himself, he strode towards the group of knights knotted around their captain. He saw exhausted faces, bloodied, beaten, but resilient. He saw grievous wounds on men still standing, yelling at the soldiers of the Fifth that they must return with them. To Tanin, only one thing mattered.

No, no, no – where is my son? Where is he?

He strode through the knights, his guts twisting themselves sickeningly. The knights were exasperated, screaming and shouting to rally men to assault Rouen. Some tried to speak to Tanin but their voices did not pierce his mind. Some tried to grasp his arm but their grips were like an untried fisherman's on wet scales. He had eyes only for one man, First Captain Solanthur Verutus. He caught the captain's eye.

"My son?" was all Tanin could say, his jaw clenched to stop the sobs of expectation coming out.

The first captain grabbed him by the arms, his face open in its urgency.

"General! Get your men ready for advance, now!" he yelled.

"My son?" repeated Tanin, his iron jaw beginning to waver and a tear streaking down his cheek as his knees began to weaken.

"He may still live, general, but not for long if we tarry here!" cried Solanthur.

Tanin's face obviously didn't register any intent to help Solanthur so the first captain shook him violently. "Break out of this, man! Uthiel and my brothers were ambushed but we saw them take refuge in a building on the outskirts of town. Their only hope is if we get the army moving forward immediately, else your son's death may be on your hands."

Those words cut through Tanin like a knife. He blinked, shook his head and turned, his sense of urgency peaking with every new heartbeat. He pumped his legs back to his men and, completely ignoring the chain of command to Lord Pomen, cried out to them to charge forwards. Immediately he grabbed the Fifth's banner bearer by the arm and began running towards Rouen. Companies began to run to form up around him.

Before him the first captain got his men together once more and stood at the forefront of the Secundan lines as they jogged towards Rouen. Had Tanin been able to think of anything else but getting to the town ahead he may have admired their courage and determination. But there was only one thing on his mind. His only son was just slightly more than a mile away, and Armenius had given him this one chance to save him.

Uthiel and his brothers looked on in abject horror as the dull light coming through the top floor window began to break through the darkness that surrounded the creature coming up the stairs towards them. It seemed to shrug away the very light like it was an anathema to the glory of the sun. The only things that stood out were those milky white eyes as they fixed their unrelenting, malice-filled glare on Uthiel.

Uthiel felt his heart skip a beat and his knees start to weaken. What was slowly and ungainly marching its way up the stairs should not have existed. It stood almost six feet tall and still wore the bloodied armour of a Grey Wolf knight. A grey tattered cloak with a large dark stain around the neck flapped wetly in the air behind him. A long black drool string ran down from his chin and spattered onto the bodies and floorboards over which its heavy step hammered down as it continued up the stairs.

Uthiel could hear something in the air, a fell voice that tore at the ears and the mind when he strained to listen to its words. The voice wasn't coming from the monster ascending towards him and his brothers, it was as if the voice came from everywhere at once and nowhere at the same time. Uthiel tried to block out the sound as he found he and his brothers involuntarily taking steps back away from the stairs.

"Wha..." began Branor.

"Is that?" continued Keldon.

"That's not him," said Uthiel, his voice involuntarily whining. "Armenius protect us, it can't be him. We saw him fall..."

The first thing to enter the room was the polished steel of a Secundan blade. It made its way into the light of the upper floor and was soon followed by the bearer. Uthiel and his brothers gasped out loud when they saw Carn's face. His flesh was pale with death and his mouth drooped open to an almost impossible size. The slackly hanging jaw was still filled with partly congealed blood. Long lines of almost black viscera dribbled from his chin, hitting the floorboards below with audible pats.

The knights continued to back away, even when the walking abomination stopped. Uthiel was transfixed by those eyes. His legs felt leaden and his swords weighed a hundred pounds each. Despair coated his mind and his will to live began to wilt. Words found their way into his mind, words that were not his own.

He felt his own mouth move without his permission, "All hope... is lost... He... is coming..."

His brothers looked at him with shock as Uthiel fought within himself to regain control. The monster in front of him didn't move. Sweat poured down the young knight's forehead as his head began to pound like a blacksmith was using it for an anvil. Just under his gorget he felt something start to burn his skin but this was like a pinprick of pain in comparison to the battle he fought within himself.

Uthiel saw only those milky white eyes, sickening parodies of his own. Desperately he pushed himself to think. He had to find a way to break free of those eyes. He needed to fight! His arms felt like they did not belong to him, as if they were beyond his control. Then, a voice. It called his name and somehow attacked the cloud covering of his mind and broke through.

"Uthiel! Brother!"

At first the voice was unrecognisable. But slowly as it called to him again it became familiar. Uthiel felt his hand move, and then his arm. Finally he felt a strong grip on his vambrance. Somehow he managed to tear his eyes away from those white orbs that had held him fast. There was Branor.

"Brother!" cried Branor, a look of absolute urgency on his face.

Branor managed no further words as the creature that stood before them distended his jaw, further than a man should have been able to, and roared a challenge. The roar was low and animalistic, like the enraged bear facing its greatest foe. There was something sickeningly primordial in the sound and Uthiel felt his gorge rise as fat speckles of semi-coagulated blood spattered his face and armour.

The hold was broken, but the true fury of the abomination in front of them was unleashed. Before anyone could react it launched itself, at a speed the eye could almost not register, at Lokhi. The young knight was taken completely by surprise and a huge rent in his armour opened at the sweep of the creature's blade. Blood exploded out in a wide arc and the young knight slammed heavily into the wall and slid to the ground crumpled and unmoving.

The creature turned to face the remaining knights, its sword held out, pointed at Uthiel in challenge. As its blue lips curled back over its teeth, Uthiel brought up his swords in readiness and felt, more than saw, his brothers start to move to his flanks. Then the beast attacked. It was like lightning in its movement and Uthiel barely managed to get his blade up in parry. The impact spun the blade from his hand.

Knowing a second slash was coming Uthiel raised one of his vambrances to block the next strike, which landed like a thunderbolt. Despite the angle he offered, which saw the sword glance down the thick outer ridge of his vambrance, Uthiel was still punched to the floor. With a yell Branor darted in and drove his blade through the monster's neck, tearing out its throat with his withdraw. He was rewarded with a sickening glare and a strike that creased his cuirass and pauldron and sent him flying across the room.

In that moment Uthiel looked to the stairs by pure chance. In the darkness he saw a skinny figure holding a staff covered in dangling fetishes. Black whisps of un-light whirled in the corners of his vision as he laid eyes upon the man and once again Uthiel found his head starting to pound. His almost translucent blue eyes snapped back to Carn just in time as the creature barrelled past Tarren and came for him again.

Uthiel dodged and struck out, Secundan steel meeting Secundan steel in a loud clash that rang up his arm. The creature didn't even notice the gouge in his stomach through his cuirass, nor the single thin rope of entrails that hung from it. It roared and leapt at him again and Uthiel very quickly found himself in a duel for his life.

Over the next few heartbeats he fought with all his skill to stay alive. He barely noticed his brothers dart in and stab into the body of the beast, whose sole purpose seemed to be to kill him. Its milky blue eyes were locked on his gorget and throat, the focus of its malice and battle fury. He cut and spun and parried and dodged. Pieces of wood exploded around him as the creature's immense strength smashed into walls where Uthiel had been only a moment ago.

Again, Uthiel landed another blow, feeling his blade cut through the creature's neck muscles and crack into the bones of the spine. Again, there was no effect as his pauldron rang with the immense force of the creature's fist. It further grappled with the armour plate and Uthiel audibly heard its fingers break and the nails being torn from fingertips. Finally, it gripped the edge of the pauldron and launched Uthiel across the room with a roar.

Uthiel hit the ground and skidded along the floorboards until he hit the wall. He pushed himself to his feet to see Branor and Keldon intercept the creature as it charged once more for Uthiel. They held it for a moment before it burst through them with an ugly, triumphant roar. Uthiel pushed himself to his feet and launched himself to the side as it crashed into the wall where he had just been.

As he ran to join the strength of his brothers away from Carn he flicked his sword out at the skinny man with the staff who had ventured out from the stairs a few feet and was chanting as if in a trance. The blade carved through the man's bicep and he cried out in pain. Simultaneously, the creature stumbled and fell to its knees.

"How do we kill it?" yelled Tarren, his sword up and ready to strike.

"We hack it to pieces!" cried out Branor.

"We must strike together," said Uthiel, his breath coming in great heaves. "He has become too great a foe for any one of us."

Carn got a foot up under himself and began to stand, those disgusting eyes locked, once more, squarely on Uthiel. In that moment, there was a clamour from down the stairs as shapes clashed together in bloody close combat. Carn straightened and moved towards them unsteadily at first but as the man with the staff's chanting began to gain volume once more he trudged forward more swiftly. From the stairs, heavy footsteps could be heard ascending.

All of a sudden, the cruel and feral visage that was Carn's reanimated face fell slack. The blade, still slick with Secundan blood clattered from his hand.

"Armenius, no," whispered a voice.

Uthiel turned as the creature collapsed to the ground in a heap. The skinny man had dropped his staff and his mouth worked without sound. Two feet of red-coated steel jutted from his midsection and his hands sliced themselves brutally as he tried to pull it out. Within moments he died and hung limp. The sword withdrew and the body collapsed to the ground. There stood First Captain Solanthur Verutus, the look on his face saying it all.

Solanthur looked to Uthiel. "Brother, what... what is going on here? Is that... Is that Carn!?"

Uthiel couldn't find the words to address the question. His eyes flickered between the prone form of Carn and his captain.

Solanthur tried again. "Uthiel, what is this? Speak to me, brother!"

Uthiel worked his mouth but it was a while before he could articulate himself. "My captain, Carn is dead. Was dead. On the ground floor."

"I know, I saw him struck by the arrow outside. How was he standing? What happened to him?" Solanthur's voice echoed a slight sense of hysteria. "Why did he attack you?"

"That wasn't Carn," came Branor's voice. "There is no way that was our brother."

Solanthur marched over to Carn's body and turned the corpse with his boot. The flesh on Carn's face had already begun to rot and further entrails had spilled out of the large gash in his stomach. A horrid smell burst out of him and Solanthur blanched and took a step backwards. The first captain stood for a moment, staring in outright horror at Carn before his eyes hardened. Taking a purposeful stride forward, Solanthur raised his blade and struck down, taking Carn's head from his shoulders.

"No way for a brother to be remembered," said Solanthur.

Uthiel voiced his agreement and heard most of his brothers do the same. It took some moments before he realised Lokhi had said nothing. He looked around desperately and found Branor already keeling over their friend. Lokhi was slumped and his head hung down over a deep gash through his cuirass. The sheer strength of the creature had cut through him like he was made of parchment.

Uthiel could see snapped ribs and ruptured organs within the wound. There was no doubt that they had lost another of their brothers to this war. Despair and rage filled Uthiel. *Are there going to be any of us left by the end of this? Are we to be picked off one by one until none remain?*

More Grey Wolves began to spill into the room and each looked to their fallen brothers with horror. One reached down to touch Carn's body as he recognised a friend. Solanthur reached out and stopped him.

"Brother, his flesh has been sullied by some evil the enemy has brought with them. We'll turn this house into his funeral pyre," said Solanthur.

"Should we take his armour?" asked the Grey Wolf.

"No, leave it. I'll not have one of our brothers wearing that armour when we know of its story," answered the first captain.

Uthiel walked over to Lokhi and with his brothers they began to pick him up. Solanthur turned his attention to them, a sad and understanding look on his face.

"Brothers, he must be left also. We must re-join the line of the Fifth and cleanse the remainder of this town. Nothing must stop us getting to Gall tomorrow."

Uthiel and his brothers nodded dumbly. *Does it matter, now? His soul is gone to the Shield Wall in the Sky. This is just an empty husk of flesh. But it still looks like Lokhi. It still looks like he could wake up.* Uthiel looked at the wound again. *By Armenius, would I want him to wake up?*

They reverently placed Lokhi's form on the floor. Uthiel drew the sword he had taken from Tadel and put it on the ground. He picked up Lokhi's fallen blade and knelt before his friend.

"My brother, it was my honour to be here when you fell. It will be my honour to retell the stories of your life around the victory tables. May Armenius greet you with open arms, my friend," said Uthiel.

Next was Branor, who knelt down painfully and repeated Uthiel's words before taking off his tabard and placing it under Lokhi's head. Keldon came next and removed one of Lokhi's pauldrons and affixed it to his armour where his previous one had been torn from him. He also repeated Uthiel's words. Finally Tarren made his way over, dragging his feet and struggling to maintain his balance.

He tried to kneel but fell to his hands and knees as his strength gave out. Knights rushed forward and helped him up.

"Quickly, get him back to the wagon column," said Solanthur. "He needs to have his wounds stitched before he bleeds out."

Keldon and Branor took their wounded brother's arms over their shoulders and walked him from the room, leaving Uthiel with Solanthur and the remainder of the Grey Wolves' first company. Uthiel ran his hands through his grimy hair and took a deep breath. Almost every set of eyes in the room was on him.

"Brother, you and your men spit in her eye again," said one of the knights.

"Not all of us," responded Uthiel.

"No, but once again you seem to have taken command of your brothers and emerged victorious," said Solanthur.

Uthiel nodded, unsure of what to say.

"Perhaps there is enough of a leader in you to lead some of our brothers?" asked Solanthur.

Uthiel was a little taken aback but did his best not to show this. "I only did my duty, Captain. To lead would be an honour, but there are surely men far more deserving under your command."

"True," mused Solanthur dismissively. "We'll be using smaller skirmish teams. You and your three brothers will be one of these teams. You will lead them."

"It would be my honour," responded Uthiel, his spirits lifting a little.

Solanthur then turned to address the rest of his men. "My brothers, today we have all fought like lions! Many of our own lie slain or grievously wounded. The time to mourn them is not now. Now, we must re-join the line. We are the hardest and toughest men Secunda has to offer, men whom the foe weeps to see and who strengthen the resolve of our friends.

"It is up to us to lead the spear tip of the advance in to Gall. Barely a third of our original number still stand. We are stretched to breaking point. Any other men would break. But I have faith in you, my brothers.

"I have faith your strength will hold true and you will follow me into the heart of the enemy and together we shall punch into his bloody chest and rip out his cold heart! Armenius watches over us this day, brothers, let us make him proud."

The knights of the first punched the air and let out one roar of approval. Uthiel smiled. These were his brothers, and they were a reflection of the mightiest warrior in the Lands of the Light. He was proud to be amongst such men.

Branor and Keldon re-entered the room and both looked to Uthiel. "Uthiel, your father is outside. He requests to see you."

Uthiel looked to his captain, who nodded his assent. "If you have an opportunity to see your father before the big push into Gall, you should take it."

Uthiel nodded his thanks to Solanthur, and then to Branor and Keldon, before leaving. He made his way through the piles of barbarian bodies as he heard his two friends being congratulated by the other knights on the toll in blood they had exacted on the enemy assault on the stairs. Downstairs, mean of the Fifth stood guard.

In the centre of the room were two figures, the Lord Pomen and General Tanin Caellar. Uthiel smiled when he saw his father but addressed his lord first.

"My lord," said Uthiel, reverently offering his hand.

Pomen reached out and gripped his forearm. "Uthiel, I have heard good things."

"Thank you, lord."

"I see you wear my ancestor's vambrances well. They suit you lad," continued Pomen. "I'll leave you with your father, I need to keep an eye on the cleansing of the town. Armenius be with you."

"And with you, lord," finished Uthiel before turning to his father.

Tanin looked his son up and down for a brief moment, and saw the hollow look of his cheeks and the barely hidden horror in his eyes, before rushing in and grasping him in an almighty hug. Uthiel winced and groaned a little as his father squeezed him harder before pushing himself back.

"My boy, I thought I'd lost you," said Tanin.

Uthiel felt like a youth again, being fussed over by his parents.

"I'm unhurt, father. You need not worry," responded Uthiel with a smile, knowing full well his father could see he was beaten and bruised.

Tanin smiled, his eyes wet. "I know. I know. Being the father of a knight is not an easy thing."

Feet began stomping down the stairs from the top floor and the voice of the first captain could be heard. "...we'll need to be at the forefront of the fighting once more. Get the men ready and then send a runner to our brothers to ask for reinforcements. We're at a third strength and that just won't do."

Uthiel looked to Tanin. Tanin sighed deeply. "You must go, my son. Your brothers will need you."

Uthiel reached out and hugged his father once more. "Until we meet again, father, may Armenius watch over you."

"And you, my son," said Tanin, before turning and leaving.

Uthiel watched his father go and then gave his attention back to his first captain, who had reached the ground floor. Solanthur looked to the young knight. "Come brother, we must away."

"It is time this pyre burned."

CHAPTER TWENTY-ONE

Nikhael stood watching Gall's city centre being transformed. Barbarian leaders whipped their tribes and slaves alike into action everywhere, erecting thousands of stout seven-foot tall trestle posts surrounding the massive castle. His dark gaze spanned up to the keep still standing tall and proud above the ruined city around it. Three of the ragged green banners of the king of Gall still fluttered in the wind, but of Gall's people there would be no more resistance.

He had enjoyed Kael's retelling of the taking of the city. The Black Wolves had moved in hundreds of men into the surrounding towns of Gall, sneaking them through the White Frontier in small groups at night and having the men and women approach towns from the direction of Secunda. Over the course of the last decade, they had moved many thousands of their countrymen into the Lands of the Light, centred on the area's defence lynchpin, Gall.

They had bought buildings within the city with reforged smuggled gold and set up weapons stockpiles within the mighty walls of Gall herself. When the barbarians had swarmed over and past the White Frontier, the thousands of insurgents within Gall had ensured no warning was received. When the unbelievable horde had arrived and besieged Gall, the soldiers of the city had thought themselves safe within the walls. That was when the men and women of the Black Lands had risen up in revolt.

It was wholesale slaughter on a level never seen before in the Lands of the Light. For six days and nights, the city held out the siege and managed to cordon most of the insurgents down to the poor quarter where the city was set alight. On the seventh morning, the sap mine that had been dug from within a purchased house near one of the guard towers was collapsed, bringing a large section of the wall down.

The hole in the wall saw the bloodiest fighting of the siege as hundreds of men butchered each other for each foot of open wall. The soldiers of Gall had managed to hold the collapsed wall section for a day and had built barricades out of fallen stone and pieces of nearby houses. That's when strange and foul creatures had started to make their presence felt within the city. Nikhael licked his lips hungrily at the thought of it.

Stories raced around the surviving population about a fell voice on the wind and creatures ripping soldiers and civilians alike screaming into the darkness. People spoke of their fallen friends rising once more to wreak havoc amongst those who still resisted. Nikhael took the most relish from the fear the Black Wolves created in their siege warfare. To hear the retellings of the looks on the citizens' faces when they saw the familiar armour and imagined themselves saved, only to have that illusion torn from them, made his mouth water.

At dusk on the eighth day, the barbarians had claimed the entirety of the wall and the Gall soldiers and their king were fighting a losing battle in a ring around the inner castle where the remaining populace of Gall huddled. This was when the Black Wolves sprung their trap. They emerged from the sewers in the middle of the populace and unleashed their nature upon the hundreds of thousands of people crammed behind the Gall lines. Nikhael felt a pang of annoyance for having not been there. *Oh, the toll I could have taken. It is most unfair.*

Kael had described the scene with such clarity that Nikhael could almost smell the metallic tang of their spilled lives. People had run from their blades and caused a rampage. The Gall lines broke as the populace were herded like cattle through from the inside and the barbarians assaulted from the outside. Every man wearing the green tabard of the Gall army who was not already inside the castle keep died that day. Kael had spoken of requiring four blades before sun-down as the meat and bones of his victims dulled the razor edge of his weapons.

The women were captured and herded together. The men who escaped slavery were exterminated. And the children, Nikhael grinned with relish at the thought of what Kael had recalled. He returned his attention to those around him. Slaves had begun to haul women bound by their wrists and ankles to be tied up to the trestles. Women in their thousands, of all ages, shapes and sizes, were trussed up as naked as the day their mothers brought them screaming into this world.

They begged and pleaded with the slave men who carried them. They screamed to be helped but the Gall men knew there was no help while the barbarians ignored them, afraid of the repercussions the Black Wolves would visit on them if they slowed in their work. There would be no saviour for these people. Tomorrow morning would be their last sunrise. Nikhael personally looked forward to running his blade across the throats of many of the pure. Tomorrow would be the day he felt most alive in his short life. *Zhar T'hur shall reward me like no other.*

Pulling out his forearm-length knife with his right hand and grasping a whetstone with his left, he spat onto the flat surface of the stone and started sharpening the blade's edge against it. He walked as he nonchalantly whittled the edge of his weapon, the sound of steel scraping on stone bringing cries from the unfortunate women shivering in the cold.

He was surprised to note that he no longer looked at the women's naked forms with any sort of attraction or lust. He viewed them now like the butcher eyes a lamb or calf, peering beneath their skin for the choicest cuts. Nikhael cared only for the possibility of the arterial spray, and ever for that spark in his darkness: the spark that poured itself into the chasm of his soul – his addiction and his beautiful curse.

He found himself standing under a middle-aged woman, her skin creased and worn but her face handsome. She was well proportioned and the stretch marks from a recent birth could still be seen on her stomach. Her face was a mask of fear, tears and snot and drool mixed over her mouth and dripped from her chin as she stared at him with hysterical eyes.

Nikhael reached up with his blade, ignoring the stretching of some of his old arrow wounds in the cold, intending to slit the woman's cheek to get just a few sacred drops of her lifeblood flowing onto his tongue. *Just a little. To whet the appetite.* His blade rested against her flesh and he smiled in anticipation. It was a mock smile, of course, intended to heighten the woman's fear. A strong grip pulled him away from the woman and Nikhael spun, ready to strike out.

The sight of Kael stayed his hand. Kael looked into the black depths of his eyes and smiled.

"You, my brother, must be one of my most favourable acquisitions of the campaign," sneered the Black Wolf through filed teeth.

Nikhael didn't respond.

"I have plans for you, little brother," continued Kael. "Plans that go so far beyond the petty whims of your Order's lords."

This piqued Nikhael's interest. He raised an eyebrow.

Kael continued. "You see all of this? Thousands of clean, innocent souls awaiting Zhar T'hur's touch through us, his chosen warriors. At dusk tomorrow we shall deliver sweet, innocent blood to Him on such a scale that our god will walk the crimson earth once more."

Nikhael finally spoke, "How? How is this possible?"

Kael smiled. His face was the picture of mischievous evil. He looked up to see a small cadre of decrepit, mostly naked but heavily tattooed, malnourished old men leaning on carved, rune-bone covered staffs. At their centre was one who seemed more disgusting than the rest with partially rotted animal skins hanging from his shoulders and a bear skull tied to the top of his head. A lean arm reached out towards Kael and Nikhael and beckoned them over.

"Come, my blank canvas, let me explain this to you," said Kael with relish.

Nikhael nodded as they walked over.

"I have been waiting and hoping to find one such as yourself, one whose soul is a great chasm that can only be momentarily filled with the glorious light of blood," said Kael. "You are such a man, such a conduit for Him to come to the earth once more. Your lords and your brothers; fodder. Some are clean enough to be touched by Zhar T'hur. They are true brothers but expendable. Some are cowards, too afraid to stand up for what they used to believe in and now just content to reap for the sake of reaping.

"There are only few mortals in this world truly ripe for Him to fill them, Nikhael, and you are one. Tomorrow, here in the heart of Gall, He will become you, and you will become Him. Nothing will be beyond your reach, power unlimited will be at your fingertips and the Black Wolves will be your lords as we rule both the Lands of Light and Blackness."

Nikhael allowed himself a grin. Inside his void the lightest of sparks began to flicker as a being of unspeakable horror and lust turned its gaze towards him with interest from above.

The remainder of the push through Rouen provided little resistance to the men of the Fifth and the knights of the Grey Wolves. The king and his personal bodyguard, now outweighing the Grey Wolves in number, had taken the centre of the line. The king himself had refused to take cover behind the lines of his men. If men were lifted to see their king before, at this Uthiel positively beamed.

Light casualties were taken among the Fifth during the advance that spanned the remainder of the afternoon and well into the night. Uthiel remembered a certain moment, when sadness at loss had become almost acceptance. *'This is war. Men die.' When did I become so bleak?*

Despite the risks of the dark, the Fifth continued its steady advance through the town until it made camp on the other side of Rouen in some farming pastures. The Seventh had split into two and had advanced alongside the Fifth's flanks on the outskirts of the town.

Uthiel could still hear Solanthur's complaints as the Grey Wolves' first company was rested behind the lines for the afternoon. They walked with the soldiers of the Seventh guarding the baggage trains. Apothecaries had walked with them for a time, checking bones for breaks and stitching up opened skin.

As Uthiel watched the first captain, he could see Solanthur getting more and more agitated at being forced back behind the lines. The king had lauded Uthiel and his brothers for their efforts but it still felt wrong to be away from the front. The first company had entered Rouen first and they should have remained at the forefront. *We are not many. But we are the best. We are wasted back here.*

For a moment Uthiel thought of the fight with Carn. The sight of his brother in such an abhorrent state had unmanned him and left a foul taste in his mouth. Too much had happened in the last six months to his men. Uthiel laughed a moment, *My men. I've got three; hardly a force to be reckoned with.*

He turned as he heard hoof beats coming from behind. Without thinking he had both blades in his hand and had turned ready to fight. Before he yelled out a challenge he saw a man clad in Secundan armour galloping at the head of twenty similarly clad priests. He smiled, honestly and warmly, as he recognised Father Trethore as the leader.

As the big priest pulled up his horse before Uthiel, the young knight drank in the sight of his centuries' old armour. It was polished to a mirror sheen and resplendent in the late evening sunlight. A helmet sat on his thigh and a massive double-handed sword was sheathed over his back. Trethore was like a walking vision back in to the beginnings of the rebirth of Secunda over four centuries ago.

"Father Trethore," acknowledged Uthiel with reverence and respect.

"Brother Uthiel, it does me good to see you alive, boy!" said Trethore, vaulting down from his saddle to stand before

Uthiel. "I see you have been elevated to first company. You'll do well by First Captain Verutus."

"The first captain is a fine man, father," replied Uthiel.

Trethore read his mood in a heartbeat. "How long has it been since you spoke to one of my Order?"

Uthiel shrugged wearily. "Not since I was back at the Grey Wolf fortress over six months ago."

Trethore nodded and turned to look at the rest of the company. "There are less than twenty of you? What happened?"

"We were ambushed at the edge of Rouen while scouting ahead for the main army, almost forty brothers gone. Two thirds of first company's strength is spent," said Uthiel.

Trethore's face grew dark and serious. "Look at your brothers, I've not seen knights so beaten up and visibly dismayed in my life!"

"Something happened..." responded Uthiel, his voice trailing off as Carn's horrible visage flashed through his subconscious once again.

"Uthiel? What happened?" questioned the priest, his voice getting stern and concerned at the same time.

"Something horrible... something that should not have walked... I pray I never see the like again," said Uthiel, his eyes distant and his voice haunted.

Trethore's eyes narrowed and he reached over to grab Uthiel by the gousset. "Uthiel, I need to you to be clearer with what you are saying."

Uthiel looked at Trethore, licking his lips nervously. "Carn... fell. An arrow though his throat. I dragged him to safety, but he died."

"Armenius knows his name. Continue, brother," said Trethore.

"They came at us, we had to leave his body behind," continued the young knight. "We stood tall and proud and killed all that attacked us. Lokhi fell."

Uthiel could see the news of Lokhi's fall sting the old priest. He'd been one of Trethore's too.

Uthiel looked up at him and he nodded in support, allowing the youth to continue. "The battle was over, we had emerged battered, but victorious. And then... then something came up the stairs... something that should not be. Carn."

Uthiel saw Trethore visibly sink.

"Carn's body came up the stairs. Only it wasn't Carn. His face was different; his flesh was that of the deceased. He moved too fast for the eye to see... he struck with the strength of a god! Were it that we could harness such power without radiating such evil..."

"Perish the thought!" spat Trethore.

Uthiel took a step back, surprised by the outburst.

Trethore took a moment, his mouth working as he looked for the words. "Brother, pray to the Eternal Lord that such an evil thing never happens to you. Did you slay the Cthonian?"

Uthiel's face twisted a little in confusion at the word. "Cthonian? Father, I do not know the word."

Trethore's voice hushed to a whisper. "Like a shaman from the stories of your youth, lad. We prayed they didn't exist but word came back from the White Frontier many years ago that spoke of brothers rising after wounds that would have felled the hardiest of soldiers in the thickest of armour. Brothers who, once they rose, took blade and claw and attacked their brothers like the very beasts of the night they started to resemble.

"They were as puppets to these Cthonians. They are men weak of body but so strong of spirit their very malice manifests in the ability to turn brother against brother after death. They turn the bloodless flesh of the fallen into creatures so foul the very air around them fills with evil.

"Most can only raise one with their chanting and witchery, but some of the stronger ones, though few in number, can raise many. If there are more of these abominations in Gall, they must be exterminated above all others for they are the purest of evil."

Uthiel nodded dumbly, trying to absorb the magnitude of what Trethore was telling him. "Yes, father, First Captain Verutus drove a blade through him and slew him. Carn fell immediately after through no effort of our own.

"Father, I must speak with you further," continued Uthiel. "In private."

Trethore put a hand on his pauldron. "Uthiel, I need to speak with the king. Once I have done so, you have my word I shall return as I can see you and your brothers need guidance."

Uthiel nodded and despondently watched the priest mount his horse and gallop towards the front lines. The young knight inwardly yearned to speak to Trethore. He needed the support; he needed to unload the anguish and heartache of the last six months. Sighing, his mind was drawn back to his fallen brethren.

As if on cue, Branor came to his side. They walked together in silence for a while and Uthiel warmed as he felt a lack of the awkwardness he and his best friend had been suffering through in each other's presence since their slaying of the barbarian warlord. He stole a quick glance at his lifelong friend and his grin broadened as he saw the light smile of Branor's face.

It was Branor that broke the silence. "It feels like a long time since I last thought of Linton."

Uthiel sighed and nodded. "Yes, I miss him."

Branor continued, as if Uthiel had not spoken. "But I saw this soldier with ears like a riverboat sail the other day..."

Both Uthiel and Branor broke into laughter.

Sniffling a little in the cold, Uthiel laughed even harder. "And do you remember Eliem and Umbar? Eliem like he was a ten year old wearing his father's armour and Umbar with a waist that resembled your Ma's muffin tops?"

The brothers, for the first time in a months, enjoyed a long piece of genuine shared levity. The memory of their three brothers, now gone to fight alongside Armenius for eternity, broke down the barriers that recognised glory and now rank had built between them.

"Lokhi," said Branor, needing to say no more.

"His loss is still so fresh Bran, I cannot think happy thoughts of him yet," sighed Uthiel.

"I agree, brother," said Branor. "I had hoped Father Trethore would stay around longer. I feel like there is a spiritual

287

weight I need lifted off my shoulders before we move in to Gall."

"You and I both," said Uthiel, turning and placing and arm around Branor. "He did say he'd be back once he's spoken to the king. I hope that is before we are moved back to the front. The first captain is chomping at the bit to get us back into the fray."

"I could do with a break, personally, all this business of raking in the glory of an army for ourselves is tiring business."

Uthiel laughed.

"I apologise for being maudlin and of foul mood of late, brother," said Branor suddenly. "I have found the grief of loss of our brothers hard to bear at times and I allowed it to spill over. You're my best friend and I should not have treated you so."

Uthiel's spirits lifted even further. "I should not have allowed my head to get so big..."

"I knew there was a reason the first captain had us all ditch our helms!" butted in Branor.

Uthiel's friend became morose again. "The way we are placed at the front of battles, there is a very good chance one or both of us will die before this week is out. I could not have our last days spent filled with this stupidity."

Uthiel ruffled Branor's hair. "My only release of stupidity will be if you actually do die."

The brothers laughed once more and walked in companionable silence for a mile or two.

Uthiel frowned thoughtfully. "What do you suppose happened to Nikhael?"

CHAPTER TWENTY-TWO

It was late afternoon and the Secundan army had set camp a few miles east of Rouen upon its surrounding plain before Trethore found his way back to Uthiel and the ragged band of knights that made up the Grey Wolves first company. He walked in with his full regalia of armour, because often finding it lifted the spirits of men just to see armour of heroes who had fought alongside the Eternal Lord.

The men were covered in bandages and hastily repaired or replaced suits of armour. Their faces were gaunt and their eyes hollow. Trethore knew what they had seen and upon coming to the fire he had expected no less. Weapons and shields sat beside almost empty sacks of food and dirty wooden food bowls. He had heard that the first captain, Uthiel, Branor, Tarren and Keldon had seen Carn at his worst, before he had fallen for the second time. These were the men he deemed needed him most.

The first captain hid his haunted visage far better than the younger men, sitting alone and staring into the fire, but the man was hurting and he needed the healing light of Armenius upon his soul. Uthiel, painted as the hero who'd slain the barbarian warlord, looked to be suffering in more than one way. Not only had he fought Carn, but he was also sagging under the responsibility of both his fame and his newfound promotion.

Uthiel did not stare at the fire, but out into the thousands of men in the camp beyond where the Grey Wolves were billeted beside the Fifth, his eyes flitting from left to right rhythmically as he followed the movements of men between camp fires. By his side sat Branor, furiously shovelling handfuls of watery stew into his mouth. The young knight stopped, mouth open and dribbling stew and his hand half filled with small chunks of some unknown foodstuff halfway between gaping maw and bowl.

Trethore laughed a little to himself, to help mask his own concerns if anything, before walking past a heavily bandaged Tarren and a lightly snoring Keldon. Other knights also lay around, either eating noisily or struggling with the day's horrors in their sleep. As his presence attracted the attention of more and more knights, the first captain broke from his staring competition with the flames and stood, a slight bow his greeting and show of respect.

Trethore took position next to the fire, being careful not to allow his cloak too close to the flame and broke his silence. "My brothers, these are hard times we face."

Those asleep woke at the sound of his voice and groggily sat up.

"On your feet, brothers," ordered Solanthur in a tired but authoritative voice.

His men obeyed immediately, rising sleepily and bowing in a show of respect for the revered priest. Trethore noted that most of them were just tired or inwardly grieving. The effect of Carn's reawakening was restricted to only a few of the knights. These few were the men who needed him most. These were the men who had seen something that few men still walking the Lands of the Light had ever born witness to.

Trethore resolved to sit with each man, but first he needed to tend to the first company as a larger flock. He signalled them to each take a knee and as one the men knelt and dipped their heads. Looking down at his countrymen, he cleared his throat and began.

"He is our father, our protector, and our shining guidance against the dark night that lingers menacingly beyond the White Frontier. Armenius hear our prayer."

"Armenius hear our prayer," rumbled the knights.

"He is our shield, our sword, our armour and the brother next to you. Armenius hear our prayer."

The rumbling of the knights repeated itself. "Armenius hear our prayer."

"He calls our fallen brothers to his side when their lives of honour and glory are at an end and they bid us sorrowful goodbyes. Armenius hear our prayer."

"Armenius hear our prayer."

"Eternal Lord, watch over your descendant as he leads us in righteous war, watch over our families, our people, and my brothers in arms."

"Eternal Lord, watch over we proud Secundans," intoned the group as they raised their eyes, fresh light flickering in the dark hollows of their red-rimmed Secundan blues.

Trethore moved through the group, speaking to individual men and sharing in their grief for lost brothers as they asked him to offer a prayer up for their lost souls. Finally he came across the first captain, who had withdrawn a few steps from his brothers to watch from afar.

"A finer group of knights I've never seen, first captain," said Trethore. "They do you credit."

Solanthur was sullen, folding his arms across his chest. "That they do, Father. The loss of so many grieves me greatly. That these men are still keen to get back to the front and finish the job speaks of the Grey Wolf spirit in a way that no speech or written word could. I am honoured to lead them."

Trethore nodded, and then changed tack. "Brother, you carry a great burden on your shoulders. I can see it in your gait. We should speak, in private."

Solanthur stared at the ground for a long while before speaking again. "You are right, one of my men had his soul torn from his body and replaced with the malice of a barbarian witch. I failed my brother when I stretched our line too far and could not arrive in force fast enough to save him. If not in life, I should have saved him in death."

"I am here to listen, not judge your leadership," said Trethore, indicating that Solanthur should continue.

Solanthur snorted and walked back a step. "My brothers need your help more than I, priest. The young knights who were Carn's charges carry the weight of drawing blade against him. I suggest you start with Uthiel, he bears many pressures already and this must be affecting him greatly."

Trethore frowned a little, taken aback by the first captain's redirection of his efforts. "As it pleases you, first captain, I shall see to your brothers first. But you and I need to talk. I shall be back later and hope you are in a more sharing mood."

Solanthur locked eyes with him for a moment. Those stereotypical blue Secundan eyes called to Trethore for help for a brief instant before they were torn away. The first captain was on his way away from the fire around which his men gathered before the priest could say anything further. Trethore sighed and turned his attention to Uthiel. The young knight was staring at the fire and poked at it with a stick, sending bright yellow embers tumbling to the dirt and then ushering them back into the flames.

Next to him, Branor had picked up his bowl and was finishing his meal hungrily. The young knight bowed to the priest. Trethore ushered him away quietly, promising to speak with him next. Branor nodded and moved away to sit with one of his brothers who was tightening a crossbow string.

"Brother, I would speak with you a moment," said Trethore

Uthiel looked up from the fire. "Yes father, how can I help?"

"I see you have received a promotion, Uthiel. I had always imagined you would go far. Your legend now precedes you. The young knight who slew the barbarian warlord in single combat," said Trethore.

Uthiel laughed to himself. The undertone of scorn was not lost on the priest. "What Lord General Thomak seems to forget to tell people is that I was part of a company that took on the warlord and his retinue. My brothers died so that I could land a killing blow."

"Is this what troubles you? Fame?" asked Trethore.

"Fame? No. That I have to convince every man that comes to speak to me about it that it wasn't me against an army by myself, yes."

"And what of Carn?" probed Trethore.

"Carn," said Uthiel, brushing back his hair and blowing out his cheeks. "Yes, the death of our group's leader... sticks in my memory as much as I try to get rid of it."

Trethore thought for a moment. This was a brother in need of a focal point for the anger within him.

Without a second thought Trethore provided him with one. "Brother, son of Secunda, knight of the Grey Wolf Order, hold on to that memory. Remember what the enemy can do to those you love. Use that anger within you, use that hate to fuel the strength of your strike. Use it to seek out the mightiest of foul foes and to smite him and know that your brothers stand by you. Let them feed off of your righteous fury! Loyal and honourable men of Secunda; we all need men like you..."

Uthiel interrupted, his gaze far off. "Loyal... honourable... funny you should use those words."

Trethore saw immediately the young knight's mind was elsewhere and bit back his anger at being so rudely interrupted as his natural inquisitiveness took over.

"Uthiel, continue. Why should those words be funny?" he asked.

The young knight seemed to snap back from his reverie with a little shock and turned his face away.

"I am sorry, father, I should not have interrupted you. I should not have spoken," said Uthiel shamefacedly.

Trethore sensed the young man was hiding something. Many decades of listening to the deepest, darkest thoughts of thousands of knights throughout the Orders of Secunda had given him a deep insight into the minds of fighting men of Uthiel's calibre. *What is it my young charge is hiding from me? What could a knight have to hide from a priest?*

"No, Uthiel, tell me why those words strike a chord with you."

The young knight looked in to his eyes for a long moment and Trethore could see the need in those eyes to speak of what he had hidden. But the look soon passed as the steel-hard portcullis of secrecy slammed down. Uthiel broke his gaze and stepped backwards and half turned away, a clear sign that the conversation was over.

"No, father, I cannot. The other brothers need you. Please see to them. Thank you for your time, it was good to see you."

The young knight turned his back and walked away before Trethore could respond. Trethore couldn't help but kick his powerful mind into overdrive. *What is he hiding that he can't tell me?* He'd known Uthiel and his brothers since they had been ten summers old. He'd helped turn their young minds into the hard-edged blades they needed to be to battle the darkness beyond the White Frontier. He thought he had forged lifelong bonds with these men; bonds of openness and honesty.

But now the young man's mind was closed to him. *What could possibly be hidden behind the brutally scarred, but still youthful face of Uthiel Caellar?* The young knight had had a harsh and undistilled introduction to battle and war, but had shone in twice taking leadership of his men and twice leading them to both survival and victory. That the boy was destined for greatness, should he survive long enough, was beyond question but a mind that was closed to the Secundan warrior priests was closed to Armenius himself.

As Trethore watched the young knight walk away from the campfire he resolved to break down that barrier and once again open the young man's mind to Armenius. Many more brothers needed his help tonight, however, and so the youth would need to wait until after the battle for Gall.

Looking around the men of the first company, many of whom still stared at his armour in wonder, he spied Branor still sitting and speaking with the knight with the crossbow. Trethore walked over to them, filing away the matter of Uthiel's secret for another time.

**

As Uthiel walked away he cursed himself inwardly for his momentary slip. He thought back to his discussion with the lord general.

"Who else knows of this message?"

"None, lord general. The message was for your ears alone."

"Good. Brother, I will have your word of honour that it will stay that way. Now."

"You have it."

He had come so close to unloading his problem to the priest. Worse, he had wanted to let the message out. Trethore had known immediately that he was hiding something, of that Uthiel was certain. He had just withheld information from an Armenian priest. Nothing good would come of doing so, Uthiel knew. But his word to the lord of his Order was sacrosanct, and he would not break it.

As he strode through knots of soldiers of the Secundan Fifth, some greeted him as they turned away from their cook fires to catch sight of the knight who had slain the warlord. Some tried to stop him to talk but he respectfully made his way past them, citing business with the general. Searching through thousands of men, it took a long time for him to find his father.

Eventually, some hours later, he found the general hunkering down near a fire trying to escape the bitter cold.

"Father!' called out Uthiel as he spied Tanin speaking with Camen, Antony and Argo.

Uthiel smiled to see his father and his three friends. Antony had lost much of the weight he'd carried the last time Uthiel had seen him at the Blue Goose in Secunda. Argo had a dirty white piece of cloth tied around his head with a deep red bloodstain on the side. Camen was drawn and looked worn out, his massive shoulders and back bent with exhaustion. Branor's father had not been a fighting man before the war, having spent his life in the mines, but had volunteered after the destruction of the Fifth at the White Frontier.

All four men turned to look at Uthiel simultaneously and as one, broad smiles crossed their worn features and the weariness of war seemed to drop off their frames. Before he knew what was happening, Antony and Argo had almost barrelled him to the ground in welcome. Camen reached in and grabbed his forearm in a warrior's welcome next before pulling him in to a hug and then Tanin hugged his boy with the intensity reserved for a father.

Uthiel beamed at his warm reception and was soon caught up in the light hearted banter common between close friends and soldiers. They mockingly bragged of their exploits and teased each other, enjoying the easy camaraderie that came with having grown up in the same Secundan neighbourhood. Uthiel laughed until his face started hurting at the way the four men joked with each other.

Finally, a still laughing Tanin turned to his three comrades. "Friends, give an old man a moment with his son?"

Antony and Argo nodded and said their goodbyes to Uthiel before leaving. Camen lingered a moment.

"What of my Bran? Does he fare well?" asked Camen.

Uthiel reached out a hand to place on Camen's shoulder. "He does. He and I have fought many skirmishes and battles together and he has done you proud. In fact, it may not be known, but he stood and fought by me when we killed the barbarian warlord."

Camen's eyebrows raised in surprise. "Really?"

"Truly. A finer example of Secundan courage and honour you'll be hard pressed to find. He is but a hundred feet or so away with the rest of our company. I'm certain a visit before the big push into Gall will do him the world of good."

Camen visibly lifted and turned to walk away before spinning back for a moment. "Armenius be with you Uthiel, it does me good to know you two stand together."

Uthiel patted Camen on the shoulder as the old soldier hurried off to see Branor. Uthiel looked back to his father.

"We'll be going up the centre tomorrow, father, I hear the Fifth will be with us," said Uthiel.

Tanin nodded. "I will be there with the Fifth, my son. We'll be holding the right flank, with the Seventh on the left and a combined mix of our under-strength units in reserve. There will be much suffering from our men if we reach Gall and the walls are held against us."

"Will the king be with us?" asked Uthiel, his face hopeful.

"The king will be right behind your Order in the centre of the line. The banner of Secunda will fly high, no matter what we find."

"What do you think has happened? Where have their armies been? Where are their people?" pushed Uthiel, concern and trepidation replacing his hopefulness.

Tanin shook his head. "I don't know, my boy. Only Armenius knows what has happened to the people of Gall, and tomorrow he will fill us in on the secret. Something has happened, of that we can be sure, but only the afternoon sun tomorrow will tell us what that is. Either way we will march tall and proud for Secunda and no matter what we find, we shall defeat it in His name."

"I almost wish tomorrow afternoon were already here," said Uthiel. "The wait is maddening."

Tanin sighed. Uthiel read disappointment upon his lined features. "Just remember to relish the moments when you can see your brothers happy and laughing and joking. For tomorrow, you may see a great many of them screaming in pain or hatred as you have not seen warfare like siege warfare, Uthiel. There are few things as brutal or bloody as trying to force a thousand men through a twenty-foot breach in a fortress city wall defended by the enemy.

"I promise you, my boy, that if we survive to reach the walls, you will see butchery that will wound your very soul. I had prayed you would never see the like. My only solace in this is that I am here and have the power to look over you, my last son, the last of my lineage, my only link to the future."

Tanin's voice cracked in the last sentence and Uthiel moved in and embraced his father.

"Do not fear," said Uthiel, pulling away from his father to look Tanin in the eye. "The king is with us and I stand with hundreds of my brothers - "

297

Tanin cut him off. "Just you wear your bloody helm and carry your shield. Look at you clumping around with your head bare and your two bloody swords..."

Now it was Uthiel's turn to cut his father off, not with words, but with laughter. Tanin tried to hold his serious face but his son's laughter was infectious and soon he was laughing too.

Uthiel stood there, a little awkwardly if he was being honest, as his father stared at him.

"I'm proud of you, boy. I shall see you inside the walls of Gall," said Tanin.

"Just you try to keep up with us father," said Uthiel, turning and walking away, excitement and fear churning within him.

Emilia gritted her teeth and stifled a cry of pain as she felt the rough rope wrench tight against her raw, freezing skin. Her teeth chattered and her heart hammered as the biting wind cut down between the rows of buildings either side of the street in which she was now securely tied to a seven foot tall trestle. Her head hung loose over one roughly cut end and the muscles running up the back of her neck were already beginning to ache.

Around her, hundreds of girls and women had similarly been tied, elevated with their heads hanging loosely and their hair whipping wildly in the wind. Barbarians worked feverishly to get more and more women tied up upon the trestles. Twisting and craning her neck, Emilia tried to look skywards. All she could see was the darkness of heavily potent storm clouds, low and pregnant and suddenly lit with sickly red lightning.

Her breathing became shorter and faster as panic began to eat away her last reserves of courage, reserves that had held fast for so long and through so much. She looked around for her mother, a cry of fear barely held in check by quivering lips as her darting eyes could not find the woman. Tears began to stream down her cheeks as she saw shapes in the darkness. Elongated limbs and disgusting tattoos. Wiry, filthy hair and empty eyes. Yellow, rotted teeth and emaciated bodies. She screamed as lighting highlighted the disgusting creatures in their fur loincloths.

One of the men that wearing a bear's skull strapped to his head whirled around and looked at her, a sickly grin crossing his mouth. A snaking tongue slid over his lips and flicked a piece of something from his grotesque beard. A bony foot took one step towards her before a booming voice dragged his attention away from her. Like a starving wolf cheated of his meal, the creature slunk away dejectedly. From above, a clap of thunder made Emilia jump. Rain began to fall onto her bare back, its icy coldness soothing the rope burns across her shoulders, buttocks and legs.

Closing her eyes and desperately pushing the pitiful cries of fear around her out of her mind, Emilia tried to bring the face of her knight to her mind. She tried to retreat to her place of inner safety where her heart pounded not for fear, but for someone. Try as she might, the young man's face just would not come to mind. Gone was the scent of his shoulder and neck as she sat astride him, his laugh, and his beautiful eyes. They were gone, replaced by nameless horrors and shadows of hope: shadows that wore Secundan knight armour with faces that bayed for blood.

Emilia wept openly and bitterly.

CHAPTER TWENTY-THREE

Uthiel stood in awe, his hand shielding his eyes, as he gaped at his first sighting of Gall from afar. The city looked like an immense crater in the ground surrounded by a wide berth of white, grey and black roofs. Above the city centre black and dark green clouds swirled around in an immense vortex, reaching down like the hand of an angry god preparing to touch the very earth. Crackling lightning flickered through the dense overhang and lit the clouds through frightening and awe inspiring hues of red and brilliant white.

The city had a diameter that made Secunda look like a small county. The fortress walls that surrounded the more ancient section of the capital city eclipsed those of Secunda in both size and majesty and the tall castle in the centre simply took the breath away. Massive bastions, almost like castles in their own right, sat like epic guardians looking over both the newer sections of the city sprawling out over the countryside and the inner quarters.

A thick blue river cut through the western approach, a wide bridge leading to the centre of the city spanning its raging gap from one densely housed area to the other. Huge bastions protected either side of the river, two on each bank. Dirt roads starting on the outer edges of the city quickly turned into dark grey cobblestone as they reached in to the more populated outer areas to resemble a tremendous spider web that led to the central hub protected by the walls and bastions.

Uthiel squinted. Close to those colossal walls, smouldering remains of seventy-foot tall siege towers sat dormant and devoid of the hundreds of barbarians who had pushed it. Arrow-coated but charcoal free versions of the same towers sat against the walls, their twenty-five foot wide assault ramps resting against the parapets. Uthiel couldn't see a single soul moving in the outer regions of the city, though at this distance, that provided little comfort.

Long tendrils of lightning began to lick at the tall iron spires atop the castles and bastions, burning away the tattered remains of flags and banners, as the storm above began to increase in intensity. Chunks of stone and masonry toppled from the buildings, shrouded in explosions of powdered and splintered rock in a show of unbelievable power. Thunder roared like the voice of the world, shaking the very ground that stretched out underneath it.

Like an army unleashing a hail of arrows at a foe, the skies opened up and released pelting rain, the wind of the vortex blowing it out from the epicentre at an unbelievable angle. As the fury of the storm intensified, further and further heavy sleet began to fall as the sky swept from a deep green and black, whipping through the air like ice blades. Like the full hatred of a dark god lording over a tainted city, pure malice hammered outwards like the ash cloud of an exploding volcano.

Uthiel swallowed, hard. *We're going in there.*

Nikhael looked up from the sacrifice grounds to the swirling sky above. His heart beat slowly and rhythmically as not even the imminent arrival of Zhar T'hur affected his cold demeanour. His gaze swept back down from the insane movements above him and lifted a hand to shield his eyes as heavy rain began to pour down and red and white lightning lit the sky up ominously. Thousands upon thousands of seven-foot tall trestles held their sacrifices fast as far as the eye could see. Thousands of houses

301

lay in ruin, not from war, but from a need of their wooden beams.

They filled the parade ground and the streets surrounding it, clogging the arterial roads like thick blood clots. Some of them screamed or squealed as the ice-cold rain lashed against their naked bodies, wrenching the last vestiges of warmth and hope from their quaking forms. Nikhael purposefully sought out their eyes and let them look within him, to see the depths of his soulless crevasse.

He licked his cracked lips at the thought of the blood drenching these streets were about to receive. He bit into those same lips until they bled as the visage of himself coated head to toe in thick, warm crimson swept through the void inside like the fleeting promise of light within. A string of drool slung down from the corner of his mouth as his sight settled on the beating throat vein of one of the sacrifices. He lost himself in that moment. *Her throat split open. Pumping arterial spray wetly spattering against me.*

"Nikhael."

"Nikhael!" came the voice again, more insistent this time.

Nikhael snapped away from his daydreaming, gradually focussing on the figures in front of him as he dragged himself back from his bloodlust obsessed fantasies. As he recognised the figures his face transformed back from an image of faint happiness to his usual blank and nonchalant expression.

"Lord Irill, Kael," he said, more than slightly frustrated at the interruption. "What do you want?"

Lord Irill raised an eyebrow at Nikhael's impudence. Kael ignored the lord, seemingly only paying attention to the young Knight Aggressor. "Today, prophecies centuries of years old come to fruition," he said with relish.

Nikhael didn't respond, but sensed that this could mean it was almost time to do away with this pointless waiting around and start slitting throats. The thought appealed to him and a wry smile creased across his face. Kael obviously mistook this as an invitation to further lengthen the time between the now and when his blade would enter the first pulsing pale neck, and continued.

"Zhar T'hur will come down from the sky. Look above, you can see his passage already beginning! His fury smites the very walls of Gall as a vision of His hatred!" Spittle flew from Kael's sneering mouth and his wild eyes portrayed a focussed rage that might have unmanned Nikhael, could he feel fear.

"He shall come at our calling and we will drench this city with the blood of the innocent as his welcome mat. Zhar T'hur shall know our names and under his leadership we shall rule the land and every delicious morsel of life on it!"

Kael paused, breathing heavily after his outburst. The Lord Irill's his eyes were locked in anticipation upon the Black Wolf like a lapdog awaiting the whim of its master. Kael still stared at Nikhael, his eyes burning like a pair of coals.

Kael turned to Irill. "Still here? Away with you. Get to your position," and then returned his attention to Nikhael as Irill ran off like he had been struck by his father for disobedience.

"Brother, time we took control of this land. It is ours to own. The Galls are gone. The Secundans are gone. The vast expanse of the Lands of the Light belong to us, Nikhael! Let us bring Zhar T'hur among us through glorious sacrifice and revel in his dark light!" yelled Kael.

Nikhael remained still. He allowed Kael's face to falter for a moment, as the Black Wolf thought he was devoid of support, before speaking.

"I look forward to shedding the blood of the innocent with you, brother," rasped Nikhael, leering with a purposeful lack of sincerity.

Kael nodded and drew his forearm-length blade of gleaming Secundan steel and set off for the first line of weeping sacrifices. Nikhael followed suit, the relish that now settled on his face unmistakable in its lust. He rolled his shoulders, stretched his arms and loosened his back as he walked to the nearest trestle. *It won't do to pull a muscle early on with such a magnificent day in front of me.*

To his left, he heard the musical rasp of a razor-edged blade over the storm as it cut through flesh, followed by the wet splattering of hot blood against hair, skin and metal with a light undertone of the choked gurgling of the already dead.

With Kael beginning the ritual, the floodgates opened and the symphony of death around Nikhael exploded to life. He closed his eyes and savoured the moment for a heartbeat before opening his black pits and drinking in the fear of the young woman strapped to the trestle above him.

In those green eyes he saw fear so intense it lit the spark within him to know he was a cause of it. He raised his blade to her neck and lightly pressed it to her skin. He watched her dribbling mouth cry and plea with him but heard nothing but his own heartbeat. Nikhael reached up his other hand and pressed a single finger to her lips. She calmed for a moment in surprise at an almost tender touch and that was all the young knight needed.

With blinding speed he pushed himself up onto his toes and grabbed a fistful of long lank hair. In the same movement he wrenched her head back and cut across the pale white flesh of her throat and opened it from ear to ear. His blade bit with such force that a shiver of pleasure rippled through him as he felt the edge scrape against the bone of her spine.

He closed his eyes as her lifeblood exploded from her initially and then continued to pump rhythmically onto him. Within the spark detonated with brilliant light and for a luscious moment, Nikhael was in absolute ecstasy. But then it faded almost as quickly as it had come. He released her hair and her dead face flopped down to look at him with sightless but terrified eyes that spoke volumes of the horror of her demise.

Nikhael sighed with release before he heard a nearby whimper. His dark red face snapped to lock on his next victim and she started screaming. The young knight smiled genuinely. Today would truly be the greatest day of his life.

As the long line of Secundans began their five mile march to the outer suburbs of Gall, the first whipping gales of rain and ice began to beat against them. Thousands of soldiers, the knights of the Grey Wolf Order and the king's personal retinue leant into the gale-force wind. Only a scant few hundred feet before them the abandoned twin peaks of the west facing twin bridge bastions speared high into the grey swirling sky.

Uthiel felt the deepest sense of trepidation as he and the three hundred-odd Grey Wolf knights led the Fifth across the massive bridge that spanned across the choppy blue river dissecting the outer regions of Gall. Units of the Seventh patrolled the flanking streets and checked into empty buildings. The odd rotting body was found, but nowhere near the number they expected of a city housing well into the hundreds of thousands. All the while, the relentless rain hammered down.

The first company strode at the front, almost fifty feet clear of the next Grey Wolves. Shields up and blades resting against their pauldrons, they moved forward, the eye slits of their bucket helms hiding darting eyes in shadow. Despite being encased in plate and chain armour, Uthiel felt less than safe within the vanguard. They had been reinforced from the other Grey Wolf companies to two-thirds strength, but even with forty brothers around him, he knew that in the tight confines of a city, they could be cut off and butchered very quickly by a smart and determined force.

His intense stare swept from thin alleys filled with garbage to vacant and dark houses that loomed either side of the street. Claustrophobia gripped him in an ice-cold fist, and not for the first time he shouldered his shield higher as the hackles on the back of his neck rose and sent a shiver down his spine. Stealing a glance at his brothers as they prepared to pass over the killing fields surrounding the bridge bastions, he saw most of them shared his mood.

Uthiel licked his lips nervously and raised his shield instinctively a little higher again as he watched the bastion's battlements for a sign of archers underneath the remnants of madly flapping banners. Branor moved next to him as they came within twenty feet of the base, and Uthiel took some strength from his friend's presence. Out of his peripheral vision he spied Keldon with his crossbow aimed up at the bastion, following very closely behind a brother new to Uthiel's command who had his shield up in protection of them both.

"It's a bloody ghost town," whispered Branor. "What in the name of Armenius happened here?"

"Where is everybody?" chimed in Keldon as he carefully stepped over a soldier's body.

"We need Tarren here with us," continued Branor. "With that ugly mug out in the open we'd hear the bastards running screaming from their hiding places."

Uthiel looked to his two brothers, inwardly chuckling but retaining his steely demeanour. "Quiet, both of you. Concentrate."

"Well he has got a face like a dropped apple pie..." trailed off Keldon as Uthiel fixed him with a harsh gaze.

That brought a couple of chuckles, which drifted to the ears of the first captain. First Captain Solanthur Verutus turned back for a moment and put a single finger up to his helm in front of where his lips would be. Uthiel shook his head, knowing that Solanthur would be discussing his men's lack of discipline later. Annoyed now, he looked to both Keldon and Branor and angrily chopped a hand across his throat for silence.

Keldon held up a hand in apology but Branor kept his gaze forwards. As they made it past the far end of the bastion, it came as a shock to the men to see the twenty-foot wide gates open. Bodies, both Gall soldier and barbarian, lay scattered around the gate.

At the first captain's order, two groups of five knights broke off from the main force and entered the gates of each bastion to scout for immediate threats while the remainder pushed on to the bridge. Uthiel spared a glance into the darkened inner corridors as he passed and saw his brothers picking through the bodies with the tips of their blades. It took them a little longer to check upstairs but soon they returned, alive and well.

Alone, and out on the bridge, the first company pushed on. Uthiel's heart beat faster and faster as the feeling of dread intensified. As they neared the halfway point of the bridge, he began to see the bodies through the sheets of cold rain. Ice white skin, covered in tattoos and furs, they were strewn in an ever-thickening carpet of death from which buried arrows jutted skywards.

Easily a hundred bodies lay strewn between the final quarter of the bridge and the burst-open doors. Around the gate the pile reached three feet deep where the soldiers of Gall and barbarians had met and butchered each other. The bodies of the barbarians far outnumbered the soldiers of Gall in their green tabards and mail hauberks.

The first company formed up at the end of the bridge. If they were attacked en masse here, it would be the best place they could hold until the main army caught up. Immediately they formed up around the first captain in two lines of twenty, reaching from one bastion wall to the other. Forty iron shields simultaneously locked in a single loud clash. Forty pairs of eyes stared out of their helm slits and up the main road that led to the city gate.

Rain sheeted down so heavily that the knights could not see more than a hundred feet out from the first company's shield wall and Uthiel squinted as once again he felt a cold shiver work its way down his back. From behind the pauldrons of his brothers in the front line, he desperately pushed his sight to pierce the downpour deeper. Behind him came the sound of galloping hooves between the rolling thunder echoing from above.

He turned and saw ten horses coming at them from the rear, deep purple cloaks trailing water as they flicked wildly in the wind. Uthiel's eyebrows rose as he saw the glorious figure at their head. The king rode with the Lord General Thomak and the Lord Pomen in tow. Seven of the king's personal guard followed in a wedge, their keen eyes ever outwards and their limbs taut and ready to leap to the defence of their king.

The broad-backed figure of Solanthur turned around for a moment as the clattering of hooves on cobblestone grabbed his attention. Through the eye slits of the first captain's helm Uthiel was sure he saw a look of surprise as the king reined in his mount five feet behind Uthiel and his brothers. With a quick call from the first captain, another group of five knights broke from the rear rank and moved back towards the king, raising their shields up high to protect the direct descendant of their god.

The king sat high and proud upon his glorious steed. The five strong shield wall protected him and his horse but allowed him to survey the road and grounds beyond the bridge. Before them was the heart of the maelstrom, lit in flashes by the lightning streaking down from above. Somewhere within those buffeting clouds of rain, something toppled and crashed heavily. Moments later a flight of black birds could be seen breaking for the sky, braving the conditions.

His eyes drawn upwards, Uthiel saw that the storm above had suddenly increased in intensity. The whirling vortex of clouds constantly flashed from black to brilliant white and then to an angry red. Lightning began to crash with ever-increasing frequency deep into the city. The crumbling of stone echoed loudly in between thunder so deep and resonating that it vibrated the very air in a man's chest.

"We need to deploy our full force beyond the mouth of the bridge immediately, my king," said the Lord Pomen. "If they catch us during the deployment of our strength we will suffer greatly. I would suggest sending out some soldiers as skirmishers and then the Grey Wolves forward second in a shield wall to establish a solid core. Then the Fifth and the Seventh will deploy either side. Once this is done, the Grey Wolves will advance up the centre with the Fifth and Seventh moving through the city towards the main gate."

Uthiel did his best to listen to the lords behind him as the rain beat an aggressive and tinny staccato on his and his brother's helms and armour.

"Agreed, Lord Pomen, but we must ensure we do not spread our strength out too far. This storm is going to play havoc with our plans to get into the city walls by nightfall," continued Thomak.

The two Grey Wolves looked to the king, who sat immobile and looking out into the fog of rain.

"Lord General Thomak," said the king. "Get me five of your keenest-eyed knights up in that bastion and find out if we can see what may lay before us."

"My king, respectfully, we need to deploy skirmishers immediately," said Thomak. "If we remain stationary, we give any enemy that may be out there time to manoeuvre into an ambush."

"If they do not wait in ambush already," cut in the king.

"It is possible, but we must find out. Either way we cannot stand still in hostile territory, my king," said Thomak.

King Faramon took a deep breath. "I understand. Get me those knights into the tower immediately, and then begin deployment of the Grey Wolves to create the centre of our line for the advance through the city. The Fifth are to separate their strength to either flank of the Wolves and the Seventh will deploy most of their strength to create a second line behind them. The remainders of the Seventh will follow with the baggage trains."

"Where shall you be, my king?" asked the Lord Pomen.

"I shall be in the centre, between the Grey Wolves and the Seventh."

"My king, you will be at risk," said Thomak.

"I will be at risk no matter where I am, my friend. If battle is to come I will not be found wanting and shall meet the enemy amongst my brother Secundans. Let us begin," said the king, turning and galloping back past the column of Grey Wolves towards the remainder of his household guard at the head of the first army units.

Uthiel heard Thomak swear under his breath.

"First Captain Verutus!" called Thomak. "Give me five of your men on top of that bastion to call down what they can see immediately please."

"Yes lord," said Solanthur before looking at Uthiel. "Brother Uthiel, you and your men on top of that bastion. Call down what you can see."

"Yes, first captain," replied Uthiel.

He turned and jogged towards the gaping maw of the bastion gate, his four brothers in tow. As he heard the marching feet of three hundred of his brothers behind him move into position, he gingerly stepped over the bodies of the fallen and passed into the darkness inside. As all light was lost to him, Uthiel heard the crash of three hundred shields locking as it was quickly drowned out by a clap of thunder.

He couldn't help but feel that the city itself was doing its best to push the light of Secunda from its tainted dark heart. Gall herself was hiding a treacherous secret and Uthiel anticipated with dread that to discover that secret would mean the death of a great many Secundans.

CHAPTER TWENTY-FOUR

Uthiel and his four brothers surged through the dark insides of the bastion. It stank of the human waste, effluent and well decomposed flesh of the Gall soldiers who had lived and died here. Uthiel's eyes had quickly accommodated the dark, the scant light allowed in through murder holes and arrow slits providing a gloomy vision of toppled furniture and skeletal corpses as they made their way through the second floor.

Uthiel raised his shield before him and readied his sword as he moved up the stairs to the third and final level. He could hear a door above banging and a shrill ice wind whipped down the stairs like the howling enraged souls of the dead trying to tear the warmth from their very bones. Uthiel set his jaw and led with his shield up the stairs until he could see the loudly banging iron-reinforced door.

He looked back to his brothers and inclined his head towards the exit as it swung open and allowed them to see the wild tempest that raged above the ground. He charged out and his brothers followed him onto the empty battlement. The rain and wind struck them with their full might and Uthiel reached out to steady himself on the stone of the wall.

"It's as if Armenius himself rages at us, brother," Keldon cried out. "I've never seen a storm of such ferocity."

Branor shrugged and Uthiel turned his gaze out towards the outer reaches of the city. The blinding and thick rain blocked the view of almost everything but the largest shapes of buildings. Uthiel leaned out and tried to see more but discovered nothing. In frustration he turned his gaze down and saw that the Grey Wolves had moved a good forty feet beyond the bastions, leaving the bulk of the Fifth in their wake.

Elements of the Fifth had begun to move out on the left in force, but congestion on the bridge caused by the king's personal retinue had stalled their movements on the right and opened a gaping hole in the Secundan line. The black banner, under which he knew his father would be standing, was just leaving the mouth of the bridge.

Also still at the mouth of the bridge, the king, Thomak and Pomen sat atop their horses with the king's seven guards and the five Grey Wolves with their shields raised in protection of their king.

A hand slapped against Uthiel's pauldron in earnest and then pointed out into the mist. Uthiel followed Branor's gloved finger as he stared out to the right of the Grey Wolves shield wall. As if the very hand of Armenius came down and offered a moment of respite, the rain slackened for a few heartbeats. Figures moved between the houses, flitting in and out of the withering banks of rain. Uthiel looked back down at the hole in the right flank, and then down to the king as the rain hammered back down with increased ferocity.

Shit.

In a moment of absolute clarity Uthiel knew what was about to happen. The delay in getting the remainder of the Fifth past the king's three hundred household guard had left a gaping hole in their deployment. The rain had blinded both the Grey Wolves and the following units to a horrible fact. There was a direct route to the three men who led not only this army, but also Secunda herself. In one fell swoop they would swipe the head off the army and leave the body leaderless.

Uthiel screamed and yelled and waved his arms but the very wind seemed to whip his voice up into the maelstrom above. In fear and frustration he tore his helm from his head and threw it at the household guard, only to see it ripped from its trajectory and sent into the river. As a wedge of barbarians broke from the city and made for the gap Uthiel knew there was nothing he could do. Keldon burst forward and fired a bolt into the path of the king.

The bolt cracked into the flagstones but so heavy was the rain and the pounding of barbarian feet that none of the men saw or heard it strike. Keldon and Uthiel looked at each other and knew their situation was hopeless.

Alerted by the sound of the charge, the king, his guards, the Grey Wolves and the men of the Fifth spotted the barbarians. Without hesitation the knights smoothly began backtracking towards the mouth of the bridge and moved their lines to intercept the charge but only managed to dam half the advance. The impact was heavy and as more barbarians broke from the city Uthiel saw more and more blood-crazed men impact the slowly retreating line of knights. To the left, a company or two of the Fifth had been immediately cut off, having made the mistake of not immediately linking their lines with the Grey Wolves.

The remainder of the assault force, well over two thousand barbarians strong, made for the king. The king's guards milled about in confusion, being trapped with the bulk of the Fifth blocking the road behind them.

A torn black banner flapped wildly behind the lines of the engaged Grey Wolves. It moved majestically, despite the storm, above a small group of the Secundan Fifth as they ran for all they were worth to intercept the line of the attack. Uthiel held his breath as he realised the king's guards and the units of the Fifth still on the bridge would be too slow to protect the king. He clenched his jaw in outright fear as he saw his father, at the head of those soldiers led by the black banner, lead a suicidal but incredibly brave assault. Tanin drew his blade and leapt into the barbarians and was quickly lost in the melee, the black banner of the Fifth following him closely.

The fight was brutal and short but it bought the king's guards enough time to section off a hundred strong wedge and drive it past the companies of the Fifth on the bridge and into the barbarians. Their momentum saw them plough through the stalled charge of the barbarians like an axe smashing its way through a block of wood. Bodies tumbled and sprawled backwards away from the knights and it galled Uthiel to see that some of those bodies that flew like broken rag dolls wore Secundan tabards.

With the space around the mouth of the bridge cleared, the Grey Wolves' first company continued their fall back and linked up with the king's guards and more elements of the Fifth. Barbarians continued to throw themselves against the shield wall in greater numbers and with greater ferocity. The knights continued to hold but already a fifth of the Grey Wolves lay slain on the field. Of the element of the Fifth left stranded when the barbarians had hit, there was no sign.

Uthiel saw none of this, his blue eyes locked squarely on the wave of fur – and leather – clad men trampling over the site where his father had stood and the black banner of the Fifth had fallen. Inside him rage and horror rose and fought each other. One demanded bloody action while the other screamed at him to mourn and curl up into a ball and weep. Uthiel savagely quelled his weakness, the handle and strap of his shield falling from his grasp as his hand reached for his second sword.

Father.

"Father!"

Without looking or speaking to his brothers, Uthiel launched himself back down the stairs and through the bastion. He sprinted as hard as he could, leaving his brothers far behind. He leapt over furniture and crushed wet bones beneath his heavy tread. Doors slammed open as he drove his shoulder into them and his cries of rage and anguish echoed behind him throughout the corridors and stairways.

His brothers were now twenty paces behind him, desperately trying to catch up. Uthiel burst out of the bastion and leapt straight into the barbarians who had pushed the

Secundans back into the mouth of the bridge, some twenty feet beyond the door he burst from. Within his first moments back out in the storm, he unleashed five whip-crack strikes and slew five warriors before they could even register he was there.

He swung and moved with a fluidity of movement engrained within his very bones and sinew. Every flick and strike of his swords drew blood and screams of surprise and pain as he drove into them like a berserker. Axes began to clang from his armour as he used his blades only to take life, allowing the souls of the Grey Wolves long dead imbued in his armour to protect his body.

Over his shoulder an axe rose to split his skull in half, but fell from a dead hand a moment before striking. Uthiel turned his gaze for a moment, spotting and then forgetting the bolt that had impaled the man's skull in from behind. Three storeys above him, Keldon pulled the string on his crossbow back again. Finally, Branor and the other Grey Wolves managed to catch up to Uthiel and together they strove through towards where a son had last seen his beloved father.

Behind him brother Palon fell, a wicked half moon axe buried up to its haft through the back of his helm. Uthiel looked back but instantly knew his man was dead. In front of him a screaming warrior fell to his knees with a crossbow bolt though his stomach. Uthiel flicked his sword out in a brutal arc that defied the eye with its speed and ended the man's life. Beneath his gorget he felt something burning his chest. As its heat intensified, his focus sharpened.

To Uthiel's left Branor hacked and slashed with his blade, leaping forward to protect his crazed friend as more axes were aimed at the charging knight. Bearded, tattooed faces flashed past, lost in sprays and explosions of gore. Steel glinted in the wan light and impacts rang off his armour. To lose his focus or drop more than a step behind Uthiel at the spear tip for a fraction of a heartbeat was to die.

This is what they were made for, what they lived for. Fear and horror conquered by courage and faith. Despite the danger, Branor let out a loud war whoop as his blood fired.

The sharp tip of an axe bit through Branor's shield and he struck out, revelling in the spray of blood his blade smacked out of the bare head of his assailant. Before him Uthiel was a whirlwind of destruction. His two blades cut into the thickening foe at an unbelievable rate and his tally of mortal blows was fearsome. His armour was taking a battering and Branor leapt forward to block a killing strike that surely would have caved in the back of his lifelong friend's bare head.

Finally, in a charge of some thirty feet that had lasted a lifetime and a heartbeat in an instant, Uthiel stopped atop a pile of bodies of the Secundan Fifth, barbarians and a spattering of king's guards and their mounts. The sheer ferocity and recklessness of their charge had pushed a gap around them and the four Grey Wolves had a heartbeat's respite. Some of the barbarians became stand-offish, halting in their assault in an odd mix of surprise and disbelief.

Whether it was the gore soaked, beaten, violent visage of Uthiel and his men standing like blood-bloated berserkers at the end of their path of crimson destruction or the unexpected appearance of such a meagre band of warriors some twenty feet out from the Secundan lines, those barbarians stood like gawking youths. At Uthiel's feet lay Tanin. That he had gone to stand by Armenius' side, there was no doubt. A ragged axe wound had cut into the corner where his unprotected neck met his shoulder.

Uthiel dropped to his knees with a cry of grief as his brothers looked around and prepared themselves to meet the Eternal Lord standing guard over the general of the Fifth and his grieving son. But Uthiel did not reach for his father. Instead he grabbed a long wooden pole. With all of his might he hefted the tattered black banner of the mighty Fifth and held it high to fly once more in its sorrowful blood drenched glory, the name of his father roaring from behind his bared teeth heard over the storm.

A roar erupted from the Secundan lines and Uthiel looked over his shoulder to see the Grey Wolves burst forward and smash into the barbarians, their zeal renewed at the sight of such brazen aggression and courage. The moment of pause by the enemy finished, but the first foe to put a foot towards the black banner reeled back as a bolt smacked into his chest. Then the barbarians charged towards Uthiel and his brothers.

With their brother Louen protecting their back, Branor and Uthiel lashed out at the charge. Uthiel struck out with all his rage and might, his legs planted firmly either side of Tanin. Branor's shield rang loudly and bucked violently as axe after axe crashed into it. Their situation was hopeless and they fought all the harder for it. The battle raged all around them like a whirling demon. The barbarians began to compress their charge as Uthiel and his brothers continued to kill. Behind them he heard the Secundan line getting closer and closer.

Uthiel stabbed out his sword to block an axe swinging down at Branor and in doing so left himself open. The impact of the first axe smacked the blade from his grip and without thinking he whipped his arm back and up. A wicked moon bladed axe struck against his vambrance with bone jarring power, dropping his arm below his head. The barbarian holding the blade drew the axe back once more for the killing blow. Uthiel knew that this must be the end.

Armenius welcome -

The blow never landed. A crimson-coated blade lashed out and cut the axe-wielding hand from the barbarian's body and then returned to cut down through his chest. Before Uthiel could react, hundreds of Grey Wolves locked shields with a crash of metal on metal to either side of him. One step further and he was one row back as Louen smoothly moved into position before him.

Step by blood-soaked step the shield wall of the Grey Wolves moved forward and cut into the hated enemy. Swords stabbed out in the lashing rain and bright polished metal shone in the wicked lightning. All of a sudden Solanthur was by his side.

"Well met brother!" cried out the first captain over the clamour of battle.

Uthiel nodded, but looked down to his father's body. "My father has fallen."

Solanthur put a hand on Uthiel's dented and bloody pauldron and removed his own helm. He put his hand on the side of Uthiel's matted hair and directed his head up to lock eyes with the young knight.

"My brother, it is the lot in life of we soldiers to die before our time is due," said Solanthur solemnly. "It is how we live in the time Armenius gives us that will see us remembered. There is a time to remember your father and a time to mourn the fallen. But now is not that time."

Uthiel's eyes hardened and he reached within his gorget, ripping something out from beneath the armour. Solanthur smiled curiously as he saw a necklace with the shape of a wolf's head attached to it come out. Uthiel leant the black banner against his shoulder as he wrapped the leather band around his palm and gripped one of his swords in the same hand. As Uthiel grabbed the banner once more and held it aloft in his left hand, Solanthur reached out and put a hand on his pauldron.

"My brother, it would be my honour if you would join me in the line," said Solanthur.

The young knight looked down as a group of men of the Fifth trudged through the rain and piles of bodies and knelt by their general's side. The Lord Pomen joined them and together they lifted his body upon their shoulders and turned back to the mouth of the bridge as the Fifth once more began its advance to the flanks. One of the men was Camen, Branor's father. With tears in his eyes he placed a hand upon Uthiel's pauldron and then bowed his head and left the front line.

Before leaving, Branor's father spared a glance for the banner. "It would have made him proud to see you carry his banner to victory."

Overhead, arrows began to soar high over the battlefield, their sleek shafts disappearing into the thick rain only to reappear like vengeful reapers and crash into the barbarians. The tide of the battle had begun to turn.

Uthiel nodded dumbly, and with Solanthur they quickly caught up to the advancing Grey Wolves' line and joined their brothers once more in war.

**

318

Nikhael was blood-drunk. Not a single piece of him or his armour existed without a thick coating of the lifeblood of the maidens of Gall. He'd taken to carrying a whetstone around with him as he moved amongst the screaming women, because already one of his blades had been blunted and he'd not have it slowing him down again.

The women and girls he killed no longer had faces, no longer had voices, no longer were people he slew. Inside, his void shone with horrible and pure incandescent light. Were he to stop and rest, were he to try and catch his breath, Nikhael might lose that which burned with life inside. This thought pushed him to further and further excesses.

No longer did he just slit the throats, now he moved under their buttocks after their neck had bled dry and stabbed into the thick vein in their thigh to get at more of the hot goodness within. There was no noise but the thudding of viscera against his body, no feeling but that of the warmth flowing over him and bursting inside the void where his soul should have been, no taste but the sweet metallic blood over his teeth and tongue and down the back of his throat. He'd never felt so alive.

Nikhael roared to the maelstrom in the sky, the mouth of its swirling vortex reaching right down through the howling rain. In the centre, a hole almost as wide as the keep itself seemed to draw the knight up into it, toward a sky darker than the blackest pitch. With the swirling clouds and the red and white lighting, the sky above the city looked like a massive pupil and raging iris of a fell god. Thunder roared back at Nikhael.

He laughed an unsmiling, barking laugh that challenged anything and anyone to try to ruin this awesome feeling. Without even realising he'd moved, he found another woman's screaming mouth above him, a fat wad of her drenched hair in his fist and his blade cutting the very life from her. Then it was another, and another and another. He'd not bothered counting but he must have cut a thousand throats already this day. Limbs that should have ached with effort roared with power.

Someone grabbed his pauldron, a shouted voice buzzing almost soundlessly in his ear. His gaze levelled at the Black Wolf who stood before him. Thick rivers of fresh steaming blood mixed with the rain and ran from his matted eyebrows onto his deep red cheeks. Before him stood Kael. Nikhael felt a brief flash of annoyance as he saw their leader so thickly coated with the life of the sacrifices he looked almost black. He saw two heads hanging by their hair from his hips. If he had taken a thousand souls, then surely Kael must have sacrificed twice that many.

Kael's lips moved but still his voice could not break the thick fog that surrounded Nikhael's mind. Nonchalantly the young Secundan tipped his head to the side, a runnel of coagulating blood trickling from his ear. Hearing some success, he did the same with his other ear.

"...are at the bridge. The barbarians are scattering. We must finish the sacrifice!" yelled Kael.

Nikhael did not speak, to do so would have been pointless as Zhar T'hur's rage unleashed its fury above, lightning bringing unholy light to almost every exposed surface in the city, and thunderclaps crashing like the death of worlds above. Without even noticing he had been doing so, the whetstone had been rasping against the dulled edge of his blade. With a soulless grin he turned, only having heard the part of Kael's message he wanted to hear, and whipped the knife up through the throat of an old woman.

CHAPTER TWENTY-FIVE

The Grey Wolves' first company were the first men to arrive at the immense gates of Gall. Stones half as tall as Uthiel made the square edges of the shattered gate. A devastated wooden door lay burned amongst blackened iron bars inside the twenty-foot tall awning. The tower above stretched high into the sky and was menacing against the backdrop of the roaring maelstrom above. Rain smashed into them from all sides, stinging their eyes with fat drops and clattering against their armour in an effort to deafen them all. To the right of the gate, the walls of Gall stretched off into the distance, massive and indestructible, to be quickly lost into the sheeting rain, while on the left the sap had brought down a large section. Knights of the second company moved off to investigate the breach and quickly disappeared into the darkness.

The stench of death was almost as thick as the downpour. Well-rotted meat and stagnant faecal matter assaulted the senses of the knights as they slowly moved under the tall gate. Around them piles of corpses, sometimes six or seven bodies deep, ringed them in to the gaping maw of Gall. Inside, the destruction was even worse. Uthiel had to climb up upon a thick carpet of barbarians and Gall soldiers who had fallen in the most brutal of bloodlettings as thousands of men had butchered each other for the ownership of the gate to the city.

Faces, dark with the leftovers of carrion birds, and white with the bones picked clean, looked up at them from eyeless sockets. Broken limbs were splayed like a burnt-out forest and the dull glint of bare metal caught what little light reached under the gate where the dark red of rust did not corrode its surface. The solid round shields of the soldiers of Gall were cracked and splintered as much as their previous bearers while many of the axes of the enemy were still buried in the bodies of the fallen.

Uthiel dipped the banner to ensure its head did not strike the arch above, and took his first step upon the rotted flesh of the fallen. Almost an hour ago, they had broken the back of the barbarians. A scant few hundred had fled the battlefield and men of the Seventh had given chase throughout the city while the Grey Wolves and the Fifth moved into the gate.

For thirty feet, Uthiel crunched his way over the dead, not noticing the lack of rain as he followed the hunched-over advance of the Grey Wolves before him. Before them the arch into the city was a dark curve, against which the bright light of a lightning strike lit up the thick mat of bodies outside that lay strewn in an ever-expanding arc around the entrance to the city like a vast rug in the cold halls of Death herself.

The city near the walls was eerily empty and completely devoid of life. The triangle banners of Gall nobles fluttered wildly from polearms whose hafts had been buried in the enemy's bodies. As they stepped out into the rain once more and formed up a shield wall, Uthiel looked to the sky. Never had he seen a storm so tumultuous in its rage. Hard drops of rain increased their intensity like a body fighting infection. The Secundans leaned into the gale and began to forge their way up the main road towards the heart of the city.

It took some time to get the remaining strength of the Grey Wolves through the gate and as they began to slowly search through the destruction of the people of Gall, the men of the Fifth began to get through and form up behind and to the side of them. The Lord General Thomak stood with the king, who had dismounted with his guard around him, and together they ordered the Fifth to move through the flanks of the city while the combined might of the knights and the king's guards, over five hundred plate-armoured warriors, marched up the centre.

As soon as the last units of the Fifth came through, almost two hours later, they began their march with the Grey Wolves in the lead. Above the black banner and the banners of the Grey Wolves, the angrily swirling vortex continued to roar its disapproval at their intention with bone shuddering claps of thunder and horribly radiant snaps of lightning. Uthiel tried to shake the rain from his eyes as he looked to the sky and frowned at what he saw.

Branor's eyes were also skyward through the slit in his helm. "It's coming down closer!" he yelled.

Uthiel nodded in agreement. It was coming down closer, of that there could be no mistake. In a moment that nearly stopped his heart, a blindingly white strike of lightning crashed into the tall metal spire of a house before them. The roof exploded out, showering the front line of men in tiny pieces of slate roof and stone. Then a second one destroyed a house across the street and it was in this light that Uthiel first saw the tall trestle constructed before them.

It was about fifty paces up the road, and had it not been for the lightning he may not have seen it through the rain and darkness. As they moved closer he saw more and more trestles, the horizontal piece of them an extra foot or two above Uthiel's soaked hair. As they got closer and closer, Uthiel felt the tension rise to an almost palpable state and a familiar tingle ran down his spine.

He tried to place the feeling as he strained his eyes at the dark silhouettes of the trestles now only twenty paces ahead of the advancing shield wall. He felt his skin crackle for a heartbeat before he heard the explosion behind him. Whirling around, he was almost blinded by the burst of light, but through the swirling afterimages of the bolt of lightning he saw Grey Wolves and king's guards alike hurled, blackened and broken, into the air by the furious thunderbolt that detonated the very cobblestones it smacked into.

Turning back to the fore, he saw them. Hundreds of trestles, and upon them were hundreds of naked white bodies with their dead hair flowing wetly in the wrath of the storm. Men yelled out in fear but knew not where to run as another house detonated under the immense force of a lighting strike and thunder rolled above in constant concussive booms of raw power. Uthiel did not move, and looked to the ground. The mud was red and it was running downhill from the city centre in a fast running stream of diluted blood and sludge.

Uthiel heard Thomak yell something unintelligible, before the men behind him began to push forwards. Uthiel tried not to look up. Men around him did the same, keeping their gazes below the horror, as they knew any moment could be their last and to see one of the faces of the women the Lands of the Light had failed in their last moments was to look at the ragged mortal wound that Gall herself had become, and despair.

Twice more, lightning struck the ranks of the Grey Wolves and the king's guards. Dozens of men fell as incandescent tongues of light leapt between the metal ranks, and explosively cooked knights alive. As they moved forward, the black banner remained tall and proud amongst the banners of the Wolves, but the men under them began to grow fearful at the full scale of the field of slaughter the city had become.

Every street was filled with trestles, and upon every trestle were the drained remains of a girl or lady of Gall. For an hour straight, they moved through the rows of trestle legs, still none wanting to look up into the wide open eyes of the dead. This horrid nightmare of butchery and madness seemed to go on forever for the Grey Wolves as they moved through forests of trestles dangling pale limbs.

Whispers of screams of terror licked the ears of the men like ghoulish lovers; such was the malice of the streets of Gall. Uthiel risked a glance to the sky above as he moved between wooden legs and cried out.

Above the very centre of the city, not two hundred paces away, the swirling epicentre of the maelstrom had constricted and dipped so low it had swallowed the top of the keep. Lightning cracked within its grey and red walls with such frequency that an unholy light flickered like a brilliant embattled flame over the core of the city, breaching the sheeting rain that flew almost horizontally now in its evil vigour.

Up ahead, Uthiel and his brothers saw dark shapes flicking amongst the forest of trestles, with the unmistakeable gait of warriors and bulk of plate armoured men. The large pauldrons on those men left no doubt as to who they were. A shrill scream carried to them. It was sharply cut off but the message was clear. Uthiel once again felt the charge before he heard the order.

Charging right into our erstwhile brothers. Right in to men that should have been fighting by our sides. He looked to his brothers either side of him. *And they don't even know.*

The first two fallen brethren didn't even notice the charging knights, such was the obsession with the warm blood splashing on to them from above. Solanthur slew both men, his blade driven with such rage and power that it cut through their cuirasses brutally. Both Black Wolves fell without a sound, one of them even giggling wetly as he tumbled.

As if sensing their arrival as one, over a hundred plate clad, blood drenched knights turned from their sacrifices and with one voice unleashed a horrific roar that mortal vocal chords should not have been able to sound. Jaws distended unnaturally, and long after breath should have been spent, their unholy scream swept through the wind and rain towards the charging knights.

The Secundan charge faltered a moment but the sight of their unwavering first captain stirred them forwards. Solanthur had his shield up and his sword raised ready to smite the foe, his legs powering him to the nearest enemy. As the first captain's crimson blade slashed down to strike, Uthiel heard the sound of chanting voices.

He looked up to see dark shapes moving arrhythmically as if they phased in and out of reality, like the strobe effect of lightning in the pitch darkness of night, upon the roofs above them. Staffs with chains and skulls and other perilous tokens of

325

the dark god clattered and whipped against bloodied skin as they twirled amongst the cacophony of the storm above.

Then came the impact. Like one immense rock smashing into another the two lines met with unbelievable force. Bodies flew and, in heroic moments that lasted less than the blink of an eye, ended with brutal finality as knight after knight fell under sword and claw and shield on both sides. Black Wolves who had scythed through the front row found themselves isolated and hacked down in the same manner as the Grey Wolves who pushed too far into the enemy.

Uthiel heard a cry of surprise behind him and turned for a moment to see some knights standing in a circle staring in abject horror at the shaggy and swaying form of one of the dead men in Secundan plate. From under matted hair, milky dead eyes stared blankly at the men around it. The chanting caught on the wind and began to intensify. The second body on the ground twitched.

"Kill it! Kill it now!" screamed Uthiel.

The knights hesitated and the creature leapt, smashing its fist through the first knight's helm. A heartbeat later two more knights were dead and the swords began to rain upon the beast as the Grey Wolves hacked it and its companion to pieces.

Uthiel growled with animalistic rage, raising the banner high before slamming its wooden pole into the ground below. The standard drove in between two cobblestones with enough force for Uthiel to release the haft and leave it freestanding, its black material billowing in the storm. He called to his men and as one his three knights split off from the line of Grey Wolves and ran towards him. Branor looked up and saw the shamans. Despite their full encasing of armour, Uthiel could see the livid rage coming from his brother in waves.

"Our brothers are soon to be attacked by powers so foul, I can barely speak of them without the need to spit," said Uthiel. "We alone have faced these horrors before and lived. We alone know what we face. We four, right now, need to save our brothers. Are you with me?"

All three of his brothers dipped their heads in unison and their tinny voices came from their helms as one. "For Armenius and the king, brother."

Uthiel smiled grimly. "For Armenius and the king."

Uthiel charged through the front door of the three-storey house. At first they met only scant resistance. Weedy barbarians flew at them, or away from them. Either way one of Uthiel's blades cut through them mercilessly.

As they reached the second floor they risked a glance out of the window. Outside, their brothers fought desperately against the berserk onslaught of the enemy. Despite his brothers' belief these were barbarians dressed in their tainted armour, Uthiel knew better. These men were traitor knights whose souls had been sold to a dark god and they fought like demons, taking three and four brothers with them screaming to their deaths and then rising again to rip into the ranks of the Grey Wolves.

The chanting had grown in volume. It buffeted them like children's fists, but grew in intensity with every step the four young Grey Wolves took towards the third storey. Uthiel snarled and leapt up the stairs with Branor in tow. They burst out onto the rooftop and the chanting turned into an incomprehensible roar of fell rage. Shamans were everywhere.

They danced and chanted and struck at themselves brutally, guttural voices roaring and whispering. Grossly distended jaws hung below disgustingly white eyes hooded under greasy dreadlocks. Odd shapes that confused the eyes nauseatingly with their sudden depth and movement had been inserted under the taut skin of these... these... men. Uthiel struggled to actually call them men as he watched their elongated, bone-thin limbs snap left and right in their twitching dance.

Uthiel felt the chain in his hand glow hot and burn into his flesh. A quick glance showed the wolf's head talisman shining bright in the darkness.

Uthiel smiled. "Brothers, Armenius is with us! Slay them all!"

He launched himself forward and had cut through three of the monsters before they turned on him. The sheer force of their chants struck at him like hammer blows. His ears rung and bled as sound pitched so high it turned to static. One shaman stood at the centre, heavy tattoos and brow sickle shaped insertions showing him as an authority amongst the monsters. His fist struck out in Uthiel's direction and, although he was over ten feet away, Uthiel flew back like he'd been struck by a sledgehammer.

He clipped Branor on the way as he flew back and both knights smashed into the ground. The shaman leader's focus set on Keldon. The knight whipped his crossbow up and fired. The bolt flew true but stopped mid flight as the shaman raised his filthy palm, fetishes swinging wildly from his wrist. With his other hand he formed a hollow fist and began to squeeze. Keldon screamed out in pain as his armour first protested and then began to buckle. The chanting of the shamans around was so loud Keldon's scream was whipped up in it and turned back against him. In a heartbeat it was cut off as his cuirass and pauldrons cracked and his body imploded, thick sprays of Secundan blood gushing from every joint and opening in his destroyed armour.

With a flash of steel, Keldon dropped as Louen launched himself at the lead shaman and smashed him from his feet bodily. Uthiel got to his feet with a cry of anguish and with Branor they both charged in after Louen. Before they could reach him the sprawling shaman leader writhed a long bladed black dagger from a fur pouch and stabbed in to the gap between Louen's gorget and helm as twenty and more shamans, their jaws still distended, leapt upon the stricken knight and tore him to pieces.

Uthiel and Branor slammed into the shamans like a pair of steel-tipped hurricanes, hacking and slashing like lunatics. The shock of their attack bit through the static roar of the chanting as carved-up shamans flew back from their frenzied destruction of Louen. The murderous evil of their chanting soon began to stutter and fail as more and more of their voices were cut from the cacophony of their malevolence.

Uthiel drove one blade through the stomach of a screaming shaman before spinning and ducking to lash out and cut the legs from under two more as they desperately grasped the air where his head had been a moment ago. Beside him, Branor stomped on the throat of one he had just smashed to the ground and crouched to hammer the lower point of his kite shield through the nose and eye socket of his foe. Uthiel came up and all of a sudden was facing the monster that had slain Keldon and Louen.

With a roar of pure burning hatred Uthiel strode forwards.

"As long as I fight in his name,
And draw the blood of those that would sully Mother Secunda, for Him..."
His right fist rose high, the glow of the wolf's head talisman bringing light to his face.
"The Eternal Lord shall be my blade!"

Uthiel's sword smashed down in a strike of such tremendous force he split the scrawny figure of the shaman from his left collarbone through and out the right hip. The shaman exploded with a clap of thunder and Uthiel was launched backwards once more, crashing to the ground and sliding into Keldon's remains.

Unsteady, he clambered to his feet and saw Branor walking towards him when incandescent light nearly blinded him. He looked away and shielded his eyes, waiting for the lightning strike to fade away, but it did not. Instead it grew brighter, pricking his skin and warming his armour despite the ongoing downpour. He forced himself to the edge of the roof that was closest to the source of the light and with an outstretched hand shading his eyes, looked towards the city centre.

It was as if the castle had disappeared into the vortex above and now a twenty-foot thick solid vertical lance of lightning stood like the tallest tower, spearing down from the sky in a continuous flow. At its base Uthiel could just make out two figures as black shadow blotches against light so bright it was as if the sun itself had fallen to the cobblestones of Gall. Pieces of stone and wood floated up from the where the light struck the ground, slowly at first until they were whipped up and lost.

In the street below, the Grey Wolves and king's guards still fought, and had been pushed back almost fifty feet by the ravenous dead but, without the shamans those fiends had fallen lifeless once more and the true sons of Secunda began to push back. At the forefront of the fighting, as ever, was First Captain Solanthur Verutus. His armour was in ruin but his body was powerful and skilful as he skewered and slashed a Black Wolf to the ground.

Uthiel's gaze spared a moment from the crash of battle to look for Keldon. There was no doubt he had passed beyond this mortal realm: where he should have been tall and broad, he had been crushed to almost two thirds his original size.

"He deserved a more glorious death," said Branor beside him sadly, able to speak with the chanting gone.

"He'll be watching over us with Armenius now," said Uthiel.

"That he will, he was a good man."

"Come Bran, there are few foes left with which to avenge our fallen brothers and I'll not allow a single one of these fiends to stand while Secundan blood stains this city."

Branor looked to Keldon once more. "I'll avenge you my friend, I swear it."

Uthiel put a hand on Branor's dented and bloodied pauldron. "Keldon Tremorne, our brother, our friend. Vengeance will be yours this night. By Armenius I swear it will be yours this very night!"

Uthiel looked back to the two black blotches at the base of the white light. Something inside him urged him to face them. Something urged him to go down and smite the foe for all he was worth. His hand burned ever more intensely, though he refused the pain its vindication and tightened his grip on his sword hilt and talisman as he and Branor turned to run down the stairs and back onto the street.

**

Around Emilia, the screams of fear intensified as the armour-clad barbarians came ever closer, a woman's life ending every time she felt her racing heart punch the inside of her chest. Her breathing was ragged and though tears of fear streamed down her cheeks, she still fought on. Ripped nails and bloodied fingers pulled and pushed at one of her bonds desperately and with all of her might.

Emilia wriggled and writhed upon the trestle, barely noticing the harsh splinters as they worked their way under her red flesh. All of a sudden, with a cry of release, the rope tying her hands together behind her back came loose. Clamping her mouth shut and cursing herself for such stupidity, she moved her head carefully around to see if any of the barbarians had heard.

All of the leather – and fur – clad ones had left a while ago, rushing towards the city gates in their thousands, leaving only the ones in stolen Secundan plate to enact their bloody sacrifice. Seeing nobody had noticed her small victory, Emilia reached upwards and felt the knot between her shoulder blades that was keeping her chest flat to the wood. She took a deep breath and calmed herself, trying to feel out the best way to unravel the knot.

Closing her eyes she pictured it, trying to match it to some of the knots her father had taught her when she was young. Her raw fingers soothed over the heavy duty binding, feeling it loop back on itself multiple times until she worked out its pattern. She gripped a piece of it and pushed gently. The position she was in saw her force her flexibility and strength to its limit just to achieve this small act.

In an instant, the knot came loose and she was bound only by a single rope looped over her buttocks and ankles. She looked around again. There were two of the disgusting enemy making their way towards her. Around her women screamed out in terror, but this only spurred the barbarians on, their movements becoming faster as they greedily bathed in both the terror and the lifeblood of the unfortunate. Upon the trestle next to her, a plump elderly woman spotted Emilia as she dropped the second rope to the ground.

Emilia locked eyes with her for a moment and saw unreasoning terror. The woman mouthed to her; *help me.*

Emilia nodded and slowly pushed her bottom backwards over bent knees while keeping her head against the trestle to keep her movements as secretive as possible. Her hands reached back and grabbed the third and final knot. She began to work on it.

"Help me!" hissed the woman.

Emilia ignored her, focussing on the knot as her fingers began to painfully pry it loose.

"Help me!" snarled the woman, getting louder as her frustration grew. "Get me out of here!"

Emilia shot her a glance, "Shut up! They'll hear you and then we'll both be killed!"

The knot unravelled and Emilia began to pull the rope from her body as she looked around and saw that the two barbarians were now thirty feet closer, having carved their way through no less than thirty innocents. Somewhere nearby but out of sight, the sound of battle began to echo.

Emilia daintily dropped to the ground and turned her back on the plump woman to see once more where the barbarians were.

"Don't you dare leave me here you little bitch!" screamed the fat woman shrilly.

Emilia turned to say something but the damage was already done. With a wordless roar, one of the barbarians ran at her drunkenly, crashing through the legs of trestles and sending their contents crashing to the ground. Emilia, standing there in naught but what she was born in, turned and fled with a muffled cry of dismay, cutting left and right through the forest of wooden legs.

Behind her, the monster smashed through the legs of the plump woman's trestle. With no limbs free to brace for the impact, she screamed once more as her face plummeted down and connected with the cobblestone in a sickening crunch that drove her jaw bone through the fatty flesh on the back of her neck.

Emilia aimed for an old butcher store and burst through its door, her wet feet sliding on the sand-covered stone floor and sending her crashing into a set of shelves. Knives and cleavers clattered to the floor around her, one slamming into her with its flat but still managing to slice her skin as it slid from her. She could hear his feet pounding towards the door. A fresh burst of terror pushed her to her feet, razor sharp knife in hand, and then under a table as she scurried to a hiding spot.

She only had a few ragged breaths to settle herself before the barbarian crashed in through the door, forearm-length knife raised and bare face snapping from left to right looking for her. His breathing was loud and harsh. Emilia clamped a hand over her mouth as she watched his booted feet step closer towards her, leaving partly congealed bloody footprints behind him. She gripped the knife in her hand harder and harder as he came closer.

Then he stopped right by her table. He stood there for a moment, his boots twitching as if he was a child with far too much energy. A fist slammed down into the table above her, a cry of frustrated rage echoing inside the walls. Emilia kept her silence, though how he had not heard her hammering heart she would never know. Then the boots turned around and the barbarian stood facing the opposite direction.

Father. Your kind killed my father. Your kind killed my mother. My sisters. My uncles. Everyone I ever knew. Your kind killed them all.

Emilia reached out with her blade, to the side of his boot near the ankle. With one fluid motion, putting all of her weight, power and pent up anger into the strike, she stabbed the blade into the side of his leg, just above and behind the ankle, with the sharp edge facing her. The barbarian howled in shock but Emilia was not done yet. With a hard flick of her wrist the blade exploded out the back of his boot and severed the tendon. The barbarian collapsed and Emilia threw herself out from under the table, urgently trying to get away from him as he fell.

A backhand lashed out and caught Emilia on the side of the face, her legs flicking out from under her and her back slamming into the sandy stone underneath her. Her breath exploded from her lungs and through blind luck she rolled away. The sharp clang of the barbarian's blade kissing the stone ground behind her let her know just how close she had been to being carved in two upon its length.

Emilia forced herself to roll again, and in doing so avoided a second knife strike but also cornered herself away from any windows or doors. The barbarian tried to stand but again stumbled, his severed tendon failing to hold him upright. As he fell Emilia dodged past the stricken monster. Despite his wound, the blade flicked out and cut into her side, bouncing off a rib and sliding clear. White pain carved through her and Emilia fell.

Looking up, Emilia spotted two things: firstly, the open door to the outside, and a heavy meat cleaver within arm's reach. Fight or fly, her choices were simple. Her fingers wrapped around the polished bone handle of the cleaver. Its heavy blade weighed her down but she hefted it over her shoulder anyway and levelled her glare at the barbarian before her.

He limped heavily forwards, his sneer drooling blood from a bitten tongue or from a Gall woman, towards the battered and bruised form of Emilia. She stood side on to him, her weight on her bent front leg, cleaver up and over her shoulder like an axe ready to split wood, and fierce eyes staring malevolently at him between matted long dark brown hair. Blood streamed down from her ribs and dribbled to the floor over her long lean legs.

The barbarian swept back his head, looking to the ceiling and laughed. It was raw and guttural and terrible to behold as his jaw distended and his tongue lolled out the side of his mouth. His eyes began to sweep back down.

"If my lady Ambar had been anything like you I'd still be in Secund..."

He never got to finish that sentence. He saw the heavy blade slicing through the air for his throat. Registered the leap she had taken to reach his height. Tried desperately to whip his head back and out of harm's way. Hoped his pauldron collar was tall enough to take the blow. Felt raw pain as never before as the heavy chopping blade cut through his neck and severed it all the way back to his spine. All this in one blink of an eye.

He reeled a few staggering steps backwards as a thick red smile appeared across his throat and then fell as the gash turned into a waterfall of blood down his gorget and cuirass. Emilia landed upon his legs as he crashed to the floor and his hands grappled for her. They grabbed a handful of her hair and yanked her face up towards his with failing strength.

Emilia wrestled and pulled, but even mortally wounded, he was far too strong for her. With a scream she hacked again with the cleaver, and then again and again. Straddling his chest with her knees, her hair free of his grasp as his hand fell to the floor devoid of its physical link to him, she arched her back and with both hands brought the blade crashing down into his face, splitting it vertically in two down to the bottom jaw.

She stood on shaky legs, her eyes glued to the grotesque form as she backed away towards the door. She retched once, twice, and then vomited at the sight. Outside, she could still hear screaming. She ran to the door and looked out to see that the second barbarian had been completely oblivious to his friend's demise and had continued down the street, having slit the throats of some twenty or thirty more women.

She was about to run in the opposite direction when something stopped her. A memory that turned her stomach and made her want to explode with rage at the same time. The barbarian had said to her:

If my Lady Ambar had been anything like you I'd still be in Secund...

...I'd still be in Secund...

...Secunda.

Her vision snapped back to the broad shoulders of the barbarian still murdering his way through the forest of women. She turned around and stormed back over to the man she had just killed, wrenching the cleaver free. With a hot breath she ran out into the rain, towards the traitorous Secundan knight.

335

CHAPTER TWENTY-SIX

Uthiel burst from the door with Branor. One glance away from the centre of the city told him that down the road, the Grey Wolves had the upper hand and were swiftly hacking through the remaining foes. The other direction still came close to blinding him but with his closest friend and Grey Wolf brother by his side Uthiel strode forward with one of his red blades in either blood soaked hand.

The rain that whipped at the two brothers was like a swarm of biting flies as every drop struck with such force on exposed skin it stung like pelting ice. They leant into the wind and trudged forward, intent on their prey. Before them the two blurry black silhouettes stood before the pillar of brutal light. Both looked to have their arms raised to the sky.

The two Secundans continued up the road, two men of the light walking towards two men steeped in dark mystery. They continued to pick their way around trestle after trestle, looking up every now and then for a sign of life but only seeing pale, cold death.

The wind and rain lashed against them vigorously and fell voices once more swooped through the sky. One of the dark figures turned away from the light, a smoky trail of luminescence being whipped away from his eyes, which now provided the only point of light on the black shadow. That figure began to stride towards them while behind it, the other dark shape remained unmoved.

Uthiel and Branor were undeterred in their advance, a stern frown upon Uthiel's face as they approached the opponent before them. In a movement that defied the eye with its speed, a blade flashed into either hand and was raised towards them in challenge. A heartbeat later the shadowed figure was charging towards them.

As the figure got closer Uthiel saw the filed teeth around a gaping mouth, the well-muscled but tattooed arms and in an instant knew who they faced. Not for the briefest moment did his heart know fear as his anger burned within like the hottest blacksmith's furnace and the coldest ice at the same time. Raw fury and the want to visit absolute brutal destruction upon his foe tempered by the iron will instilled by his training.

"Kael!" yelled Uthiel.

Kael smiled in recognition and pulled up in his charge only ten feet away from Uthiel and Branor.

"Young Grey Wolves," he sneered. "Not sated by the beating I delivered to you months ago, you've come to allow me to sacrifice you to Zhar T'hur."

The very name of the dark god was like a blow against Uthiel's mind. It clawed and scrabbled at him, seeking to pull the raging beast within out from under the iron clad discipline that held it in check. Images of murder, depraved slaughter, and hateful sacrifice flicked past him at the sound and Uthiel dropped to his knee, pressing the back of his forearm to his forehead.

Beside him Branor also struggled, a long fleck of drool slipping from the bottom of his helmet and groans of pain and rage accompanied the straining tendons of his body as he fought to control his rising bloodlust. Above both of them Kael smiled wickedly and drew a blade across his cheek to spill his own blood.

"For you, my god, these two are for you to take and own."

337

Uthiel roared in pent up rage as he struggled to his feet. The sky above flashed to match the pillar of light and one word blasted into his mind.

MINE

Uthiel and Branor were flung back and crashed into the forest of trestles behind them, collapsing three or four with their heavy impacts. Uthiel had dropped his swords and clutched his head with both hands as he fought to retain his soul. Beside him Branor was convulsing, his helmet had been flung from his head and his eyes had rolled back in his head.

With a sheer effort of will, Uthiel reached out and grabbed one of his swords. A few heartbeats later he put a foot under himself and staggered forwards to lay his hand on another. In what seemed an eternity he struggled to his feet, a thin trickle of crimson dribbling from his ear. His limbs felt like they were frozen. The warm glow from the talisman flickered in time with his heart and then once again burned strong as he gripped his blade with renewed strength. The light gave warmth to his limbs. Pain prickled but it reminded him he was alive in this nightmare. And if he was alive, he had brothers to avenge.

He looked back to Branor. His brother was on his hands and knees, heaving and dry retching and screaming incoherently with rage. Uthiel turned away and took a step towards Kael. Where Uthiel looked like a castle sat upon his shoulders, weighing him down, Kael moved with the grace of a lion, loosening up his thickly blood-coated shoulders and arms as he approached.

"I'm going to enjoy cutting you pieces, one bloody lesson at a time!" shouted Kael, his smile pure evil as he stretched his neck left, and then right.

Summoning all of his strength and concentration, Uthiel leapt forwards and swung at Kael. Kael didn't even deign to raise his blade in defence, swaying backwards and laughing as his sword whipped up and carved through Uthiel's pauldron like it was made of paper. Uthiel cried out as his blood sprayed out away from his body, was sucked up into the wind and fed into the incandescent light behind Kael. Something that was no longer human groaned in pleasure and anticipation. Something that was so far beyond humanity, and yet so far below it.

Before Uthiel could react, another blade licked out and sliced through his cuirass, leaving a burning line of blood across his chest. Once again, Kael was playing with him and dodged backwards nimbly as Uthiel wildly lashed out at him. Uthiel stepped forward and struck out again and again. While Kael avoided or parried each blow with ease, Uthiel felt his control and focus begin to return as he moved through the attacking combinations he'd trained so hard to grasp.

He began to move more fluidly and managed to land a glancing blow upon a blood-encrusted pauldron. Kael laughed and spun away, unharmed. Uthiel followed him and their blades met in a series of constant clashes that connected with blinding speed. Uthiel was one moment on the front foot, then defending and ducking, before springing forwards to strike out again. Kael mirrored his moves seemingly with ease, but the scowl of concentration and effort on his face spoke otherwise.

A blade sliced across Uthiel's thigh, just between his mail skirt and greaves. Uthiel stumbled but righted himself in time to stop a decapitating swing that his angled sword guided over his head. The unsuspected carry-through took Kael by surprise and Uthiel rose and drove his knee into Kael's midriff, lifting the big man off his feet. With a desperate slash he carved deep into the Black Wolf's bicep, cutting through the muscle and hitting bone.

Kael roared, but not in pain, as one of his blades clattered to the cobblestones. Pleasure crossed his face as the wind whipped his blood back and into the bright beam. Uthiel looked over Kael's shoulder and saw the light had intensified and become slimmer, almost half its original width. That moment of curiosity almost cost him his life and Kael attacked as if the cost of his grievous wound had only seen to drive him further into madness-born strength.

Uthiel defended himself desperately, swerving and ducking as Kael struck at him with sword and knee and foot. The young knight was desperate as Kael hacked at him with enough power to fell a tree. Then Uthiel saw his chance. A brief moment of hesitation as Kael moved to strike with his wounded arm without thinking and the last piece of connecting muscle in his bicep snapped with the strain and flicked back within his flesh. In that moment Uthiel struck out and cut Kael's sword wielding hand from his arm.

In the same move he slammed his shoulder into Kael. The Black Wolf was flung onto his back. Uthiel leapt forwards, dropping one sword to the ground and gripping the other with both hands and with all his might drove it into and through Kael's midriff and into the stone below. Kael grappled at him with useless limbs, his sharp-toothed mouth spitting blood and profanity in equal portions. Uthiel twisted the blade with a cry of rage and release, then fell to his knees.

Kael was chuckling and gurgling, his blind eyes snapping open and shut. "Zhar T'hur knows your rage. He knows your lust, and he wants your soul."

Kael laughed harder and convulsed. "And he shall have it."

With a cry of rage Uthiel drew his forearm-length blade and drove it down and through the side of Kael's head, just above the ear, pinning his hated foe in a second place to the cobblestone and ending this one monster's hold over Secunda.

Above him, the pillar of light flickered explosively, tossing debris throughout the city as one moment it was there burning with livid hatred, and the next moment there was but an after image only to be once again replaced by the searing lance of fire. Something triggered within Uthiel and he turned back to Branor as the lone figure at the base of the light began to turn.

"Bran!" bellowed Uthiel. "It's them! It's' the Black Wolves! They hold this storm and this power to this place! We must slay them all! Bran!"

But Branor was not there.

"Bran?"

Something slammed into Uthiel's side and smashed him into the ground. Fingers tore at his face and powerfully wrestled with the plates of his armour. A dark shape punched and struck at him and shouted in pain and pleasure as Uthiel moved and a fist struck the cobblestones with the power of a trained warrior behind it.

Uthiel punched back and reached for his knife, cursing as he glimpsed it still buried up to the hilt in the side of Kael's head. He lifted his forearms and blocked the rending fingernails, desperately kicking his feet to get him out from under the demon who straddled him. Human teeth snapped as his face, the owner of them snarling like a rabid animal. Spitting saliva slapped against Uthiel's forehead and spilled into his eyes.

Uthiel managed to put a knee between him and this monster and with a desperation-filled effort, launched the thing off him. It landed with a clatter of plate armour against cobblestone. Uthiel stood and quickly found his sword as the demon before him slowly and menacingly stood up.

The tattered remnants of a grey tabard hung from around the man's neck, which sat deep within the protection of the tall thick collar of two large pauldrons. A dented and rent cuirass covered the man's stocky physique and unkempt hair dangled over his eyes and face, which finished in a jaw quivering with pent up rage and undistilled hate.

Curled lips worked soundlessly over bared and bloodied teeth, while scratched hands clenched and unclenched. Under the armour of Secunda, the man's body was a coiled-up spring of potential death. Uthiel tensed, ready for the imminent fight. The wind whipped the man's hair out of his face and Uthiel's knees buckled, his spirit broken.

"Brother," rasped Branor's voice through a cracked grin.

Only it wasn't Branor's voice. Nowhere in the noise that came from that man's mouth was the cheeky, happy, supportive voice that had never left Uthiel's side in all of his years of life. Gone were the memories of cavorting with maidens or drinking ale or laughing with their friends and family or competing during their training. All that remained was bloody betrayal.

Branor spoke again, smaller voices whirling within the sound. "Join me, accept the dark-light. You cannot imagine its wonders."

Branor took a step towards Uthiel.

"Let it take away fear. Let it destroy hope. Make filthy notions like honour and duty melt into nothing."

Branor stopped and shuddered, then vomited blood, "No! Uthiel, run! Rrr..."

Uthiel's lifelong friend dropped to his knees, wrestling himself, clubbing at the side of his head with his fist. Uthiel watched on in horror as Branor tore at his clothes and armour and hair, screaming shrilly one moment then laughing with rage the next. Uthiel knew what he had to do.

Levering himself up by leaning on his, sword he stumbled forwards. Branor fell to the ground and writhed, white froth spilling from his lips and eyes rolling back in his head once more as he fought his mind and his body. Uthiel gripped his blade and knelt next to his friend. A light golden glow spread against his friend's face as the wolf's head talisman hung over him.

Uthiel looked down at it, genuinely surprised to see it still wrapped around his hand. Branor had stopped shaking.

"Kill me, Uthiel, I can't beat it," whispered Branor. "Please, brother. End me."

A tear spilled down Uthiel's cheek. "Bran, no, please. You can beat it. Just fight!"

"It's too strong for me, end this while some of me still lives under the Eternal Lord's light," said Branor.

"Don't make me do this Bran, you're all I've got left!" shouted Uthiel. "Fight!"

"I can't!" sobbed Branor. "I've seen it and I know who lords over the Black Lands. I know who chips away at the Lands of the Light with foul deeds. I have seen it and it has seen me! I know of Zhar T'hur!"

With that the light faded from Branor's eyes and the rage returned. A hand whipped up and grabbed Uthiel's gorget and a deep guttural growl started deep within in his breast. Uthiel struck his friend on the head. Branor's skin split and his head slammed back into the ground. Uthiel wiped the pommel of his blade of his friend's blood.

"I may not be able to save you, my friend, but once I am done there may be others who can pull the taint out of you and return you to me," said Uthiel as he turned to face down his last enemy.

He'd not even seen the man move but the last Black Wolf was not at the base of now drastically flickering and fading light. Uthiel looked around, peering into alleys and houses, even up to rooftops to spot his quarry. Then, pain and weightlessness. Ribs breaking and metal cracking and crumpling. Whistling wind and biting rain, light flashing as he nauseatingly tumbled end over end towards it. And finally, explosively painful impact.

The sound of his bones grinding and his glorious plate armour screeching against the cobblestones rent Uthiel's ears as he slid towards the flashing spear of light. The heat of it burnt his hair and eyebrows as his slide arrested some five feet away from its scorching impact. Uthiel tried to scrabble away but a leather boot slammed into his chest and shoved him flat to the ground.

Above him a gore-coated god of bloodshed stood triumphant. Uthiel looked up, striking his vambrance against the boot with all his might to no effect.

"You waste your effort," said a voice steeped in torture and self-loathing.

Uthiel could do nothing to move the boot on his chest.

"A hundred thousand and more maidens sacrificed so that He can walk amongst us once more and you slay His acolyte and endanger His return."

Uthiel kicked his legs as the light behind his head dissipated for a moment and the rain coolly smacked into his hair and face.

"Without the acolyte, only your blood will slake his thirst. Hah! To think, there is a king and lords and generals just down the road and well within my power to slay and He wants you!?"

The spear of light blasted down behind his head once more. Only the man pinning him to the ground seemed unaffected as the strength of the strike tried to throw Uthiel back to the gates. Uthiel screamed out in hopelessness and agony as the power of a god washed over him once more.

The pressure of the boot on his chest buckled Uthiel's cuirass and he felt his ribs crack once more. His eyes wide open, he looked into his foe's face and the walls of his mind came crashing down as yet another of his brothers revealed his hand in this horrible slaughter.

"Nikhael?"

As far as Branor was gone, Nikhael was a thousand times worse. Of the young, loyal friend with the faraway eyes he'd loved as a brother when younger, there was nothing left. Nothing at all. The horrible realisation tumbled through Uthiel's mind and as it did he felt claws tear at him on the inside as something viciously gained purchase within him. Despair is what it loved to snack upon and in Uthiel, a fraction of Zhar T'hur's immeasurable malice licked its lips in anticipation.

Nikhael's eyes burned into Uthiel's, draining the life from him.

"Oh yes, brother," he said with relish, raising his sight and his arms to the sky. "My god is going to enjoy you, Uthiel, and then he is going to come to rule these lands and I shall be his right hand!"

"No!" screamed Branor as he impacted Nikhael in a powerful driving tackle that launched both of them past Uthiel just as the searing spear of light disappeared into the sky. Uthiel twisted up and around onto his front and saw the desperate fight as Branor pummelled his fists into Nikhael. Above, the clouds lit up.

In that moment Branor looked up, his eyes clear and his old self looking at Uthiel. Branor smiled and shouted something to Uthiel as Kael struggled beneath him.

"Until we both stand at His side, brother."

Then, in an explosion of light that lasted but a moment, Uthiel was thrown backwards without the force of Nikhael's unnatural strength to hold him down. Once more he skidded over the cobblestones and once again he crashed into fallen trestles and broken-limbed pale bodies of the dead. Before he had stopped moving, Uthiel was pushing himself up.

"Branor!" he cried. "No, my brother! No! Bran!"

Uthiel ignored the pain of his body and stumbled forward to the edge of the immense crater the raw power of Zhar T'hur had gouged into the soil of Gall herself. Of Branor and Nikhael there was no sign, not even a smouldering piece of armour. Nothing. Uthiel looked to the sky. The storm had already begun to dissipate and through the failing blackness, streaks of light blue were pushing through.

The harsh wind changed to a breeze and the pelting rain eased to a sprinkle. Uthiel fell on to his bottom and then onto his back amongst the destruction. Empty. All of his men, all of his friends, his father, Branor. He had nothing left. Uthiel wanted to cry, he wanted to scream and curse the gods, but he couldn't. He could barely even breathe. Uthiel fell back and lay flat, closing his eyes and praying that one of his broken ribs would end him somehow.

Just take me, Armenius. Please, all I have is already by your side.

Uthiel listened hard, his mind full of turmoil. But through the raging ocean of grief he heard them.

Stay a while, my son, there is much yet for you to do, said one voice.

Secunda will need you in the coming days, my brother, said another.

Despite his grief, Uthiel smiled in sad recognition as somebody gently placed their small hands under his head and raised it up. He opened his eyes and looked into a face he had long since lost hope of seeing. Someone who, with only her presence, brought a smile of happiness to his face despite all he had lost. A soft touch made its way down his scarred face and he smiled as her name came to his lips. With a sigh his eyes clouded over and closed, exhaustion finally taking its toll.

Emilia stroked the side of her lover's face. She could not describe the unbelievable happiness she had felt at finding him. The fear of watching him almost killed by other knights in this final battle, and the absolute relief as what she observed from hiding showed him to be the loyal and honest man she had given herself to a lifetime ago waged internal war with the anger of what she had uncovered.

Traitors. Traitors in the Secundan ranks. Knights.

She had watched him betrayed by his closest friend, and then saved by the same man. Watched him call out the name of a traitor knight he had once known in disbelief. Heard his cry of anguish as Branor was vaporised. Watched as his spirit was shattered more than once in the space of one short battle. Her naked body shivered in the cold as she hugged Uthiel to her chest, straining with his armoured and unconscious weight, ignoring the pain of a jagged edge as it worked her flesh raw.

Emilia had lost everything she had known; from her family down to her very clothes she had absolutely nothing left. Despairingly, she looked down and found her spirit becalmed by his face once more, as it had so many times over the last few months. It was beaten and scarred and gaunt and filled with pain even in its slackness, but it was still him.

She dragged her cleaver close to her. She would start over. She would protect him as he lay helpless, and she would start over.

She had Uthiel; shattered, broken Uthiel and a lifetime to build on their short time together.

They need only survive.

EPILOGUE

Uthiel sat upon the wagon as it made its way through the Secundan war camp outside of Gall. He sat among the hundreds of wounded under the bright morning sky as they were taken to a place of safer rest and recovery. The memory of burying his father and his friends in the plains outside of Gall amongst well over two thousand Secundans was still fresh but despite his grief, he smiled as Emilia gripped his hand from beside him. He looked from her beautiful face to the sky and in the soothing rays of the sun he could feel Tanin and Branor watching over him, side by side with the Eternal Lord.

"Smiling, brother?" asked the wounded knight beside him. "I've not seen a smile upon your ugly face for many days."

Uthiel laughed, and then winced as his ribs and shoulder flared with pain. He looked to his brother knight.

"I imagine not, my brother, there has been little to smile about these past months," said Uthiel wistfully.

"They say the king still lives," said Tarren. "That he is grievously burned but his Secundan strength and his link to the Eternal Lord keeps him alive. That's something, at least."

Uthiel was a little shocked by this. The last he had seen of the king, the man had been burned a grotesque mix of black

347

and pink. He was well on his way to the Shield Wall in the Sky. Men had already dropped to their knees to pray for his release from his mortal pain. There were bereaved tears and curses, but there was no one left to curse. No foe was left alive to be the focus of their rage.

Uthiel remembered he had struggled over to the Lords Thomak and Pomen, both men who had taken their eyes off their stricken king for but a heartbeat to register his presence. Their faces were deeply creased with worry as they turned their attention back to the king. Uthiel heard them speak in low voices as he turned to walk away.

"Will he make it?" asked Thomak.

"He's tough. If Armenius has deigned it to be he will live to lead us back to the White Frontier and beyond," responded Pomen.

Thomak rubbed at his eyes with both hands. "We've struck the enemy an almighty blow these last few months. He's emptied his land in an attempt to get a foothold in our lands and he has failed. He has cost us over half our fighting strength and all of Gall, but he has failed."

"Have you heard from the other Orders? We need their consolidated strength. We are spread too thin."

"A rider from the Order of the White Rose has come in from Lemug. They have been victorious and cleansed the whole way to the White Frontier. Of the four other armies, there has been no word, though we now know what has happened to the Knights Aggressor," said Thomak with disgust.

"It does us all shame to find their bodies amongst the fallen. As if Kael and his men weren't bad enough... We may never wipe the stain of their treachery from our nation's honour. By the Eternal Lord, I may never see a sun rise again where I am not sickened by what has happened to our knight Orders. How could we all have allowed this to happen?"

Pomen paused for a while, as if finding the best way to approach his next comment. "Have they all been burned?"

Thomak did not respond, only nodding as his eyes remained on the apothecaries tending to their king.

Uthiel had walked away. He wanted to hear no more.

Breaking from his reverie, Uthiel placed a hand on Tarren's shoulder and wrapped an arm around Emilia on the other side, drawing her close to him. He felt her snuggle in to him and warmed to the touch.

"May Armenius watch over us, my friends," said Uthiel, mustering all the outward cheer he could. *In the days ahead we'll need your protection, my Eternal Lord.*

Father Trethore walked through the main street, feeling his spirit torn asunder by the sheer volume of death. A hundred thousand women and girls sacrificed, and Armenius only knew what they had done with the menfolk who had not died upon the walls. Gall city alone had boasted well over two hundred and fifty thousand people and her surrounding lands that again and more.

He shook his head as he watched work teams pull down the bodies and drag them to the burning pits. The stench of death was horrible and he was of a mind to put Gall to the torch. As the most experienced and trusted Armenian priest in the field, he had been made responsible for the reconsecration of this tainted city. *And if I cannot bring it back to the light I will burn it to the ground!*

He took a deep calming breath and looked down at the long list of names on his cuirass, drawing on his forefathers' strength to calm his mind and his spirit. He saw his father there, and smiled to think of the man: tall and strong and pure, just as an Armenius priest should be.

He turned wistfully and by chance glanced down an alley. Something glinted in the shadows and caught his eye and his interest. It was a shadow, a form, a silhouette that sat darker than the rest of the shadow lit only by the glint of metal. Trethore began to walk towards the shape, tilting his head.

A moment later he realised what it was and his hand reached for his sword. It stopped short when he saw the three crossbow bolts jutting from its chest. He saw the blood-covered visage of the barbarian in Secundan knight armour. Something inside him ignited. He stormed into the alley and drew his forearm-length blade.

With quick movements he cut at the armour joins and began to tear the pauldrons and then the cuirass from the body.

You sully our armour with your barbarian filth!

Finally he grabbed at the hauberk and roughly hauled at it.

You are not worthy! How dare...

Trethore stopped dead as pale, dead bare skin came out from under the mail. There, burned into the flesh upon the man's ribs decades ago and scarred pink, was a wolf's head.

ABOUT THE AUTHOR

Thank you for reading Shield of Secunda, my first novel. I hope you enjoyed the blood-soaked ride, and got a good insight into the worlds I love to read and write about.

I'm a pretty average guy from Sydney, Australia, with an obsessive (and probably compulsive) approach to all things reading and writing.

I grew up reading Gemmell, Tolkein, Abnett, McNeill, Abercrombie, and so many more. History, fantasy, sci-fi, thriller, horror, anything I could get my hands on, I read – and in turn was influenced by.

Come find me on my website, Twitter, or Facebook. I look forwards to getting to know you a bit better on this crazy ride towards becoming a full time author.

- Adrian Collins
www.adriancollins.com.au
https://twitter.com/ACollinsAuthor
https://www.facebook.com/AdrianCollins.Author?ref=hl

www.ingramcontent.com/pod-product-compliance
Lightning Source LLC
Chambersburg PA
CBHW030403180626
46812CB00005B/1906